Terry Pratchett is the acclaimed creator of the global bestselling
Discworld series, the first of which, *The Colour of Magic*, was published in
1983. In all, he is the author of fifty bestselling books. His novels have been
widely adapted for stage and screen, and he is the winner of multiple prizes,
including the Carnegie Medal, as well as being awarded a knighthood for
services to literature. Worldwide sales of his books now stand at 70 million,
and they have been translated into thirty-seven languages.

# INTRODUCING DISCWORLD

The Discworld Series is a continuous history of a world not totally
unlike our own except that it is a flat disc carried on the backs of four
elephants astride a giant turtle floating through space, and that it is peopled
by, among others, wizards, dwarves, policemen, thieves, beggars, vampires
and witches. Within the history of Discworld there are many individual
stories, which can be read in any order, but reading them in sequence
can increase your enjoyment through the accumulation of all the fine
detail that contributes to the teeming imaginative complexity of this
brilliantly conceived world.

# The Discworld® series

## Have you read them all?

———————— **Other books about Discworld** ————————

THE SCIENCE OF DISCWORLD
(with Ian Stewart and Jack Cohen)

THE SCIENCE OF DISCWORLD II: THE GLOBE
(with Ian Stewart and Jack Cohen)

THE SCIENCE OF DISCWORLD III:
DARWIN'S WATCH
(with Ian Stewart and Jack Cohen)

THE NEW DISCWORLD COMPANION
(with Stephen Briggs)

NANNY OGG'S COOKBOOK
(with Stephen Briggs, Tina Hannan and Paul Kidby)

THE PRATCHETT PORTFOLIO
(with Paul Kidby)

THE DISCWORLD ALMANAK
(with Bernard Pearson)

THE UNSEEN UNIVERSITY CUT-OUT BOOK
(with Alan Batley and Bernard Pearson)

WHERE'S MY COW?
(illustrated by Melvyn Grant)

THE ART OF DISCWORLD
(with Paul Kidby)

THE WIT AND WISDOM OF DISCWORLD
(compiled by Stephen Briggs)

THE FOLKLORE OF DISCWORLD
(with Jacqueline Simpson)

─────────────── **Discworld maps** ───────────────

THE STREETS OF ANKH-MORPORK
(with Stephen Briggs, painted by Stephen Player)

THE DISCWORLD MAPP
(with Stephen Briggs, painted by Stephen Player)

A TOURIST GUIDE TO LANCRE – A DISCWORLD MAPP
(with Stephen Briggs, illustrated by Paul Kidby)

DEATH'S DOMAIN
(with Paul Kidby)

A complete list of Terry Pratchett ebooks and audio books as well as other books
based on the Discworld series – illustrated screenplays, graphic novels,
comics and plays – can be found on
**www.terrypratchett.co.uk**

─────────────── **Non-Discworld books** ───────────────

THE DARK SIDE OF THE SUN

STRATA

THE UNADULTERATED CAT (illustrated by Gray Jolliffe)

GOOD OMENS (with Neil Gaiman)

─────────── **Non-Discworld novels for younger readers** ───────────

THE CARPET PEOPLE

TRUCKERS

DIGGERS

WINGS

ONLY YOU CAN SAVE MANKIND*

JOHNNY AND THE DEAD

JOHNNY AND THE BOMB

NATION

*www.ifnotyouthenwho.com

# I Shall Wear Midnight

## Terry Pratchett

A DISCWORLD® NOVEL

CORGI BOOKS

**I SHALL WEAR MIDNIGHT**
**A CORGI BOOK 978 0 552 16605 8**

First published in Great Britain by Doubleday,
an imprint of Random House Children's Publishers UK
A Random House Group Company

Doubleday edition published 2010
Corgi edition published 2011
This edition published 2012

1 3 5 7 9 10 8 6 4 2

The Random House Group Limited supports the Forest Stewardship Council
(FSC®), the leading international forest certification organization. Our books
carrying the FSC label are printed on FSC®-certified paper. FSC is the only forest
certification scheme endorsed by the leading environmental organizations,
including Greenpeace. Our paper procurement policy can be found at
www.randomhouse.co.uk/environment.

MIX
Paper from
responsible sources
FSC® C016897

Set in 12/14.5pt Minion by Falcon Oast Graphic Art Ltd.

Corgi Books are published by Random House Children's Publishers UK,
61–63 Uxbridge Road, London W5 5SA

www.**kids**at**random**house.co.uk
www.**totally**random**books**.co.uk
www.**random**house.co.uk

Addresses for companies within The Random House Group Limited can be found
at: www.randomhouse.co.uk/offices.htm

THE RANDOM HOUSE GROUP Limited Reg. No. 954009

A CIP catalogue record for this book is available from the British Library.

Printed and bound by CPI Group (UK) Ltd, Croydon, CR0 4YY

# I Shall Wear Midnight

CHAPTER 1

# A Fine Big Wee Laddie

Why was it, Tiffany Aching wondered, that people liked noise so much? Why was noise so important?

Something quite close sounded like a cow giving birth. It turned out to be an old hurdy-gurdy organ, hand-cranked by a raggedy man in a battered top hat. She sidled away as politely as she could, but as noise went, it was sticky; you got the feeling that if you let it, it would try to follow you home.

But that was only one sound in the great cauldron of noise around her, all of it made by people and all of it made by people trying to make noise louder than the other people making noise. Arguing at the makeshift stalls, bobbing for apples or frogs,* cheering

* This was done blindfolded.

the prize fighters and a spangled lady on the high wire, selling candyfloss at the tops of their voices and, not to put too fine a point on it, boozing quite considerably.

The air above the green downland was thick with noise. It was as if the populations of two or three towns had all come up to the top of the hills. And so here, where all you generally heard was the occasional scream of a buzzard, you heard the permanent scream of, well, everyone. It was called *having fun*. The only people not making any noise were the thieves and pickpockets, who went about their business with commendable silence, and they didn't come near Tiffany; who would pick a witch's pocket? You would be lucky to get all your fingers back. At least, that was what they feared, and a sensible witch would encourage them in this fear.

When you were a witch, you were all witches, thought Tiffany Aching as she walked through the crowds, pulling her broomstick after her on the end of a length of string. It floated a few feet above the ground. She was getting a bit bothered about that. It seemed to work quite well, but nevertheless, since all around the fair were small children dragging balloons, *also* on the end of a piece of string, she couldn't help thinking that it made her look more than a little bit silly, and something that made one witch look silly made *all* witches look silly.

On the other hand, if you tied it to a hedge some-where, there was bound to be some kid who would untie the string and get on the stick for a dare, in which case most likely he would go straight up all the way to the top of the atmosphere where the air froze, and while she could in theory call the stick back, mothers got very touchy about having to thaw out their children on a bright late-summer day. That would not look good. People would talk. People always talked about witches.

She resigned herself to dragging it again. With luck, people would think she was joining in with the spirit of the thing in a humorous way.

There was a lot of etiquette involved, even at something so deceptively cheerful as a fair. She was the witch; who knows what would happen if she forgot someone's name or, worse still, got it wrong? What would happen if you forgot all the little feuds and factions, the people who weren't talking to their neighbours and so on and so on and a lot more so and even further on? Tiffany had no understanding at all of the word 'minefield', but if she had, it would have seemed kind of familiar.

She was the witch. For all the villages along the Chalk she was the witch. Not just her own village any more, but for all the other ones as far away as Ham-on-Rye, which was a pretty good day's walk from here. The area that a witch thought of as her own, and for whose people she did what was needful, was called a steading, and as steadings went, this one was pretty good. Not many witches got a whole geological out-crop to themselves, even if this one was mostly covered in grass, and the grass was mostly covered in sheep. And today the sheep on the downs were left by themselves to do whatever it was that they did when they were by themselves, which would presumably be pretty much the same as they did if you were watching them. And the sheep, usually fussed and herded and generally watched over, were now of no interest whatsoever, because right here the most wonderful attraction in the world was taking place.

Admittedly, the scouring fair was only one of the world's most wonderful attractions if you didn't usually ever travel more than about four miles from home. If you lived around the Chalk you were bound to meet everyone that you knew\* at the fair. It was quite often where you met the person you were likely to marry. The girls certainly all wore their best dresses, while the boys wore expressions of hopefulness and their hair smoothed down with cheap hair pomade or, more usually, spit. Those who had opted for spit generally came off better since the cheap pomade was very cheap indeed and would often melt and run in the hot weather, causing the young men not to be of interest to the young women, as they had fervently hoped, but to the flies, who would make their lunch off their scalps.

However, since the event could hardly be called 'the fair where you went in the hope of getting a kiss and, if your luck held, the promise of another one', the fair was called the scouring.

---

\* Speaking as a witch, she knew them very well.

The scouring was held over three days at the end of summer. For most people on the Chalk, it was their holiday. This was the third day, and most people said that if you hadn't had a kiss by now you might as well go home. Tiffany hadn't had a kiss, but after all, she was *the witch*. Who knew what they might get turned into?

If the late-summer weather was clement, it wasn't unusual for some people to sleep out under the stars, and under the bushes as well. And that was why if you wanted to take a stroll at night it paid to be careful so as not to trip over someone's feet. Not to put too fine a point to it, there was a certain amount of what Nanny Ogg – a witch who had been married to three husbands – called *making your own entertainment*. It was a shame that Nanny lived right up in the mountains, because she would have loved the scouring and Tiffany would have loved to see her face when she saw the giant.*

He – and he was quite definitely a he, there was no possible doubt about that – had been carved out of the turf thousands of years before. A white outline against the green, he belonged to the days when people had to think about survival and fertility in a dangerous world.

Oh, and he had also been carved, or so it would

---

* Later on, Tiffany realized that all the witches had probably flown across the giant, especially since you could hardly miss him if you were flying from the mountains to the big city. He kind of stood out, in any case. But in Nanny Ogg's case, she would probably turn round to look at him again.

appear, before anyone had invented trousers. In fact, to say that he had no trousers on just didn't do the job. His lack of trousers filled the world. You simply could not stroll down the little road that passed along the bottom of the hills without noticing that there was an enormous, as it were, lack of something – e.g. trousers – and what was there instead. It was definitely a figure of a man without trousers, and certainly not a woman.

Everyone who came to the scouring was expected to bring a small shovel, or even a knife, and work their way down the steep slope to grub up all the weeds that had grown there over the previous year, making the chalk underneath glow with freshness and the giant stand out boldly, as if he wasn't already.

There was always a lot of giggling when the girls worked on the giant.

And the reason for the giggling, and the circumstances of the giggling, couldn't help but put Tiffany in mind of Nanny Ogg, who you normally saw somewhere behind Granny Weatherwax with a big grin on her face. She was generally thought of as a jolly old soul, but there was a lot more to the old woman. She had never been Tiffany's teacher *officially*, but Tiffany couldn't help learning things from Nanny Ogg. She smiled to herself when she thought that. Nanny knew all the old, dark stuff – old magic, magic that didn't need witches, magic that was built into people and the landscape. It concerned things like death, and marriage, and betrothals. And promises that were promises even if there was no one to hear them. And all those things that make people touch wood and never, ever walk under a black cat.

You didn't need to be a witch to understand it. The world around you became more – well, more real and fluid, at those special times. Nanny Ogg called it *numinous* – an uncharacteristically solemn word from a woman who was much more likely to be saying, 'I would like a brandy, thank you very much, and could you make it a double while you are about it.' And she had told Tiffany about the old days, when it seemed that witches had a bit more fun. The things that you did around the changing of the seasons, for example; all the customs that were now dead except in folk memory which, Nanny Ogg said, is deep and dark and breathing and never fades. Little rituals.

Tiffany especially liked the one about the fire. Tiffany liked fire. It was her favourite element. It was considered so powerful, and so scary to the powers of darkness, that people would even get married by jumping over a fire together.* Apparently it helped if you said a little chant, according to Nanny Ogg, who lost no time in telling Tiffany the words, which immediately stuck in Tiffany's mind; a lot of what Nanny Ogg told you tended to be sticky.

But those were times gone by. Everybody was more

---

* Obviously, Tiffany thought, when jumping over a fire together, one ought to be concerned about wearing protective clothing and having people with a bucket of water to hand, just in case. Witches may be a lot of things, but first and foremost, they are practical.

respectable now, apart from Nanny Ogg and the giant.

There were other carvings on the Chalk lands too. One of them was a white horse that Tiffany thought had once broken its way out of the ground and galloped to her rescue. Now she wondered what would happen if the giant did the same thing, because it would be very hard to find a pair of pants sixty feet long in a hurry. And on the whole, you'd *want* to hurry.

She'd only ever giggled about the giant once, and that had been a very long time ago. There were really only four types of people in the world: men and women and wizards and witches. Wizards mostly lived in universities down in the big cities and weren't allowed to get married, although the reason why not totally escaped Tiffany. Anyway, you hardly ever saw them around here.

Witches were definitely women, but most of the older ones Tiffany knew hadn't got married either, mostly because Nanny Ogg had already used up all the eligible husbands, but also probably because they didn't have time. Of course, every now and then, a witch might marry a grand husband, like Magrat Garlick, as was, of Lancre had done, although by all accounts she only did herbs these days. But the only young witch Tiffany knew who had even had time for courting was her best friend up in the mountains: Petulia – a witch who was now specializing in pig magic, and was soon going to marry a nice young man who was shortly going to inherit his father's pig farm,* which meant he was practically an aristocrat.

But witches were not only very busy, they were also *apart*; Tiffany had learned that early on. You were among people, but not the *same* as them. There was always a kind of distance or separation. You didn't have to work at it, it happened anyway. Girls she had known when they were all so young they used to run about and play with only their vests on would make a tiny little curtsy to her when she passed them in the lane, and even elderly men would touch their forelock, or probably what they thought was their forelock, as she passed.

This wasn't just because of respect, but because of a kind of fear as well. Witches had secrets; they were there to help when babies were being born. When you got married, it was a good idea to have a witch standing by (even if you weren't sure if it was for good luck or to prevent bad luck), and when you died there would be a witch there too, to show you the way. Witches had secrets they never told . . . well, to people

---

* Possibly Petulia's romantic ambitions had been helped by the mysterious way the young man's pigs were forever getting sick and required treating for the scours, the blind heaves, brass neck, floating teeth, scribbling eyeball, grunge, the smarts, the twisting screws, swivelling and gone knees. This was a terrible misfortune, since more than half of those ailments are normally never found in pigs, and one of them is a disease known only in freshwater fish. But the neighbours were impressed at the amount of work Petulia put in to relieve their stress. Her broomstick was coming and going at all hours of the day and night. Being a witch, after all, was about dedication.

who weren't witches. Among themselves, when they could get together on some hillside for a drink or two (or in the case of Mrs Ogg, a drink or nine), they gossiped like geese.

*But never about the real secrets, the ones you never told, about things done and heard and seen. So many secrets that you were afraid they might leak. Seeing a giant without his trousers was hardly worth commenting on compared to some of the things that a witch might see.*

No, Tiffany did not envy Petulia her romance, which surely must have taken place in big boots, unflattering rubber aprons and the rain, not to mention an awful lot of 'oink'.

She did, however, envy her for being so *sensible*. Petulia had got it all worked out. She knew what she wanted her future to be, and had rolled up her sleeves and made it happen, up to her knees in 'oink' if necessary.

Every family, even up in the mountains, kept at least one pig to act as a garbage can in the summer and as pork, bacon, ham and sausages during the rest of the year. The pig was *important*; you might dose Granny with turpentine when she was poorly, but when the pig was ill you sent immediately for a pig witch, and paid her too, and paid her well, generally in sausages.

On top of everything else, Petulia was a specialist pig borer, and indeed she was this year's champion in the noble art of boring. Tiffany thought you couldn't put it better; her friend could sit down with a pig and talk to it gently and calmly about extremely boring things until some strange pig mechanism took over, whereupon it would give a happy little yawn and fall over, no longer a living pig and ready to become a very important contribution to the family's diet for the following year. This might not appear the best of outcomes for the pig, but given the messy and above all noisy way pigs died *before* the invention of pig boring, it was definitely, in the great scheme of things, a much better deal all round.

Alone in the crowd, Tiffany sighed. It was hard, when you wore the black, pointy hat. Because, like it or not, the witch *was* the pointy hat, and the pointy hat was the witch. It made people *careful* about you. They would be respectful, oh yes, and often a little bit nervous, as if they expected you to look inside their heads, which as a matter of fact you could probably do, using the good old witch's standbys of First Sight and Second Thoughts.* But these weren't really magic. Anyone could learn them if they had a lick of sense, but sometimes even a lick is hard to find. People are often so busy living that they never stopped to wonder *why*. Witches did, and that meant them being needed: oh yes, needed – needed practically all the time, but not, in a very polite

---

* First Sight means that you can see what really is there, and Second Thoughts mean thinking about what you are thinking. And in Tiffany's case, there were sometimes Third Thoughts and Fourth Thoughts, although these were quite difficult to manage and sometimes led her to walk into doors.

and definitely unspoken way, not *exactly* wanted.

This wasn't the mountains, where people were very used to witches; people on the Chalk could be friendly, but they weren't friends, not *actual* friends. The witch was different. The witch knew things that you did not. The witch was another kind of person. The witch was someone that perhaps you should not anger. The witch was not like other people.

Tiffany Aching was the witch, and she had made herself the witch because they needed one. Everybody needs a witch, but sometimes they just don't know it.

And it was working. The storybook pictures of the drooling hag were being wiped away, every time Tiffany helped a young mother with her first baby, or smoothed an old man's path to his grave. Nevertheless, old stories, old rumours and old picture books still seemed to have their own hold on the memory of the world.

What made it more difficult was that there was no tradition of witches on the Chalk – none would ever have settled there when Granny Aching had been alive. Granny Aching, as everybody knew, was a wise woman, and wise enough not to be a witch. Nothing ever happened on the Chalk that Granny Aching disapproved of, at least not for more than about ten minutes.

So Tiffany was a witch alone.

And not only was there no longer any support from the mountain witches like Nanny Ogg, Granny Weatherwax and Miss Level, but the people of the

Chalk weren't very familiar with witches. Other witches would probably come and help if she asked, *of course*, but although they wouldn't say so, this might mean that you couldn't cope with responsibility, weren't up to the task, weren't sure, *weren't good enough.*

'Excuse me, miss?' There was a nervous giggle. Tiffany looked round and there were two little girls in their best new frocks and straw hats. They were looking at her eagerly, with perhaps just a hint of mischief in their eyes. She thought quickly and smiled at them.

'Oh yes, Becky Pardon and Nancy Upright, yes? What can I do for the two of you?'

Becky Pardon shyly produced a small bouquet from behind her back and held it out. Tiffany recognized it, of course. She had made them herself for the older girls when she was younger, simply because it was what you did, it was part of the scouring: a little bunch of wild flowers picked from the downland, tied in a bunch with – and this was the important bit, the magic bit – some of the grass pulled up as the fresh chalk was exposed.

'If you put this under your pillow tonight, you will dream of your beau,' said Becky Pardon, her face quite serious now.

Tiffany took the slightly wilting bunch of flowers with care. 'Let me see . . .' she said. 'We have here sweet mumbles, ladies' pillows, seven-leaf clover – very lucky – a sprig of old man's trousers, jack-in-the-wall, oh – love-lies-bleeding and . . .'

13

She stared at the little white and red flowers.

The girls said, 'Are you all right, miss?'

'Forget-me-lots!'* said Tiffany, more sharply than she had intended. But the girls hadn't noticed, so she continued to say, brightly, 'Quite unusual to see it here. It must be a garden escapee. And, as I'm sure you both know, you have bound them all together with strips of candle rush, which once upon a time people used to make into rush lights. What a lovely surprise. Thank you both very much. I hope you have a lovely time at the fair . . .'

Becky raised her hand. 'Excuse me, miss?'

'Was there something else, Becky?'

Becky went pink, and had a hurried conversation with her friend. She turned back to Tiffany, looking slightly more pink but nevertheless determined to see things through.

'You can't get into trouble for asking a question, can you, miss? I mean, just asking a question?'

It's going to be 'How can I be a witch when I'm grown up?' Tiffany thought, because it generally was. The young girls saw her on her broomstick and thought that was what being a witch was. Out loud she said, 'Not from me, at least. Do ask your question.'

Becky Pardon looked down at her boots. 'Do you have any passionate parts, miss?'

* The forget-me-lots is a pretty red and white flower usually given by young ladies to signal to their young men that they never wanted to see them again ever, or at least until they'd learned to wash properly and got a job.

Another talent needful in a witch is the ability not to let your face show what you're thinking, and especially not allowing it, no matter what, to go as stiff as a board. Tiffany managed to say, without a single wobble in her voice and no trace of an embarrassed smirk, 'That is a very interesting question, Becky. Can I ask you why you want to know?'

The girl looked a lot happier now that the question was, as it were, out in the public domain.

'Well, miss, I asked my granny if I could be a witch when I was older, and she said I shouldn't want to, because witches have no passionate parts, miss.'

Tiffany thought quickly in the face of the two solemn owlish stares. These are farm girls, she thought, so they had certainly seen a cat have kittens and a dog have puppies. They'd have seen the birth of lambs, and probably a cow have a calf, which is always a noisy affair that you can hardly miss. They know what they are asking me about.

At this point Nancy chimed in with, 'Only, if that is so, miss, we would quite like to have the flowers back, now we've shown them to you, because perhaps it might be a bit of a waste, meaning no offence.' She stepped back quickly.

Tiffany was surprised at her own laughter. It had been a long time since she had laughed. Heads turned to see what the joke was, and she managed to grab both the girls before they fled, and spun them round.

'Well done, the pair of you,' she said. 'I like to see some sensible thinking every now and again. Never hesitate to ask a question. And the answer to your question is that witches are the same as everybody else when it comes to passionate parts, but often they are so busy rushing around that they never have time to think about them.'

The girls looked relieved that their work had not been entirely in vain and Tiffany was ready for the next question, which came from Becky again. 'So, do you have a beau, miss?'

'Not right at the moment,' Tiffany said briskly, clamping down on her expression lest it give anything away. She held up the little bouquet. 'But who knows, if you've made this properly, then I'll get another one, and in that case you will be better witches than me, that is for certain.' They both beamed at this dreadful piece of outright flannel, and it stopped the questions.

'And now,' said Tiffany, 'the cheese rolling will be starting at any minute. I'm sure you won't want to miss that.'

'No, miss,' they said in unison. Just before they left, full of relief and self-importance, Becky patted Tiffany on her hand. 'Beaus can be very difficult, miss,' she said with the assurance of, to Tiffany's certain know-ledge, eight years in the world.

'Thank you,' said Tiffany. 'I shall definitely bear that in mind.'

When it came to the entertainment offered at the fair, such as people making faces through a horse collar or fighting with pillows on the greasy pole or even the bobbing for frogs, well, Tiffany could take them or leave them alone, and in fact much preferred to leave them alone. But she always liked to see a good cheese roll – that is to say, a good cheese roll all the way down a slope of the hill, although not across the giant because no one would want to eat the cheese afterwards.

They were hard cheeses, sometimes specially made for the cheese-rolling circuit, and the winning maker of the cheese that reached the bottom unscathed won a belt with a silver buckle and the admiration of all.

Tiffany was an expert cheese-maker, but she had never entered. Witches couldn't enter that sort of competition because if you won – and she knew she had made a cheese or two that *could* win – everyone would say that was unfair because you were a witch; well, that's what they would think, but very few would *say* it. And if you didn't win, people would say, 'What kind of witch can't make a cheese that could be beat by simple cheeses made by simple folk like we?'

There was a gentle movement of the crowd to the start of the cheese rolling, although the frog-bobbing stall still had a big crowd, it being a very humorous and reliable source of entertainment, especially to those people who weren't actually bobbing. Regrettably, the man who put weasels down his trousers, and apparently had a personal best of nine weasels, hadn't been there this year, and people were wondering if he had lost his touch. But sooner or later everyone would drift over to the start line for the cheese rolling. It was a tradition.

The slope here was very steep indeed and there was

always a certain amount of boisterous rivalry between the cheese-owners, which led to pushing and shoving and kicking and bruises; occasionally you got a broken arm or leg. All was going as normal as the waiting men lined up their cheeses, until Tiffany saw, and seemed to be the only one to see, a dangerous cheese roll up all by itself. It was black under the dust and there was a piece of grubby blue and white cloth tied to it.

'Oh, no,' she said. 'Horace. And where you are, trouble can't be far behind.' She spun around, carefully searching for signs of what should not be there. 'Now you just listen to me,' she said under her breath. 'I know at least one of you must be somewhere near. This isn't for you, it's just about people. Understand?'

But it was too late. The Master of the Revels, in his big floppy hat with lace around the brim, blew his whistle and the cheese rolling, as he put it, *commenced* – which is a far grander word than *started*. And a man with lace around his hat was never going to use a short word where a long word would do.

Tiffany hardly dared to look. The runners didn't so much run as roll and skid behind their cheeses. But she could hear the cries that went up when the black cheese not only shot into the lead, but occasionally turned round and went back uphill again in order to bang into one of the ordinary innocent cheeses. She could just hear a faint grumbling noise coming from it as it almost shot to the top of the hill.

Cheese-runners shouted at it, tried to grab at it and flailed at it with sticks, but the piratical cheese scythed onwards, reached the bottom again just ahead of the terrible carnage of men and cheeses as they piled up, then rolled gently back up to the top and sat there demurely while still gently vibrating.

At the bottom of the slope, fights were breaking out among the cheese-jockeys who were still capable of punching somebody, and since everyone was now watching that, Tiffany took the opportunity to snatch up Horace and shove him into her bag. After all, he was hers. Well, that was to say, she had made him, although something odd must've got into the mix since Horace was the only cheese that would eat mice and, if you didn't nail him down, other cheeses as well. No wonder he got on so well with the Nac Mac Feegles,* who had made him an honorary member of the clan. He was their kind of cheese.

Surreptitiously, hoping that no one would notice, Tiffany held the bag up to her mouth and said, 'Is this any way to behave? Aren't you ashamed?' The bag wobbled a little bit, but she knew that the word 'shame' was not in Horace's vocabulary, and neither was anything else. She lowered the bag and moved a little way from the crowd and said, 'I know you are here, Rob Anybody.'

* If you do not yet know who the Nac Mac Feegles are: 1) be grateful for your uneventful life; and 2) be prepared to beat a retreat if you hear anyone about as high as your ankles shout 'Crivens!' They are, strictly speaking, one of the faerie folk, but it is probably not a good idea to tell them this if you are looking forward to a future in which you still have your teeth.

There he was, sitting on her shoulder. She could smell him. Despite the fact that they generally had little to do with bathing, except when it rained, the Nac Mac Feegles always smelled something like slightly drunk potatoes. 'The kelda wanted me tae find out how ye were biding,' said the Feegle chieftain. 'You havenae bin tae the mound to see her these past two weeks,' he went on, 'and I think she is afeared that a harm may come tae ye, ye are working sae hard an' all.'

Tiffany groaned, but only to herself. She said, 'That is very kind of her. There is always so much to do; surely the kelda knows this. It doesn't matter what I do, there is always more to be done. There is no end to the wanting. But there is nothing to worry about. I am doing fine. And please don't take Horace out again in public – you know he gets excited.'

'Well, in point of fact, it says up on that banner over there that this is for the folk of these hills and we is more than folk. We is *folklore*! Ye cannae argue with the lore! Besides, I wanted tae come and pay my ain respects to the big yin without his breeks. He is a fine big wee laddie and nae mistake.' Rob paused, and then said quietly, 'So I can tell her that ye are quite well in yourself, aye?' There was a certain nervousness to him, as if he would like to have said more but knew it wouldn't be welcome.

'Rob Anybody, I would be very grateful if you would do just that,' said Tiffany, 'because I have a lot of people to bandage, if I'm any judge.'

Rob Anybody, suddenly looking like a man on a thankless errand, frantically said the words he had been told by his wife to say: 'The kelda says there's plenty more fish in the sea, miss!'

And Tiffany stood perfectly still for a moment. And then, without looking at Rob, said quietly, 'Do thank the kelda for her angling information. I have to get on, if you don't mind, Rob. *Do* thank the kelda.'

Most of the crowd was reaching the bottom of the slope by now, to gawk or rescue or possibly attempt some amateur first aid on the groaning cheese-runners. For the onlookers, of course, it was just another show; you didn't often see a satisfying pile-up of men and cheeses, and – who knew? – there might be some really interesting casualties.

Tiffany, glad of something to do, did not have to push her way through; the pointy black hat could create a path through a crowd faster than a holy man through a shallow sea. She waved the happy crowd away, with one or two forceful pushes for those of slow uptake. As a matter of fact, as it turned out, the butcher's bill wasn't too high this year, with one broken arm, one broken wrist, one broken leg and an enormous number of bruises, cuts and rashes being caused by people sliding most of the way down – grass isn't always your friend. There were several young men clearly in distress as a result, but they were absolutely definite that they were not going to discuss their injuries with a lady, thank you all the same, so she told them to put a cold compress on the afflicted area, wherever it was, when they got home, and watched them walk unsteadily away.

Well, she'd done all right, hadn't she? She had used her skills in front of the rubbernecking crowd and, according to what she overheard from the old men and women, had performed well enough. Perhaps she imagined that one or two people were embarrassed when an old man with a beard to his waist said with a grin, 'A girl who can set bones would have no trouble finding a husband,' but that passed, and with nothing else to do, people started the long climb back up the hill . . . and then the coach came past, and then, which was worse, it stopped.

It had the coat of arms of the Keepsake family on the side. A young man stepped out. Quite handsome in his way, but also so stiff in his way that you could have ironed sheets on him. This was Roland. He hadn't gone more than a step when a rather un-pleasant voice from inside the coach told him that he should have waited for the footman to open the door for him, and to hurry up, because they didn't have all day.

The young man hurried towards the crowd and there was a general smartening-up because, after all, here came the son of the Baron, who owned most of the Chalk and nearly all their houses, and although he was a decent old boy, as old boys go, a little politeness to his family was definitely a wise move . . .

'What happened here? Is everybody all right?' he said.

Life on the Chalk was generally pleasant and the relationship between master and man was one of mutual respect; but nevertheless, the farm workers had inherited the idea that it could be unwise to have too many words with powerful people, in case any of those words turned out to be a word out of place. After all, there was still a torture chamber in the castle and even though it hadn't been used for hundreds of years . . . well, best to be on the safe side, best to stand back and let the witch do the talking. If she got into trouble, she could fly away.

'One of those accidents that was bound to happen, I'm afraid,' said Tiffany, well aware that she was the only woman present who had not curtsied. 'Some broken bones that will mend and a few red faces. All sorted out, thank you.'

'So I see, so I see! Very well done, young lady!'

For a moment Tiffany thought she could taste her teeth. *Young lady*, from . . . him? It was almost, but not entirely, insulting. But no one else seemed to have noticed. It was, after all, the kind of language that nobs use when they are trying to be friendly and jolly. He's trying to talk to them like his father does, she thought, but his father did it by instinct and was good at it. You can't talk to people as though they are a public meeting. She said, 'Thank you kindly, sir.'

Well, not too bad so far, except that now the coach door opened again and one dainty white foot touched the flint. It was her: Angelica or Letitia or something else out of the garden; in fact Tiffany knew full well it was Letitia, but surely she could be excused just a tiny touch of nasty in the privacy of her own head? Letitia!

What a name. Halfway between a salad and a sneeze. Besides, who was Letitia to keep Roland away from the scouring fair? He should have been there! His father would have been there if the old man possibly could! And look! Tiny white shoes! How long would they last on somebody who had to do a job of work? She stopped herself there: *a bit* of nasty was enough.

Letitia looked at Tiffany and the crowd with something like fear and said, 'Do let's get going, can we please? Mother is getting vexed.'

And so the coach left and the hurdy-gurdy man thankfully left and the sun left, and in the warm shadows of the twilight some people stayed. But Tiffany flew home alone, up high where only bats and owls could see her face.

## CHAPTER 2

# Rough Music

She got one hour's sleep before the nightmare began.

What she remembered most of all about that evening was the thumping of Mr Petty's head against the wall and the banisters as she hauled him bodily out of his bed and dragged him by his filthy nightshirt down the stairs. He was a heavy man and half asleep, the other half of him being dead drunk.

The important thing was not to give him any time to think, even for one moment, as she towed him behind her like a sack. He was three times her weight, but she knew about leverage. You couldn't be a witch if you couldn't manoeuvre someone who was heavier than you. You would never be able to change an invalid's sheets otherwise. And now he slithered down the last few steps into the cottage's tiny kitchen, and threw up on the floor.

She was quite glad about that; lying in stinking vomit was the very least the man deserved, but she had to be quick to take charge, before he had time to compose himself.

The terrified Mrs Petty, a mouse of a woman, had run screaming along the lanes to the village pub as soon as the beating had begun, and Tiffany's father had sent a lad to wake Tiffany up. Mr Aching was a man with considerable foresight and must have known that the beery cheerfulness after a day at the fair could be the undoing of everybody, and as Tiffany sped towards the cottage on her broomstick, she had heard the rough music begin.

She slapped Petty's face. 'Can you hear that?' she demanded, waving her hand towards the darkened window. 'Can you hear it? That's the sound of the rough music, and they are playing it for you, Mister Petty, for you. And they have sticks! And they have stones! They have everything they can pick up, and they have their fists and your daughter's baby died, Mister Petty. You beat your daughter so hard, Mister Petty, that the baby died, and your wife is being comforted by some of the women and everybody knows that you have done it, *everybody* knows.'

She stared into his bloodshot eyes. His hands had closed automatically into fists because he had always been a man who thought with them. Soon he would try to use them; she knew it, because it was easier to punch than think. Mr Petty had punched his way through life.

The rough music was getting nearer slowly, because it's hard to walk across fields on a dark night when you've had a skinful of beer, no matter how righteous you are currently feeling. She had to hope that they did not go into the barn first, because they would hang him there and then. If he was *lucky*, they would just hang him. When she had looked into the barn and seen that murder had been done, she knew that, without her, it would be done again. She had put a charm on the girl to take her pain away, holding it just above her own shoulder. It was invisible, of course, but in her mind's eye it burned a fiery orange.

'It was that boy,' mumbled the man, with vomit trickling down his chest. 'Coming round here, turning her head so as she wouldn't listen to her mum or me. And her being only thirteen. It's a scandal.'

'William is thirteen too,' said Tiffany, trying to keep her voice level. It was difficult; the rage was bursting to get out. 'Are you trying to tell me that she was too young for a bit of romance, but young enough to be beaten so hard that she bled from places where no one should bleed?'

She couldn't tell if he had really come to his senses, because the man had so few of them at the best of times, it was hard to know if he had any at all.

'It wasn't right, what they were doing,' he said. 'A man's got to have discipline in his own house, after all, ain't that right?'

Tiffany could imagine the fiery language in the pub as the overture to the music got wound up. There were not very many weapons in the villages of the Chalk, but there were such things as reaping hooks and scythes and thatching knives and big, big hammers. They weren't weapons – until you hit somebody with them. And everyone knew about old Petty's temper, and the number of times his wife told the neighbours that she had got her black eye by walking into a door.

Oh, yes – she could imagine the conversation in the pub, with the beer joining in and people remembering where all those things that weren't weapons were hanging in their sheds. Every man was king in his little castle. Everyone knew about that – well, at least every *man* – and so you minded your own business when it came to another man's castle until the castle began to stink, and then you had to do something about it lest all castles should fall. Mr Petty was one of the neighbourhood's sullen little secrets, but it was not a secret any more.

'I am your only chance, Mr Petty,' she said. 'Run away. Grab what you can and run away right now. Run away to where they've never heard of you, and then run a bit further, just to be on the safe side, because I will not be able to stop them, do you understand? Personally, I could not care less what happens to your miserable frame but I do not wish to see good people get turned into bad people by doing a murder, so you just leg it across the fields and I won't remember which way you went.'

'You can't turn me out of my own house,' he mumbled, finding some drunken defiance.

'You've lost your house, your wife, your daughter . . . and your grandson, Mr Petty. You will find no friends here this night. I am just offering you your life.'

'It was the drink what done it!' Petty burst out. 'It was done in drink, miss!'

'But you drank the drink, and then you drank another drink, and another drink,' she said. 'You drank the drink all day at the fair and you only came back because the drink wanted to go to bed.' Tiffany could feel only coldness in her heart.

'I'm sorry.'

'Not good enough, Mr Petty, not good enough at all. Go away and become a better person and then, maybe, when you come back as a changed man, people here might find it in their hearts to say hello to you, or at least to nod.'

She had been watching his eyes, and she knew the man. Something inside him was boiling up. He was ashamed, bewildered and resentful, and in those circumstances the Pettys of the world struck out.

'Please don't, Mr Petty,' she said. 'Do you have any idea what would happen to you if you hit a witch?'

She thought to herself, With those fists, you could probably kill me with a punch and that is why I intend to keep you scared.

'You set the rough music on me, didn't ya?'

She sighed. 'No one controls the music, Mr Petty,

you know that. It just turns up when people have had enough. No one knows where it starts. People look around, and catch one another's eye, and give each other a little nod, and other people see that. *Other* people catch *their* eye and so, very slowly, the music starts and somebody picks up a spoon and bangs it on a plate, and then somebody else bangs a jug on the table and boots start to stamp on the floor, louder and louder. It is the sound of anger, it is the sound of people who have had enough. Do you want to face the music?'

'You think you're so clever, don't ya?' Petty snarled. 'With your broomstick and your black magic, ordering *ordin-ery* folks about.'

She almost admired him. There he was, with no friends in the world, covered in his own sick and – she sniffed: yes, there was urine dripping from the bottom of his nightshirt – yet he was stupid enough to talk back like that. 'Not clever, Mr Petty, just cleverer than you. And that's not hard.'

'Yeah? But clever gets you into trouble. Slip of a gel like you, pokin' about in other people's business . . . What are you going to do when the music comes for *you*, eh?'

'Run, Mr Petty. Get out of here. It's your last chance,' she said. And it probably was; she could hear individual voices now.

'Well, would your majesty let a man put his boots on?' he said sarcastically. He reached down for them beside the door, but you could read Mr Petty like a very small book, one with fingermarks on all the pages and a piece of bacon as a bookmark.

He came up with fists swinging.

She took one step backwards, caught his wrist and let the pain out. She felt it flow down her arm, leaving it tingling, into her cupped hand and into Petty: all his daughter's pain in one second. It flung him clear across the kitchen and it must have burned away everything inside him except animal fear. He rushed at the rickety back door like a bull, broke through it and headed off into the darkness.

She staggered back into the barn, where a lamp was burning. According to Granny Weatherwax, you did not feel the pain that you carried, but it was a lie. A necessary lie. You did feel the pain that you carried, and because it wasn't *actually* your pain you could somehow bear it, but its departure left you feeling weak and shocked.

When the charging, clanging mob arrived, Tiffany was sitting quietly in the barn with the sleeping girl. The noise went all around the house but did not go inside; that was one of the unwritten rules. It was hard to believe that the anarchy of the rough music had rules, but it did; it might go on for three nights, or stop at one, and no one came out of the house when the music was in the air and no one came sneaking home and went back into the house either, unless it was to beg for forgiveness, understanding or ten minutes to pack their bags and run away. The rough music was never organized. It seemed to occur to everybody at once. It played when a village thought that a man had beaten his wife too hard, or his dog too savagely, or if a married man and a married woman forgot that they were married to somebody else. There were other, darker crimes against the music too, but they weren't talked about openly. Sometimes people could stop the music by mending their ways; quite often they packed up and moved away before the third night.

Petty would not have taken the hint; Petty would have come out swinging. And there would have been a fight, and someone would have done something stupid, that is to say even more stupid than what Petty would have done. And then the Baron would find out and people might lose their livelihood, which would mean they would have to leave the Chalk and go perhaps as much as ten miles to find work and a new life among strangers.

Tiffany's father was a man of keen instinct and he gently opened the barn door a few minutes later when the music was dying down. She knew it was a bit embarrassing for him; he was a well-respected man, but somehow, now, his daughter was more important than he was. A witch did not take orders from anybody, and she knew that he got teased about it by the other men.

She smiled and he sat down on the hay next to her while the wild music found nothing to beat, stone or hang. Mr Aching didn't waste words at the best of times. He looked around and his gaze fell on the little bundle, hastily wrapped in straw and sacking, that Tiffany had put where the girl would not see it. 'So it's true, she was with child, then?'

'Yes, Dad.'

Tiffany's father appeared to look at nothing at all. 'Best if they don't find him,' he said after a decent interval.

'Yes,' said Tiffany.

'Some of the lads were talking about stringing him up. We would have stopped them, of course, but it would have been a bad business, with people taking sides. It's like poison in a village.'

'Yes.'

They sat in silence for a while. Then her father looked down at the sleeping girl. 'What have you done for her?' he asked.

'Everything I can,' said Tiffany.

'And you did that taking-away-pain thingy you do?'

She sighed. 'Yes, but that's not all I shall have to take away. I need to borrow a shovel, Dad. I'll bury the poor little thing down in the woods, where no one will know.'

He looked away. 'I wish it wasn't you doing this, Tiff. You're not sixteen yet and I see you running around nursing people and bandaging people and who knows what chores. You shouldn't have to be doing all of that.'

'Yes, I know,' said Tiffany.

'*Why?*' he asked again.

'Because other people don't, or won't, or can't, that's why.'

'But it's not *your* business, is it?'

'I make it my business. I'm a witch. It's what we do. When it's nobody else's business, it's *my* business,' Tiffany said quickly.

'Yes, but we all thought it was going to be about whizzing around on brooms and suchlike, not cutting old ladies' toenails for them.'

'But people don't understand what's needed,' said Tiffany. 'It's not that they are bad; it's just that they don't think. Take old Mrs Stocking, who's got nothing in the world except her cat and a whole lot of arthritis. People were getting her a bite to eat often enough, that is true, but no one was noticing that her toenails were so long they were tangling up inside her boots and so she'd not been able to take them off for a year! People around here are OK when it comes to food and the occasional bunch of flowers, but they are not around when things get a little on the messy side. Witches notice these things. Oh, there's a certain amount of whizzing about, that's true enough, but mostly it's only to get quickly to somewhere there is a mess.'

Her father shook his head. 'And you like doing this?'

'Yes.'

'*Why?*'

Tiffany had to think about this, her father's eyes never leaving her face. 'Well, Dad, you know how Granny Aching always used to say, "Feed them as is hungry, clothe them as is naked, and speak up for them as has no voices"? Well, I reckon there is room in there for "Grasp for them as can't bend, reach for them as can't stretch, wipe for them as can't twist", don't you? And because sometimes you get a good day that makes up for all the bad days and, just for a moment, you hear the world turning,' said Tiffany. 'I can't put it any other way.'

Her father looked at her with a kind of proud puzzlement. 'And you think that's worth it, do you?'

'Yes, Dad!'

'Then I am proud of you, jiggit, you are doing a man's job!'

He'd used the pet name only the family knew, and so she kissed him politely and did not tell him that he was unlikely to see a man doing the job that she did.

'What are you all going to do about the Pettys?' she asked.

'Your mum and me could take Mrs Petty and her daughter in and . . .' Mr Aching paused and gave her a strange look, as if she frightened him. 'It's never simple, my girl. Seth Petty was a decent enough lad when we were young. Not the brightest piggy in the litter, I'll grant you that, but decent enough in his way. It was his dad who was a madman; I mean, things were a bit rough and ready in those days and you could expect a clip around the head if you disobeyed, but Seth's dad had a thick leather belt with two buckles on it, and he would lay into Seth just for looking at him in a funny way. No word of a lie. Always used to say that he would teach him a lesson.'

'It seems that he succeeded,' Tiffany said, but her father held up a hand.

'And then there was Molly,' he went on. 'You couldn't say that Molly and Seth were made for one another, because in truth neither of them were rightly made for anybody, but I suppose they were sort of happy together. In those days, Seth was a drover, driving the flocks all the way to the big city sometimes. It wasn't the kind of job you needed much learning for, and it might be that some of the sheep were a bit brighter than he was, but it was a job that needed doing, and he picked up a wage and no one thought the worse of him for that. The trouble was, that meant he left Molly alone for weeks at a time, and . . .' Tiffany's father paused here, looking embarrassed.

'I know what you're going to tell me,' said Tiffany, to help him out, but he took care to ignore this.

'It's not that she was a bad girl,' he said. 'It's just that she never really understood what it was all about, and there wasn't anyone to tell her, and you got all kinds of strangers and travellers passing through all the time. Quite handsome chaps, some of them.'

Tiffany took pity on him, sitting there looking miserable, embarrassed about telling his little girl things his little girl shouldn't know.

So she leaned over and kissed him on the cheek again. 'I *know*, Dad, *I really do know*. Amber isn't actually his daughter, right?'

'Well, I never said that, did I? She might be,' said her father awkwardly.

And that would be the trick, wouldn't it, Tiffany thought. Maybe if Seth Petty had known one way or the other, he might have come to terms with the *perhaps*. Maybe. You never know.

But he didn't know, either, and there would be some days when he thought he did know and some days when he thought the worst. And for a man like Petty, who was a stranger to thinking, the dark thoughts would roll around in his head until they tangled up his brain. And when the brain stops thinking, the fist steps in.

Her father was watching her very closely. 'You know about this sort of thing?' he said.

'We call it going round the houses. Every witch does it. Please try and understand me, Dad. I have seen horrible things, and some of them all the more horrible because they were, well, normal. All the little secrets behind closed doors, Dad. Good things and nasty things I am not going to tell you about. It's just part of being a witch! You learn to sense things.'

'Well, you know, life is not exactly a bed of roses for any of us . . .' her father began. 'There was the time when—'

'There was this old woman up near Slice,' Tiffany interrupted him. 'And she died in her bed. Nothing particularly bad about that, really: she had just run out of life. But she lay there for two months before anyone wondered what had happened. They are a bit strange

37

over in Slice. The worst part of it was that her cats couldn't get out and started eating her; I mean, she was cat-mad and probably would not have minded, but one of them had kittens in her bed. In her actual bed. It was really very difficult to find the kittens homes in places where people hadn't already heard the story. They were beautiful kittens too, lovely blue eyes.'

'Er,' her father began. 'When you say "in her bed", you mean . . .'

'With her still in it, yes,' said Tiffany. 'I've had to deal with dead people, yes. You throw up a bit first time, and then you just realize that death is, well, part of life. It is not so bad if you think of it as a list of things to do, and do them one at a time. You might have a bit of a cry as well, but that's all part of it.'

'Didn't anyone help you?'

'Oh, a couple of ladies helped me when I knocked on their doors, but really she was nobody's business. It can happen like that. People disappear in the cracks.' She paused. 'Dad, we're still not using the old stone barn, are we? Can you get some of the lads to clean it out for me?'

'Of course,' said her father. 'Do you mind if I ask why?'

Tiffany heard his politeness; he was talking to a witch. 'I think I'm having a kind of idea,' she said. 'And I think I can make good use of that barn. It's only a thought, and it won't do any harm to have it tidied up in any case.'

'Well, I still feel mightily proud when I see you

rushing all over the place on that broomstick of yours,' said her father. 'That's magic, isn't it?'

Everyone wants magic to exist, Tiffany thought to herself, and what can you say? No, there isn't? Or: Yes, there is, but it's not what you think? Everyone wants to believe that we can change the world by snapping our fingers. 'The dwarfs make them,' she said. 'I don't have a clue how they work. Staying on them, that's the trick.'

The rough music had died down now, possibly because there was nothing for it to do, or perhaps because – and this was quite likely – if the rough musicians got back to the pub soon, there might be time for another drink before it closed.

Mr Aching stood up. 'I think we should take this girl home, don't you?'

'Young woman,' corrected Tiffany, leaning over her. 'What?'

'Young woman,' said Tiffany. 'She deserves that, at least. And I think I should take her somewhere else first. She needs more help than I can give her. Can you please go and scrounge some rope? I've got a leather strap on the broomstick, of course, but I don't think it will be enough.' She heard a rustling from the hayloft above, and smiled. Some friends could be so reliable.

But Mr Aching looked shocked. 'You are taking her away?'

'Not far. I have to. But look, don't worry. If Mum makes up an extra bed I'll soon have her back.'

Her father lowered his voice. 'It's them, isn't it? Do they still follow you?'

'Well,' Tiffany said, 'they say they don't, but you know what little liars the Nac Mac Feegle are!'

It had been a long day, and not a good one, otherwise she would not have been so unfair, but – strangely – there was no giveaway reply from above. To her surprise, a lack of Feegle was suddenly almost as distressing as an overdose.

And then, to her delight, a small voice said, 'Ha ha ha, she didnae catch us oot that time, aye, lads? We kept as quiet as little mices! The big wee hag didnae suspect a thing! Lads? Lads?'

'Daft Wullie, I swear ye dinnae have enough brains to blow your nose,' said a similar but angry voice. 'What part o' "nae one is tae say one wee word" did ye nae understand? Och, crivens!'

This last remark was followed by the sounds of a scuffle.

Mr Aching glanced nervously at the roof and leaned closer. 'You know your mother is very worried about you? You know she's just been a grandma again. She's very proud of them all. And you too, of course,' he added hurriedly. 'But all this witchy business, well, that's not the sort of thing a young man looks for in a wife. And now that you and young Roland . . .'

Tiffany dealt with this. Dealing was part of witch-craft too. Her father looked so miserable that she put on her cheerful face and said, 'If I was you, Dad, I would go home and get a decent night's sleep. I'll sort things out. Actually, there's a coil of rope over there, but I'm certain I won't need to use it now.'

He looked relieved at this. The Nac Mac Feegle could be pretty worrying to those who did not know them very well, although now she thought about it, they could be pretty worrying however long you had known them; a Feegle in your life very soon changed it.

'Have you been here all this time?' she demanded, as soon as her father had hurried off.

For a moment it rained bits of hay and whole Feegles.

The problem with getting angry at Nac Mac Feegles was that it was like getting angry at cardboard or the weather; it didn't make any difference. She had a go anyway, because by now it was sort of traditional.

'Rob Anybody! You promised not to spy on me!'

Rob held up a hand. 'Ah weel, there ye have it, right enough, but it is one of them miss apprehensions, miss, 'cause we wasn't spying at all, was we, lads?'

The mass of little blue and red shapes that now covered the floor of the barn raised their voices in a chorus of blatant lying and perjury. It slowed down when they saw her expression.

'Why is it, Rob Anybody, that you persist in lying when you are caught red-handed?'

'Ah weel, that's an easy one, miss,' said Rob Anybody, who was technically the head man of the Nac Mac Feegles. 'After all, ye ken, what would be the point of lyin' when you had nae done anything wrong? Anyway, now I am mortally wounded to my giblets on account of me good name being slandered,' he said, grinning. 'How many times have I lied to you, miss?'

'Seven hundred and fifty-three times,' said Tiffany. 'Every time you promise not to interfere in my business.'

'Ah weel,' said Rob Anybody, 'ye are still our big wee hag.'

'That may or may not be the case,' said Tiffany haughtily, 'but I am a lot more big and considerably less wee than I used to be.'

'And a lot more hag,' said a jolly voice. Tiffany did not have to look to know who was talking. Only Daft Wullie could put his foot in it as far up as his neck. She looked down at his beaming little face. And he never did quite understand what it was that he was doing wrong.

Hag! It didn't sound pretty, but every witch was a hag to the Feegles, however young she was. They didn't mean anything by it – well, *probably* didn't mean anything by it, but you could never tell for certain – and sometimes Rob Anybody grinned when he said it, but it was not their fault that to anyone not six inches tall the word meant someone who combed her hair with a rake and had worse teeth than an old sheep. Being called a hag when you are nine can be sort of funny. It isn't quite so amusing when you are nearly sixteen and have had a very bad day and very little sleep and could really, really do with a bath.

Rob Anybody clearly noticed this, because he turned to his brother and said, 'Ye will bring to mind, brother o' mine, that there was times when ye should stick your head up a duck's bottom rather than talk?'

Daft Wullie looked down at his feet. 'Sorry, Rob. I couldnae find a duck the noo.'

The head man of the Feegles glanced down at the girl on the floor, sleeping gently under her blanket, and suddenly everything was serious.

'If we had been here when that leathering was happening, it would have been a bad day for him, I'll tell ye,' said Rob Anybody.

'Just as well that you weren't here, then,' said Tiffany. 'You don't want to find people coming up to your mound with shovels, do you? You keep away from bigjobs, you hear me? You make them nervous. When people get nervous, they get angry. But since you're here you can make yourselves useful. I want to get this poor girl up to the mound.'

'Aye, we know,' said Rob. 'Was it not the kelda herself who was sending us down here to find you?'

'She knew about this? *Jeannie* knew about this?'

'I dinnae ken,' said Rob nervously. He always got nervous when talking about his wife, Tiffany knew. He loved her to distraction, and the thought of her even frowning in his direction turned his knees to jelly. The life of all the other Feegles was generally about fighting, stealing and boozing, with a few extra bits like getting food, which they mostly stole, and doing the laundry, which they mostly did not do. As the kelda's husband, Rob Anybody had to do the Explaining as well, and that was never an easy job for a Feegle. 'Jeannie has the kenning o' things, ye ken,' he said, not looking directly at Tiffany. She felt sorry for him then; it must be better to be between a rock and a hard place than to be between a kelda and a hag, she thought.

CHAPTER 3

# Those Who Stir in Their Sleep

The moon was well up and turned the world into a sharp-edged jigsaw of black and silver as Tiffany and the Feegles headed up onto the downs. The Nac Mac Feegles could move in absolute silence when they wanted to; Tiffany had been carried by them herself, and it was always a gentle ride, and really quite pleasant, especially if they had had a bath in the last month or so.

Every shepherd on the hills must have seen the Feegle mound at some time or other. No one ever talked about it. Some things were best left unspoken, such as the fact that the loss of lambs on the down where the Feegles lived was much less than it was in more distant parts of the Chalk, but on the other hand a *few* sheep would disappear; they would be the weak lambs or the very old ewes (Feegles liked old strong mutton, the kind that you could chew for hours) – the flocks were guarded, and guards took their pay. Besides, the mound was very close to all that remained of Granny Aching's shepherding hut, and that was almost holy ground.

Tiffany could smell the smoke leaking up through the thorn bushes as they got nearer. Well, at least it was a blessing that she would not have to slide down the hole to get into it; that sort of thing was all very well when you were nine, but when you were nearly sixteen it was undignified, the ruination of a good dress and, although she would not admit this, far too tight for comfort.

But Jeannie the kelda had been making changes. There was an old chalk pit quite close to the mound, reached by a passageway underground. The kelda had got the boys working on this with bits of corrugated iron and tarpaulin which they had 'found' in that very distinctive way they had of 'finding' things. It still looked like a typical upland chalk pit, because brambles and Climbing Henry and Twirling Betty vines had been trained over it so that barely a mouse would be able to find its way inside. Water could get in though, dripping down the iron and filling barrels down below; there was a much larger space now for cooking, and even enough room for Tiffany to climb down if she remembered to shout out her name first, when hidden hands pulled strings and opened the way through the impassable brambles as if by magic. The kelda had her own private bathroom down there; the Feegles themselves took a bath only when something reminded them, such as an eclipse of the moon.

Amber was whisked down the hole and Tiffany waited impatiently close to the right spot in the bramble forest until the thorns magically 'moved aside'.

Jeannie, the kelda, almost as round as a football, was waiting for her, a baby under each arm.

'I am very pleased to see you, Tiffany,' she said, and for some reason that sounded odd and out of place. 'I have told the boys tae go and let off steam outside,' the kelda went on. 'This is woman's work, and not a pretty errand at that, I'm sure ye will agree. They have laid her down by the fire and I have started to put the soothings on her. I do think she will bide fine, but it was a good job that ye have done this night. Your famous Mistress Weatherwax her own self could not have done a better job.'

'She taught me to take away pain,' said Tiffany.

'Ye dinnae say?' said the kelda, giving Tiffany a strange look. 'I hope ye never have occasion to regret the day she did ye that . . . kindness.'

At this point several Feegles appeared down the tunnel that led into the main mound. They looked uneasily from their kelda to their hag, and a very reluctant spokesfeegle said, 'Not to be barging in or anything, ladies, but we was cooking up a wee late-night snack, and Rob said to ask if the big wee hag would like a wee tasty?'

Tiffany sniffed. There was a definite scent in the air,

and it was the kind of scent you get when you have sheep meat in close conjunction with, for example, a roasting pan. All right, she thought, we know they do it, but they might have the good manners not to do it in front of me!

The spokesfeegle must have realized this because, while wringing the edge of his kilt madly with both hands, as a Feegle generally did when he was telling an enormous lie, he added, 'Weel, I think I did hear that maybe a piece of sheep kind of accidentally fell intae the pan when it was cooking and we tried to drag it oot but – well, ye ken what sheep is like – it panicked and fought back.' At this point the speaker's obvious relief at being able to cobble some kind of excuse together led him to attempt greater heights of fiction, and he went on: 'It is my thinking that it must have been suicidal owing to having nothing to do all day but eat grass.'

He looked hopefully at Tiffany to see if this had worked, just as the kelda cut in sharply and said, 'Wee Honeymouth Jock, just you go in there and say that the big wee hag would like a mutton sandwich, OK?' She looked up at Tiffany and said, 'No arguing, girl. Ye look tae me to be all but swaying for want of a decent hot meal. I ken well that witches looks after everybody but theirselves. Run ye along, boys.'

Tiffany could still feel a tension in the air. The kelda's solemn little gaze stayed fixed on her, and then Jeannie said, 'Can you remember yesterday?'

It sounded like a silly question, but Jeannie was never silly. It was worth thinking about, although

Tiffany yearned for some suicidal sheep and a decent night's sleep.

'Yesterday – well, I suppose it's the day before yesterday now – I was called over to Buckle-Without,' she said thoughtfully. 'The blacksmith there had not been careful with his forge, and it had broken open and shot hot coals all down his leg. I treated him and took away the pain, which I put in his anvil. For the doing of this, I was paid twenty-four pounds of potatoes, three cured deerskins, half a bucket of nails, one old but serviceable sheet good enough to make bandages and one small jar of hedgehog fat which his wife swore was a capital remedy for inflammation of the pipes. I also had a good helping of stew with the family. Then, since I was in the vicinity, I went on to Buckle-With-Many, where I saw to Mr Gower's little problem. I mentioned to him about the hedgehog fat, and he said it was a wonderful cure for the unmentionables, and traded me one whole ham for the jar. Mrs Gower made me tea and allowed me to pick a bushel basket of love-in-a-pickle, which grows more freely in her garden than I have ever seen it grow anywhere else.' Tiffany paused a moment. 'Oh yes, and then I stopped off at Wits End to change a poultice, and then I went and saw to the Baron, and then, of course, the rest of the day was my own, hah! But on the whole it was not a bad day, as days go, as people were too busy thinking about the fair.'

'And as days go, the day has gone,' said the kelda, 'and no doubt it was a busy and useful one. But all day

I had premonitions about ye, Tiffany Aching.' Jeannie held up a small nut-brown hand as Tiffany began to protest, and went on, 'Tiffany, ye must know that I watch over you. Ye are the hag o' the hills, after all, and I have the power to watch ye in my heid, to keep an eye on ye, because somebody must. I know ye know this because ye are clever, and I know that ye pretend to me that ye do not know, just as I pretend not to know that I know, and I am sure that ye know that too, yes?'

'I might have to work all that out with a pencil and paper,' Tiffany said, trying to laugh it off.

'It is nae funny! I can see ye clouded in my heid. Danger around ye. And the worst of it is, I cannae see from whence it comes. And that is not right!'

Just as Tiffany opened her mouth, half a dozen Feegles came scurrying down the tunnel from the mound, carrying a plate between them. Tiffany couldn't help noticing, because witches always noticed things if they possibly can, that the blue decoration around the edge of the plate looked very much like that on her mother's second-best dinner service. The rest of the plate was obscured by a large piece of mutton, along with jacket potatoes. It smelled wonderful, and her stomach took over her brain. A witch took her meals where she could, and was happy to get them.

The meat had been cut in half, although the half for the kelda was slightly smaller than the half for Tiffany. Strictly speaking, you cannot have a half that is smaller than the other half, because it wouldn't be a half, but human beings know what it means. And keldas always had a huge appetite for their size, because they had babies to make.

This wasn't the time to talk anyway. A Feegle offered Tiffany a knife which was, in fact, a Feegle claymore, and then held up a rather grubby tin can with a spoon stuck in it.

'Relish?' he suggested shyly.

This was a bit posh for a Feegle meal, although Jeannie was civilizing them somewhat, in so far as you could civilize a Feegle. At least they were getting the right idea. Nevertheless, Tiffany understood enough to be wary.

'What's in it?' she asked, knowing that this was a dangerous question.

'Oh, wonderful stuff,' said the Feegle, rattling the spoon in the can. 'There's crabapple, there is, and mustard seed and horseradish and snails and wild herbs and garlic and a sprinkling of Johnny-come-lately—' But he had gabbled one word a bit too quickly for Tiffany's taste.

'Snails?' she interrupted.

'Oh aye, yes, very nourishing, full of vit'mins and min'rals, ye ken, and those wee pro-teenies, and the nice thing is, with enough garlic, they taste of garlic.'

'What do they taste of if you *don't* use garlic?' said Tiffany.

'Snails,' said the kelda, taking pity on the waiter, 'and I have to say they are good eating, my girl. The boys let them out at night to graze on wild cabbage and dog lettuce. They are quite tasty, and I think ye might approve of the fact that there is no stealing involved.'

Well, that was a good thing, Tiffany had to admit. Feegles did steal, joyously and repeatedly, as much for sport as anything else. On the other hand, to the right people, in the right place, at the right time, they could be *very* generous, and this was, fortunately, happening right now.

'Even so, Feegles farming?' she said aloud.

'Oh no,' said the spokesfeegle, while his fellows behind him pantomimed insulted distaste by making 'yuk' noises and sticking their fingers down their throat. 'It is nae farming, it is livestock herding, as is suitable for them who is free o' spirit and likes to feel the wind up their kilt. Mind ye, the stampedes can be a wee bit embarrassing.'

'Have some, please do,' the kelda pleaded. 'It will encourage them.'

In fact, the new Feegle cuisine was quite tasty. Perhaps it's true what they say, thought Tiffany, that anything goes with garlic. Except custard.

'Don't mind my boys,' said Jeannie when they had both eaten their fill. 'The times are changing and I think they know it. For ye too. How do ye feel?'

'Oh, you know. The usual,' said Tiffany. 'Tired, flustered and upset. That sort of thing.'

'Ye work too hard, my girl. I fear ye do not have enough to eat, and I can certainly see ye don't get enough sleep. When did ye last sleep the night in a proper bed, I wonder? Ye ken that ye must have sleep;

ye cannae think properly without some time to rest. I fear ye will soon need all the strength ye can muster. Would ye like me to put the soothings on ye?'

Tiffany yawned again. 'Thank you for offering, Jeannie,' she said, 'but I don't think I need them, if it's all the same to you.' There was a pile of greasy fleeces in the corner that had probably not long before belonged to sheep who had decided to say goodbye to the cruel world and commit suicide. They looked very inviting. 'I had better go and see to the girl.' Tiffany's legs did not seem to want her to move. 'Still, I expect she is as safe as houses in a Feegle mound.'

'Oh, no,' said Jeannie softly as Tiffany's eyes shut. 'Much, *much* safer than houses.'

When Tiffany was actually snoring, Jeannie walked slowly up and into the mound itself. Amber was curled up near the fire, but Rob Anybody had stationed some of the older and wiser Feegles around her. This was because the evening fighting was going on. The Nac Mac Feegle fought as often as they breathed, and generally at the same time. It was by way of being a way of life, in a way. Besides, when you were only a few inches tall, you had the whole world to fight and so you might as well learn early.

Jeannie sat down by her husband and watched the brawling for a while. Young Feegles were bouncing off the walls, their uncles and one another. Then she said, 'Rob, do ye think we are bringing our boys up properly?'

Rob Anybody, who was sensitive to Jeannie's mood, glanced across at the sleeping girl.

'Oh aye, no doubt about it— Hey, did ye no' see that? Slightly-more-wee-than-wee-Jock-Jock kicked Daft Wullie in the pog! Wonderful dirty fightin', and he's still only three inches high!'

'He is going to make a grand warrior one day, Rob, that's true enough,' said Jeannie, 'but . . .'

'I always tell them,' Rob Anybody went on excitedly as the young Feegle flew over their heads, 'that the way to success is always to attack only people who are much bigger than ye are! Important rule!'

Jeannie sighed as another young Feegle smacked into the wall, shook his head and rushed back into the fight. It was almost impossible to hurt a Feegle. Any human who tried to stamp on a Feegle would find that the little man he thought was under his boot was now in fact climbing up his trouser leg, and after that the day could only get worse. Besides, if you saw one Feegle, there were probably many more around that you hadn't spotted, and they had certainly spotted *you*.

Perhaps the bigjobs have bigger problems because they're bigger than us, the kelda thought. She sighed inwardly. She would never let her husband know this, but sometimes she did wonder whether a young Feegle might profitably be taught something like, well, accountancy. Something that didnae mean ye had to bounce off the walls, and didnae mean you had to fight all the time. But then, would he still be a Feegle?

'I'm feared for the big wee hag, Rob,' she said. 'Something is wrong.'

'She wanted to be a hag, lassie,' said Rob. 'Now she

has to dree her weird, same as us. She is a bonny fighter, ye ken. She kissed the Lord of the Winter to his death and banged the Queen o' the Elves with a frying pan. And I mind the time that invisible beastie got into her heid, and she wrestled it and sent it away. She fights.'

'Oh, I ken that well enough,' said the kelda. 'She kissed the face o' winter and made springtime come again. It was a great thing that she did, sure enough, but she had the mantle of the summer about her. It was that power she dealt to him, not just her own. She did it well, mind, I can think of none who would have done it better, but she must beware.'

'What enemy can she have that we cannae face with her?' Rob asked.

'I cannae tell,' said the kelda, 'but in my heid, it seems like this. When she kissed the winter, it shook me to my roots; it seemed like it shook the world and I cannae but wonder that there might be those who stirred in their slumber. You mak' certain, Rob Anybody, to keep more than one eye on her.'

CHAPTER 4

# The Real Shilling

Tiffany woke hungry and to the sound of laughter. Amber was awake and, against all probability, happy.

Tiffany found out why when she managed to squeeze most of herself into the tunnel that led to the mound. The girl was still lying curled up on one side, but a group of young Feegles were entertaining her with somersaults and handsprings and occasionally tripping one another up in humorous ways.

The laughter was younger than Amber was; it sounded like the chuckle a baby makes when it sees shiny things in pretty colours. Tiffany did not know how the soothings worked, but they were better than anything a witch could do; they seemed to settle people down and make them better from inside their head outwards. They made you well and, best of all, they made you forget. Sometimes, it seemed to Tiffany, the kelda talked about them as if they were alive – living thoughts perhaps, or kindly living creatures that somehow took away the bad things.

'She's doing well,' said the kelda, appearing out of nowhere. 'She will bide fine. There will be nightmares as the darkness comes out. The soothings can't do everything. She's coming back into herself now, right from the start, and that's the best thing.'

It was still dark but dawn edged the horizon. Tiffany had a dirty job to do before daylight.

'Can I leave her here with you for a little while?' she said. 'There's a small task that needs doing.'

I shouldn't have gone to sleep, she thought as she climbed out of the pit. I should have gone right back! I shouldn't have left the poor little thing there!

She tugged the broomstick out of the thorn bushes around the mound, and stopped dead. Someone was watching her; she could feel it on the back of her neck. She turned sharply, and saw an old woman all in black, quite tall, but leaning on a walking-stick. Even as Tiffany looked, the woman vanished, slowly, as if evaporating into the scenery.

'Mistress Weatherwax?' Tiffany said to the empty air, but that was silly. Granny Weatherwax would not be seen dead with a walking-stick, and certainly wouldn't be seen alive with one. And there was movement in the corner of her eye. When she spun round again there was a hare, right up on her* hind legs, watching her with interest and no sign of fear.

It was what they did, of course. The Feegles didn't hunt them, and the average sheepdog would run out of legs before a hare ran out of breath. The hare had no stuffy burrow to be trapped in; speed was where a hare lived, shooting across the landscape like a dream of the wind – she could afford to sit and watch the slow world go by.

This one burst into flames. She blazed for a moment and then, entirely unharmed, sped away in a blur.

All right, thought Tiffany as the broomstick came free, let's approach this from the point of view of common sense. The turf isn't scorched and hares are not known for bursting into flames, so— She stopped as a tiny trapdoor flicked open in her memory.

*The hare runs into the fire.*

Had she seen that written down anywhere? Had she heard it as part of a song? A nursery rhyme? What had the hare got to do with anything? But she was a witch, after all, and there was a job to do. Mysterious omens could wait. Witches knew that mysterious omens were around all the time. The world was always very nearly drowning in mysterious omens. You just had to pick the one that was convenient.

Bats and owls steered effortlessly out of Tiffany's way as she sped over the sleeping village. The

* Whatever sex a hare is, to the true countryman, all hares are referred to as 'her'.

Petty house was on the very edge. It had a garden. Every house in the village had a garden. Most of them had a garden full of vegetables or, if the wife had the upper hand, half vegetables and half flowers. The Petty house was fronted by a quarter of an acre of stinging nettles.

That had always annoyed Tiffany right down to her country boots. How hard would it have been to grub up the weeds and put in a decent crop of potatoes? All they needed was muck, and there was plenty of that in a farming village; the trick was to stop it getting into the house. Mr Petty could have made an effort.

He had been back to the barn, or at least somebody had. The baby was now on top of the heap of straw. Tiffany had come prepared with some old, but still serviceable linen, which was at least better than sacking and straw. But somebody had disturbed the little body, and put flowers around it, except that the flowers were, in fact, stinging nettles. They had also lit a candle in one of the tin-plate candlesticks that every house in the village owned. A candlestick. A light. On a pile of loose straw. In a barn full of tinder-dry hay and more straw. Tiffany stared in horror, and then heard the grunt overhead.

A man was *hanging* from the barn's rafters.

They creaked. A little dust and some shreds of hay floated down. Tiffany caught them quickly and picked up the candle before the next fall of wisps set the whole barn alight. She was about to blow it out when it struck her that this would leave her in the dark with the gently spinning figure that may or may not be a corpse. She put it down ever so carefully by the door and scrabbled around to find something sharp. But this was Petty's barn, and everything was blunt, except a saw.

It had to be him up there! Who else could it be? 'Mr Petty?' she said, clambering into the dusty rafters.

There was something like a wheeze. Was this good?

Tiffany managed to hook one leg round a beam, leaving one hand free to wield the saw. The trouble was that she needed two more hands. The rope was tight round the man's neck, and the blunt teeth of the saw bounced on it, making the man swing even more. And he was beginning to struggle too, the fool, so that the rope not only swung, but twisted as well. In a moment, she would fall down.

There was a movement in the air, a flash of iron, and Petty dropped like a rock. Tiffany managed to hold her balance long enough to grab a dusty rafter and half climb and half slither after him.

Her fingernails clawed at the rope round his neck but it was as tight as a drum . . . and there should have been a flourish of music because suddenly Rob Anybody was there, right in front of her; he held up a tiny, shiny claymore and looked at her questioningly.

She groaned inwardly. What good are you, Mr Petty? What good have you been? You can't even hang yourself properly. What good will you ever do? Wouldn't I be doing the world and you a favour by letting you finish what you began?

That was the thing about thoughts. They thought themselves, and then dropped into your head in the hope that you would think so too. You had to slap them down, thoughts like that; they would take a witch over if she let them. And then it would all break down, and nothing would be left but the cackling.

She had heard it said that, before you could understand anybody, you needed to walk a mile in their shoes, which did not make a whole lot of sense because, probably *after* you had walked a mile in their shoes you would understand that they were chasing you and accusing you of the theft of a pair of shoes – although, of course, you could probably outrun them owing to their lack of footwear. But she understood what the proverb *actually* meant, and here was a man one breath away from death. She had no option, no option at all. She had to give him that breath, for the sake of a handful of nettles; something inside the wretched hulk had still managed to be good. It was a tiny spark, but it was there. And there was no argument.

Hating herself deep down for being so soppy, she nodded at the Big Man of the Feegle clan. 'All right,' she said. 'Try not to hurt him too much.'

The sword sparkled; and the cut was made with the delicacy of a surgeon, although the surgeon would have washed his hands first.

The rope actually sprang out as the Feegle severed it, and shot away as though it was a serpent. Petty gasped air so hard that the candle flame by the door seemed to flatten for a moment.

Tiffany got up off her knees and brushed herself down. 'What did you come back for?' she said. 'What were you looking for? What did you expect to find?'

Mr Petty lay there. There wasn't even a grunt in reply. It was hard to hate him now, wheezing on the floor.

Being a witch meant you had to make choices, usually the choices that ordinary people did not want to make or even to know about. So she washed his face with a bit of torn cloth moistened from the pump outside and wrapped the dead child in the rather larger and cleaner bit of cloth that she had brought for the purpose. It wasn't the best of shrouds, but it was honest and civilized. She reminded herself, in a dreamy kind of way, that she needed to build up her store of makeshift bandages and realized how grateful she should be. 'Thank you, Rob,' she said. 'I don't I think I could have managed by myself.'

'I reckon that maybe ye could,' said Rob Anybody, while they both knew that she couldn't. 'It just so happened that I was passing by, ye ken, and not following ye at all. One of them coincidences.'

'There have been a lot of those coincidences lately,' said Tiffany.

'Aye,' said Rob, grinning, 'it must be another coincidence.'

It was impossible to embarrass a Feegle. They just couldn't grasp the idea.

He was watching her. 'What happens now?' he said.

That was *the* question, wasn't it. A witch needed to make people believe she knew what to do next, even if she didn't. Petty was going to live, and the poor child was not going to stop being dead. 'I'll take care of things,' she said. 'It's what we do.'

Only it's just me; there is no 'us', she thought as she flew through the mists of morning to the place of flowers. I wish, I wish there was.

In the hazel woods there was a clearing of flowers from early spring to late autumn. There was meadowsweet and foxglove and old man's trousers and Jack-jump-into-bed and ladies' bonnets and three-times-Charlie and sage and southernwood and pink yarrow and ladies' bedstraw and cowslips and primroses and two types of orchid.

It was where the old lady that they had called the witch was buried. If you knew where to look, you could see what little was left of her cottage underneath all that greenery, and if you really knew where to look, you could see the place where she had been buried. If you really and truly knew where to look, you could find the spot where Tiffany had buried the old lady's cat too; there was catnip growing on it.

Once upon a time, the rough music had come for the old woman and her cat, oh yes it had, and the people walking to its drumming had dragged her out into the snow and pulled down the rickety cottage and burned her books because they had pictures of stars in them.

And why? Because the Baron's son had gone missing and Mrs Snapperly had no family and no teeth and, to be honest, cackled a bit as well. And that made her a witch, and the people of the Chalk didn't trust witches, so she was pulled out into the snow, and while the fire ate up the thatch of the cottage, page after page of stars crackled and crinkled into the night sky while the men stoned the cat to death. And that winter, after she had hammered on doors that remained closed to her, the old woman died in the snow, and because she had to be buried somewhere, there was a shallow grave where the old cottage used to be.

But the old woman had nothing to do with the loss of the Baron's son, had she? And soon after, Tiffany had gone all the way to a strange fairyland to bring him back, hadn't she? And nobody talked about the old lady these days, did they? But when they walked past the place in the summer, the flowers filled the air with delight and bees filled it with the colours of honey.

No one talked about it. After all, what would you say? Rare flowers growing on the grave of the old woman and catnip growing where the Aching girl had buried the cat? It was a mystery, and maybe a judgement, although whose judgement it was, on whom, for what and why, was best not thought about, let alone discussed. Nevertheless, wonderful flowers growing over the remains of the possible witch – how could that happen?

Tiffany didn't ask that question. The seeds had been

expensive to buy and she had had to go all the way to Twoshirts to get them, but she had vowed that every summer the brilliance in the wood would remind people that there had been an old lady they had hounded to death and been buried there. She did not quite know why she thought that was important, but she was certain to the centre of her soul that it was.

When she had finished digging the deep but sad little hole in a patch of love-in-a-hurry, Tiffany looked around to make certain that no early-morning traveller was watching and used both hands to fill the hole with dirt, moving dead leaves and transplanting some forget-me-lots. They weren't really right here, but they grew fast and that was important because . . . *someone was watching her*. It was important not to look round. She knew she couldn't be seen. In all her life she had met only one person who was better than her at not being seen, and that was Granny Weatherwax. It was still misty too, and she would have heard if anyone had come along the path. It wasn't a bird or animal, either. *They* always felt different.

A witch should never have to look around because they should *know* who was behind them. Usually she could work it out, but every sense she had told her that no one but Tiffany Aching was there, and somehow, in some strange way, it felt wrong.

'Too much to do, not enough sleep,' she said aloud, and thought she heard a faint voice say, 'Yes.' It was like an echo except there was nothing for it to echo from. She flew away as fast as she could make the broomstick go, which, not being very fast at all, at least served to prevent it looking as though she was running away.

Going nuts. Witches didn't often talk about it, but they were aware of it all the time.

Going nuts; or, rather *not* going nuts, was the soul and centre of witchcraft, and this was how it worked. After a while, a witch, who almost always worked by herself in the tradition of witches, had a tendency to go . . . strange. Of course, it depended on the length of time and the strength of mind of the witch, but sooner or later they tended to get confused about things like right and wrong and good and bad and truth and consequences. That could be very dangerous. So witches had to keep one another normal, or at least what was normal for witches. It didn't take very much: a tea party, a singsong, a stroll in the woods, and somehow everything balanced up, and they could look at adverts for gingerbread cottages in the builder's brochure without putting a deposit on one.

On top of everything else Tiffany was worried about going nuts. It was two months since she had last been up into the mountains and three months since she had last seen Miss Tick, the only other witch you ever saw down here. There wasn't time to go visiting. There was always too much to do. Perhaps that was the trick of it, Tiffany thought. If you kept yourself busy you wouldn't have *time* to go nuts.

The sun was well up when she got back to the Feegle

mound and she was shocked to see Amber sitting out on the side of the mound, surrounded by Feegles and laughing. The kelda was waiting for Tiffany by the time she had garaged the broomstick in the thorn bushes.

'I hope ye do not mind,' she said when she saw Tiffany's face. 'The sunshine is a great healer.'

'Jeannie, it was wonderful of you to put the soothings on her, but I don't want her to see too much of you. She might tell people.'

'Oh, it will all seem like a dream tae her, the soothings will see to that,' said Jeannie calmly, 'and who will take much heed of a wee girl prattling about the fairies?'

'She is thirteen!' said Tiffany. 'It's not supposed to happen!'

'Is she no' happy?'

'Well, yes, but . . .'

There was a steely look in Jeannie's eye. She had always been very respectful to Tiffany, but respect requires respect in its turn. It was Jeannie's mound, after all, and probably her land as well.

Tiffany settled for saying, 'Her mother will be worrying.'

'Is that so?' said Jeannie. 'And did her mam worry when she left the poor thing taking a beating?'

Tiffany wished the kelda wasn't so astute. People used to tell Tiffany that she was so sharp she would cut herself, but the kelda's steady grey gaze could chop iron nails.

'Well, Amber's mother is . . . she's not very . . . clever.'

'So I hear,' said Jeannie, 'but most beasts is short on brains, and yet still the doe will stand her ground to defend her fawn, and a fox for her cub will face down the dog.'

'Humans are more complicated,' said Tiffany.

'So it seems,' said the kelda, her voice chilly just for that moment. 'Well, the soothings is working fine, so maybe the girl needs to be back in your complicated world?'

Where her father is still alive, Tiffany reminded herself. I know he is. He was bruised, but he was breathing, and I hope to goodness he sobers up. And is this problem ever going to end? It has to be sorted out! I've got other things to do! And I've got to go and see the Baron this afternoon!

Tiffany's father met them when they walked into the farmyard; Tiffany generally left the broomstick tied to a tree just outside, in theory because flying overhead frightened the chickens, but mostly because she was never able to land very gracefully and certainly didn't want an audience.

He looked from Amber to his daughter. 'Is she all right? She looks a bit . . . dreamy.'

'She's had something to calm her down and make her feel better,' said Tiffany, 'and she shouldn't run around.'

'Her mum has been in a dreadful state, you know,'

Tiffany's father went on reproachfully, 'but I told her you were looking after Amber in a very safe place.'

There was more than a hint of 'You are sure about that, aren't you?' in the way he spoke, and Tiffany was careful to ignore it, and simply said, 'I was.' She tried to imagine Mrs Petty in a dreadful state, and it didn't work. Every time she had ever seen the woman she had a look of baffled apprehension, as if life had too many puzzles and you just had to wait until the next one hit you.

Tiffany's father pulled his daughter to one side and lowered his voice. 'Petty came back in the night,' he hissed, 'and they say that someone tried to kill him!'

'*What?*'

'True as I'm standing here.'

Tiffany turned to Amber. The girl was staring at the sky as if hoping patiently for something interesting to happen.

'Amber,' she said carefully, 'you know how to feed chickens, don't you?'

'Oh yes, miss.'

'Well, go and feed ours, will you? There's grain in the barn.'

'Your mum fed them hours ago—' her father began, but Tiffany dragged him away quickly.

'When did this happen?' she asked, watching Amber walking obediently into the barn.

'Some time last night. Mrs Petty told me. He was beaten badly. In that rackety old barn. Right where we were sitting last night.'

'Mrs Petty went back? After everything that happened? What does she see in him?'

Mr Aching gave a shrug. 'He is her husband.'

'But everyone knows he beats her up!'

Her father looked a bit embarrassed. 'Well,' he said, 'I suppose to some women any husband is better than none.'

Tiffany opened her mouth to reply, looked into her father's eyes and saw the truth of what he had said. She had seen some of them up in the mountains, worn out by too many children and not enough money. Of course, if they knew Nanny Ogg, something could be done about the children at least, but you still found the families who sometimes, in order to put food on the table, had to sell the chairs. And there was never anything you could do about it.

'Mr Petty wasn't beaten up, Dad, although it wouldn't be such a bad idea if he was. I found him trying to hang himself, and I cut him down.'

'He's got two broken ribs, and bruises all over him.'

'It was a long way down, Dad – he was choking to death! What should I have done? Let him swing? He has lived to see another day, whether he deserves to or not! It's not my job to be an executioner! There was a bouquet, Dad! Weeds and nettles! His hands were swollen with nettle stings! There's at least some part of him that deserves to live, do you see?'

'But you did steal the baby away.'

'No, Dad, I stole away *with* the baby. Listen, Dad, do get it right. I buried the child, which was dead. I saved the man who was dying. I did those things, Dad. People might not understand – might make up stories. I don't care. You do the job that is in front of you.'

There was a clucking, and Amber walked across the yard with the chickens following her in a line. The clucking was being done by Amber, and as Tiffany and her father watched, the chickens marched back and forth as if under the command of a drill sergeant. The girl was giggling to herself in between clucks, and after managing to get the chickens to walk solemnly in a circle she looked up at Tiffany and her father as if nothing had happened and led the fowls back into the barn.

After a pause Tiffany's father said, 'That did just happen, didn't it?'

'Yes,' said Tiffany. 'I have no idea why.'

'I've been talking to some of the other lads,' said her father, 'and your mother has been talking to the women. We'll keep an eye on the Pettys. Things have been let go that shouldn't have. People can't expect to leave everything to you. People mustn't think that you can fix everything, and if you'll take my advice, neither will you. There are some things a whole village has to do.'

'Thanks, Dad,' said Tiffany, 'but I think I had better go and see to the Baron now.'

Tiffany could only just remember ever seeing the Baron as a well man. Nor did anyone seem to know what was wrong with him. But, like many other invalids she had seen, he somehow kept on going, living in a holding pattern and waiting to die.

She had heard one of the villagers call him a creaking door which never slammed; he was getting worse now, and in her opinion it was not going to be very long before his life slammed shut.

But she could take away the pain, and even frighten it a little so it wouldn't come back for a while.

Tiffany hurried to the castle. The nurse, Miss Spruce, was waiting when she arrived, and her face was pale.

'It's not one of his good days,' she said, then added with a modest little smile, 'I have been praying for him all morning.'

'I'm sure that was very kind of you,' said Tiffany. She had taken care to keep any sarcasm out of her voice, but she got a frown from the nurse anyway.

The room Tiffany was ushered into smelled like sickrooms everywhere: all too much of people, and not enough air. The nurse stood in the doorway as if she was on guard. Tiffany could feel her permanently suspicious gaze on the back of her neck. There was more and more of that sort of attitude about. Sometimes you got wandering preachers around who didn't like witches, and people would listen to them. It seemed to Tiffany that people lived in a very strange world sometimes. Everybody knew, in some mysterious way, that witches ran away with babies and blighted crops, and all the other nonsense. And at the same time, they would come running to the witch when they needed help.

The Baron lay in a tangle of sheets, his face grey, his hair totally white now, with little pink patches where it had all gone. He looked neat, though. He had always been a neat man, and every morning one of the guards would come and give him a shave. It cheered him up, as far as anyone could tell, but right now he looked straight through Tiffany. She was used to this; the Baron was what they called 'a man of the old school'. He was proud and did not have the best of tempers, but he would stand up for himself at all times. To him, the pain was a bully, and what do you do to bullies? You stood up to them, because they always ran away in the end. But the pain didn't know about *that* rule. It just bullied even more. And the Baron lay with thin white lips; Tiffany could hear him *not* screaming.

Now, she sat down on a stool beside him, flexed her fingers, took a deep breath, and then received the pain, calling it out of the wasted body and putting it into the invisible ball just above her shoulder.

'I don't hold with magic, you know,' said the nurse from the doorway.

Tiffany winced like a tightrope walker who has just felt someone hit the other end of the rope with a big stick. Carefully, she let the flow of pain settle down, a little bit at a time.

'I mean,' said the nurse, 'I know it makes him feel better, but where does all this healing power come from, that's what I'd like to know?'

'Perhaps it comes from all your praying, Miss

Spruce,' said Tiffany sweetly, and was glad to see the moment of fury on the woman's face.

But Miss Spruce had the hide of an elephant. 'We must be sure that we don't get involved with dark and demonic forces. Better a little pain in this world than an eternity of suffering in the next!'

Up in the mountains there were sawmills driven by water, and they had big circular saws that spun so fast they were nothing but a silver blur in the air . . . until an absent-minded man forgot to pay attention, when it became a *red* disc and the air was raining fingers.

Tiffany felt like that now. She needed to concentrate and the woman was determined to go on talking, while the pain was waiting for just one moment's lack of attention. Oh well, nothing for it . . . she threw the pain at a candlestick beside the bed. It shattered instantly, and the candle flashed into flame; she stamped on it until it went out. Then she turned to the astonished nurse.

'Miss Spruce, I am sure that what you have to say is very interesting, but on the whole, Miss Spruce, I don't really care what you think about anything. I don't mind you staying in here, Miss Spruce, but what I do mind, Miss Spruce, is that this is very difficult and can be dangerous for me if it goes wrong. Go away, Miss Spruce, or stay, Miss Spruce, but most of all, *shut up*, Miss Spruce, because I've only just started and there is still a lot of pain to shift.'

Miss Spruce gave her another look. It was fearsome.

Tiffany returned this with a look of her own, and if

there is one thing that a witch learns how to do, it is *how* to look.

The door shut behind the enraged nurse.

'Talk quietly – she listens at doors.'

The voice came from the Baron, but it was hardly a voice at all; you could just hear in it the tones of someone used to command, but now it was cracked and failing, every word pleading for enough time to say the *next* word.

'I'm sorry, sir, but I must concentrate,' said Tiffany. 'I would hate for this to go wrong.'

'Of course. I shall remain silent.'

Taking away pain was dangerous, difficult and very tiring, but there was, well, a wonderful compensation in seeing the grey face of the old man come back to life. There was already some pinkness to his skin, and it was fleshing out as more and more pain flowed out of him and through Tiffany and into the new little invisible ball floating above her right shoulder.

Balance. It was all about balance. That had been one of the first things that she had learned: the centre of the seesaw has neither up nor down, but upness and downness flow through it while it remains unmoved. You had to be the centre of the seesaw so that pain flowed *through* you, not *into* you. It was very hard. But she could do it! She prided herself on it; even Granny Weatherwax had grunted when Tiffany had showed her one day how she had mastered the trick. And a grunt from Granny Weatherwax was like a round of applause from anybody else.

But the Baron was smiling. 'Thank you, Miss Tiffany Aching. And now, I would like to sit in my chair.'

This was unusual, and Tiffany had to think about it. 'Are you sure, sir? You are still very weak.'

'Yes, everybody tells me that,' said the Baron, waving a hand. 'I can't imagine why they think I don't know. Help me up, Miss Tiffany Aching, for I must speak to you.'

It wasn't very difficult. A girl who could heave Mr Petty out of his bed had little problem with the Baron, whom she handled like a piece of fine china, which he resembled.

'I do not think that you and I, Miss Tiffany Aching, have had more than the simplest and most practical of conversations in all the time you have been seeing to me, yes?' he said when she had him settled with his walking-stick in his hands so that he could lean on it. The Baron was not a man to lounge in a chair if he could sit on the edge of it.

'Well, yes, sir, I think you are right,' said Tiffany carefully.

'I dreamed I had a visitor here last night,' said the Baron, giving her a wicked little grin. 'What do you think of that then, Miss Tiffany Aching?'

'At the moment I have no idea, sir,' said Tiffany, thinking, Not the Feegles! Let it not be the Feegles!

'It was your grandmother, Miss Tiffany Aching. She was a fine woman, and extremely handsome. Oh yes. I was rather upset when she married your grandfather, but I suppose it was for the best. I miss her, you know.'

'You do?' said Tiffany.

The old man smiled. 'After my dear wife passed on, she was the only person left who would dare to argue with me. A man of power and responsibility nevertheless needs somebody to tell him when he is being a bloody fool. Granny Aching fulfilled that task with commendable enthusiasm, I must say. And she needed to, because I was often a bloody fool who needed a kick up the arse, metaphorically speaking. It is my hope, Miss Tiffany Aching, that when I am in my grave you will perform the same service to my son Roland who, as you know, is inclined to be a bit too full of himself at times. He will need somebody to kick him up the arse, metaphorically speaking, or indeed in real life if he gets altogether all too snotty.'

Tiffany tried to hide a smile, then took a moment to adjust the spin of the ball of pain as it hovered companionably by her shoulder. 'Thank you for your trust in me, sir. I shall do my best.'

The Baron gave a polite little cough and said, 'Indeed, at one point I harboured hopes that you and the boy might make a more . . . intimate arrangement?'

'We are good friends,' said Tiffany carefully. 'We were good friends and I trust that we will continue to be . . . good friends.' She hurriedly had to stop the pain wobbling dangerously.

The Baron nodded. 'Jolly good, Miss Tiffany Aching, but please don't let the bond of friendship prevent you from giving him a righteous kick up the arse if he needs one.'

'I will take some pleasure in doing so, sir,' said Tiffany.

'Well done, young lady,' said the Baron, 'and thank you for not chiding me for using the word "arse" or asking me the meaning of the word "metaphorical".'

'No, sir. I know what "metaphorical" means, and "arse" is a traditional usage – nothing to be ashamed of.'

The Baron nodded. 'It has a commendable grown-up sharpness to it. "*Ass*", on the other hand, is quite frankly for spinsters and little children.'

Tiffany turned the words on her tongue for a moment, and said, 'Yes, sir. I think that is probably the long and the short of it.'

'Very good. Incidentally, Miss Tiffany Aching, I cannot conceal my interest in the fact that you do not curtsy in my presence these days. Why not?'

'I am a witch now, sir. We don't do that sort of thing.'

'But I am your baron, young lady.'

'Yes. And I am your witch.'

'But I have soldiers out there who will come running if I call. And I am sure you know, too, that people around here do not always respect witches.'

'Yes, sir. I know that, sir. And I am your witch.'

Tiffany watched the Baron's eyes. They were a pale blue, but right now there was a foxy glint of mischief in them.

The worst thing you could possibly do right now,

she told herself, would be to show any kind of weakness at all. He's like Granny Weatherwax: he tests people.

As if he was reading her mind exactly at that point, the Baron laughed. 'Then you are your own person, Miss Tiffany Aching?'

'I don't know about that, sir. Just lately I feel as if I belong to everybody.'

'Hah,' said the Baron. 'You work very hard and conscientiously, I'm told.'

'I am a witch.'

'Yes,' said the Baron. 'So you have said, clearly and consistently and with some considerable repetition.' He leaned both skinny hands on his walking-stick and looked at her over the top of them. 'It is true then, is it?' he said. 'That some seven years ago you took an iron skillet and went into some sort of fairyland, where you rescued my son from the Queen of the Elves – a most objectionable woman, I have been given to understand?'

Tiffany hesitated about this. 'Do you want it to be so?' she said.

The Baron chuckled and pointed a skinny finger at her. 'Do I want it to be? *Indeed!* A good question, Miss Tiffany Aching, who is a witch. Let me think . . . let us say . . . I want to know the truth.'

'Well, the bit about the frying pan is true, I must admit, and well, Roland had been pretty well knocked about so I, well, had to take charge. A bit.'

'A . . . bit?' said the old man, smiling.

'Not an unreasonably large bit,' said Tiffany quickly.

'And why didn't anybody tell me this at the time, pray?' said the Baron.

'Because you are the Baron,' said Tiffany simply, 'and boys with swords rescue girls. That's how the stories go. That's how stories work. No one really wanted to think the other way round.'

'Didn't you mind?' He wasn't taking his eyes off her, and he hardly seemed to blink. There was no point in lying.

'Yes,' she said. 'A bit.'

'Was it a reasonably large bit?'

'I would say so, yes. But then I went off to learn to be a witch, and it didn't seem to matter any more. That's the truth of it, sir. Excuse me, sir, who told you this?'

'Your father,' said the Baron. 'And I am grateful to him for telling me. He came to see me yesterday, to pay his respects, seeing as I am, as you know, dying. Which is, in fact, another truth. And don't you dare tell him off, young lady, witch or otherwise. Promise me?'

Tiffany knew that the long lie had hurt her father. She'd never really worried about it, but it had worried him.

'Yes, sir, I promise.'

The Baron was silent for a moment, staring at her. 'You know, Miss Tiffany Aching, who is, by regular repetition, a witch, I am at a time when my eyes are cloudy, but my mind, somehow, sees further than you think. But perhaps it is not too late for me to make amends. Under my bed is a chest bound with brass. Go and open it. Go on! Do that now.'

Tiffany pulled out the chest, which felt as if it was full of lead.

'You will find some leather bags,' said the old man behind her. 'Take one of them out. It will contain fifteen dollars.' The Baron coughed. 'Thank you for saving my son.'

'Look, I can't take—' Tiffany began, but the Baron banged his stick on the floor.

'Shut up and listen, please, Miss Tiffany Aching. When you fought the Queen of the Elves, you were not a witch and therefore the tradition against witches taking money does not apply,' he said sharply, his eyes glittering like sapphires. 'With regard to your personal services to myself, I believe you have been paid in food and clean used linen, second-hand footwear and firewood. I trust my housekeeper has been generous? I told her not to stint.'

'What? Oh, oh yes, sir.' And that was true enough. Witches lived in a world of second-hand clothes, old sheets (good for making bandages), boots with some life left in them and, of course, hand-me-downs, hand-me-outs, hand-me-ups, hand-me-rounds and hand-me-overs. In such a world, the pickings to be had from a working castle were like being given the key to a mint. As for the money . . . she turned the leather bag over and over in her hands. It was very heavy.

81

'What do you do with all that stuff, Miss Tiffany Aching?'

'What?' she said absentmindedly, still looking at the bag. 'Oh, er, trade it, pass it on to people who need it . . . that sort of thing.'

'Miss Tiffany Aching, you are suddenly vague. I believe that you were engrossed in thinking that fifteen dollars isn't much, is it, for saving the life of the Baron's son?'

'No!'

'I'll take that as a "yes" then, shall I?'

'*You will take it from me as a no, sir! I am your witch!*' She glared at him, panting. 'And I am trying to balance a rather difficult ball of pain, sir.'

'Ah, Granny Aching's granddaughter. I humbly beg your forgiveness, as I occasionally should have asked for hers. But nevertheless, will you please do me the favour and honour of taking that bag, Miss Tiffany Aching, and putting its contents to such use as you may determine in memory of me. I'm sure it's more money than you have ever seen before.'

'I don't often see any money at all,' she protested, stunned by this.

The Baron banged his stick on the floor again, as if applauding. 'I doubt very much if you have ever seen money like this,' he said merrily. 'You see, although there are fifteen dollars in the bag, they are not the dollars that you are used to, or would be if you were used to them at all. They are *old* dollars, from before they started mucking about with the currency. The modern dollar is mostly brass, in my opinion, and contains as much gold as sea water. These, however, are the real shilling, if you'll excuse my little joke.'

Tiffany excused his little joke, because she didn't get it. He smiled at her puzzlement. 'In short, Miss Tiffany Aching, if you take these coins to the right dealer, he should pay you, oh, I would estimate somewhere in the region of five thousand Ankh-Morpork dollars. I don't know what that would be in terms of old boots, but quite possibly it could buy you an old boot the size of this castle.'

And Tiffany thought: I can't take this. Apart from anything else the bag had become *extremely* heavy. Instead, she said, 'That's far too much for a witch.'

'But not too much for a son,' said the Baron. 'Not too much for an heir, not too much for continuity down the generations. Not too much for removing a lie from the world.'

'But it can't buy me another pair of hands,' said Tiffany, 'or change one second of the past.'

'Nevertheless, I must insist that you take it,' said the Baron, 'if not for your sake, then for mine. It will take a burden off my soul and, believe me, it could do with a bit of shining up at this time, don't you agree? I am going to die soon, am I not?'

'Yes, sir. Very soon, I think, sir.'

Tiffany was beginning to understand something about the Baron by now, and she wasn't surprised when he laughed.

'You know,' he said, 'most people would have said, "Oh, no, old chap, you've got ages yet, you will be up and out of here in no time, lots of life left in you!"'

'Yes, sir. I'm a witch, sir.'

'And in this context that means . . . ?'

'I try very hard not to have to tell lies, sir.'

The old man shifted in his chair, and was suddenly solemn. 'When the time comes . . .' he began, and hesitated.

'I will keep you company, sir, if you wish,' said Tiffany.

The Baron looked relieved. 'Have you ever seen Death?'

She had been expecting this and was ready. 'Usually you just feel him passing, sir, but I have seen him twice, in what would have been the flesh, if he had any. He's a skeleton with a scythe, just like in the books – in fact, I think it's *because* that's what he looks like in the books. He was polite but firm, sir.'

'I'll bet he is!' The old man was silent for a little while and then went on. 'Did he . . . drop any hints about the afterlife?'

'Yes, sir. Apparently it contains no mustard, and I got the impression that it contains no pickles either.'

'Really? Bit of a blow, that. I suppose that chutney is out of the question?'

'I did not go into the subject of pickled condiments in any depth, sir. He had a big scythe.'

There was a loud knocking at the door, and Miss Spruce called loudly, 'Are you all right, sir?'

'In tip-top condition, dear Miss Spruce,' said the Baron loudly, then lowered his voice to say conspiratorially, 'I believe our Miss Spruce does not like you very much, my dear.'

'She thinks I'm unhygienic,' said Tiffany.

'Never really understood about all that nonsense,' said the Baron.

'It's quite easy,' said Tiffany. 'I have to stick my hands in the fire at every opportunity.'

'What? You put your hands in the *fire*?'

Now she was sorry she had mentioned it, but she knew the old man would not now be satisfied until she had shown him. She sighed and crossed over to the fireplace, pulling a large iron poker out of its stand. She admitted to herself that she liked showing off this trick occasionally, and the Baron would be an appreciative audience. But should she do it? Well, the fire trick was not that complicated and the balance of the pain was fine, and it wasn't as if the Baron had much time left.

She drew a bucket of water from the little well at the far end of the room. The well had frogs in it, and therefore so did the bucket, but she was kind and dropped them back into their well. No one likes boiling a frog. The bucket of water was not strictly necessary, but it did have a part to play. Tiffany coughed theatrically. 'Do you see, sir? I have one poker and one bucket of cold water. Cold metal poker, cold bucket of water. And now . . . I hold in my left hand the poker, and I stick my right hand into the hottest part of the fire, like *this*.'

The Baron gasped as flames burst around her hand and the tip of the poker in her other hand suddenly glowed red hot.

With the Baron suitably impressed, Tiffany dowsed the poker in the bucket of water, from which erupted a cloud of steam. Then she stood in front of the Baron, holding up her right hand, quite unscathed.

'But I saw flames come up!' said the Baron, his eyes wide. 'Well done! Very well done! Some sort of trick, yes?'

'More of a skill, sir. I put my hand in the fire and sent the heat into the poker. I just moved the heat around. The flame you saw was caused by the burning of bits of dead skin, dirt, and all those nasty, invisible little biting things that unhygienic people might have on their hands . . .' She paused. 'Are you all right, sir?' The Baron was staring at her. 'Sir? Sir?'

The old man spoke as if he was reading from an invisible book: '*The hare runs into the fire. The hare runs into the fire. The fire, it takes her, she is not burned. The fire, it loves her, she is not burned. The hare runs into the fire. The fire, it loves her, she is free* . . . It all comes back to me! How did I ever forget it! How did I *dare* to forget it? I told myself I would remember it for ever, but time goes on and the world fills up with things to remember, things to do, calls on your time, calls on your memory. And you forget the things that were important, the real things.'

Tiffany was shocked to see tears streaming down his face.

'I remember it all,' he whispered, his voice punctuated with sobs. 'I remember the heat! I remember the hare!'

At which point the door banged open and Miss Spruce stepped into the room. What happened next took a moment, but seemed to Tiffany to go on for an hour. The nurse looked at her holding the poker, and then at the old man in tears, then at the cloud of steam, then back to Tiffany as she let the poker go, and then back to the old man, and then back to Tiffany as the poker landed in the hearth with a *clang* that echoed around the world. And then Miss Spruce took a deep breath like a whale preparing to dive to the bottom of the ocean and screamed, 'What do you think you are doing to him? Get out of here, you brazen hussy!'

Tiffany's ability to speak came back quickly, and then grew into an ability to shout. 'I am not brazen and I don't huss!'

'I'm going to fetch the guards, you black and midnight hag!' the nurse screamed, heading for the door.

'It's only eleven thirty!' Tiffany shouted after her and hurried back to the Baron, totally at a loss as to what to do next. The pain shifted. She could feel it. She wasn't keeping her mind straight. Things were getting out of balance. She concentrated for a moment and then, trying to smile, turned to the Baron.

'I'm very sorry if I have upset you, sir,' she began, and then realized that he was smiling through his tears and his whole face seemed full of sunlight.

'Upset me? Good gracious no, I'm not upset.' He tried to pull himself upright in the chair and pointed towards the fire with a trembling finger. 'I am, in fact, set up! I feel alive! I am young, my dear Miss Tiffany Aching! I remember that perfect day! Can you not see me? Down in the valley? A perfect, crisp September day. A little boy in the tweed jacket that was far too itchy, as I recall, yes, was far too itchy and smelled of wee! And my father was singing "The Larks They Sang Melodious", and I was trying to harmonize, which of course I couldn't do then because I had about as much voice as a rabbit, and we were watching them burn the stubbles. There was smoke everywhere, and as the fire swept along, mice, rats, rabbits and even foxes were running towards us away from the flames. Pheasants and partridges were taking off like rockets at the last minute, as they do, and suddenly there was no sound at all and I saw this hare. Oh, she was a big one – did you know that country people used to think all hares were female? – and she just stood there, looking at me, with bits of burning grass falling around us, and the flames behind her, and she was looking directly at me, and I will swear that when she knew that she had caught my eye, she flicked herself into the air and jumped straight into the fire. And of course I cried like anything, because she was so fine. And my father picked me up and said he'd tell me a little secret, and he taught me the hare song, so that I would know the truth of it, and stop crying. And then later on, we walked over the ashes and there was no dead hare.' The old man turned his head awkwardly towards her, and beamed, really beamed. He *shone*.

Where is that coming from? Tiffany wondered. It's too yellow for firelight, but the curtains are shut. It's always too gloomy in here, but now it is the light of a crisp September day . . .

'I remember doing a crayon picture of it when we got home, and my father was so proud of it he took it all around the castle so that everybody could admire it,' the old man went on, as enthusiastic as a boy. 'A child's scrawl, of course, but he talked about it as if it were a work of genius. Parents do such things. I found it among his documents after he died, and in fact, if you are interested, you will find it in a leather folder within the money chest. It is, after all, a precious thing. I've never told anyone else that,' said the Baron. 'People and days and memories come and go but that memory has always been there. No money that I could give you, Miss Tiffany Aching, who is the witch, could ever repay you for bringing back to me that wonderful vision. Which I shall remember until the day I—'

For a moment the flames on the fire stood still and the air was cold. Tiffany was never actually sure that she ever saw Death, not actually *saw*; perhaps in some strange way it had all happened inside her head. Though wherever he was, well, he was there.

WASN'T THAT APPROPRIATE? Death said.

Tiffany didn't step back. There was no point. 'Did you *arrange* that?' she asked.

MUCH AS I WOULD LIKE TO TAKE THE CREDIT, OTHER FORCES ARE AT WORK. GOOD MORNING TO YOU, MISS ACHING.

Death left, and the Baron followed, a little boy in his new tweed jacket, which was terribly itchy and sometimes smelled of wee,* following his father across the smoking field.

Then Tiffany placed her hand on the dead man's face and, with respect, closed his eyes, where the light of burning fields was dimming.

---

* The old cloth-makers used urine as a mordant for the dyes used in making woollen clothes, so that the colours would be fixed and not run; as a result, they can be a bit smelly for years. Not even Miss Tick could have explained it better and stayed so calm, although she would probably have used the term 'evacuated bodily juices'.

CHAPTER 5

# The Mother of Tongues

There should have been a moment of peace; in fact there was a moment of metal. Some of the castle guard were approaching, their armour making even more noise than armour usually does because none of it fitted properly. There hadn't been any battles here for hundreds of years, but they still wore armour, because it seldom needed mending and didn't wear out.

The door was pushed open by Brian, the sergeant. He wore a complicated expression. It was the expression of a man who has just been told that an evil witch, whom he has known since she was a kid, has killed the boss, and the boss's son is away, and the witch is still in the room, and a nurse, whom he does not like very much, is prodding him in the bottom and shouting, 'What are you waiting for, man? Do your duty!'

All this was getting on his nerves.

He gave Tiffany a sheepish look. 'Morning, miss, is everything all right?' Then he stared at the Baron in his chair. 'He's dead then, is he?'

Tiffany said, 'Yes, Brian, he is. He died only a couple of minutes ago, and I have reason to believe that he was happy.'

'Well, that's good then, I suppose,' said the sergeant, and then his face twisted into tears so that the next words were gulped and damp. 'You know, he was really very good to us when my nan was ill; he had hot meals sent over to her every day, right up until the end.'

She held his unprotesting hand and looked over his shoulder. The other guards were crying too, and crying all the more because they knew they were big strong men, or so they hoped, and shouldn't cry at all. But the Baron had always been there, part of life, like the sunrise. All right, maybe he'd give you a dressing-down if you were asleep on duty or had a blunt sword (despite the fact that no guard in living memory had needed to use his sword for anything more than levering the lid off a tin of jam), but when all was said and done, he was the Baron and they were his men and now he was gone.

'Ask her about the poker!' screamed the nurse behind Brian. 'Go on, ask her about *the money*!'

The nurse could not see Brian's face. Tiffany could. He had probably been prodded in the bottom again, and was suddenly livid.

'Sorry, Tiff . . . I mean, miss, but this lady here says

she thinks you done a murder and a robbery,' he said, and his face added that its owner right now was not thinking the same thing and didn't want to get into trouble with anyone, especially Tiffany.

Tiffany rewarded him with a little smile. Always remember you are a witch, she told herself. Don't start shouting your innocence. You *know* you are innocent. You don't have to shout *anything*. 'The Baron was kind enough to give me some money for . . . looking after him,' she said, 'and I suppose Miss Spruce must have inadvertently heard him doing so and formed a wrong impression.'

'It was a lot of money!' Miss Spruce insisted, red in the face. 'The big chest under the Baron's bed was open!'

'All that is true,' said Tiffany, 'and it would appear that Miss Spruce was accidentally hearing for quite some time.'

Some of the guards sniggered, which made Miss Spruce even more angry, if that were possible. She pushed her way forward.

'Do you deny that you were standing there with a poker and your hand on fire?' she demanded, her face as red as a turkey.

'I would like to say something, please,' said Tiffany. 'It's rather important.' She could feel the impatient pain now, fighting to get free. Her hands felt clammy.

'You were doing black magic, admit it!'

Tiffany took a deep breath. 'I don't know what that is,' she said, 'but I know I am holding just above my shoulder the last pain that the Baron will ever know, and I have to get rid of it soon, and I can't get rid of it in here, what with all these people. Please? I need an open space right now!' She pushed Miss Spruce out of the way and the guards swiftly stood aside for her, to the nurse's extreme annoyance.

'Don't let her go! She will fly away! That's what they do!'

Tiffany knew the layout of the castle very well; everybody did. There was a courtyard down some steps, and she headed there rapidly, feeling the pain stirring and unfolding. You had to think of it as a kind of animal that you could keep at bay, but that only worked for so long. About as long as . . . well, now, in fact.

The sergeant appeared beside her, and she grabbed his arm. 'Don't ask me why,' she managed to say through gritted teeth, 'but throw your helmet in the air!'

He was bright enough to follow orders, and spun the helmet into the air like a soup plate. Tiffany hurled the pain after it, feeling its dreadful silkiness as it found its freedom. The helmet stopped in midair as if it had hit an invisible wall, and dropped onto the cobblestones in a cloud of steam and bent almost in half.

The sergeant picked it up and immediately dropped it again. 'It's bloody hot!' He stared at Tiffany, who was leaning against the wall and trying to catch her breath. 'And you've been taking away pain like that *every day*?'

She opened her eyes. 'Yes, but I normally get plenty of time to find somewhere to dump it. Water and rock aren't very good, but metal is quite reliable. Don't ask me why. If I try to think about how it works, it doesn't work.'

'And I've heard that you can do all kinds of tricks with fire too?' said Sergeant Brian admiringly.

'Fire is easy to work with if you keep your mind clear, but pain . . . pain fights back. Pain is alive. Pain is the enemy.'

The sergeant gingerly attempted to reclaim his helmet, hoping that by now it was cool enough to hold. 'I will have to make certain I knock the dent out of it before the boss sees it,' he began. 'You know what a stickler he is for smartness . . . Oh.' He stared down at the ground.

'Yes,' said Tiffany, as kindly as she could. 'It's going to take a bit of getting used to, isn't it?' Wordlessly, she handed him her handkerchief, and he blew his nose.

'But you can take away pain,' he began, 'so does that mean you can . . . ?'

Tiffany held up a hand. 'Stop right there,' she said. 'I know what you're going to ask, and the answer is no. If you chopped your hand off I could probably make you forget about it until you tried to eat your dinner, but things like loss, grief and sadness? I can't do that. I wouldn't *dare* meddle with them. There is something called "the soothings", and I know only one person in the world who can do that, and I'm not even going to ask her to teach me. It's too deep.'

'Tiff . . .' Brian hesitated and looked around as though he expected the nurse to appear and prod him from behind again.

Tiffany waited. Please don't ask, she thought. You've known me all your life. You can't possibly think . . .

Brian looked at her pleadingly. '*Did* you . . . take anything?' His voice tailed off.

'No, of course not,' Tiffany said. 'What maggot's got into your head? How *could* you think such a thing?'

'Dunno,' said Brian, flushing with embarrassment.

'Well, that's all right then.'

'I suppose I had better make sure the young master knows,' said Brian after another good nose-blow, 'but all I know is that he's gone to the big city with his—' He stopped again, embarrassed.

'With his fiancée,' said Tiffany determinedly. 'You can say it out loud, you know.'

Brian coughed. 'Well, you see, we thought . . . well, we all thought that you and him were, well, you know . . .'

'We have always been friends,' said Tiffany, 'and that's all there is to it.'

She felt sorry for Brian, even though he too often opened his mouth before he got it attached to his brain, so she patted him on the shoulder. 'Look, why don't I fly down to the big city and find him?'

He almost melted with relief. 'Would you do that?'

'Of course. I can see you have a lot to do here, and it will take a load off your mind.'

Admittedly it will put the load on mine, she thought as she hurried away through the castle. The news had spread. People were standing around, crying or just looking bewildered. The cook ran up to her just as she was leaving. 'What am I to do? I've got the poor soul's dinner on the stove!'

'Then take it off and give it to someone who needs a good dinner,' said Tiffany briskly. It was important to keep her tone cool and busy. The people were in shock. She would be too, when she had the time, but right at this moment it was important to bounce people back into the world of the here and now.

'Listen to me, all of you,' and her voice echoed around the big hall. 'Yes, your baron is dead but you still have a baron! He will be here soon with his . . . lady, and you must have this place spotless for them! You all know your jobs! Get on with them! And remember him kindly and clean the place up for *his* sake.'

It worked. It always did. A voice that sounded as if its owner knew what she was doing could get things done, especially if its owner was wearing a pointy black hat. There was a sudden rush of activity.

'I suppose you think you've got away with it, do you?' said a voice behind her.

Tiffany waited a moment before turning round, and when she did turn round, she was smiling. 'Why, Miss Spruce,' she said, 'are you still here? Well, perhaps there are some floors that need scrubbing?'

The nurse was a vision of fury. 'I do not scrub floors, you arrogant little—'

'No, you don't scrub anything, do you, Miss Spruce? I've noticed that! Now, Miss Flowerdew, who was here before you, now she *could* scrub a floor. *She* could scrub a floor so that you could see your face in it, although in your case, Miss Spruce, I can imagine why that would not appeal. Miss Jumper, who we had before her, would even scrub floors with sand, white sand! She chased dirt like a terrier chasing a fox!'

The nurse opened her mouth to speak, but Tiffany didn't allow the words any space. 'The cook has told me that you are a very religious woman, always on your knees, and that is fine by me, absolutely fine, but didn't it ever occur to you to take a mop and bucket down there with you? People don't need prayers, Miss Spruce; they need you to do the job in front of you, Miss Spruce. And I have had enough of you, Miss Spruce, and especially of your lovely white coat. I think Roland was very impressed by your wonderful white coat, but I am not, Miss Spruce, because *you never do anything that will get it dirty.*'

The nurse raised a hand. 'I could *slap* you!'

'No,' said Tiffany firmly. 'You couldn't.'

The hand stayed where it was. 'I have never been so insulted before in my life!' screamed the enraged nurse.

'Really?' said Tiffany. 'I'm genuinely surprised.' She turned on her heel, left the nurse standing and marched over to a young guard who had just come into the hall. 'I've seen you around. I don't think I know who you are. What's your name, please?'

The trainee guard gave what he probably thought was a salute. 'Preston, miss.'

'Has the Baron been taken down to the crypt, Preston?'

'Yes, miss, and I've took down some lanterns and some cloths and a bucket of warm water, miss.' He grinned when he saw her expression. 'My grandma used to do the laying out when I was a little boy, miss. I could help, if you wanted.'

'Did your *grandma* let you help?'

'No, miss,' said the young man. 'She said men weren't allowed to do that sort of thing unless they had a certificate in doctrine.'

Tiffany looked puzzled for a moment. 'Doctrine?'

'You know, miss. Doctrine: pills and potions and sawing off legs and similar.'

Light dawned. 'Oh, you mean doctoring. I should hope not. This isn't about making the poor soul better. I will do it by myself, but thank you for asking, anyway. This is women's work.'

Exactly *why* it is women's work I don't know, she said to herself as she arrived in the crypt and rolled up her sleeves. The young guard had even thought to bring down a dish of soil and a dish of salt.* Well done, your granny, she thought. At last someone had taught a boy something useful!

She cried as she made the old man 'presentable' as Granny Weatherwax called it. She always cried. It was

---

* The soil and the salt were an ancient tradition to keep ghosts away. Tiffany had never seen a ghost, so they probably worked, but in any case they worked on the minds of people, who felt better for knowing that they were there, and once you understood that, you understood quite a lot about magic.

a needful thing. But you didn't do it where anyone else could see, not if you were a witch. People wouldn't expect that. It would make them uneasy.

She stood back. Well, the old boy looked better than he had done yesterday, she had to admit. As a final touch, she took two pennies out of her pocket and laid them gently over his eyelids.

Those were the old customs, taught to her by Nanny Ogg, but now there was a new custom, known only to her. She leaned on the edge of the marble slab with one hand and held the bucket of water in the other. She stayed there, motionless, until the water in the bucket began to boil and ice was forming on the slab. She took the bucket outside and tipped its contents down the drain.

The castle was bustling when she had finished, and she left people to get on with things. She hesitated as she stepped out of the castle and stopped to think. People often didn't stop to think. They thought as they went along. Sometimes it was a good idea. Just to stop moving, in case you moved the wrong way.

Roland was the Baron's only son and, as far as Tiffany knew, his only relative, or at least his only relative who was allowed to come anywhere near the castle; after some horrible and expensive legal fighting, Roland had succeeded in banishing the dreadful aunts, the Baron's sisters who, frankly, even the old Baron thought were as nasty a pair of old ferrets as any man should find down the trousers of his life. But there was another person who should know, who was in no conceivable way at all kin to the Baron, but was nevertheless, well, someone who should know something as important as this, as soon as possible. Tiffany headed up to the Feegle mound to see the kelda.

Amber was sitting outside when Tiffany arrived, doing some sewing in the sunlight.

'Hello, miss,' she said cheerfully. 'I'll just go and tell Mrs Kelda that you're here.' And with that she disappeared down the hole as easily as a snake, just as Tiffany had once been able to do.

Why had Amber gone back there? Tiffany wondered. She had taken her to the Aching farm to be safe. Why had the girl walked up the Chalk to the mound? How had she even remembered where it was?

'Very interesting child, that,' said a voice, and the Toad* stuck his head out from under a leaf. 'I must say you look extremely flustered, miss.'

'The old Baron is dead,' said Tiffany.

'Well, only to be expected. Long live the Baron,' said the Toad.

'He's not going to live long,' said Tiffany. 'He's dead.'

---

* The Toad had no other name but that of the Toad and had joined the Feegle clan some years previously, and found life in the mound much to be preferred over his former existence as a lawyer or, to be precise, as a lawyer who had got too smart in the presence of a fairy godmother. The kelda had offered several times to turn him back, but he always refused. The Feegles themselves considered him the brains of the outfit since he knew words that were longer than he was.

'No,' croaked the Toad. 'It's what you're supposed to say. When a king dies, you have to immediately announce that there is another king. It's important. I wonder what the new one will be like. Rob Anybody says that he's a wet nelly who is not fit to lick your boots. And has scorned you very badly.'

Whatever the circumstances of the past, Tiffany was not going to let that go by unchallenged. 'I don't need anybody to lick anything for me, thank you very much. Anyway,' she added, 'he's not *their* baron, is he? The Feegles pride themselves on not having a lord.'

'You are correct in your submission,' said the Toad ponderously, 'but you must remember that they also pride themselves on having as much as possible to drink at the slightest possible excuse, which leaves them of an uncertain temper, and that the Baron quite definitely believes that he is, *de facto*, the owner of all the property hereabouts. A claim that stands up in law. Although I am sorry to say that I can no longer do the same. But the girl, now, she is something strange. Haven't you noticed?'

Haven't I noticed? Tiffany thought quickly. What should I have noticed? Amber was just a kid;* she had seen her around – not so quiet as to be worrying, not so noisy as to be annoying. And that was it. But then she thought, The chickens. That was strange.

'She can speak Feegle!' said the Toad. 'And I don't

---

* That was to say, from Tiffany's point of view, that meant a couple of years younger than Tiffany.

mean all that crivens business; that's just the patois. I mean the serious old-fashioned stuff that the kelda speaks, the language they spoke from wherever it was they came from before they came from there. I am sorry, with preparation I am sure I could have made a better sentence.' He paused. 'I don't understand a word of Feegle myself, but the girl seems to have just picked it up. And another thing, I'll swear she's been trying to talk to me in Toad. I'm not much good at it myself, but a little bit of understanding did come with the ... shape change, as it were.'

'Are you saying that she understands unusual words?' said Tiffany.

'I'm not certain,' said the Toad. 'I think she under-stands meaning.'

'Are you sure?' said Tiffany. 'I've always thought she was a bit simple.'

'Simple?' said the Toad, who seemed to be enjoying himself. 'Well, as a lawyer I can tell you that something that looks very simple indeed can be incredibly com-plicated, especially if I'm being paid by the hour. The sun is simple. A sword is simple. A storm is simple. Behind everything simple is a huge tail of complicated.'

Amber poked her head out of the hole. 'Mrs Kelda says to meet her in the chalk pit,' she said excitedly.

There was a faint cheering coming from the chalk pit as Tiffany lowered herself gingerly through the careful camouflage.

She liked the pit. It seemed impossible to be truly

unhappy there, with the damp white walls cradling her and the light of the blue day pricking through the briars. Sometimes, when she was much younger, she had seen the ancient fish swimming in and out of the chalk pit, ancient fish from the time when the Chalk was the land under the waves. The water had gone long ago, but the souls of the ghost fish hadn't noticed. They were as armoured as knights and ancient as the chalk. But she didn't see them any more. Perhaps your eyesight changes as you get older, she thought.

There was a strong smell of garlic. A large part of the bottom of the pit was full of snails. Feegles were walking carefully among them, painting numbers on their shells. Amber was sitting next to the kelda, with her hands clasped round her knees. Seen from above, it looked for all the world like a sheepdog trials, but with less barking and a lot more stickiness.

The kelda spotted Tiffany, and raised a tiny finger to her lips, followed by a brief nod at Amber, who was now engrossed in the proceedings. Jeannie patted the space on the other side of her, and said, 'We are watching the lads putting our brand on the livestock, ye ken.' There was a slight touch of strangeness to her voice. It was the kind of voice a grown-up uses when it tells a child 'We are having fun, *aren't we?*', in case the child hasn't reached that conclusion yet. But Amber really did look as if she was enjoying herself. It occurred to Tiffany that being around the Feegles seemed to make Amber happy.

She got the impression that the kelda wanted to

keep the conversation light, so she simply asked, 'Why mark them? Who's going to try to steal them?'

'Other Feegles, of course. My Rob reckons they will be queuing up to steal our snails while they are left unprotected, ye ken.'

Tiffany was mystified. 'Why would they be unprotected?'

'Because my lads, ye ken, will be away stealing *their* livestock. It's an old Feegle tradition, it means everyone gets in lots of fighting, rustling and stealing and, of course, the all-time favourite, boozing.' The kelda winked at Tiffany. 'Well, it keeps the lads happy, and stops them fretting and getting under our feet, ye ken.'

She winked at Tiffany again and patted Amber on the leg, and said something to her in the language that sounded like a very old version of Feegle. Amber answered in the same language. The kelda nodded meaningfully at Tiffany and pointed to the other end of the pit.

'What did you just say to her?' said Tiffany, looking back at the girl, who was still watching the Feegles with the same smiling interest.

'I told her that you and I were going to have a conversation for grown-ups,' said the kelda, 'and she just said the boys were very funny, and I don't know how, but she has picked up the Mother of Tongues. Tiffany, I only use it to a daughter and the gonnagle,* ye ken, and I was talking to him on the mound last night

* see Glossary, page 417.

when she joined in! She picked it up just by listening! That shouldn't happen! That's a rare gift she has, and no mistake. She must ken the meanings in her head, and that's magic, missy, it's the pure quill and no mistake.'

'How could it happen?'

'Who knows?' said the kelda. 'It's a gift. And if ye take my advice, ye will set this girl to training.'

'Isn't she a bit too old to be starting?' said Tiffany.

'Put her to the craft, or find some channel for her gift. Believe me, my girl, I wouldnae want ye to believe that beating a girl nigh on to death is a good thing, but who kens how our paths are chosen? And so she ended up here, with me. She has the gift of understandin'. Would she have found it else? Ye know full well that the meaning of life is to find your gift. To find your gift is happiness. Never tae find it is misery. Ye said she's a bit simple: find her a teacher who can bring out the complicated in her. The girl learned a difficult language just by listening to it. The world sore needs folk that can do that.'

It made sense. Everything the kelda said made sense.

Jeannie paused and then said, 'I am very sorry the Baron is dead.'

'I'm sorry,' Tiffany said. 'I meant to tell you.'

The kelda smiled at her. 'Do you think a kelda would need to be told something like that, my girl? He was a decent man, and ye did right by him.'

'I've got to go and find the new Baron,' said Tiffany.

'And I'll need the boys to help me find him. There's thousands of people in the city, and the lads are very good at finding things.'* She glanced up at the sky. Tiffany had never flown all the way to the big city before and didn't much fancy flying there in the darkness. 'I shall leave at first light. But first of all, Jeannie, I think I'd better take Amber back home. You'd like that, wouldn't you, Amber,' she said hopelessly . . .

Three quarters of an hour later, Tiffany flew her stick back down towards the village, the screams still ringing in her head. Amber wasn't going back. She had, in fact, made her reluctance to leave the mound abundantly clear by bracing her arms and legs in the hole and staying there screaming at the top of her voice every time Tiffany gave a gentle pull; when she let go, the girl went back to sit next to the kelda. So that was that. You try to make plans for people, and the people make other plans.

However you looked at it, Amber had parents; pretty awful parents, you might say, and you might add that that was giving them the best of it. At least they had to know that she was safe . . . And in any case, what possible harm could come to Amber in the care of the kelda?

\* \* \*

* She kept to herself any thought about the fact that what they were most good at finding was things that belonged to other people. It was true, though, that the Feegles could hunt like dogs, as well as drink like fish.

Mrs Petty slammed the door shut when she saw that it was Tiffany on the step, then opened it again almost immediately, in a flood of tears. The place stank, not just of stale beer and bad cooking but also of helplessness and bewilderment. A cat, the mangiest that Tiffany had ever seen, was almost certainly another part of the problem.

Mrs Petty was frightened out of whatever wits she had and dropped to her knees on the floor, pleading incoherently. Tiffany made her a cup of tea, which was no errand for the squeamish, given that such crockery as the cottage possessed was piled up in the stone sink, which was otherwise filled with slimy water that occasionally bubbled. Tiffany spent several minutes of heavy scrubbing before she had a cup she'd care to drink from, and even then something was rattling inside the kettle.

Mrs Petty sat on the one chair that had all four legs and babbled about how her husband was really a good man provided his dinner was on time and Amber wasn't naughty. Tiffany had grown used to that sort of desperate conversation when she was 'going round the houses' up in the mountains. They were generated by fear – fear of what would happen to the speaker when they were left alone again. Granny Weatherwax had a way of dealing with this, which was to put the fear of Granny Weatherwax into absolutely everyone, but Granny Weatherwax had had years of being, well, Granny Weatherwax.

Careful non-aggressive questioning brought news

that Mr Petty was asleep upstairs, and Tiffany simply told Mrs Petty that Amber was being looked after by a very kind lady while she *healed*. Mrs Petty started to cry again. The misery of the place was getting on Tiffany's nerves too, and she tried to stop herself being cruel; but how hard was it to slosh a bucket of cold water over a stone floor and swoosh it out of the door with a broom? How hard was it to make some soap? You could make quite a serviceable one out of wood ash and animal fat. And, as her mother had said once, 'No one is too poor to wash a window,' although her father, just to annoy her mother, occasionally changed it to, 'No one is too poor to wash a widow.' But where could you start with this family? And whatever it was that was in the kettle was still rattling, presumably trying to get out.

Most of the women in the villages had grown up to be tough. You needed to be tough to bring up a family on a farm labourer's wages. There was a local saying, a sort of recipe for dealing with a troublesome husband. It was: 'Tongue pie, cold barn and the copper stick.' It meant that a troublesome husband got a nagging instead of his dinner, he would be shoved out to the barn to sleep, and if he raised his hand to his wife, he might get a good wallop from the long stick every cottage had for stirring the washing in the wash-tub. They usually learned the error of their ways before the rough music played.

'Wouldn't you like a short holiday away from Mr Petty?' Tiffany suggested.

The woman, pale as a slug and skinny as a broom,

looked horrified. 'Oh no!' she gasped. 'He wouldn't know what to do without me!'

And then . . . it all went wrong, or rather, a lot more wrong than it was already. And it was all so innocent, because the woman was so downcast. 'Well, at least I can clean your kitchen for you,' Tiffany said cheerfully. It would have been fine if she had simply grabbed a broom and got to work but, oh no, she had to go and look up at the grey, cobweb-filled ceiling and say, 'All right, I know you're here, you always follow me, so make yourself useful and clean this kitchen thoroughly!' Nothing happened for a few seconds, and then she heard, because she was listening for it, a muffled conversation from up near the ceiling.

'Did ye no' hear that? She kens we is here! How come she always gets it right?'

A slightly different Feegle voice said, 'It's because we *always* follow her, ye wee dafty!'

'Oh aye, I ken that well enough, but my point is, did we not promise faithfully not to follow her around any more?'

'Aye, it was a solemn oath.'

'Exactly, and so I cannae but be a wee bit disappointed that the big wee hag will nae take heed of a solemn promise. It's a wee bit hurtful to the feelings.'

'But we *have* broken the solemn oath; it's a Feegle thing.'

A third voice said, 'Look lively, ye scunners, it's the tapping o' the feets!'

A whirlwind hit the grubby little kitchen.* Foaming water swirled across Tiffany's boots, which had indeed been tapping. It has to be said that no one could create a mess more quickly than a party of Feegles, but strangely, they could clean one up as well, without even the help of bluebirds and miscellaneous woodland creatures.

The sink emptied in an instant and filled again with soap suds. Wooden plates and tin mugs hummed through the air as the fire burst into life. With a *bang bang bang* the log box filled. After that, things speeded up, and a fork shuddered in the wall beside Tiffany's ear. Steam rose like a fog, with strange noises coming out of it; the sunlight flooded in through the suddenly clean window, filling the room with rainbows; a broom shot past pushing the last of the water in front of it; the kettle boiled; a vase of flowers appeared on the table – some of them, admittedly, upside down – and suddenly the room was fresh and clean and no longer smelled of rotted potatoes.

Tiffany looked up at the ceiling. The cat was holding onto it by all four paws. It gave her what was definitely a look. Even a witch can be out-looked by a cat that has had it up to here, and is still *up* here.

Tiffany finally located Mrs Petty under the table, with her hands over her head. When she had finally

* Tiffany had earned the admiration of other witches by persuading the Feegles to do chores. The unfortunate fact was that Feegles would do any chore, provided it was loud, messy and flamboyant. And, if possible, included screams.

been persuaded to come out and sit down on a nice clean chair in front of a cup of tea from a wonderfully clean mug, she was very keen to agree that there had been a great improvement, although later on Tiffany couldn't help but admit that Mrs Petty would probably have agreed to absolutely anything if only Tiffany would go away.

Not a success, then, but at least the place was a whole lot cleaner and Mrs Petty was bound to be grateful when she'd had time to think about it. A snarl and a thump that Tiffany heard as she was leaving the ragged garden was probably the cat, parting company with the ceiling.

Halfway back to the farm, carrying her broomstick over her shoulder, she thought aloud, 'Perhaps that was a bit stupid.'

'Dinnae fash yourself,' said a voice. 'If we had had the time we could have made some bread as well.' Tiffany looked down, and there was Rob Anybody, along with half a dozen others known variously as the Nac Mac Feegle, the Wee Free Men and, sometimes, the Defendants, the Culprits, people wanted by the police to help them with their enquiries and sometimes as 'that one, second on the left, I swear it was him.'

'You keep on following me!' she complained. 'You always promise not to and you always do!'

'Ah, but ye dinnae take into account the geas that is laid on us, ye ken. Ye are the hag o' the hills and we must always be ready to protect ye and help ye, no matter what *ye* say,' said Rob Anybody stoutly. There was a rapid shaking of heads among the other Feegles, causing a fallout of bits of pencil, rats' teeth, last night's dinner, interesting stones with holes in, beetles, promising bits of snot tucked away for leisurely examination later, and snails.

'Look,' said Tiffany, 'you can't just go around helping people whether they want you to or not!'

Rob Anybody scratched his head, put back the snail that had fallen out and said, 'Why not, miss? *You* do.'

'I don't!' she said aloud, but inside an arrow struck her heart. I wasn't kind to Mrs Petty, was I? she thought. Yes, it was true that the woman seemed to have the brains as well as the demeanour of a mouse, but filthy though it was, the stinking house was Mrs Petty's house, and Tiffany had burst in with a lot of, well, not to put too fine a point on it, Nac Mac Feegles, and just messed it up, even if it was less of a mess than it had been before. I was brusque and bossy and self-righteous. My mother could have handled it better. If it comes to that, probably any other woman in the village could have handled it better, but I am the witch and I blundered in and blundered about and scared the wits out of her. Me, a slip of a girl with a pointy hat.

And the other thing she thought about herself was that if she didn't actually lie down very soon, she was going to fall over. The kelda was right; she *couldn't* remember when she'd last slept in a proper bed, and there was one waiting for her at the farm. And, she thought suddenly and guiltily, she still had to let her own parents know that Amber Petty was back with the Feegles . . .

There's always something, she thought, and then there's another something on top of the something, and then there is no end to the somethings. No wonder witches were given broomsticks. Feet just couldn't do it by themselves.

Her mother was tending to Tiffany's brother Wentworth, who had a black eye.

'He's been fighting the big boys,' her mother complained. 'Got a black eye, didn't we, Wentworth?'

'Yes, but I did kick Billy Teller in the fork.'

Tiffany tried to starve a yawn. 'What have you been fighting for, Went? I thought you were more sensible.'

'They said you was a witch, Tiff,' said Wentworth. And Tiffany's mother turned with a strange expression on her face.

'Yes, well, I am,' said Tiffany. 'That's my job.'

'Yeah, but I doubt you do the kind of things they said you was doing,' said her brother.

Tiffany met her mother's gaze. 'Were these bad things?' she said.

'Hah! That's not the half of it,' said Wentworth. Blood and snot covered his shirt, where it had dripped from his nose.

'Wentworth, you go upstairs to your room,' Mrs Aching ordered – and probably, Tiffany thought, not even Granny Weatherwax would have been able to speak an order that was so instantly obeyed. And so full of the implicit threat of doomsday if it was not.

When the boots of the reluctant boy had disappeared around the staircase, Tiffany's mother turned to her youngest daughter, folded her arms and said, 'It's not the first time he's been in a fight like this.'

'It's all down to the picture books,' said Tiffany. 'I'm trying to teach people that witches aren't mad old women who go around putting spells on people.'

'When your dad comes in, I'll get him to go and have a word with Billy's dad,' said her mother. 'Billy's a foot taller than Wentworth but your dad . . . he's two foot taller than Billy's dad. There won't be any fighting. You know your dad. He's a calm man, your dad. Never seen him punch a man more than about twice, never has to. He'll keep people calm. They'll be calm or else. But something's not quite right, Tiff. We're all very proud of you, you know, what you're doing and everything, but it's getting to people somehow. They're saying some ridiculous things. And we're having difficulties selling the cheeses. And everybody knows you are the best at cheeses. And now, Amber Petty. You think it is right that she is running around there with . . . them?'

'I hope so, Mum,' said Tiffany. 'But the girl has a very strong mind of her own and, Mum, when it comes right down to it, all I can do is the best that I can.'

Later that night, Tiffany, dozing in her ancient bed, could hear her parents talking very quietly in the room below. And although, of course, witches didn't cry, she had an overwhelming urge to do so.

## CHAPTER 6

# The Coming of the Cunning Man

Tiffany was angry at herself for oversleeping. Her mother actually had to bring her up a cup of tea. But the kelda had been right. She hadn't been sleeping properly and the ancient but homely bed had just closed around her.

Still, it could have been worse, she told herself as they set off. For example, there could have been snakes on the broomstick. The Feegles had been only too glad, as Rob Anybody put it, to 'feel the wind beneath their kilts'. Feegles were probably better than snakes, but that was only a guess. They would do things like run from one side of the stick to the other to look at interesting things they were flying over, and on one occasion she glanced over her shoulder to see about ten of them hanging onto the back of the stick or, to put it more precisely, one of them was hanging onto the back of the stick and then one was hanging onto *his* heels and one was hanging onto his heels, and so on, all the way to the last Feegle. They were having fun, screaming with laughter, their kilts indeed flapping in the wind. Presumably the thrill of it made up for the danger and the lack of a view, or at least, of a view that anyone else would want to look at.

One or two actually did lose their grip on the bristles, floating away and down while waving at their brothers and making *Yahoo!* noises and generally treating it as a big game. Feegles tended to bounce when they hit the ground, although sometimes they damaged it a little. Tiffany wasn't worried about their journey home; undoubtedly there would be lots of dangerous creatures prepared to jump out on a little running man, but by the time he got home there would in fact be considerably fewer of them. Actually, the Feegles were – by Feegle standards – pretty well behaved on the flight, and didn't actually set fire to the broomstick until they were about twenty miles from the city, an incident heralded by Daft Wullie saying 'Whoops!' very quietly, and then guiltily trying to conceal the fact that he'd set fire to the bristles by standing in front of the blaze to hide it.

'You've set fire to the broomstick again, haven't you, Wullie,' Tiffany stated firmly. 'What was it that we learned last time? We *don't* light fires on the broomstick for no good reason.'

The broomstick began to shake as Daft Wullie and

his brothers tried to stamp out the flames. Tiffany searched the landscape below them for something soft and preferably wet to land on.

But it was no use getting angry with Wullie; he lived in a Wullie-shaped world of his own. You had to try thinking diagonally.

'I just wonder, Daft Wullie,' she said as the broomstick developed a nasty rattle, 'if, working together, we might find out why my broomstick is on fire? Do you think it might be something to do with the fact that you are holding a match in your hand?'

The Feegle looked at the match as if he had never seen one before, and then put it behind his back and stared at his feet, which was quite brave of him in the circumstances. 'Don't really know, miss.'

'You see,' said Tiffany as the wind whipped around them, 'without enough bristles I can't steer very well, and we are losing height but still regrettably going quite fast. Perhaps you could help me with this conundrum, Wullie?'

Daft Wullie stuck his little finger in his ear and wiggled it about as if rummaging in his own brain. Then he brightened up. 'Should we no' land, miss?'

Tiffany sighed. 'I would like to do that, Daft Wullie, but, you see, we are going quite fast and the ground is not. What we have in those circumstances is what they call *a crash*.'

'I wasnae considering that ye should land in the dirt, miss,' said Wullie. He pointed down, and added, 'I was just considering that ye might like to land on *that*.'

Tiffany followed the line of his pointing finger. There was a long white road below them, and on it, not too far ahead, was something oblong, moving almost as fast as the broomstick itself. She stared, listening to her brain calculating, and then said, 'We will still have to lose *some* speed . . .'

And that was how a smouldering broomstick carrying one terrified witch and about two dozen of the Nac Mac Feegles, holding their kilts out to slow themselves down, landed on the roof of the Lancre-to-Ankh-Morpork parcel express.

The coach had good springs and the driver got the horses back under control quite quickly. There was silence as he climbed down from his seat, while white dust began to settle back on the road. He was a heavy-looking man who winced at every step, and in one hand he held a half-eaten cheese sandwich and in the other an unmistakable length of lead pipe. He sniffed. 'My supervisor will have to be told. Damage to paintwork, see? Got to do a report when it's damage to paintwork. I hate reports, never been a man what words come to with ease. Got to do it, though, when it's damage to paintwork.' The sandwich and, more importantly, the lead pipe disappeared back into his very large overcoat, and Tiffany was amazed at how happy she felt about that.

'I really am very sorry,' she said as the man helped her down from the coach roof.

'It's not me, you understand, it's the paintwork. I tell them, look, I tell them there's trolls, there's dwarfs, huh, and you know how *they* drive, eyes half closed most of the time 'cause of them not liking the sun.'

Tiffany sat still as he inspected the damage and then looked up at her and noticed the pointy hat.

'Oh,' he said flatly. 'A witch. First time for everything, I suppose. Do you know what I'm carrying in here, miss?'

What could be the worst thing? Tiffany thought. She said, 'Eggs?'

'Hah,' said the man. 'That we should be so lucky. It's mirrors, miss. One mirror, in point of fact. Not a flat one, either; it's a ball, they tell me. It's all packed up very snug and sound, or so they say, not knowing that somebody was going to drop out of the sky on it.' He didn't sound angry, just worn out, as if he permanently expected the world to hand him the dirty end of the stick. 'It was made by the dwarfs,' he added. 'They say it cost more than a thousand Ankh-Morpork dollars, and you know what it's for? To hang up in a dance hall in the city, where they intend to dance the waltz, which a well-brought-up young lady such as you should not know about, on account of the fact, it says in the paper, that it leads to depravity and goings-on.'

'My word!' said Tiffany, thinking that something like this was expected of her.

'Well, I suppose I'd better go and see what the damage is,' said the driver, laboriously opening the back of the coach. A large box filled quite a lot of the space. 'It's mostly packed with straw,' he said. 'Give me a hand to get it down, will you? And if it tinkles, we're both in trouble.'

It turned out not to be as heavy as Tiffany expected. Nevertheless, they lowered it gently onto the road and the coachman rummaged among the straw inside, bringing out the mirror ball, holding it aloft like a rare jewel which, indeed, it resembled. It filled the world with sparkling light, dazzling the eyes and sending beams of flashing rays across the landscape. And at this point the man screamed in pain and dropped the ball, which shattered into a million pieces, filling the sky just for a moment with a million images of Tiffany, while he, curling up, landed on the road, raising more white dust and making little whimpering noises as the glass dropped around him.

In slightly less than an instant, the moaning man was surrounded by a ring of Feegles, armed to whatever teeth they still possessed with claymores, more claymores, bludgeons, axes, clubs and at least one more claymore. Tiffany had no idea where they had been hiding; a Feegle could hide behind a hair.

'Don't hurt him,' she shouted. 'He wasn't going to hurt me! He's very ill! But make yourselves useful and tidy up all this broken glass!' She crouched down in the road and held the man's hand. 'How long have you had jumping bones, sir?'

'Oh, I've been a martyr to them these past twenty years, miss, a martyr,' the coachman moaned. 'It's the jolting of the coach, you see. It's the suspenders – they don't work! I don't think I get more than just one decent night's sleep in five, miss, and that's the truth; I have a little snooze, turn over, like you do, and there's this little click and then it's agony, believe me.'

Except for a few dots on the edge of sight, there was no one else around apart from, of course, for a bunch of Nac Mac Feegles who, against all common sense, had perfected the art of hiding behind one another.

'Well, I think I may be able to help you,' Tiffany said.

Some witches used a shamble to see into the present, and, with any luck, into the future as well. In the smoky gloom of the Feegle mound, the kelda was practising what she called the *hiddlins* – the things you did and passed on but, on the whole, passed them on as a secret. And she was acutely aware of Amber watching with clear interest. A strange child, she thought. She sees, she hears, she understands. What would we give for a world full of people like her? She had set up the cauldron* and lit a small fire underneath the leather.

The kelda closed her eyes, concentrated and read the memories of all the keldas who had ever been and would ever be. Millions of voices floated through her brain in no particular order, sometimes soft, never very loud, often tantalizingly beyond her reach. It was a wonderful library of information, except that all the

* A message from the author: not all cauldrons are metal. You can boil water in a leather cauldron, if you know what you are doing. You can even make tea in a paper bag if you are careful and know how to do it. But please don't, or if you do, don't tell anyone I told you.

books were out of order and so were all the pages, and there wasn't an index *anywhere*. She had to follow threads that faded as she listened. She strained as small sounds, tiny glimpses, stifled cries, currents of meaning pulled her attention this way and that . . . And there it was, in front of her as if it had always been there, coming into focus.

She opened her eyes, stared at the ceiling for a moment, and said, 'I look for the big wee hag and what is it that I see?'

She peered forward into the mists of memories old and new, and jerked her head back, nearly knocking over Amber, who said, with interest, '*A man with no eyes?*'

'Well, I think I may be able to help you, Mr, er . . .'

'Carpetlayer, miss. William Glottal Carpetlayer.'

'Carpetlayer?' said Tiffany. 'But you're a coachman.'

'Yes, well, there's a funny story attached to *that*, miss. Carpetlayer, you see, is my family name. We don't know how we got it because, you see, *none of us have ever laid a carpet!*'

Tiffany gave him a kind little smile. 'And . . . ?'

Mr Carpetlayer gave her a puzzled look. 'And what? That *was* the funny story!' He started to laugh, and screamed again as a bone jumped.

'Oh yes,' said Tiffany. 'Sorry I'm a bit slow.' She rubbed her hands together. 'And now, sir, I will sort out your bones.'

The coach horses watched with quiet interest as she

helped the man up, lending a hand as he took off his huge overcoat (with many a grunt and minor scream) and stood him so that his hands rested on the coach.

Tiffany concentrated, feeling the man's back through his thin vest and – yes, there it was, a jumping bone.

She stepped across to the horses, whispering a word into each fly-flicking ear, just to be on the safe side. Then she went back to Mr Carpetlayer, who was waiting obediently, not daring to move. As she rolled up her sleeves, he said, 'You're not going to turn me into anything unnatural, are you, miss? I wouldn't want to be a spider. Mortally afraid of spiders, and all my clothes are made for a man with two legs.'

'Why in the world would you think I'd turn you into anything, Mr Carpetlayer?' said Tiffany, gently running her hand down his spine.

'Well, saving your honour's presence, miss, I thought that's what witches do, miss – nasty things, miss, earwigs and all that.'

'Who told you that?'

'Can't rightly say,' said the coachman. 'It's just sort of . . . you know, what everybody knows.'

Tiffany placed her fingers carefully, found the jumping bone, said, 'This might smart a little,' and pushed the bone back into place. The coachman screamed again.

His horses tried to bolt, but their legs were not doing business as usual, not with the word still ringing in their ears. Tiffany had felt ashamed at the time, a year ago, when she had acquired the knowing of the horseman's word; but then again, the old blacksmith she had helped to his death, with kindness and without pain, well, *he* had felt ashamed that he had nothing with which to pay her for her painstaking work, and you *had* to pay the witch, the same as you had to pay the ferryman, and so he had whispered into her ear the horseman's word, which gave you the control of any horse that heard it. You couldn't buy it, you couldn't sell it, but you could give it away and still keep it, and even if it'd been made of lead it would have been worth its weight in gold. The former owner had whispered in her ear, 'I promised to tell no man the word, and I ain't!' And he was chuckling as he died, his sense of humour being somewhat akin to that of Mr Carpetlayer.

Mr Carpetlayer was also pretty heavy, and had slipped gently down the side of the coach and—

*'Why are you torturing that old man, you evil witch? Can you not see that he's in dreadful pain?'*

Where had he come from? A shouting man, his face white with fury, his clothes as dark as an unopened cave or – and the word came to Tiffany suddenly – as a crypt. There had been no one around, she was sure of it, and no one on either side except the occasional farmer watching the stubbles burn as they cleared the land.

But his face was now a few inches from hers. And he was real, not some kind of monster, because monsters don't usually have little blobs of spittle on their lapel. And then she noticed – he stank. She'd never smelled anything so bad. It was physical, like an iron bar, and it seemed to her that she wasn't smelling it with her nose, but with her mind. A foulness that made the average privy as fragrant as a rose.

'I'm asking you politely to step back, please,' said Tiffany. 'I think you might have got hold of the wrong idea.'

'*I assure you, fiendish creature, that I have only the* right *idea! And that is to return you to the miserable and stinking hell from which you spawned!*'

All right, a madman, thought Tiffany, but if he—

Too late. The man's waggling finger got too close to her nose, and suddenly the empty road contained a lifetime's supply of Nac Mac Feegles. The man in black flailed at them, but that sort of thing does not work very well with a Feegle. He *did* manage, despite the Feegle onslaught, to shout, '*Be gone, nefarious imps!*'

Every Feegle head turned hopefully when they heard this. 'Oh aye,' said Rob Anybody. 'If there's any imps aboot, we are the boys to deal with them! Your move, mister!' They leaped at him and ended up in a heap on the road behind him, having passed straight through. They automatically punched one another as they staggered up, on the basis that if you're having a good fight you don't want to spoil the rhythm.

The man in black glanced at them and then paid them no attention whatsoever.

Tiffany stared down at the man's boots. They

gleamed in the sunlight, and that was wrong. She had been standing in the dust of the road for only a few minutes and her boots were grey. And there was the ground that the man was standing on, and *that* was wrong too. Very wrong, on a hot, cloudless day. She glanced at the horses. The word was holding them, but they were trembling with fear, like rabbits in the gaze of a fox. Then she closed her eyes and looked at him with First Sight, and *saw*. And said, 'You cast no shadow. I knew something wasn't right.'

And now she looked directly into the man's eyes, almost hidden under the wide hat brim and . . . he . . . had . . . no eyes. The understanding dawned on her like ice melting . . . No eyes at all, not ordinary eyes, not blind eyes, no eye sockets . . . just two holes in his head: she could see right through to the smouldering fields beyond. She didn't expect what happened next.

The man in black glared at her again and hissed, '*You are the witch. You are the one. Wherever you go, I will find you.*'

And then he vanished, leaving only a pile of fighting Feegles in the dust.

Tiffany felt something on her boot. She looked down, and a hare, which must have fled the burning stubbles, stared back at her. They held each other's gaze for a second, and then the hare jumped into the air like a leaping salmon and headed off across the road. The world is full of omens and signs; and a witch did indeed have to pick the ones that were important. Where could she begin here?

Mr Carpetlayer was still slumped against the coach, totally ignorant of what had just happened. So was Tiffany in a way, but she *would* find out. She said, 'You can get up again now, Mr Carpetlayer.'

He did so very gingerly, grimacing as he waited for the lightning strokes of agony all down his back. He shifted experimentally, and gave a little jump in the dust, as if he was squashing an ant. That seemed to work, and he tried a second jump and then, throwing his arms out wide, he shouted 'Yippee!' and spun like a ballerina. His hat fell off and his hobnailed boots smacked into the dust and Mr Carpetlayer was a very happy man as he twirled and hopped, very *nearly* turned a cartwheel, and when it turned out to be about half a cartwheel, he rolled back onto his feet, picked up the astonished Tiffany and danced her along the road, shouting, 'One two three, one two three, one two three,' until she managed to shake herself loose, laughing. 'Me and the wife is going to go out tonight, young lady, and we are going to go waltzing!'

'But I thought that led to depraved behaviour?' said Tiffany.

The coachman winked at her. 'Well, we can but hope!' he said.

'You don't want to overdo it, Mr Carpetlayer,' she warned.

'As a matter of fact, miss, I rather think I do, if it's all the same to you. After all the creaking and groaning and not sleeping hardly at all, I think I would like to overdo it a little, or if possible a lot! Oh, what a good girl to think of the horses,' he added. 'That shows a kind nature.'

'I am pleased to see you in such fine spirits, Mr Carpetlayer.'

The coachman did a little twirl in the middle of the road. 'I feel twenty years younger!' He beamed at her, and then his face clouded just a little. 'Er . . . how much do I owe you?'

'How much will the damage to the paintwork cost me?' said Tiffany.

They looked at one another, and then Mr Carpetlayer said, 'Well, I can't ask you for anything, miss, given that it was me that busted the mirror ball.'

A little tinkling sound made Tiffany look behind them, where the mirror ball, apparently unharmed, was spinning gently and, if you looked carefully, just *above* the dirt.

She knelt down on a road totally free of broken glass and said, apparently to nothing at all, 'Did you stick it back together again?'

'Oh aye,' said Rob Anybody happily from behind the ball.

'But it was smashed to smithereens!'

'Oh aye, but a smithereen is easy, ye ken. See, the tinier bits are, the more they all fit together again. Ye just hae to give them a little push and the wee molly cules remembers where they should be and they sticks together again, nae problemo! Ye dinnae have to act surprised, we dinnae just smash things.'

Mr Carpetlayer stared at her. 'Did you do that, miss?'

'Well, sort of,' said Tiffany.

'Well I should say so!' said Carpetlayer, all smiles. 'So I says *quid pro quo*, give and take, knock for knock, tit for tat, one thing for another, an eye for an eye and me for you.' He winked. 'I'll say it worked out even, and the company can put their paperwork where the monkey put his jumper – what you say to that, eh?' He spat on his hand and held it out.

Oh dear, thought Tiffany, a handshake with spit seals an unbreakable accord; thank goodness I have a reasonably clean handkerchief.

She nodded speechlessly. And there had been a broken ball, and now it appeared to have mended itself. The day was hot, a man with holes where his eyes should be had vanished into nothing . . . Where would you even begin? Some days you trimmed toe-nails, removed splinters and sewed up legs, and some days were days like this.

They shook hands, rather damply, the broomstick was shoved among the bundles behind the driver, Tiffany climbed up alongside him, and the journey continued, dust rising up from the road as it passed and forming strangely unpleasant shapes until it settled down again.

After a while Mr Carpetlayer said, in a careful kind of voice, 'Er, that black hat you've got on, are you going to carry on wearing it?'

'That's right.'

'Only, well, you are wearing a nice green dress and, if I may say so, your teeth are lovely and white.' The man seemed to be wrestling with a problem.

'I clean them with soot and salt every day. I can recommend it,' said Tiffany.

It was turning into a difficult conversation. The man seemed to reach a conclusion. 'So you are not *really* a witch then?' he said hopefully.

'Mr Carpetlayer, are you *scared* of me?'

'That's a scary question, miss.'

Actually it is, Tiffany thought. Aloud, she said, 'Look, Mr Carpetlayer, what's this all about?'

'Well, miss, since you ask, there have been some stories lately. You know, about babies being stolen, that sort of thing. Kids running off and that.' He brightened up a bit. 'Still, I expect those were wicked *old* ... you know, with, like, hooked noses, warts and evil black dresses – not nice girls like you. Yes, that's just the sort of thing *they* would do!' Having sorted out that conundrum to his satisfaction, the coachman said little for the rest of the journey, although he did whistle a lot.

Tiffany, on the other hand, sat quietly. For one thing, she was now very worried, and for another thing she could just about hear the voices of the Feegles back among the mail bags, reading* other

---

* Jeannie, a modern kelda, had encouraged literacy among her sons and brothers. With Rob Anybody's example to follow, they had found the experience very worthwhile, because now they could read the labels on bottles before they drank them, although this didn't make too much of a difference, because unless

people's letters to each other. She had to hope that they were putting them back in the right envelopes.

The song went: '*Ankh-Morpork! It's a wonderful town! The trolls are up and the dwarfs are down! Slightly better than living in a hole in the ground! Ankh-Morpork! It's a wonderfuuuuuulllll townnn!*'

It wasn't, really.

Tiffany had only been there once before and didn't like the big city very much. It stank, and there were too many people, and far too many places. And the only green was on the surface of the river, which could only be called mud because a more accurate word would not have been printable.

The coachman pulled up outside one of the main gates, even though they were open.

'If you take my advice, miss, you'll take your hat off and walk in by yourself. That broomstick looks like firewood now, in any case.' He gave her a nervous grin. 'Best of luck, miss.'

'Mr Carpetlayer,' she said loudly, aware of people around her. 'I do hope that when you hear people talk about witches, you will mention that you met one and she made your back better – and, may I suggest, saved your livelihood. Thank you for the ride.'

'Oh well, I'll definitely tell people I met one of the good ones,' he said.

there was a skull and crossbones on it, a Feegle would probably drink it anyway, and even then it would have to be a very scary skull and crossbones.

* * *

With her head held high, or at least as high as is appropriate when you are carrying your own damaged
broomstick over your shoulder, Tiffany walked into
the city. The pointy hat got one or two glances, and
perhaps a couple of frowns, but mostly people didn't
look at her at all; in the country, everyone you meet is
someone you know or a stranger worth investigating,
but here it seemed there were so many people that it
was a waste of time even to look at them at all, and
possibly dangerous in any case.

Tiffany bent down. 'Rob, you know Roland, the
Baron's son?'

'Ach, the wee streak o' nothing,' said Rob
Anybody.

'Well, nevertheless,' said Tiffany, 'I know you can
find people and I would like you to go and find him
for me now please.'

'Would you no' mind if we had just the one wee drink
while we are looking?' said Rob Anybody. 'A man could
drown o' thirst around here. I can't remember a time
when I wasn't bogging for a wee dram or ten.'

Tiffany knew that it would be foolish to say either
yes or no and settled for, 'Just the one then. When
you've found him.'

There was the faintest of whooshing noises behind
her, and no more Feegles. Still, they would be easy to
find; you just had to listen for breaking glass. Oh yes,
breaking glass that repaired itself. Another mystery:
she had looked at the mirror ball very carefully as they

put it back in its box, and there hadn't been even a scratch on it.

She glanced up at the towers of Unseen University, crammed with wise men in pointy hats, or at least men in pointy hats, but there was another address, well known to witches, which was in its own way just as magical: Boffo's Joke Emporium, number four, Tenth Egg Street. She had never been there, but she did get a catalogue occasionally.

People started to notice her more when she got off the main streets and made her way through the neighbourhoods, and she could feel eyeballs on her as she walked over the cobbles. People weren't angry or unfriendly as such. They were just . . . watching, as if wondering what to make of her, and she had to hope that it was not, for example, stew.

There wasn't a bell on the door of Boffo's Joke Emporium. There was a whoopee cushion, and for most of the people who came to buy things in the emporium, a whoopee cushion, perhaps in conjunction with a generous dollop of fake sick, was the last word in entertainment, which indeed it is, unfortunately.

But real witches often needed boffo too. There were times when you had to *look* like a witch, and not every witch was good at it and was just too busy to get her hair in a mess. So Boffo's was where you bought your fake warts and wigs, stupidly heavy cauldrons and artificial skulls. And, with any luck, you might get the address of a dwarf who could help you repair your broomstick.

Tiffany stepped inside and admired the deep-throated farting of the whoopee cushion, pushed her way round and more or less through a ludicrous fake skeleton with glowing red eyes, and reached the counter, at which point somebody blew a squeaker at her. It disappeared, to be replaced by the face of a small, worried-looking man, who said, 'Did you by any chance find that even remotely amusing?'

His voice suggested that he expected the answer to be 'no' and Tiffany saw no reason to disappoint him. 'Absolutely not,' she said.

The man sighed and pushed the unfunny squeaker down the counter. 'Alas, no one ever does,' he said. 'I'm sure I'm doing something wrong somewhere. Oh well, what can I do for you, miss— Oh – you are a *real* one, aren't you? I can always tell, you know!'

'Look,' said Tiffany, 'I've never ordered anything from you, but I used to work with Miss Treason, who . . .'

But the man wasn't listening to her. Instead he was shouting at a hole in the floor. 'Mother? We've got a real one!'

A few seconds later, a voice by Tiffany's ear said, 'Derek is sometimes mistaken and you might have found the broomstick. You are a witch, aren't you? Show me!'

Tiffany vanished. She did it without thinking – or, rather, thinking so fast that her thoughts had no time to wave to her as they flashed by. Only when the man, who was apparently Derek, was staring open-mouthed at nothing at all did she realize that she had faded into the foreground so quickly because disobeying *that* voice behind her would definitely be an unwise thing to do. A witch was standing behind her: most definitely a witch, and a skilled one too.

'*Very* good,' said the voice approvingly. 'Very good indeed, young woman. I can still see you, of course, because I was watching very carefully. My word, a real one.'

'I'm going to turn round, you know,' Tiffany warned.

'I don't recall saying that you couldn't, my dear.'

Tiffany turned round and was faced with the witch of nightmares: battered hat, wart-encrusted nose, claw-like hands, blackened teeth and – Tiffany looked down – oh yes, big black boots. You did not have to be very familiar with Boffo's catalogue to see that the speaker was wearing the full range of cosmetics in the 'Hag in a Hurry' range (*'Because you're Worthless'*).

'I think we should continue this conversation in my workshop,' said the horrible hag, disappearing into the floor. 'Just stand on the trapdoor when it comes back up, will you? Make some coffee, Derek.'

When Tiffany arrived in the basement, the trapdoor working wonderfully smoothly, she found what you would expect in the workshop of the company that made everything needed by a witch who felt she needed some boffo in her life. Rows of rather scary hag masks were hanging on a line, benches were full of brightly coloured bottles, racks of warts had been laid out to dry, and various things that went *bloop* were doing so in a big cauldron by the fireplace. It was a proper cauldron too.*

The horrible hag was working at a bench, and there was a terrible cackle. She turned round, holding a small square wooden box with a piece of string sticking out of it. 'First-class cackle, don't you think? A simple thread and resin arrangement with a sounding board because, quite frankly, cackling is a bit of a pain in the neck, don't you think? I believe I can make it work by clockwork too. Let me know when you've seen the joke.'

'Who *are* you?' Tiffany burst out.

The hag had put the box on her workbench. 'Oh dear,' she said, 'where are my manners?'

'I don't know,' said Tiffany, who was getting a bit fed up. 'Perhaps the clockwork has run down?'

The hag grinned a black-toothed grin. 'Ah, sharpness. I like that in a witch, but not *too* much.' She held out a claw. 'Mrs Proust.'

The claw was less clammy than Tiffany had

---

* Most people who cook with cauldrons use them as a kind of double boiler, with small saucepans filled with water around the edge, picking up the heat of the big cauldron into which perhaps you might put a leg of pork weighted down, and possibly a few dumplings in a bag. This way, quite a large meal for several people can be cooked quite cheaply all in one go, including the pudding. Of course, it meant you had to stomach a lot of boiled food – but eat it up, it's good for you!

expected. 'Tiffany Aching,' she said. 'How do you do?' Feeling that something further was expected of her, Tiffany added, 'I used to work with Miss Treason.'

'Oh yes, a fine witch,' said Mrs Proust. 'And a good customer. Very keen on her warts and skulls, as I recall.' She smiled. 'And since I doubt that you want to get hagged up for a girls' night out, I must assume you need my help? The fact that your broomstick has about half the bristles needed for aerodynamic stability confirms my initial surmise. Incidentally, have you seen the joke yet?'

What should she say? 'I think so . . .'

'Go on then.'

'I'm not going to say until I'm sure,' said Tiffany.

'Very wise,' said Mrs Proust. 'Well, let's get your broomstick mended, shall we? It will mean a little stroll, and if I was you I would leave your black hat behind.'

Instinctively Tiffany grabbed at the brim of her hat. 'Why?'

Mrs Proust frowned, causing her nose to very nearly catch her chin. 'Because you might find . . . No, I know what we can do.' She rummaged on the workbench and, without asking any permission, stuck something on Tiffany's hat, right at the back. 'There,' she said. 'No one will take any notice now. Sorry, but witches are a little bit unpopular at the moment. Let's get that stick of yours repaired as soon as possible, just in case you need to leave in a hurry.'

Tiffany pulled off her hat and looked at what Mrs Proust had stuck in the hat band. It was a brightly coloured piece of cardboard on a string and it said: *Apprentice witch hat with evil glitter. Size 7. Price: AM$2.50. Boffo! A name to conjure with!!!*

'What's all this?' she demanded. 'You've even sprinkled evil glitter on it.'

'It's a disguise,' said Mrs Proust.

'What? Do you think any self-respecting witch would walk down the street wearing a hat like this?' said Tiffany angrily.

'Of course not,' said Mrs Proust. 'The best disguise for a witch is a rather cheap witch's outfit! Would a real witch buy clothes from a shop that also does a pretty good trade in naughty Fido jokes, indoor fireworks, laughable pantomime wigs and – our best and most profitable line – giant inflatable pink willies, suitable for hen nights? That would be unthinkable! It's boffo, my dear, pure, unadulterated boffo! *Disguise, subterfuge and misdirection* are our watchwords. All watchwords. And, *Amazing value for money,* they're our watchwords too. *No refunds under any circumstances,* they're important watchwords. As is our policy of dealing terminally with shoplifters. Oh, and we also have a watchword about people smoking in the shop, although that's not a very important word.'

'What?' said Tiffany who, out of shock, had not heard the list of watchwords because she was staring at the pink 'balloons' hanging from the ceiling. 'I thought they were piglets!'

Mrs Proust patted her hand. 'Welcome to life in the big city, my dear. Shall we go?'

'Why *are* witches so unpopular at the moment?' asked Tiffany.

'It's amazing the ideas people get into their heads sometimes,' said Mrs Proust. 'Generally speaking, I find it best just to keep your head down and wait until the problem goes away. You just need to be careful.'

And Tiffany thought that she did indeed need to be careful. 'Mrs Proust,' she said. 'I think I know the joke by now.'

'Yes, dear?'

'I thought you were a real witch disguising herself as a fake witch . . .'

'Yes, dear?' said Mrs Proust, her voice like treacle.

'Which would be quite amusing, but I think there's another joke, and it's not really very funny.'

'Oh, and what would that be, dear?' said Mrs Proust in a voice which now had sugary gingerbread cottages in it.

Tiffany took a deep breath. 'That really is *your* face, isn't it? The masks you sell are masks of *you*.'

'Well spotted! Well spotted, my dear! Only, you didn't spot it exactly, did you? You felt it, when you shook hands with me. And— But come on now, we'll get your broomstick over to those dwarfs.'

When they stepped outside, the first thing Tiffany saw was a couple of boys. One of them was poised to throw a stone at the shop window. He spotted Mrs Proust and a sort of dreadful silence descended. Then the witch said, 'Throw it, my lad.'

The boy looked at her as if she was mad.

'I said throw it, my lad, or the worst will happen.'

Clearly assuming now that she was mad, the boy threw the stone, which the window caught and threw back at him, knocking him to the ground. Tiffany saw it. She saw the glass hand come out of the glass and catch the stone. She saw it throw the stone back. Mrs Proust leaned over the boy, whose friend had taken to his heels, and said, 'Hmm, it will heal. It won't if I ever see you again.' She turned to Tiffany. 'Life can be very difficult for the small shopkeeper,' she said. 'Come on, it's this way.'

Tiffany was a bit nervous about how to continue the conversation and so she opted for something innocent, like, 'I didn't know there were any *real* witches in the city.'

'Oh, there's a few of us,' said Mrs Proust. 'Doing our bit, helping people when we can. Like that little lad back there, who will now have learned to mind his own business and it does my heart good to think that I may have dissuaded him from a lifetime of vandalism and disrespect for other people's property that would, you mark my words, have resulted in him getting a new collar courtesy of the hangman.'

'I didn't know you *could* be a witch in the city,' said Tiffany. 'I was told once that you need good rock to grow witches, and everyone says the city is built on slime and mud.'

'And masonry,' said Mrs Proust gleefully. 'Granite and marble, chert and miscellaneous sedimentary deposits, my dear Tiffany. Rocks that once leaped and flowed when the world was born in fire. And do you see the cobbles on the streets? Surely every single one of them, at some time, has had blood on it. Everywhere you look, stone and rock. Everywhere you can't see, stone and rock! Can you imagine what it feels like to reach down with your bones and feel the living stones? And what did we make from the stone? Palaces, and castles and mausoleums and gravestones, and fine houses, and city walls, oh my! Not just in this city either. The city is built on itself, all the cities that came before. Can you imagine how it feels to lie down on an ancient flagstone and feel the power of the rock buoying you up against the tug of the world? And it's mine to use, all of it, every stone of it, and that's where witchcraft begins. The stones have life, and I'm part of it.'

'Yes,' said Tiffany. 'I know.'

Suddenly Mrs Proust's face was a few inches from hers, the fearsome hooked nose almost touching her own, the dark eyes ablaze. Granny Weatherwax could be fearsome, but at least Granny Weatherwax *was*, in her way, handsome; Mrs Proust was the evil witch from the fairy stories, her face a curse, her voice the sound of the oven door slamming on the children. The sum of all night-time fears, filling the world.

'Oh, you know, do you, little witch in your jolly little dress? What is it that you know? What is it that you really *know*?' She took a step back, and blinked. 'More than I suspected, as it turns out,' she said, relaxing. 'Land under wave. In the heart of the chalk, the flint. Yes, indeed.'

\* \* \*

Tiffany had never seen dwarfs on the Chalk, but up in the mountains they were always around, generally with a cart. They bought, and they sold, and for witches they made broomsticks. Very *expensive* broomsticks. On the other hand, witches seldom ever bought one. They were heirlooms, passed down the generations from witch to witch, sometimes needing a new handle, sometimes needing new bristles, but, of course, always remaining the same broomstick.

Tiffany's stick had been left to her by Miss Treason. It was uncomfortable and not very fast and had the occasional habit of going backwards when it rained, and when the dwarf who was in charge of the clanging, echoing workshop saw it, he shook his head and made a sucking noise through his teeth, as if the sight of the thing had really spoiled his day and he might have to go away and have a little cry.

'Well, it's elm, isn't it,' he said to an uncaring world in general. 'It's a lowland wood, your elm, heavy and slow, and of course there's your beetles to consider. Very prone to beetles, your elm. Struck by lightning, was it? Not a good wood for lightning, your elm. Attracts it, so they say. Tendency to owls as well.'

Tiffany nodded and tried to look knowledgeable; she had made up the lightning strike, because the truth, while a valuable thing, was just too stupid, embarrassing and unbelievable.

Another, and almost identical, dwarf materialized behind his colleague. 'Should have gone for ash.'

'Oh yes,' said the first dwarf gloomily. 'Can't go wrong with ash.' He prodded Tiffany's broomstick and sighed again.

'Looks like it's got the start of bracket fungus in the base joint,' the second dwarf suggested.

'Wouldn't be surprised at anything, with your elm,' said the first dwarf.

'Look, can you just patch it up enough to get me home?' Tiffany asked.

'Oh, we don't "patch things up",' said the first dwarf loftily or, rather, metaphorically loftily. 'We do a bespoke service.'

'I just need a few bristles,' said Tiffany desperately, and then, because she forgot she hadn't been going to admit to the truth, 'Please? It wasn't my fault the Feegles set fire to the broomstick.'

Up until that point, there had been quite a lot of background noises in the dwarf workshop as dozens of dwarfs had been working away on their own benches and not taking much heed of the discussion, but now there was a silence, and in that silence a single hammer dropped to the floor.

The first dwarf said, 'When you say Feegles, you don't mean *Nac Mac Feegles*, do you, miss?'

'That's right.'

'The wild ones? Do they say . . . *Crivens*?' he asked very slowly.

'Practically all the time,' said Tiffany. She thought she ought to make things clear and added, 'They are my friends.'

'Oh, are they?' said the dwarf. 'And are any of your little friends here at this moment?'

'Well, I told them to go and find a young man of my acquaintance,' said Tiffany, 'but they are probably in a pub by now. Are there many pubs in the city?'

The two dwarfs looked at one another. 'About three hundred, I should say,' said the second dwarf.

'That many?' said Tiffany. 'Then I don't expect they'll come looking for me for at least half an hour.'

And suddenly the first dwarf was all frantic good humour. 'Well, where are our manners?' he said. 'Anything for a friend of Mrs Proust! Tell you what: it will be our pleasure to give you our express service *gratis* and for nothing, including free bristles and creosote at no charge whatsoever!'

'Express service meaning you leave straight away afterwards,' said the second dwarf flatly. He took off his iron helmet, wiped the sweat off the inside with his handkerchief and put it back on his head quickly.

'Oh yes, indeed,' said the first dwarf. 'Right away; that's what express *means*.'

'Friends with the Feegles, are you?' said Mrs Proust as the dwarfs hurried to deal with Tiffany's broom-stick. 'They don't have many, I understand. But talking of friends,' she continued in a suddenly chatty tone, 'you did meet Derek, didn't you? He's my son, you know. I met his father in a dance hall with very bad lighting. Mr Proust was a very kind man who was always gracious enough to say that kissing a lady with-out warts was like eating an egg without salt. He passed on twenty-five years ago, of the crisms. I am very sorry I couldn't help him.' Her face brightened. 'But I'm glad to say that young Derek is the joy of my' – she hesitated – 'middle age. A wonderful lad, my dear. It's going to be some lucky girl who takes her chance on young Derek, I can tell you. He's totally devoted to his work and pays such attention to detail. Do you know, he tunes all the whoopee cushions every morning and frets if any of them are wrong. And conscientious? When we were developing our forth-coming "Pearls of the Pavement" hilarious artificial dog poo collection, he must have spent weeks follow-ing just about every type of dog in the city with a notebook, a scoop and a colour chart, just to get everything exactly right. A very meticulous lad, clean in his ways, with all his own teeth. And very careful about his company . . .' She gave Tiffany a hopeful but rather sheepish look. 'This isn't working, is it?'

'Oh dear, did it show?' said Tiffany.

'I heard the spill words,' said Mrs Proust.

'What's a spill word?'

'You don't know? A spill word is a word that some-body *almost* says, but doesn't. For a moment they hover in the conversation but aren't spoken – and may I say that in the case of my son Derek, it is as well that you didn't say them aloud.'

'I'm really very sorry,' said Tiffany.

'Yes, well, be told,' said Mrs Proust.

Five minutes later, they walked out of the workshop

with Tiffany towing a fully functional broomstick behind her.

'Actually,' said Mrs Proust as they walked, 'now I come to think about it, your Feegles remind me a lot of Wee Mad Arthur. Tough as nails and about the same size. Haven't heard him say "Crivens", though. He's a policeman in the Watch.'

'Oh dear, the Feegles really don't like policemen,' said Tiffany, but she felt she ought to balance this somewhat, so she added, 'But they are very loyal, mostly helpful, good-natured in the absence of alcohol, honourable for a given value of honour and, after all, they did introduce the deep-fried stoat to the world.'

'What's a stoat?' said Mrs Proust.

'Well, er . . . you know a weasel? It's very much like a weasel.'

Mrs Proust raised her eyebrows. 'My dear, I treasure my ignorance of stoats *and* weasels. Sounds like countryside stuff to me. Can't abide countryside. Too much green makes me feel bilious,' she said, giving Tiffany's dress a shuddering glance.

At which point, on some celestial cue, there was a distant cry of 'Crivens!' followed by the ever-popular sound, at least to a Feegle, of breaking glass.

CHAPTER 7

# Songs in the Night

When Tiffany and Mrs Proust got to the source of the shouting, the street was already covered with a rather spectacular layer of broken glass, and worried-looking men with armour and the kind of helmet that you could eat your soup out of in an emergency. One of them was putting up barricades. Other watchmen were clearly unhappy about being on the wrong side of the barricades, especially since at that moment an extremely large watchman came flying out of one of the pubs that occupied almost all of one side of the street. The sign on it proclaimed it to be the King's Head, but by the look of it, the King's Head now had a headache.

The watchman took what remained of the glass with him, and when he landed on the pavement, his helmet, which could have held enough soup for a large family and all their friends, rolled off down the street making a *gloing! gloing!* noise.

Tiffany heard another watchman shout, 'They got Sarge!'

As more watchmen came running from both ends of the street, Mrs Proust tapped Tiffany on the shoulder and said sweetly, 'Tell me again about their good points, will you?'

I'm here to find a boy and tell him that his father is dead, said Tiffany to herself. Not to pull the Feegles out of yet another scrape!

'Their hearts are in the right place,' she said.

'I don't doubt it,' said Mrs Proust, who looked as though she was enjoying herself no end, 'but their arses are on a pile of broken glass. Oh, here come the reinforcements.'

'I don't think they will do much good,' said Tiffany – and to her surprise turned out to be wrong.

The guards were fanning out now, leaving a clear path to the pub entrance; Tiffany had to look hard to see a small figure walking purposely along it. It looked like a Feegle, but it was wearing . . . She stopped and stared . . . Yes, it was wearing a watchman's helmet slightly bigger than the top of a salt cellar, which was unthinkable. A legal Feegle? How could there be such a thing?

Nevertheless, it reached the doorway of the pub and shouted, 'You scunners are all under arrest! Now this is how it's going to go, ye ken: ye can hae it the hard way, or . . .' He paused for a moment. 'No, that's about it, aye,' he finished. 'I don't know any other way!' And with that he sprang through the doorway.

Feegles fought all the time. For them, fighting was a hobby, exercise and entertainment all combined.

Tiffany had read in Professor Chaffinch's famous book on mythology that many ancient peoples thought that when heroes died they went to some kind of feasting hall, where they would spend all eternity fighting, eating and boozing.

Tiffany thought that this would be rather boring by about day three, but the Feegles would love it, and probably even the legendary heroes would throw them out before eternity was half done, having first shaken them down to get all the cutlery back. The Nac Mac Feegle were indeed ferocious and fearsome fighters, with the minor drawback – from their point of view – that seconds into any fight, sheer enjoyment took over, and they tended to attack one another, nearby trees and, if no other target presented itself, themselves.

The watchmen, after reviving their sergeant and finding his helmet for him, sat down to wait for the noise to die away, and it seemed that it was after only a minute or two that the tiny watchman came back out of the stricken building, dragging by one leg Big Yan, a giant among Feegles and now, it appeared, fast asleep. He was dropped, the policeman went back in again and came out with an unconscious Rob Anybody over one shoulder, and Daft Wullie over the other.

Tiffany stared, with her mouth open. *This could not be happening.* The Feegles *always* won! *Nothing* beats a Feegle! They were *unstoppable*! But there they were: stopped, and stopped by a creature so small that he looked like one half of a salt and pepper set.

When he had run out of Feegles, the little man ran back into the building and came out very quickly, carrying a turkey-necked woman who was trying to hit him with her umbrella, a fruitless endeavour since he was balancing her carefully over his head. She was followed by a trembling young maidservant, clutching a voluminous carpet bag. The little man put the woman down neatly alongside the pile of Feegles, and while she screamed at the watchmen to arrest him, went back inside and came out again, balancing three heavy suitcases and two hat boxes.

Tiffany recognized the woman, but not with any pleasure. She was the Duchess, the mother of Letitia, and fairly fearsome. Did Roland really understand what he was letting himself in for? Letitia herself was all right, if you liked that kind of thing, but her mother apparently had so much blue blood in her veins that she ought to explode, and right now looked as if that was going to happen. And how *appropriate* that the Feegles should have trashed the very building that the nasty old baggage was staying in. How lucky could one witch get? And what would the Duchess think about Roland and his watercolour-painting wife-to-be being left in the building unchaperoned?

This question was answered by the sight of the little

man dragging both of them out of the building by some very expensive clothing. Roland was wearing a dinner jacket slightly too big for him, while Letitia's apparel was simply a mass of flimsy frills upon frills, in Tiffany's mind *not* the clothing of anyone who was any use whatsoever. Hah.

Still more watchmen were turning up, presumably because they had dealt with Feegles before and had had the sense to walk, not run, to the scene of the crime. But there was a tall one – more than six feet in height – with red hair and wearing armour so polished that it blinded, who was taking a witness statement from the owner; it sounded like a long-drawn-out scream to the effect that the watchmen should make this terrible nightmare not have happened.

Tiffany turned away and found herself staring directly into the face of Roland.

'*You? Here?*' he managed. In the background, Letitia was bursting into tears. Hah, just like her!

'Look, I have to tell you something very—'

'The floor fell in,' said Roland before she could finish, like someone still in a dream. 'The actual floor actually fell in!'

'Look, I must—' she began again, but this time Letitia's mother was suddenly in front of Tiffany.

'I know you! You're his witch girl, yes? Don't deny it! How dare you follow us here!'

'How did they make the floor fall in?' Roland demanded, his face white. 'How did you make the floor fall in? Tell me!'

And then the smell came. It was like being hit, unexpectedly, with a hammer. Under her bewilderment and horror Tiffany sensed something else: a stink, a stench, a foulness in her mind, dreadful and unforgiving, a compost of horrible ideas and rotted thoughts that made her want to take out her brain and wash it.

That's him: the man in black with no eyes! And the smell! A toilet for sick weasels couldn't smell worse! I thought it was bad last time, but that was a bed of primroses! She looked around desperately, hoping against hope not to see what she was looking for.

Letitia's sobs were getting louder, and mixing very badly with the sounds of the Feegles groaning and swearing as they started to wake up.

The mother-in-law-to-be grabbed Roland by his jacket. 'Come away from her right now; she is nothing but a—'

'*Roland, your father is dead!*'

That silenced everybody, and Tiffany was suddenly in a thicket of stares.

Oh dear, she thought. It shouldn't have happened like this.

'I'm sorry,' she managed in the accusing silence. 'There was nothing I could do.' She saw colour flow into his face.

'But you were looking after him,' said Roland, as if trying to work out a puzzle. 'Why did you stop keeping him alive?'

'All I could do was take the pain away. I'm so very sorry, but that's all I could do. I'm sorry.'

'But you're a witch! I thought you were good at it, you're a witch! Why did he die?'

*What did the bitch do to him? Do not trust her! She is a witch! Do not suffer a witch to live!*

Tiffany didn't hear the words; they seemed to crawl across her mind like some kind of slug, leaving slime behind it, and later she wondered how many other minds it had crawled across, but now she felt Mrs Proust grip her by the arm. She saw Roland's face contort into fury, and she remembered the screaming figure on the road, shadowless in full sunlight, delivering abuse as if it was vomit and leaving her with a sick feeling that she would never be able to get clean again.

And the people around her had a worried, hunted look, like rabbits who have smelled a fox.

Then she saw him. Hardly visible, at the edge of the crowd. There they were, or rather there they weren't. The two holes in the air staring at her just for a moment, before vanishing. And not knowing where they had gone made them worse.

She turned to Mrs Proust. 'What is *that*?'

The woman opened her mouth to answer, but the tall watchman's voice said, 'Excuse me, ladies and gentlemen, or rather just one gentleman in fact. I am Captain Carrot, and since I am the duty officer this evening, the doubtful pleasure of dealing with this incident falls to me, and so . . .' He opened his notebook, pulled out a pencil, and gave them a confident smile. 'Who is going to be the first to help me unravel this little conundrum? To begin with, I would very much like to know what a bunch of Nac Mac Feegle are doing in *my* city, apart from recovering?'

The glint off his armour hurt the eyes. And also he smelled strongly of soap, and that was good enough for Tiffany.

She began to raise her hand, but Mrs Proust grabbed it and held it firmly. This caused Tiffany to shake off Mrs Proust even more firmly and then say in a voice firmer than the grip, 'That would be me, Captain.'

'And you would be . . . ?'

Running away as soon as possible, Tiffany said to herself, but spoke up with, 'Tiffany Aching, sir.'

'Off to a hen night, are you?'

'No,' said Tiffany.

'Yes!' said Mrs Proust quickly.

The captain put his head on one side. 'So only one of you is going? That doesn't sound like much fun,' he said, with his pencil poised over the page.

This was clearly too much for the Duchess, who pointed an accusing finger at Tiffany; it trembled with anger. 'It is as clear as the nose on your face, Officer! This . . . this . . . this *witch* knew we were travelling down to the city in order to buy jewellery and gifts, and clearly, I repeat *clearly*, conspired with her imps to rob us!'

'I never did!' Tiffany yelled.

The captain held up a hand, as if the Duchess was a

line of traffic. 'Miss Aching, did you indeed encourage Feegles into the city?'

'Well, yes, but I didn't really intend to. It was a sort of spur-of-the-moment thing. I didn't intend—'

The captain held up his hand again. 'Stop talking, please.' He rubbed his nose. Then he sighed. 'Miss Aching, I'm arresting you on suspicion of . . . well, I'm just feeling suspicious. Besides, I am well aware that it is impossible to lock up a Feegle who doesn't want to be locked up. If they are friends of yours, I *trust*' – he looked around meaningfully – 'they will not do anything to get you into *further* trouble and, with luck, all of us will be able to get a decent night's sleep. My fellow officer, Captain Angua, will escort you down to the Watch House. Mrs Proust, would you be so good as to go along with them and explain the way of the world to your young friend?' Captain Angua stepped forward; she was female and beautiful and blonde – and . . . odd.

Captain Carrot turned to her ladyship. 'Madam, my officers will be happy to escort you to any other hotel or inn of your choice. I see that your maidservant is holding a rather strong-looking bag. Would this be containing the jewellery of which you spoke? In which case, can we ascertain that it has *not* been stolen?'

Her ladyship was not happy about this, but the captain cheerfully did not notice, in that very professional way policemen have of not seeing things they don't want to see. And there was a definite sense that he wouldn't have paid much attention in any case.

It was Roland who opened the bag and held the purchase up to the light. The tissue paper was carefully pulled off, and in the light of the lamps something sparkled so brilliantly that it seemed not only to reflect the light but to generate it too, somewhere inside its glowing stones. It was a tiara. Several of the watchmen gasped. Roland looked smug. Letitia looked objectionably winsome. Mrs Proust sighed. And Tiffany . . . went back in time, just for a second. But in that second she was a little girl again, reading the well-thumbed book of fairy stories that all her sisters had read before her.

But she had seen what they had not seen; she had seen through it. It lied. No, well, not exactly lied, but told you truths that you did not want to know: that only blonde and blue-eyed girls could get the prince and wear the glittering crown. It was built into the world. Even worse, it was built into your hair colouring. Redheads and brunettes sometimes got more than a walk-on part in the land of story, but if all you had was a rather mousy shade of brown hair you were marked down to be a servant girl.

Or you could be the witch. Yes! You didn't have to be stuck in the story. You could change it, not just for yourself, but for other people. You could change the story with a wave of your hand.

She sighed anyway, because the jewelled headdress was such a wonderful thing. But the sensible witch part of her said, 'How often would you wear it, miss? Once in a blue moon? Something as expensive as that will spend all its time in a vault!'

'Not stolen then,' said Captain Carrot happily. 'Well, that's good, isn't it? Miss Aching, I suggest you tell your little chums to follow you quietly, yes?'

Tiffany looked down at the Nac Mac Feegle, who were silent, as if in shock. Of course, when about thirty deadly fighters found themselves being beaten into submission by one tiny man, it takes a while to come up with a face-saving excuse.

Rob Anybody looked up at her with a very rare expression of shame. 'Sorry, miss. Sorry, miss,' he said. 'We just had considerably too much of the booze. And ye ken, the more ye have of the booze, you ken ye want to have even more of the booze, until ye falls over, which is when ye know ye've had enough of the booze. By the way, what the heel is *crème-de-menthe*? A nice green colour, ye ken, I must have drunk a bucket of that stuff! I suppose there is no point in saying we are verrae sorry? But ye ken, we did find the useless streak of rubbish for ye.'

Tiffany looked up at what remained of the King's Head. Flickering in the torchlight it looked like some kind of skeleton of a building. Even as she watched, a large beam began to creak and dropped apologetically onto a pile of broken furniture.

'I told you to find him; I didn't tell you you were supposed to pull the doors off,' she said. She folded her arms, and the little men huddled even closer together; the next stage of female anger would be the tapping o' the feets, which generally led them to burst into tears and walk into trees. Now, though, they formed up neatly behind her and Mrs Proust and Captain Angua.

The captain nodded at Mrs Proust and said, 'I'm sure we can all agree that handcuffs won't be necessary – yes, ladies?'

'Oh, you know me, Captain,' said Mrs Proust.

Captain Angua's eyes narrowed. 'Yes, but I don't know anything about your little friend. I would like you to carry the broomstick, Mrs Proust.'

Tiffany could see there was no point in arguing, and handed the stick over without complaining. They walked on in silence apart from the muted mumbling of the Nac Mac Feegles.

After a while the captain said, 'Not a good time to be wearing pointy black hats, Mrs Proust. There's been another case, out on the plains. Some dead and alive hole you would never go to. They beat up an old lady for having a book of spells.'

'No!'

They turned to look at Tiffany, and the Feegles walked into her ankles.

Captain Angua shook her head. 'Sorry, miss, but it's true. Turned out to be a book of Klatchian poetry, you know. All that wiggly writing! I suppose it looks like a spell book for those inclined to think that way. She died.'

'I blame *The Times*,' said Mrs Proust. 'When they put that sort of thing in the paper, it gives people ideas.'

Angua shrugged. 'From what I hear the people who did it weren't much for reading.'

'You've got to stop it!' said Tiffany.

'How, miss? We are the *City* Watch. We don't have any real jurisdiction outside the walls. There are places out there in the woods that we probably haven't even heard of. I don't know where this stuff comes from. It's like some mad idea dropping out of the air.' The captain rubbed her hands together. 'Of course, we don't have any witches in the city,' she said, 'although there are quite a lot of hen nights, eh, Mrs Proust?' And the captain winked. She really winked, Tiffany was certain of it, in the same way she had been certain that Captain Carrot really did not like the Duchess very much.

'Well, I think real witches would soon stop it,' Tiffany said. 'They certainly would in the mountains, Mrs Proust.'

'Oh, but we don't *have* real witches in the city. You heard the captain.' Mrs Proust glared at Tiffany and then hissed, 'We do not argue around the normal people. It makes them jittery.'

They stopped outside a large building with blue lamps on either side of the doors. 'Welcome to the Watch House, ladies,' said Captain Angua. 'Now, Miss Aching, I shall have to lock you in a cell, but it will be a clean one – no mice, hardly at all – and if Mrs Proust will keep you company, then, shall we say, I might be a bit forgetful and leave the key in the lock, do you understand? Please do not leave the building, because you will be hunted.' She looked directly at Tiffany and added, 'And no one should be hunted. It is a terrible thing, being hunted.'

She led them through the building and down to a row of surprisingly cosy-looking cells, gesturing for them to go inside one of them. The door of the cell clanged behind her and they heard the sound of her boots as she went back down the stone corridor.

Mrs Proust walked over to the door and reached through the bars. There was a tinkle of metal and her hand came back in with the key in it. She put it in the keyhole on this side, and turned it. 'There,' she said. 'Now we are doubly safe.'

'Och, crivens!' said Rob Anybody. 'Will ye no' look at us? Slammed up in the banger!'

'Again!' said Daft Wullie. 'I dinnae ken if I will ever look m'self in the face.'

Mrs Proust sat back down and stared at Tiffany. 'All right, my girl, what was that we saw? No eyes, I noticed. No windows into the soul. No soul, perhaps?'

Tiffany felt wretched. 'I don't know! I met him on the road here. The Feegles walked right through him! He seems like a ghost. And he stinks. Did you smell it? And the crowd were turning on us! What harm were we doing?'

'I'm not certain he's a him,' said Mrs Proust. 'He might even be an it. Could be a demon of some sort, I suppose . . . but I don't know much about them. Small-trade retail is more my forte. Not that that can't be a bit demonic at times.'

'But even Roland turned on me,' said Tiffany. 'And we've always been . . . friends.'

'Ah-ha,' said Mrs Proust.

'Don't you ah-ha me,' snapped Tiffany. 'How dare you ah-ha me. At least I don't go around making witches look *ridiculous*!'

Mrs Proust slapped her. It was like being hit with a rubber pencil. 'You're a rude slip of a girl, you young hussy. And I go around keeping witches *safe*.'

Up in the shadows of the ceiling, Daft Wullie nudged Rob Anybody and said, 'We cannae let somebody smack oor big wee hag, eh, Rob?'

Rob Anybody put a finger to his lips. 'Ah weel, it can be a wee bit difficult with womenfolk arguing, ye ken. Keep right oot of it, if ye'll tak' ma advice as a married man. Any man who interferes in the arguin' of women is gonnae find both of them jumping up and doon on him in a matter o' seconds. I'm nae talkin' about the foldin' of the arms, the pursin' of the lips and the tappin' of the feets. I'm talking about the smacking around with the copper stick.'

The witches stared at one another. Tiffany felt suddenly disorientated, as if she had gone from A to Z without passing through the rest of the alphabet.

'Did that just happen, my girl?' said Mrs Proust.

'Yes, it did,' said Tiffany sharply. 'It still stings.'

Mrs Proust said, 'Why did we do it?'

'To tell the truth, I hated you,' said Tiffany. 'Just for a moment. It frightened me. I just wanted to be rid of you. You were just—'

'All wrong?' said Mrs Proust.

'That's right!'

'Ah,' said Mrs Proust. 'Discord. Turning on the witch. Always blame the witch. Where does it start? Perhaps we have found out.' Her ugly face stared at Tiffany, then she said, 'When did you become a witch, my girl?'

'I think it was when I was about eight,' said Tiffany. And she told Mrs Proust the story about Mrs Snapperly, the witch in the hazel woods.

The woman listened carefully and settled down on the straw. 'We know it happens sometimes,' she said. 'Every few hundred years or so, suddenly everyone thinks witches are bad. No one knows why it is. It just seems to happen. Have you been doing anything lately that might attract attention? Any especially important piece of magic or something?'

Tiffany thought back and then said, 'Well, there was the hiver. But he wasn't all that bad. And before that there was the Queen of the Fairies, but that was ages ago. It was pretty awful too, but generally speaking, I think hitting her over the head with a frying pan was the best thing I could have done at the time. And, well, I suppose I'd better say that a couple of years ago, I did kiss the winter . . .'

Mrs Proust had been listening to this with her mouth open, and now she said, 'That was *you*?'

'Yes,' said Tiffany.

'Are you sure?' said Mrs Proust.

'Yes. It was me. I was there.'

'What was it like?'

'Chilly, and then damp. I didn't want to have to do it. I'm sorry, OK?'

'About two years ago?' said Mrs Proust. 'That's interesting. The trouble seemed to start around then, you know. Nothing particularly major; it was just as though people didn't respect us any more. Just something in the air, you might say. I mean, that kid with the stone this morning. Well, he would never have dared try that a year ago. People always gave me a nod when I passed by in those days. And now they frown. Or they make some little sign, just in case I bring bad luck. The others have told me about this too. What's it been like where you are?'

'Can't really say,' said Tiffany. 'People were a bit nervous of me, but on the whole I suppose I was related to a lot of them. But everything felt odd. And I thought that was how it had to feel. I'd kissed the winter, and everybody knew it. Honestly, they do go on about it. I mean, it was only *once*.'

'Well, people are packed a little more closely together around here. And witches have long memories. I mean, not individual witches, but all the witches put together can remember the really bad times. When wearing a pointy hat got a stone thrown at you, if not something worse. And when you go back further than that ... It's like a disease,' Mrs Proust said. 'It sort of creeps up. It's in the wind, as if it goes from person to person. Poison goes where poison's welcome. And there's always an excuse, isn't there, to throw a stone at the old lady who looks funny. It's always easier to blame somebody. And once you've called someone a witch, then you'd be amazed how many things you can blame her for.'

'They stoned her cat to death,' said Tiffany, almost to herself.

'And now there's a man without a soul who's following you. And the stink of him makes even witches hate witches. You don't feel inclined to set fire to me, by any chance, Miss Tiffany Aching?'

'No, of course not,' said Tiffany.

'Or press me flat on the ground with lots of stones on me?'

'What are you talking about?'

'It wasn't just stones,' said Mrs Proust. 'You hear people talk about witches being burned, but I don't reckon many real witches ever did get burned unless they were tricked in some way; I think it was mostly poor old women. Witches are mostly too soggy, and it was probably a wicked waste of good timber. But it's very easy to push an old lady down to the ground and take one of the doors off the barn and put it on top of her like a sandwich and pile stones on it until she can't breathe any more. And that makes all the badness go away. Except that it doesn't. Because there are other things going on, and other old ladies. And when they run out, there are always old men. Always strangers. There's always the outsider. And then, perhaps, one day, there's always you. That's when the madness stops. When there's no one left to be mad. Do you know, Tiffany Aching, that I felt it when you kissed the winter? Anyone with an ounce of magical talent felt something.' She paused and her eyes narrowed. Now she was staring at Tiffany. 'What did you wake up, Tiffany Aching? What rough thing opened the eyes that it had not got and wondered who you were? What have you brought upon us, Miss Tiffany Aching? *What have you done?*'

'You think that . . .' Tiffany hesitated and then said, 'That he is after *me*?'

She closed her eyes so that she couldn't see the accusing face, and remembered the day she had kissed the winter. There had been terror, and dreadful apprehension, and the strange feeling of being warm whilst surrounded by ice and snow. And as for the kiss, well, it had been as gentle as a silk handkerchief falling on a carpet. Until she had poured all the heat of the sun into the lips of winter and melted him into water. Frost to fire. Fire to frost. She'd always been good with fire. Fire had always been her friend. It wasn't as if the winter had ever died; there had been other winters since, but not so bad, never so bad. And it hadn't just been a snog. She had done the right thing at the right time. It was what you did. Why had she had to do it? Because it was her fault; because she had disobeyed Miss Treason and joined in a dance that wasn't just a dance but the curving of the seasons and the turning of the year.

And, with horror, she wondered: Where does it end? You do one foolish thing and then one thing to put it right, and when you put it right something else goes wrong. Where did it ever stop? Mrs Proust was watching her as though fascinated.

'All I did was dance,' said Tiffany.

Mrs Proust put a hand on her shoulder. 'My dear, I think you will have to dance again. Could I suggest you do something very sensible at this point, Tiffany Aching?'

'Yes,' said Tiffany.

'Listen to my advice,' said Mrs Proust. 'I don't usually give things away, but I feel quite chipper about catching that lad who kept breaking my windows. So I'm in the mood for a good mood. There is a lady who I am sure would be very keen to talk to you. She lives in the city, but you'll never find her no matter how hard you try. She will find you, though, in the blink of a second, and my advice is that when she does, you listen to everything she might tell you.'

'So how *do* I find her?' said Tiffany.

'You're feeling sorry for yourself and not listening,' said Mrs Proust. 'She will find you. You'll know it when she does. Oh my word, yes.' She reached into a pocket and produced a small round tin, the lid of which she flicked open with a black fingernail. The air suddenly felt prickly. 'Snuff?' she said, offering the tin to Tiffany. 'Dirty habit, of course, but it clears the tubes and helps me think.' She took a pinch of the brown powder, tipped it onto the back of the other hand and sniffed it up with a sound like a honk in reverse. She coughed and blinked once or twice and said, 'Of course, brown bogeys are not to everybody's liking, but I suppose they add to that nasty witch look. Anyway, I expect they'll soon give us dinner.'

'They're going to feed us?' said Tiffany.

'Oh yes, they're a decent bunch, although the wine last time was a bit off in my opinion,' said Mrs Proust.

'But we're in prison.'

'No, my dear, we're in the police cells. And, though nobody's saying it, we're locked in here for our protection. You see, everyone else is locked *out*, and although they sometimes act dumb, policemen can't help being clever. They know that people need witches; they need the unofficial people who understand the difference between right and wrong, and when right is wrong and when wrong is right. The world needs the people who work around the edges. They need the people who can deal with the little bumps and inconveniences. And little problems. After all, we are almost all human. Almost all of the time. And almost every full moon Captain Angua comes to me to make up a prescription for her hardpad.'

The snuff tin was produced again.

After a while Tiffany said, 'Hardpad is a disease of dogs.'

'And werewolves,' said Mrs Proust.

'Oh. I thought there was something odd about her.'

'She stays on top of it, mind you,' said Mrs Proust. 'She shares lodgings with Captain Carrot and doesn't bite anybody – although, come to think about it, she possibly bites Captain Carrot, but least said soonest mended, I'm sure you will agree. Sometimes what is legal isn't what is right, and sometimes it needs a witch to tell the difference. And sometimes a copper too, if you have the right kind of copper. Clever people know this. Stupid people don't. And the trouble is, stupid people can be oh so very clever. And by the way, miss, your boisterous little friends have escaped.'

'Yes,' Tiffany said. 'I know.'

'Isn't that a shame, despite the fact that they faithfully promised the Watch to stay?' Mrs Proust evidently did like to retain a reputation for nastiness.

Tiffany cleared her throat. 'Well,' she said, 'I suppose Rob Anybody would tell you that there are times when promises should be kept and times when promises should be broken, and it takes a Feegle to know the difference.'

Mrs Proust grinned hugely. 'You could almost be from the city, Miss Tiffany Aching.'

If you needed to guard something that didn't need guarding, possibly because no one in their right mind would want to steal it, then Corporal Nobbs of the City Watch was, for want of a better way of describing him, and in the absence of any hard biological evidence to the contrary, your man. And now he stood in the dark and crunching ruins of the King's Head, smoking a horrible cigarette made by rolling up all the stinking butts of previously smoked cigarettes into some fresh cigarette paper and sucking the horrible mess until some kind of smoke appeared.

He never noticed the hand that lifted his helmet off, hardly even felt the forensic blow to the head, and certainly did not feel the calloused little hands that placed the helmet back on his head as they lowered his sleeping body to the ground.

'OK,' said Rob Anybody in a hoarse whisper, looking around at the blackened timbers. 'Now, we don't have much time, ye ken, so—'

'Well, well, I just knew that you wee scunners would come back here if I waited long enough for ye,' said a voice in the dark. 'As a dog returneth to his vomit and a fool to his folly, so the criminal returns to the scene of his crime.'

The watchman known as Wee Mad Arthur struck a match, which was, for a Feegle, a pretty good torch. There was a clink as something that was the size of a shield for a Feegle, but would have been a badge for a human policeman, landed on the floor in front of him. 'That's tae show you wee fools that I'm nae on duty, OK? Cannae be a policeman withoot a badge, ain't that so? I just wanted tae see why ye wee dead-beats talks properly, like what I do, because ye ken, I'm no' a Feegle.'

The Feegles looked at Rob Anybody, who shrugged and said, 'What the heel do you think ye are, then?'

Wee Mad Arthur ran his hands through his hair, and nothing fell out. 'Well, my ma an' poppa told me I was a gnome, like them—'

He stopped talking because the Feegles were hooting and slapping their legs with mirth, which tends to go on for a long time.

Wee Mad Arthur watched for a little while before shouting, 'I do not find this funny!'

'Will ye no' listen to yourself?' said Rob Anybody, wiping his eyes. 'Ye are speaking Feegle, sure enough! Did yer mammy and yer pappy nae tell ye? We Feegles are born knowing how to speak! Crivens! It's just like a dog knowing how to bark! Ye cannae tell me ye are a gnome! Ye'll be telling me ye are a pixie next!'

Wee Mad Arthur looked down at his boots. 'My dad made me these boots,' he said. 'I couldnae bring mesel' to tell him I didnae like boots on my feet. The whole family had been making and repairing shoes for hundreds of years, ye ken, and I wasnae good at the cobbling at all, and then one day all the elders of the tribe called me together and told me I was a lost foundling. They was moving to a new camp, and they ha' found me, a tiny wee bairn, greeting by the road, right next to a sparrowhawk that I had strangled to death after it had snatched me from me cradle; they reckoned it was taking me home to feed me tae its chicks. And the old gnomes put their hats together, and said that while they were very happy to let me stay, what with being able to bite foxes to death and everything, it might be time for me to go out into the big world and find out who my people were.'

'Well, laddie, ye have found them,' said Rob Anybody, slapping him on the back. 'Ye did well to listen to a load of old cobblers. That was wisdom they told you, sure enough.'

He hesitated for a moment, and then went on, 'However, it's a wee bitty difficult that ye are – no offence meant – a policeman.' He jumped back slightly, just in case.

'Granted,' said Wee Mad Arthur with satisfaction. 'Whereas ye are a bunch of thieving drunken reprobates and scoff-laws with no respect for the law whatsoever!'

The Feegles nodded happily, although Rob Anybody said, 'Would you no' mind adding the words drunk and disorderly? We wouldnae want to be sold short here.'

'And what about the snail-rustling, Rob?' said Daft Wullie happily.

'Weel,' said Rob Anybody, 'in actual point of fact, the snail-rustling is still in the early stages of development at this time.'

'Have you no good points?' said Wee Mad Arthur desperately.

Rob Anybody looked puzzled. 'We kind of thought them *is* our good points, but if you want to get picky, we never steal from them as has nae money, we has hearts of gold, although maybe – OK, mostly – somebody else's gold, and we did invent the deep-fried stoat. That must count for something.'

'How is that a good point?' said Arthur.

'Weel, it saves some other poor devil having tae do it. It's what ye might call a taste explosion; ye take a mouthful, taste it, and then there is an explosion.'

Despite himself, Wee Mad Arthur was grinning. 'Have you boys got no shame?'

Rob Anybody matched him grin for grin. 'I

couldnae say,' he replied, 'but if we have, it probably belonged tae somebody else.'

'And what about the poor wee big lassie locked up and down in the Watch House?' said Wee Mad Arthur.

'Oh, she'll bide fine till the morning,' said Rob Anybody, as loftily as he could in the circumstances. 'She is a hag o' considerable resource.'

'Ye think so? You wee scunners punched an entire pub to death! How can anyone put *that* right?'

This time Rob Anybody gave him a longer, more thoughtful look before saying, 'Well, Mr Policeman, it seems ye are a Feegle and a copper. Well, that's the way the world spins. But the big question for the pair of ye is: are you a sneak and a snitch?'

In the Watch House the shift was changing. Somebody came in and shyly handed Mrs Proust quite a large plate of cold meats and pickles, and a bottle of wine with two glasses. After a nervous look at Tiffany, the watchman whispered something to Mrs Proust, and in one movement she'd taken a small packet out of her pocket and shoved it into his hand. Then she came back and sat down on the straw again.

'And I see he's had the decency to open the bottle and let the wine breathe for a while,' she said, and added, when she saw Tiffany's glance, 'Lance Constable Hopkins has a little problem that he'd rather his mother never found out about and I make a rather helpful ointment. I don't charge him, of course. One hand washes the other, although in the case of young Hopkins I hope he scrubs it first.'

Tiffany had never drunk wine before; at home you drank small beer or small cider, which had just enough alcohol to kill off the nasty invisible tiny biting things, but not enough alcohol to make you more than a bit silly.

'Well,' she said, 'I never thought prison would be like this!'

'Prison? I told you, my dear girl, this isn't prison! If you want to know what a prison is like, visit the Tanty! That's a dark place if you like! In here the watchmen don't gob in your grub – at least when you're watching, and certainly never in mine, you can be sure of that. The Tanty is a tough place; they like to think that anyone who gets put in there will think more than twice before doing anything that will get them put in there again. And they've tidied it up a bit these days, and not everybody who goes in comes out in a pine box, but the walls still scream silently to those with hearing. I hear them.' She opened her snuffbox with a click. 'And worse than the screaming is the sound of the canaries in D wing, where they lock up the men who they don't dare hang. They bang up each one by himself in a little room, and they give him a canary as company.' At this point Mrs Proust took a pinch of snuff, at such speed and volume that Tiffany was surprised that it didn't come out of her ears.

The box's lid snapped back down. 'Those men, mark you, are not your average murderer – oh no, they killed people for a hobby, or for a god or for something to do, or because it wasn't a very nice day. They did worse things than just murder, but murder was how it always ended. I see you haven't touched your beef...? Oh well, if you're quite sure...' Mrs Proust paused with rather a large piece of heavily pickled lean beef on her knife and went on: 'Funny thing, though, these cruel men used to look after their canaries, and cried when they died. The warders used to say it was all a sham; they said it gave them the creeps, but I'm not sure. When I was young, I used to run errands for the warders and I would look at those great heavy doors and I would listen to the little birds, and I would wonder what it is that makes the difference between a good man and a man so bad that no hangman in the city – not even my dad, who could have a man out of his cell and stone-cold dead in seven and a quarter seconds – would dare to put a rope round his neck in case he escaped from the fires of evil and came back with a vengeance.' Mrs Proust stopped there and shivered, as if shaking off the memories. 'That's life in the big city, my girl; it's not an easy bed of sweet primroses, like in the country.'

Tiffany wasn't very happy with being called a girl again, but that wasn't the worst of it. 'Sweet primroses?' she said. 'It wasn't sweet primroses the other day when I had to cut down a hanged man.' And she had to tell Mrs Proust all about Mr Petty and Amber. And about the bouquet of nettles.

'And your dad told you about the beatings?' said Mrs Proust. 'Sooner or later, it's all about the soul.'

The meal had been tasty, and the wine surprisingly strong. And the straw was a lot cleaner than you might have expected. It had been a long day, piled on top of other long days. 'Please,' Tiffany said, 'can we get some sleep? My father always says that things will look better in the morning.'

There was a pause. 'Upon reflection,' Mrs Proust said, 'I think your father will turn out to be wrong.'

Tiffany let the clouds of tiredness take her. She dreamed about canaries singing in the dark. And perhaps she imagined it, but she thought she woke up for a moment and saw the shadow of an old lady looking at her. It certainly wasn't Mrs Proust, who snored something terrible. The shape was there for a moment, and then it vanished. Tiffany remembered: the world is full of omens, and you picked the ones you liked.

## CHAPTER 8

# The King's Neck

Tiffany was woken by the squeak of the cell door opening. She sat up and looked around. Mrs Proust was still asleep, and snoring so hard that her nose wobbled. Correction: Mrs Proust *appeared* to be asleep. Tiffany liked her, in a wary kind of way, but could she trust her? Sometimes she seemed to almost . . . read her mind.

'I don't read minds,' said Mrs Proust, turning over.

'Mrs Proust!'

Mrs Proust sat up and started to pull bits of straw off her dress. 'I *don't* read minds,' she said, flicking the straw onto the floor. 'I really have keen, but not supernatural, skills which I have honed to the sharpest of edges, and don't you forget it, please. I hope to goodness they're going to give us a cooked breakfast.'

'No problem there – what would ye like us to fetch for ye?'

They looked up to see the Feegles sitting on the beam overhead, and dangling their feet happily.

Tiffany sighed. 'If I asked you what you were doing last night, would you lie to me?'

'Absolutely not, on our honour as Feegles,' said Rob Anybody, with his hand on where he thought his heart was.

'Well, that seems conclusive,' said Mrs Proust, standing up.

Tiffany shook her head and sighed again. 'No, it's not quite as simple as that.' She looked up at the beam and said, 'Rob Anybody, was the answer you gave me just then truthful? I'm asking you as the hag o' the hills.'

'Oh aye.'

'And that one?'

'Oh aye.'

'And that one?'

'Oh aye.'

'And that one?'

'Oh . . . well, only a tiny wee lie, ye ken, hardly a lie, just something that it wouldnae be good for ye tae know.'

Tiffany turned to Mrs Proust, who was grinning. 'The Nac Mac Feegles feel that the truth is so precious that it shouldn't be waved about too much,' she said apologetically.

'Ah, people after my own heart,' said Mrs Proust,

and then, remembering herself, she added, 'If I had one, that is.'

There was a sound of heavy boots, which got nearer and no less heavy very quickly, and turned out to belong to a tall and skinny watchman, who touched his helmet politely to Mrs Proust and gave Tiffany a nod.

'Good morning, ladies! My name is Constable Haddock and I have been told to tell you that you've been let go with a warning,' he said. 'Although I have to tell you that no one quite knows what to warn you about, as far as I can tell, so if I was you, I'd consider myself generally in the situation of being warned, as it were, in a general and generically non-specific way, and hopefully slightly chastened by the experience, no offence meant, I'm sure.' He coughed, and went on, after giving Mrs Proust a nervous look, 'And Commander Vimes has asked me to make it clear that the individuals known jointly as the Nac Mac Feegle are to be out of this city by sunset.'

There was a chorus of complaints from the Feegles on the beam, who in Tiffany's opinion were as good at astonished indignation as they were at drunkenness and thievery:

'Och, ye wouldnae pick on us if we was big!'

'It wasnae us! A big boy did it and ran awee!'

'I wasnae there! Ye can ask them! They wasnae there either!'

And otherrr excuses o' that ilk, ye ken.

Tiffany banged her tin plate on the bars until they subsided into silence. Then she said, 'Excuse me, please, Constable Haddock. I'm sure they're all very sorry about the pub—' she began, and he waved a hand at her.

'If you'll take my advice, miss, you would just leave quietly and not talk to anybody about pubs.'

'But look . . . we all know that they smashed up the King's Head, and—'

The constable stopped her again. 'I went past the King's Head this morning,' he said, 'and it was very definitely not smashed up. In fact, there were crowds of people there. Everyone in the city is going to have a look at it. The King's Head is just like it's always been, as far as I can see, with just the one tiny little detail which is, to wit, that it is now back to front.'

'What do you mean, "back to front"?' said Mrs Proust.

'I mean that it is the wrong way round,' said the policeman patiently, 'and when I was over there just now, you can bet they weren't calling it the King's *Head* any more.'

Tiffany's forehead wrinkled. 'So . . . they're calling it the King's *Neck*?'

Constable Haddock smiled. 'Well, yes, I can see you are a well-brought-up young lady, miss, because most of the people out there are calling it the King's—'

'I cannot abide smut!' said Mrs Proust severely.

Really? Tiffany thought. With half a shop window full of pink inflatable wossnames and other mysterious items that I didn't get a chance to see very clearly? But I suppose it would be a strange world if we were all the same, and especially if we were all the same as Mrs Proust.

And overhead she could hear the susurration of the Nac Mac Feegles, with Daft Wullie making more noise than usual. 'I told ye, didn't I tell ye, I said this lot is back to front, I said, but no, ye would nae pay heed! I may be daft, but I'm no' stupid.'

The King's Head, or at least whatever part of the king's anatomy it now was, was not very far away, but the witches had to push their way through the crowds when they were at least a hundred yards away, and many of the people making up the crowd were holding pint mugs in their hands. Mrs Proust and Tiffany both wore hobnailed boots, a boon to anyone who must get through a crowd in a hurry and there, in front of them was, for want of a better word – although the Feegles would have used a different word, and indeed the Feegles would not have hesitated to use a different word – was, in fact, the King's Back, which came as a relief. Standing in front of the back door, which was now doing the duty formerly left to the front door, and handing out mugs of beer with one hand while taking money with the other, was Mr Wilkin, the landlord. He looked like a cat on the day it rained mice.

Every now and again he managed to find time in this heroic endeavour to say a few words to a skinny but purposeful-looking lady who was writing things down in a notebook.

Mrs Proust nudged Tiffany. 'See her? That's Miss Cripslock of *The Times*, and over there' – she pointed at a tall man in the uniform of the Watch – 'see there, the man she's talking to is Commander Vimes of the City Watch. Decent man, always looks grumpy, won't stand any nonsense. This is going to be interesting, because he doesn't like kings of any sort; one of his ancestors chopped off the head of the last king we had.'

'That's dreadful! Did he deserve it?'

Mrs Proust hesitated for a moment, and then said, 'Well, if it's true about what they found in his private dungeon, then the answer is "yes" in great big letters. They put the commander's ancestor on trial anyway, because chopping heads off kings always causes a certain amount of comment, apparently. When the man stood in the dock, all he said was, "Had the beast a hundred heads I would not have rested until I had slain every last one." Which was taken as a guilty plea. He was hanged, and then much later they put up a statue to him, which tells you more about people than you might wish to know. His nickname was Old Stoneface, and as you can see, it runs in the family.'

Tiffany could, and this was because the commander was moving purposefully towards her, his expression that of a man who had a lot of things to do, all of them more important than what he was having to do right now. He gave a respectful little nod to Mrs Proust, and tried unsuccessfully not to glare at Tiffany.

'Did you do this?'

would think it had always been like that. He is daft, ye ken.'

'Sometimes daft works,' said Tiffany. She looked around . . . And there *he* was, the man with no eyes, walking through the crowd, *walking through the crowd*, as if they were ghosts, but she could see that they felt his presence in some way; one man brushed his hand across his face, as if feeling the footsteps of a fly; another one slapped at his own ear. But afterwards they were . . . changed. When their eyes saw Tiffany they narrowed, and the ghostly man headed towards her and the whole of the crowd became one huge frown. And here came the stench, trailing behind him and turning the daylight grey. It was like the bottom of a pond, where things had died and rotted for centuries.

Tiffany looked around desperately. The turning of the King's Head had filled the street with the curious and the thirsty. People were trying to go about their business, but were being hemmed in by the crowd in front and the crowd behind them and, of course, by the people with trays and little carts who swarmed through the city and would try to sell something to anyone who stood still for more than two seconds. She could feel the menace in the air, but in fact it was more than a menace – it was hatred, growing like a plant after rain, and still the man in black came nearer. It scared her. Of course, she had the Feegles with her, but generally speaking the Feegles got you out of trouble by getting you into a different kind of trouble.

The ground moved quite suddenly underneath her. There was a metallic scraping noise, and the bottom dropped out of her world, but only by about six feet. As she staggered in the gloom under the pavement, someone pushed past her with a cheerful 'Excuse me.' There were more inexplicable metal noises and the round hole now above her head vanished in darkness.

'Real piece of luck there,' said the polite voice. 'The only one we're going to get today, I fancy. Please try not to panic until I have lit the safety lantern. If you want to panic thereafter, that is entirely up to you. Stay close to me and when I say, "Walk as fast as possible while holding your breath," do so, for the sake of your sanity, your throat, and possibly your life. I don't care if you understand or not – just do it, because we may not have much time.'

A match flared. There was a small popping noise and a green-blue glow in the air just in front of Tiffany. 'Only a bit of marsh gas,' said the invisible informant. 'Not too bad, nothing to worry about yet, but stay close, mind you!'

The green-blue glow began to move very fast, and Tiffany had to walk quickly to keep up, which was no mean feat, because the ground beneath her boots was, by turns, like gravel, mud or occasionally a liquid of some sort but probably not a sort that you would want to know about. Here and there, in the distance, there were tiny little glows of other mysterious lights, like will-o'-the-wisps you sometimes got over marshy ground.

'Do keep up!' said the voice ahead of her.

Soon Tiffany lost all sense of direction and, for that matter, time.

Then there was a click and the figure was outlined against what looked like a perfectly ordinary doorway, except that it was in an arch, and so the door itself came to a point at the top.

'Please be so good as to wipe your feet very thoroughly on the mat just inside; it pays to take precautions down here.'

Behind the still shadowy figure, candles were lighting themselves, and now they illuminated someone in heavy, stiff clothing, big boots and a steel helmet on her head – although, as Tiffany watched, the figure carefully lifted the helmet off. She shook out her ponytail, which suggested that she was young, but her hair was white, suggesting that she was old. She was, Tiffany thought, one of those people who picks for themselves a look that suits them and doesn't get in the way, and never changes it until they die. There were wrinkles too, and Tiffany's guide had the preoccupied air of somebody who is trying to think of several things at once; and by the look on her face she was trying to think of everything. There was a small table in the room, set with a teapot, cups and a pile of small cupcakes.

'Do come on in,' said the woman. 'Welcome. But where are my manners? My name is Miss . . . Smith, for the moment. I believe Mrs Proust may have mentioned me? And you are in the Unreal Estate, quite possibly the most unstable place in the world. Would you like some tea?'

Things tend to look better when the world has stopped spinning and you have a warm drink in front of you, even if it's standing on an old packing case.

'I'm sorry it's not a palace,' said Miss Smith. 'I never stay here for more than a few days at a time, but I do need to be close to the University, and to have absolute privacy. This was a little cottage outside the University walls, you see, and the wizards just used to chuck all their waste over: after a while, all the different bits of magical rubbish started to react with one another in what I can only call unpredictable ways. Well, what with talking rats, and people's eyebrows growing up to six feet long, and shoes walking around by themselves, the people that lived nearby ran away, and so did their shoes. And since there was no one complaining any more, the University simply chucked even more stuff over the wall. Wizards are like cats going to the toilet in that respect; once you've walked away from it, it isn't there any more.

'Of course, it then became a free-for-all, with just about anybody throwing over just about anything and running away very quickly, often pursued by shoes, but not always successfully. Would you like a cupcake? And don't worry, I bought them off quite a reliable baker tomorrow, so I know they're fresh, and I pretty much tamed the magic around here a year ago. It wasn't too hard; magic is largely a matter of balance, but of course you'd know that. Anyway, the upshot is that there is such a magical fog over this place that I doubt if even a god could see into it.' Miss Smith delicately ate half a cupcake, and balanced the other half on her saucer. She leaned closer to Tiffany. 'How did it feel, Miss Tiffany Aching, when you kissed the winter?'

Tiffany stared at her for a moment. 'Look, it was just a peck, OK? Certainly no tongues!' Then she said, 'You are the person that Mrs Proust said was going to find me, aren't you?'

'Yes,' said Miss Smith. 'I would hope that is obvious. I could give you a long, complicated lecture,' she continued brusquely, 'but I think it would be better if I told you a story. I know you have been taught by Granny Weatherwax, and she will tell you that the world is made up of stories. I had better admit that this one is one of the nasty ones.'

'I am a witch, you know,' said Tiffany. 'I have seen nasty things.'

'So you may think,' said Miss Smith. 'But for now I want you to picture a scene, more than a thousand years ago, and imagine a man, still quite young, and he is a witchfinder and a book-burner and a torturer, because people older than him who are far more vile than him have told him that this is what the Great God Om wants him to be. And on this day he has found a woman who is a witch, and she is beautiful, astonishingly beautiful, which is rather unusual among witches, at least in those days—'

'He falls in love with her, doesn't he?' Tiffany interrupted.

'Of course,' said Miss Smith. 'Boy meets girl, one of the greatest engines of narrative causality in the multiverse, or as some people might put it, "It had to happen." I would like to continue this discourse without interruptions, if you don't mind?'

'But he is going to have to kill her, isn't he?'

Miss Smith sighed. 'Since you ask, not necessarily. He thinks that if he rescues her and they can get to the river, then they might have a chance. He is bewildered and confused. He has never had feelings like this before. For the first time in his life, he is really having to think for himself. There are horses not far away. There are a few guards, and some other prisoners, and the air is full of smoke because there is a pile of burning books, which is making people's eyes water.'

Tiffany leaned forward in her seat, listening to the clues, trying to work out the ending in advance.

'There are some apprentices that he is training, and also some very senior members of the Omnian church who have come to watch and bless the proceedings. And finally there are a number of people from the nearby village who are cheering very loudly because it is not them who are going to be killed and generally they don't get much entertainment. In fact, it's pretty much another day at the office, except that the girl being tied to the stake by the apprentices has caught his eye and is now watching him very carefully, not saying a word, not even screaming a word, not yet.'

'Does he have a sword?' asked Tiffany.

'Yes, he does. May I continue? Good. Now, he walks towards her. She is staring at him, not shouting, just watching, and he is thinking . . . what is he thinking? He is thinking, "Could I take on both of the guards? Will the apprentices obey me?" And then, as he gets nearer, he wonders if they could make it to the horses in all this smoke. And this is a moment eternally frozen in time. Huge events await his decision. One simple deed either way, and history will be different, and you are thinking it depends on what he does next. But you see, what he is thinking doesn't matter, because she knows who he is and what he has done, and the bad things that he has done and is famous for, and as he walks towards her, uncertain, she knows him for what he is, even if he wishes he wasn't, and reaches with both hands smoothly through the wicker basket they've put around her to keep her upright, and grabs him, and holds him tight as the torch drops down onto the oily wood and the flames spring up. She never takes her eyes off him, and never loosens her grip . . . Would you like a fresh cup of tea?'

Tiffany blinked away smoke and flames and shock. 'And how do *you* know so much about it, please?' she said.

'I was there.'

'A thousand years ago?'

'Yes.'

'How did you get there?'

'I walked,' said Miss Smith. 'But that is not the

point. The point is that then was the death – and birth – of the thing we call the Cunning Man. And he was still a man, to begin with. He was terribly injured, of course. For quite some time. And witchfinding went on – oh my word, didn't it just. You couldn't tell who the other witchfinders feared most: the witches, or the wrath of the Cunning Man if they didn't find him the witches he demanded and believe me, with the Cunning Man on your heels, you will find as many witches as he wants, oh yes.

'And the Cunning Man himself could always find witches. It was quite amazing. You would have some quiet little village where everybody got on reasonably well and no one had noticed any witches at all. But when the Cunning Man arrived, suddenly there were witches everywhere, but unfortunately not for very long. He believed that witches were the reason for just about everything bad that happened, and that they stole babies and caused wives to run away from their husbands, and milk to go sour. I think my favourite one was that witches went to sea in eggshells in order to drown honest sailors.' At this point Miss Smith held up a hand. 'No, don't say that it would be impossible for even a small witch to get inside an eggshell without crushing it, because that is what we in the craft would call a *logical argument* and therefore no one who wanted to believe that witches sank ships would pay any attention to it.

'It couldn't go on, of course. People can be very stupid, and people can be easily frightened, but sometimes you find people who aren't that stupid and aren't that fearful, and so the Cunning Man is thrust out of the world. Thrown out like the rubbish he is.

'But that wasn't the end of him. So great, so fearsome was his hatred for anything that he thought of as witchcraft that he somehow managed to live on despite finally having no body. Though there was no skin to him, no bone any more, his rage was such that he lived on. As a ghost, perhaps. And, every so often, finding someone who would let him in. There are plenty of people out there whose poisonous minds will open for him. And there are those who would rather be behind evil than in front of it, and one of them wrote for him the book known as *The Bonfire of the Witches.*

'But when he takes over a body – and believe me, in the past, there are those unpleasant people who have thought that their terrible ambitions would be furthered by allowing him to do so – the owner of the body soon finds they have no control at all. They become a part of him too. And not until it is too late do they realize that there is no escape, no release. Except death . . .'

'Poison goes where poison's welcome,' said Tiffany. 'But it looks as though it can push its way in, welcome or not.'

'I'm sorry,' said Miss Smith, 'but I will say "Well done." You *are* as good as they say. There really is nothing physical now to the Cunning Man. Nothing you can see. Nothing you can possess. And while he often kills those who have been so generous in their hospitality, he nevertheless still appears to thrive. Without a body to call his own, he drifts on the wind and, I suppose, sleeps in some way. And if he does, I know what he dreams of. He dreams of a beautiful young witch, the most powerful of all the witches. And he thinks of her with such hatred that, according to elasticated string theory, it goes all the way round the universe and comes back from a different direction so that it seems to be a kind of love. And he wants to see her again. In which case, she will almost certainly die.

'Some witches – real flesh and blood witches – have tried to fight him and have won. And sometimes they tried, and died. And then one day, a girl called Tiffany Aching, because of her disobedience, kissed the winter. Which, I have to say, no one has ever done before. And the Cunning Man woke up.' Miss Smith put down her cup. 'As a witch, you know you must have no fear?'

Tiffany nodded.

'Well, Tiffany, you must *make* a place for fear, fear under control. We think that the head is important, that the brain sits like a monarch on the throne of the body. But the body is powerful too, and the brain cannot survive without it. If the Cunning Man takes over your body, I don't think you would be able to fight him. He would be like nothing you have met before. To be caught will be, ultimately, to die. What is worse, to be his creature. In which case, death will be a longed-for release. And there you have it, Miss Tiffany Aching. He wakes up, he drifts, he looks for her. He looks for *you*.'

'Well, at least we've found her,' said Rob Anybody. 'She's somewhere in that festering midden.'

The Feegles stood with their mouths open in front of the bubbling, suppurating mess of the Unreal Estate. Mysterious things plopped, spun and exploded under the debris.

'It will be certain death to go in there,' said Wee Mad Arthur. 'Certain death! You'll be doomed.'

'Oh aye, we're all doomed sooner or later,' said Rob Anybody jovially. He sniffed. 'What the heel is that stink?'

'Sorry, Rob, that was me,' said Daft Wullie.

'Ach no, I ken your smell,' Rob said. 'But I ken I smelled it before. It was that walking gawky that we smelled on the road. Ye ken? All in black. Very lacking in the eyeball department. Bad cess to him, and bad cess he smelled. And I recollect he used very bad words about oor big wee hag. My Jeannie said we must stay close to the big wee hag and I reckon this scunner needs a bath.'

Wee Mad Arthur precipitated matters. 'Weel, Rob, ye going in there is against the law, ye ken?' He pointed to an ancient and half-melted sign on which, just readable, were the words: ACCESS STRICTLY FORBIDDEN. BY ORDER.

Rob Anybody stared at it. 'Ach, now you give me nae

choice at all,' he said, 'and you made me remember that we're all dead already.* *Charge!'*

There were dozens of questions that Tiffany could ask but the one struggling to the top was: 'What will happen if the Cunning Man catches up with me?'

Miss Smith stared at the ceiling for a moment. 'Well, I suppose from his point of view, it will be rather like a wedding. From your point of view, it will be exactly like being dead. No, worse, because you will be inside, looking out at what he can do with all your powers and all your skills to all the people that you know. Did we have the last cupcake?'

I'm not going to show any fear, said Tiffany to herself.

'I'm glad to hear that,' said Miss Smith out loud.

Tiffany leaped off the chair in a rage. 'Don't you dare do that, Miss Smith!'

'I'm sure there was one more cupcake,' said Miss Smith, and then added, 'That's the spirit, Miss Tiffany Aching.'

'You know, I did defeat a hiver. I can look after myself.'

'And your family? And everybody you know? From

---

* In truth, the Nac Mac Feegle believe that the world is such a wonderful place that in order to have got into it they must have been very good in another existence and had arrived in, as it were, heaven. Of course, they appeared to die sometimes, even here, but they like to think of it as going off to be born again. Numerous theologians had speculated that this was a stupid idea, but it was certainly more enjoyable than many other beliefs.

an attack that they won't even know is happening? You don't understand. The Cunning Man isn't a man, although he was once, and now he's not even a ghost. He is an idea. Unfortunately he is an idea whose time has come.'

'Well, at least I know when he's near me,' Tiffany said thoughtfully. 'There's a dreadful stink. Even worse than the Feegles.'

Miss Smith nodded. 'Yes, it's coming from his mind. It's the smell of corruption – corruption of thinking and of action. Your mind picks it up and doesn't know what to do with it, so it files it under "stink". All the magically inclined can smell it; but when people encounter it, it changes them, makes them a little bit like him. And so trouble follows wherever he goes.'

And Tiffany knew exactly what kind of trouble she meant, even though her memories shot her back in time to before the Cunning Man had woken again.

In her mind's eye she could see the black-edged pieces blowing back and forth in the late-autumn wind, which sighed with despair in her mind's ear, and worst of all, oh yes, worst of all, her mind's nose snuffed up the sharp acrid stink of ancient, half-burned paper. In her memory some of the pieces fluttered in the pitiless wind like moths that had been swatted and broken, but were still hopelessly trying to fly.

And there were stars on them.

People had marched to the rough music and roughly dragged out the cracked old woman whose only crime, as far as Tiffany could see, was that she had no teeth left and smelled of wee. They had thrown stones, they had smashed windows, they had killed the cat, and all this had been done by good people, nice people, people that she knew and met every day, and they had done all these things which, even now, they never talked about. It was a day that somehow had vanished from the calendar. And on that day, with a pocketful of charred stars, not knowing what it was she was doing, but determined to do it, she had become a witch.

'You said that others have fought him?' she said now to Miss Smith. 'How did they manage it?'

'That last cupcake was still in the bag with the baker's name on it, I'm sure of it. You're not sitting on it, are you?' Miss Smith cleared her throat and said, 'By being very powerful witches, by understanding what it means to be a powerful witch, and by taking every chance, using every trick and, I suspect, understanding the Cunning Man's mind before he understands theirs. I have trudged through a long time to learn about the Cunning Man,' she added, 'and the one thing I can tell you for certain is that the way to kill the Cunning Man is with cunning. You will need to be more cunning than he is.'

'He can't be that cunning if he's taken all this time to find me,' said Tiffany.

'Yes, that puzzles me,' said Miss Smith. 'And it should puzzle you. I would have expected it to have taken him a very long time. More than two years, anyway. He's either been very clever – and frankly he has nothing to be clever with – or somehow something else has drawn you to his attention. Someone magical, I would guess. Do you know any witches who aren't your friend?'

'Certainly not,' said Tiffany. 'Are any of the witches who have defeated him still alive?'

'Yes.'

'I was wondering, if I found one – perhaps they could tell me how they did it?'

'I've told you. He's the Cunning Man. Why should he fall for the same trick twice? You have to find your own way. Those who have trained you would expect nothing less.'

'This isn't some kind of test, is it?' said Tiffany, and then felt embarrassed at how lame that sounded.

'Don't you remember what Granny Weatherwax always says?' said Miss Smith.

'*Everything is a test.*' They said it together with one voice, looked at one another and laughed.

At which point, there was a squawk. Miss Smith opened the door and a small white chicken walked in, looked around curiously and exploded. Where it had been was an onion, fully rigged with mast and sails.

'I'm sorry you had to see that,' said Miss Smith. She sighed. 'Happens all the time, I'm afraid. The Unreal Estate is never static, you see. All the magic, banging together, bits of spells winding themselves around other spells, whole new spells being created that nobody has ever thought of before . . . it's a mess. It generates things quite randomly. Yesterday I found a book on growing chrysanthemums, printed in copper on water. You would think it would tend to slosh about a bit, but it all seemed to hang together until the magic ran out.'

'That was bad luck for the chicken,' said Tiffany nervously.

'Well, I can guarantee that it wasn't a chicken two minutes ago,' said Miss Smith, 'and now it's probably enjoying being a seagoing vegetable. Now perhaps you can see why I don't spend too much time down here. I had an incident with a toothbrush once that I will not forget in a hurry.' She pushed open the door still further, and Tiffany saw the shamble.

There was no mistaking a shamble.* Well, there was at first and she mistook it for a heap of rubbish.

'It's amazing what you can find in your pockets if you're in a magical junk yard,' said Miss Smith calmly.

Tiffany stared at the giant shamble again. 'Isn't that

---

* A witch made a shamble out of anything you happened to have in your pockets, but if you care about appearances, you paid attention to the things you 'accidentally' had in your pockets. It wouldn't make any difference to how the shamble worked, but if there were going to be other people around, then a mysterious nut, or an interesting bit of wood, a piece of lace and a silver pin suggested 'witch' rather more flatteringly than did, say, a broken shoelace, a torn piece of paper bag, half a handful of miscellaneous and unspeakable fluff, and a handkerchief which had been used so many times that, dreadfully, it needed both hands to fold it. Tiffany generally kept one pocket just for shamble ingredients, but if Miss Smith had made this shamble the same way, then she had pockets larger than a wardrobe; it nearly touched the ceiling.

a horse's skull?* And isn't that a bucket of tadpoles?'

'Yes. Something alive always helps, don't you find?'

Tiffany's eyes narrowed. 'But *that* is a wizard's staff, isn't it? I thought they stopped working if a woman touched one!'

Miss Smith smiled. 'Well, I've had mine ever since I was in my cradle. If you know where to look, you can see the marks I made when I was teething. It's *my* staff and it works, although I have to say it started to work better when I took the knob off the end. It didn't do anything practical and it upsets the balance. Now, will you *stop* standing there with your mouth open?'

Tiffany's mouth clamped shut, and then sprang open again. A penny had dropped and it felt as if it had dropped from the moon. 'You're her, aren't you? You must be, you're her! Eskarina Smith, right? The only woman who ever became a wizard!'

'Somewhere inside, I suppose so, yes, but it seems such a long time ago, and you know, I never really felt like a wizard, so I never really worried about what anyone said. And anyway, I had the staff, and no one could take that away from me.' Eskarina hesitated for a moment, and then went on, 'That's what I learned at university: to be me, just what I am, and not worry about it. That knowledge is an invisible magical staff, all by itself. Look, I don't really want to talk about this. It brings back bad memories.'

'Please forgive me,' said Tiffany. 'I just couldn't stop

* A horse's skull always looks scary, even if someone has put lipstick on it.

myself. I'm very sorry if I have dredged up any scary recollections.'

Eskarina smiled. 'Oh, the scary ones are *never* a problem. It's good ones that can be difficult to deal with.' There was a click from the shamble. Eskarina stood up and walked over to it. 'Oh dear, of course, only the witch that makes it can read her own shamble, but trust me when I say that the way the skull has turned and the position of the pincushion along the axis of the spinning wheel mean that he is very close. Almost right on top of us, in fact. Or the random magic in this place may be confusing him, and you seem to be everywhere and nowhere, so he'll go away soon and try to pick up the trail somewhere else. And, as I mentioned, somewhere on the trail he will eat. He'll get into some fool's head, and some old lady or some girl who is wearing quite dangerous cult symbols without an inkling of what they really mean will suddenly find herself hounded. Let us hope she can run.'

Tiffany looked around, bewildered. 'And what happens will be my fault?'

'Is that the sarcastic whine of a little girl or the rhetorical question of a witch with her own steading?'

Tiffany began to reply, and then stopped. 'You can travel in time, can't you?' she said.

'Yes.'

'Then you know what I'm going to answer?'

'Well, it's not quite as simple as that,' said Eskarina, and looked slightly uncomfortable for a moment, much to Tiffany's surprise and, it has to be said, delight. 'I know, let me see, there are fifteen different replies you might make, but I don't know which one it will be until you make it, because of the elasticated string theory.'

'Then all I will say,' said Tiffany, 'is thank you very much. I am sorry to have taken up your time. But I need to be getting on; I have so many things to do. Do you know what the time is?'

'Yes,' said Eskarina. 'It is a way of describing one of the notional dimensions of four-dimensional space. But for your purposes, it's about ten forty-five.'

That seemed to Tiffany to be a bafflingly complicated way of answering the question, but as she opened her mouth to say so, the shamble collapsed and the door opened to let in a stampede of chickens – which did not, however, explode.

Eskarina grabbed Tiffany's hand, shouting, 'He has found you! I don't know how!'

A chicken half jumped, half flapped and half tumbled onto the wreck of the shamble and crowed: *Cock-a-doodle-crivens!*

Then the chickens exploded; they exploded into Feegles.

On the whole there wasn't a great deal of difference between the chickens and the Feegles, since both run around in circles making a noise. An important distinction, however, is that chickens are seldom armed. The Feegles, on the other hand, are armed all the time, and once they had shaken off the last of their feathers

203

they fell to fighting one another out of embarrassment – and for something to do.

Eskarina took one look at them and kicked at the wall behind her, revealing a hole which a person might just be able to crawl through, and snapped at Tiffany: 'Go! Get him away from here! Get on the stick as soon as you can and go! Don't worry about me! Don't be afraid, you will be all right! You just have to help yourself.'

Heavy, nasty smoke was filling the room. 'What do you mean?' Tiffany managed, struggling with the stick.

'*Go!*'

Not even Granny Weatherwax could command Tiffany's legs so thoroughly.

She went.

## CHAPTER 9

# The Duchess and the Cook

Tiffany liked flying. What she objected to was being in the air, at least at a height greater than her own head. She did it anyway, because it was ridiculous and unbecoming to witchcraft in general to be seen flying so low that her boots scraped the tops off ant hills. People laughed, and sometimes pointed. But now, navigating the stick through the ruined houses and gloomy, bubbling pools, she ached for the open sky. It was a relief when she slid out from behind a stack of broken mirrors to see good clean daylight, despite the fact that she had emerged next to a sign which said: IF YOU ARE CLOSE ENOUGH TO READ THIS SIGN, YOU REALLY, REALLY, SHOULDN'T BE.

That was the last straw. She tipped the stick until it was leaving a groove in the mud behind it, and ascended like a rocket, clinging desperately to the strap, which was creaking, to avoid slipping off. She heard a small voice say, 'We are experiencing some turbulence, ye ken. If ye look to the right and tae the left ye will see that there are no emergency exits—'

The speaker was interrupted by another voice, which said, 'In point o' fact, Rob, the stick has got emergency exits all round, ye ken.'

'Oh aye,' said Rob Anybody, 'but there is such a thing as style, OK? Just waiting until ye have nearly hit the ground and stepping off makes us look like silly billys.'

Tiffany hung on, trying not to listen, and also trying not to kick Feegles, who had no sense of danger, feeling as they always did that they were more dangerous than anything else.

Finally she had the broomstick flying level and risked a look down. There seemed to be a fight going on outside whatever it was they were going to decide was the new name of the King's Head, but you couldn't see any sign of Mrs Proust. The witch of the city was a woman of resource, wasn't she? Mrs Proust could look after herself.

Mrs Proust *was* looking after herself, by running very fast. She hadn't waited a second once she sensed the danger, but headed for the nearest alley as the smog rose around her. The city was always full of smokes and smogs and fumes, easy work for a witch who had the knack. They were the breath of the city, and its halitosis, and she could play them like a foggy piano. And now she leaned against a wall and got some breath of her own.

She had felt it building up like a thunderstorm in a city that was normally remarkably easy-going. Any woman who even looked like a witch was becoming a target. She had to hope that old and ugly women everywhere were going to be as safe as she was.

A moment later, a couple of men burst out of the smog, one of them holding a large stick; the other one didn't need a stick, because he was huge and therefore was his own stick.

As the man with the stick ran towards her, Mrs Proust tapped her foot on the pavement and the stone under the man's feet tilted up, tripping him so that he landed safely on his chin with a *crack*, the stick rolling away.

Mrs Proust folded her arms and glared at the heavy man. He wasn't as stupid as his friend, but his fists were opening and closing and she knew it would only be a matter of time. She tapped her foot on the stones again before he plucked up courage.

The big man was trying to work out what might happen next, but didn't expect the equestrian statue*

* There is a lot of folklore about equestrian statues, especially the ones with riders on. There is said to be a code in the number and placement of the horse's hooves: if one of the horse's hooves is in the air, the rider was wounded in battle; two legs in the air means that the rider was killed in battle; three legs in the air indicates that the rider got lost on the way to the battle; and four legs in the air means that the sculptor was very, very clever. Five legs in the air means that there's probably at least one other horse standing behind the horse

of Lord Alfred Rust – famed for bravely and valiantly losing every military engagement in which he had ever taken part – to gallop out of the fog on bronze hooves and kick him so hard between the legs that he flew backwards and knocked his head on a lamppost before sliding to the ground.

Mrs Proust then recognized him as a customer who sometimes bought itching powder and exploding cigars from Derek; it didn't do to kill customers. She picked him up, groaning, by his hair, and whispered into his ear, 'You weren't here. Nor was I. Nothing happened, and you did not see it.' She thought for a moment and, because business is business added, 'And when you next go past Boffo's Joke Emporium, you will be taken with its range of extremely droll, practical jokes for all the family, and this week's new "Pearls of the Pavement" naughty Fido jokes for the connoisseur who takes his laughter seriously. I look forward to the pleasure of your custom. P.S. our new range of "thunderbolt" exploding cigars are a laugh a minute, and please do try our hilariously funny rubber chocolate. Take a moment also to browse in our new gentlemen's necessaries department for all that is best in moustache waxes, moustache cups, cut-throat razors, a range of first-class snuffs, ebony-backed nose-hair clippers and our ever-popular

you're looking at; and the rider lying on the ground with his horse lying on top of him with all four legs in the air means that the rider was either a very incompetent horseman or owned a very bad-tempered horse.

glandular trousers, supplied in a plain wrapper and limited to one pair per customer.'

Satisfied, Mrs Proust let the head fall backwards and was forced to accept that unconscious people don't buy anything, so she turned her attention to the previous owner of the stick, who was groaning. Well, yes, it was the fault of the man with no eyes, she thought, and perhaps that might be an excuse, but Mrs Proust wasn't known for her forgiving nature. 'Poison goes where poison's welcome,' she said to herself. She snapped her fingers, then climbed onto the bronze horse, taking a cold but comfortable seat in the late Lord Rust's metal lap. Clanking and groaning, the bronze horse walked away into the bank of smog that followed Mrs Proust all the way back to her shop.

Back in the alleyway, though, it seemed to be snowing, until you realized that what was falling from the sky onto the unconscious bodies had previously been in the stomachs of the pigeons who were now flocking in from every quarter of the city at Mrs Proust's command. She heard them and smiled grimly. 'In this neighbourhood we don't just watch!' she said with satisfaction.

Tiffany felt better when the reek and smoke of the city was behind them again. How do they *live* with the smell? she wondered. It's worse than a Feegle's spog.*

But now there were fields below her, and although

* See Glossary, page 417.

the smoke from the burning stubbles reached this high, it was a fragrance compared to the world within the city walls.

And Eskarina Smith lived there . . . well, sometimes lived there!

Eskarina Smith! She really was real! Tiffany's mind raced almost as fast as the broomstick itself. Eskarina Smith! Every witch had heard something about her, but no two witches agreed.

Miss Tick had said that Eskarina was the girl that got a wizard's staff by mistake!

The first witch ever trained by Granny Weatherwax! Who got her into Unseen University by giving the wizards there a piece of her – that is to say, Granny Weatherwax's – mind. Quite a large piece, if you listened to some of the stories, which included tales of magical battles.

Miss Level had assured Tiffany that she was some kind of fairy story.

Miss Treason had changed the subject.

Nanny Ogg had tapped the side of her nose conspiratorially and whispered, 'Least said, soonest mended.'

And Annagramma had loftily assured all the young witches that Eskarina had existed, but was dead.

But there was one story that just would not go away and curled around truth and lies like honeysuckle. It told the world that the young Eskarina had met at the University a young man called Simon who, it seemed, had been cursed by the gods with almost every possible ailment that mankind was prone to. But, because the gods have a sense of humour, even though it's a rather strange one, they had granted him the power to understand – well – everything. He could barely walk without assistance, but was so brilliant that he managed to keep the whole universe in his head.

Wizards with beards that went down to the floor would flock to hear him talk about space and time and magic as if they were all part of the same thing. And young Eskarina had fed him and cleaned him and helped him get about and learned from him – well – everything.

And, the rumours went, that she had learned secrets that made the mightiest of magics look like nothing more than conjuring tricks. And the story was true! Tiffany had talked to it and had cupcakes with it, and there really was a woman, then, who could walk through time and make it take orders from her. Wow!

Yes, and there was something very strange about Eskarina – a sense not that she wasn't all there, but that somehow she was everywhere else at the same time; and at this point Tiffany saw the Chalk on the skyline, shadowy and mysterious, like a beached whale. It was still a long way off, but her heart leaped. That was *her* ground; she knew every inch of it, and part of her was always there. She could face *anything* there. How could the Cunning Man, some old ghost, beat her on her own ground? She had family there, more than she could count, and friends, more than . . .

211

well, not so many now that she was a witch, but that was the way of the world.

Tiffany was aware of somebody climbing up her dress. This was not the problem it might have been; a witch would not, of course, dream of not wearing a dress, but if you were going to ride on a broomstick you definitely invested in some really tough pants, if possible with some padding. It made your bum look bigger but it also made it warmer, and at a hundred feet above the ground, fashion rather took second place to comfort. She glanced down. There was a Feegle there, wearing a watchman's helmet, which appeared to have been hammered out of the top of an old salt cellar, an equally small breastplate and, amazingly, trousers and boots. You never normally saw boots on a Feegle.

'You're Wee Mad Arthur, aren't you? I saw you at the King's Head! You're a policeman!'

'Oh aye.' Wee Mad Arthur grinned a grin that was pure Feegle. 'It's a grand life in the Watch, and the money is good. A penny goes a lot further when it buys you food for a week!'

'So are you coming over here to keep our lads in order? Are you planning to stay?'

'Oh no, I dinnae believe so. I like the city, ye ken. I like coffee that is nae made from them wee acorns and I goes to the theatre and the opera and the ballet.' The broomstick wobbled a little. Tiffany had heard of ballet, and had even seen pictures in a book, but it was a word that somehow did not fit in any sentence which included the word 'Feegle'.

'Ballet?' she managed.

'Oh aye, it's grand! Last week I saw *Swan on a Hot Tin Lake*, a reworking of a traditional theme by one of our up-and-coming young performance artists; and the day after that, of course, there was a re-interpretation of *Die Flabbergast* at the Opera House; and ye ken, they had a whole week of porcelain at the Royal Art Museum, with a free thimble of sherry. Oh aye, it's the city of culture, right enough.'

'Are you *sure* that you are a Feegle?' said Tiffany in a fascinated voice.

'That's what they tell me, miss. There is nae law says I cannot be interested in culture, is there? I told the lads that when I go back I will take them along to see the ballet for themselves.'

The stick seemed to fly itself for a while as Tiffany stared at nothing, or rather at a mental picture of Feegles in a theatre. She had never been inside one herself, but she had seen pictures and the thought of Feegles among ballerinas was so unthinkable that it was better to just let her mind boggle and then forget about it. She remembered in time that she had a broomstick to land, and brought it down very neatly near the mound.

To her shock there were guards outside it. Human guards.

She stared in disbelief. The Baron's guards never came up onto the downland. Never! It was unheard of! And ... she felt the anger rising – *one of them was holding a shovel.*

She jumped off the stick so fast that it was left to skim over the turf, scattering Feegles until it fetched up against an obstruction, shaking off the last few Feegles that had managed to hang on.

'You hold onto that shovel, Brian Roberts!' she screamed at the sergeant of the guard. 'If you let it cut the turf there will be a reckoning! How dare you! Why are you here? And *nobody* is to cut *anybody* into pieces, do you all understand?'

This last order was to the Feegles, who had surrounded the men with a ring of small, but ever so sharp, swords. A Feegle claymore was so sharp that a human might not know his legs had been cut off until he tried to walk. The guards themselves suddenly had the look of men who knew they were supposed to be big and strong but were now faced with the realization that 'big' or 'strong' wouldn't be nearly enough. They'd heard the stories, of course – oh yes, everyone on the Chalk had heard the stories about Tiffany Aching and her little . . . helpers. But they had only been stories, hadn't they? Until now. And they were threatening to run up their trousers.

In a shocked silence, Tiffany looked around, panting for breath. Everyone was watching her now, which was better than everyone fighting, wasn't it?

'Very well,' she said like a schoolteacher who is only just satisfied with the naughty class. She added a sniff, which would usually be translated to mean: I'm only *just* satisfied, mark you. She sniffed again. 'Very well, then. Is anybody going to tell me what's going on here?'

The sergeant actually raised his hand. 'Can I have a word in private, miss?' Tiffany was impressed that he had even been able to speak, given that his mind was trying to suddenly make sense of what his eyes were telling him.

'Very well, follow me.' She spun round suddenly, causing both guards and Feegles to jump. 'And nobody, and I mean *nobody*, is to dig up anybody's home or cut off anybody's legs while we are gone, is that understood? I *said*, is that understood?' There was a mumbled chorus of yeses and oh ayes, but it didn't include one from the face she was looking down at. Rob Anybody was trembling with rage and crouching ready to spring. 'Did you hear me, Rob Anybody?'

He glared at her, eyes ablaze. 'I will give ye nae promise on that score, miss, hag though you may be! Where is my Jeannie? Where are the others? These scunners hae swords! What were they going to do with them? I will have an answer!'

'Listen to me, Rob,' Tiffany began, but stopped. Rob Anybody's face was dripping tears, and he was pulling desperately at his beard as he fought the horrors of his own imagination. They were an inch from a war, Tiffany reckoned.

'Rob Anybody! I am the hag o' these hills and I put an oath on you not to kill these men until I tell you to! Understand?'

There was a crash as one of the guards fell over backwards in a faint. Now the girl was talking to the creatures! And about killing them! They weren't used to this sort of thing. Usually the most exciting thing that happened was that the pigs got into the vegetable garden.

The Big Man of the Feegles hesitated as his spinning brain digested Tiffany's order. True, it wasn't an order to kill anybody right now, but at least it held out the possibility that he might be able to do so very soon, so he could free his head from the terrible pictures in his mind. It was like holding a hungry dog on a leash of cobweb, but at least it bought her time.

'You will see that the mound has not been touched,' said Tiffany, 'so whatever may have been intended has not yet been achieved.' She turned back to the sergeant, who had gone white, and said, 'Brian, if you want your men to live with all their arms and legs, you will tell them right now, and very carefully, to put down their weapons. Your lives depend on the honour of one Feegle and he is driving himself mad with horror. Do it now!'

To Tiffany's relief he gave the command, and the guards – glad to have their sergeant ordering them to do something that every atom in their bodies was telling them was *exactly* what they should be doing – dropped their weapons from their shaking hands. One even raised his arms in the universal sign of surrender. Tiffany pulled the sergeant a little way away from the glowering Feegles and whispered, 'What do you think you are doing, you stupid idiot?'

'Orders from the Baron, Tiff.'

'The Baron? But the Baron is—'

'Alive, miss. He's been back for three hours. Drove through the night, they say. And people have been talking.' He looked down at his boots. 'We were . . . we were, well, we were sent up here to find the girl that you gave to the fairies. Sorry, Tiff.'

'Gave? *Gave?*'

'I didn't say it, Tiff,' said the sergeant, backing away, 'but, well, you hear stories. I mean, no smoke without fire, right?'

Stories, thought Tiffany. Oh yes, once upon a time there was a wicked old witch . . . 'And you think they apply to me, do you? Am I on fire or just smoking?'

The sergeant shifted uneasily and sat down. 'Look, I'm just a sergeant, OK? The young Baron's given me orders, yes? And his word is law, right?'

'He may be the law down there. Up here, it's me. Look over there. Yes, there! What do you see?'

The man looked where she pointed and his face paled. The old cast-iron wheels and stove with its short chimney were clearly visible, even though a flock of sheep was happily grazing around them as usual. He leaped to his feet as if he had been sitting on an ant's nest.

'Yes,' said Tiffany with some satisfaction. 'Granny Aching's grave. Remember her? People said she was a wise woman, but at least they had the decency to make up better stories about her! Proposing to cut the turf? I'm amazed that Granny doesn't rise up through the turf and bite your bum! Now take your men down

the hill a little way and I will sort this out, you understand? We don't want anyone to get jumpy.'

The sergeant nodded. It was not as if he had any
other option.

As the guards moved away, dragging their unconscious colleague with them and trying not to look
like, well, guards who were turning a walk away as
closely into a *running* away as was possible, Tiffany
knelt down by Rob Anybody and lowered her voice.

'Look, Rob, I *know* about the secret tunnels.'

'What scunner told ye about the secret tunnels?'

'I am the hag o' the hills, Rob,' said Tiffany sooth-
ingly. 'Shouldn't I know about the tunnels? You are
Feegles, and no Feegle will sleep in a house with only
one entrance, right?'

The Feegle was calming down a bit now. 'Oh aye, ye
have a point there.'

'Then can I please suggest you go and fetch young
Amber? Nobody is going to touch the mound.'

After a little hesitation, Rob Anybody sprang into
the entrance hole and was gone. It took some time for
him to return – time Tiffany thankfully used by
getting the sergeant to come back and help her gather
up the guards' dropped weapons – and when Rob did
resurface he was accompanied by a great many more
Feegles and the kelda. And also by a rather reluctant
Amber, who blinked nervously in the daylight and
said, 'Oh, crivens!'

Tiffany knew that her own smile was false when she
said, 'I've come to take you home, Amber.' Well, at least

I'm not stupid enough to say something like 'Won't that be nice?' she added to herself.

Amber glared at her. 'Ye willnae get me back in that place,' she announced, 'and ye can stick it where the monkey put his jumper!'

And I don't blame you, thought Tiffany, but now I can pass for being a grown-up and I have to say some stupid grown-up things . . .

'But you do have a mother and father, Amber. I'm sure they miss you.'

She winced at the look of scorn the girl gave her.

'Oh aye, and if the old scunner misses me he'll aim another blow!'

'Maybe we can go together, and help him change his ways?' Tiffany volunteered, despising herself, but the image of those thick fingers heavy with nettle stings from that awful bouquet wouldn't go away.

This time Amber actually laughed. 'Sorry, mistress, but Jeannie told me you were clever.'

What was it that Granny Weatherwax had said once? *Evil begins when you begin to treat people as things.* And right now it would happen if you thought there was a thing called a father, and a thing called a mother, and a thing called a daughter, and a thing called a cottage, and told yourself that if you put them all together you had a thing called a happy family.

Aloud, she said, 'Amber, I want you to come with me to see the Baron, so that he knows you are safe. After that, you can do as you please. That's a promise.'

Tiffany felt a knocking on her boot, and looked down

at the kelda's worried face. 'Can I have a wee word with ye?' said Jeannie. Beside her, Amber was crouching down so that she could hold the kelda's other hand.

Then Jeannie spoke again, if it was speech, and not song. But what could you sing that stayed in the air, so that the next note twisted around it? What could be sung that seemed to be a living sound that sung itself right back to you?

And then the song was gone, leaving only a hole and a loss.

'That's a kelda song,' said Jeannie. 'Amber heard me singing it to the little ones. It's part of the soothings, and she understood it, Tiffany! I gave her nae help but she understood it! I know the Toad has tol' ye this. But do ye ken what I am telling ye now? She recognizes meaning, and learns it. She is as close to being a kelda as any human could be. *She is a treasure not to be thrown away!*'

The words came out with unusual force for the kelda, who was usually so softly spoken. And Tiffany recognized it as helpful information that, ever so nicely, was a kind of threat.

Even the journey off the downland and into the village had to be negotiated. Tiffany, holding Amber by the hand, walked past the waiting guards and continued on, much to the embarrassment of the sergeant. After all, if you have been sent to bring somebody in, then you are going to look pretty silly if they go and bring themselves in by, as it were, themselves. But on the other hand, if Tiffany and Amber walked behind the guards, it looked as though they were being driven; this was sheep country, after all, and everybody knew, didn't they, that the sheep walked in front and a shepherd walked behind.

Finally they compromised on a rather awkward method where they all moved forward with a certain amount of revolving and shuffling that made it look as if they were travelling by square dance. Tiffany had to spend a lot of the time stopping Amber from giggling.

That was the funny part. It would have been nice if the funny part could have lasted longer.

'Look, I was only told to fetch the girl,' said the sergeant desperately as they walked through the castle gates. 'You don't have to come.' He said this in a way which meant: *Please, please, don't barge in and show me up in front of my new boss.* But it didn't work.

The castle was what was once called a-bustle, which meant extremely busy, with cross people running around at cross purposes in every direction except straight up. There was going to be a funeral and then there was going to be a wedding, and two big occasions so close together could test the resources of a small castle to the utmost, especially since people who would come a long way for one would probably stay for the other, saving time but causing extra work for everybody. But Tiffany was glad for the absence, now, of Miss Spruce, who had been altogether too unpleasant by half and had never been one to get her hands dirty.

And then there would always be the problem of seating. Most of the guests would be aristocrats, and it was vitally important that no one had to sit next to somebody who was related to someone who had killed one of their ancestors at some time in the past. Given that the past is a very big place, and taking into account the fact that everybody's ancestors were generally trying to kill everybody else's ancestors, for land, money or something to do, it needed very careful trigonometry to avoid another massacre taking place before people had finished their soup.

None of the servants seemed to pay any particular attention to Tiffany, Amber or the guards, though at one point Tiffany thought she saw someone making one of those tiny little signs people make when they think they need protection from evil – *here, in her place!* – and she had the strong feeling that somehow the people were not paying attention in a very *definite* way of not paying attention, as if looking at Tiffany might be dangerous to the health. When Tiffany and Amber were ushered into the Baron's study, it seemed that he was not going to take much notice of them either. He was bent over a sheet of paper that covered the whole of his desk, and was holding in his hand a bundle of different coloured pencils.

The sergeant coughed, but even choking to death would not have shaken the Baron's concentration. Finally, Tiffany shouted 'Roland!' quite loudly. He spun round, his face red with embarrassment and a side order of anger.

'I would prefer "my lord", Miss Aching,' he said sharply.

'And I would prefer "Tiffany", Roland,' said Tiffany, with a calmness that she knew annoyed him.

He laid down his pencils with a click. 'The past is past, Miss Aching, and we are different people. It would be just as well if we remembered that, don't you think?'

'The past was only yesterday,' said Tiffany, 'and it would be just as well if you remembered that there was a time when I called you Roland and you called me Tiffany, don't *you* think?' She reached up to her neck and pulled off the necklace with the silver horse that he had given her. It felt like a hundred years ago now, but this necklace had been *important*. She had even stood up to Granny Weatherwax for this necklace! And now she held the necklace like an accusation. 'The past needs to be remembered. If you do not know where you come from, then you don't know where you are, and if you don't know where you are, then you don't know where you're going.'

The sergeant looked from one to the other, and with that instinct for survival that any soldier develops by the time he's become a sergeant, decided to leave the room before things started getting thrown.

'I'll just go and see to the, er . . . the . . . things that need seeing to, if that's OK?' he said, opening and closing the door so quickly that it slammed back tightly on the last syllable. Roland stared at it for a moment, and then turned.

'I know where I am, Miss Aching. I am standing in my father's shoes, and he is dead. I have been running this estate for years, but everything I did, I did in his name. Why did he die, Miss Aching? He wasn't all that old. I thought you could do magic!'

Tiffany looked down at Amber, who was listening with interest. 'Is this best discussed later?' she said. 'You wanted your men to bring you this girl, and here she is, healthy in mind and body. And I did not, as you say, give her to the fairies: she was a guest of the Nac Mac Feegle, whose help you have had on more than one occasion. And she went back there of her own free will.' She looked carefully at Roland's face, and said, 'You don't remember them, do you?'

She could see that he didn't, but his mind was struggling with the fact that there was definitely something that he *should* have remembered. He was a prisoner of the Fairy Queen, Tiffany reminded herself. Forgetfulness can be a blessing, but I wonder what horrors were in his mind when the Pettys told him that she had taken their girl to the Feegles. To *fairies*. How could I imagine what he felt?

She softened her voice a little. 'You remember something vague about fairies, yes? Nothing bad, I hope, but nothing very clear, as if perhaps it was something you read in a book, or a story that somebody told you when you were little. Am I right?'

He glowered at her, but the spill word that he had strangled on his lips told her that she *was* right.

'They call it the last gift,' she said. 'It's part of the

soothings. It is for when it is best for everybody that you forget things that were too awful, and also the things that were too wonderful. I'm telling you this, *my lord*, because Roland is still in there somewhere. By tomorrow you will forget even what I have told you. I don't know how it works, but it works for nearly everybody.'

'You took the child from her parents! They came to see me as soon as I arrived this morning! *Everyone* came to see me this morning! Did you kill my father? Did you steal money from him? Did you try to throttle old Petty? Did you beat him with nettles? Did you fill his cottage with demons? I can't believe I just asked you that question, but Mrs Petty appears to think so! Personally, I don't know what to think, especially since some fairy woman might be messing around with my thoughts! Do you understand me?'

While Tiffany was trying to put together some kind of coherent answer, he flopped down in the ancient chair behind the desk and sighed.

'I have been told you were standing over my father with a poker in your hand, and that you demanded money from him,' he said sadly.

'That's not true!'

'And would you tell me if it was?'

'No! Because there never would *be* a was! I would never do such a thing! Well, perhaps I was standing over him . . .'

'Ah-ha!'

'Don't you dare ah-ha me, Roland, don't you dare!

Look, I know people have been telling you things, but they are not true.'

'But you just admitted that you were standing over him, yes?'

'It's simply that he wanted me to show him how I keep my hands clean!' She regretted this as soon as she said it. It was true, but what did that matter? It didn't *sound* true. 'Look, I can see that it—'

'And you didn't steal a bag of money?'

'No!'

'And you don't know anything about a bag of money?'

'Yes, your father asked me to take one out of the metal chest. He wanted to—'

Roland interrupted her. 'Where is that money now?' His voice was flat and without expression.

'I have no idea,' said Tiffany. And as his mouth opened again, she shouted, 'No! You will listen, understand? Sit there and listen! I attended your father for the better part of two years. I liked the old man and I would do nothing to hurt him or you. He died when it was his time to die. When that time comes, there is nothing anyone can do.'

'Then what is magic for?'

Tiffany shook her head. 'Magic, as you call it, kept the pain away, and don't you dare think that it came without a price! I have seen people die, and I promise you your father died well, and thinking of happy days.'

Tears were streaming down Roland's face, and she sensed his anger at being seen like that, stupid anger, as if tears made him less of a man and less of a baron.

She heard him mutter, 'Can you take away this grief?'

'I'm sorry,' she replied quietly. 'Everyone asks me. And I would not do so even if I knew how. *It belongs to you.* Only time and tears take away grief; that is what they are for.'

She stood up and took Amber's hand; the girl was watching the Baron intently.

'I'm going to take Amber home with me,' Tiffany announced, 'and you look as if you need a decent sleep.'

This didn't get a response. He sat there, staring at the paperwork as if hypnotized by it. That wretched nurse, she thought. I might have known she would make trouble. Poison goes where poison's welcome, and in Miss Spruce's case, it would have been welcomed with cheering crowds and possibly a small brass band. Yes, the nurse would have invited the Cunning Man in. She was exactly the sort of person who would let him in, give him power, envious power, jealous power, prideful power. But I know I haven't done anything wrong, she told herself. Or have I? I can only see my life from the inside, and I suppose that on the inside nobody does anything wrong. Oh, blast it! Everybody brings their troubles to the witch! But I can't blame the Cunning Man for *everything* people have said. I just wish there was somebody – other than Jeannie – to talk to who would take no notice of the pointy hat. So what do I do now? Yes, what do I do now, Miss Aching? What would you advise, Miss Aching, who is so good at making decisions for other people? Well, I would advise that you get some sleep as well. You didn't sleep too well last night, what with Mrs Proust being a champion snorer, and an awful lot has happened since then. Also, I cannot remember when you last ate regular meals, and may I also point out that you are talking to yourself?

She looked down at Roland slumped in the chair, his gaze far away. 'I said I am taking Amber home with me for now.'

Roland shrugged. 'Well, I can hardly stop you, can I?' he said sarcastically. 'You *are* the witch.'

Tiffany's mother uncomplainingly made up a bed for Amber, and Tiffany dropped off to sleep in her own bed at the other end of the big bedroom.

She woke up on fire. Flames filled the entire room, flickering orange and red but burning as gently as the kitchen stove. There was no smoke, and although the room felt warm, nothing was actually burning. It was as if fire had just dropped in for a friendly visit, not for business. Its flames rustled.

Enthralled, Tiffany held a finger to the flame and raised it as if the little flame was as harmless as a baby bird. It seemed to get colder but she blew on it anyway, and it plopped back into life.

Tiffany got carefully out of the burning bed, and if this was a dream it was making a very good job of the tinkles and pings that the ancient bed traditionally made. Amber was lying peacefully on the other bed under a blanket of flame; as Tiffany watched, the girl turned over and the flames moved with her.

Being a witch meant that you didn't simply run around shouting just because your bed was on fire. After all, it was no ordinary fire, a fire that did not harm. So it's in my head, she thought. Fire that does no harm. *The hare runs into the fire . . .* Somebody is trying to tell me something.

Silently, the flames went out. There was an almost imperceptible blur of movement in the window and she sighed. The Feegles never gave up. Ever since she was nine years old, she had known that they watched over her at night. They still did, which was why she bathed in a hip-bath behind a sheet. In all probability she hadn't got anything that the Nac Mac Feegles would be interested in looking at, but it made her feel better.

*The hare runs into the fire . . .* It certainly sounded like a message that she had to work out, but who from? From the mysterious witch who had been watching her, maybe? Omens were all very well, but sometimes it would help if people just wrote things down! It never paid, though, to ignore those little thoughts and coincidences: those sudden memories, little whims. Quite often they were another part of your mind, trying hard to get a message through to you – one that you were too busy to notice. But it was bright daylight outside and puzzles could wait. Other things couldn't. She'd start at the castle.

'My dad beat me up, didn't he?' said Amber in a

matter-of-fact voice as they walked towards the grey towers. 'Did my baby die?'

'Yes.'

'Oh,' said Amber in the same flat voice.

'Yes,' said Tiffany. 'I'm sorry.'

'I can sort of remember, but not exactly,' said Amber. 'It's all a bit . . . fuzzy.'

'That's the soothings working. Jeannie has been helping you.'

'I understand,' said the girl.

'You do?' said Tiffany.

'Yes,' said Amber. 'But my dad, is he going to get into trouble?'

He would if I told how I found you, Tiffany thought. The wives would see to it. The village people had a robust attitude to the punishing of boys, who almost by definition were imps of mischief and needed to be tamed, but hitting a girl that hard? Not good. 'Tell me about your young man,' she said aloud instead. 'He is a tailor, isn't he?'

Amber beamed, and Amber could light up the world with a smile. 'Oh yes! His grandad learned him a lot before he died. He can make just about anything out of cloth, can my William. Everyone around here says he should be put to an apprenticeship and he'd be a master himself in a few years.' Then she shrugged. 'But masters want paying for the learning of the knowing, and his mum is never going to find the money to buy him an indenture. Oh, but my William has wonderful fine fingers, and he helps his mum with the sewing of her corsets and making beautiful wedding dresses. That means working with satins and suchlike,' said the girl proudly. 'And William's mum is much complimented on the fineness of the stitching!' Amber beamed with second-hand pride. Tiffany looked at the glowing face, where the bruises, despite the kelda's soothing touch, were still quite plain.

So the boyfriend is a tailor, she thought. To big beefy men like Mr Petty, a tailor was hardly a man at all, with his soft hands and indoor work. And if he stitched clothes for ladies too, well, that was even more shame that the daughter would be bringing to the unhappy little family.

'What do you want to do now, Amber?' she said.

'I'd like to see my mum,' said the girl promptly.

'But supposing you meet your dad?'

Amber turned to her. 'Then I'll understand . . . please don't do anything nasty to him, like turn him into a pig or something?'

A day as a pig might help him mend his ways, thought Tiffany. But there was something of the kelda in the way that Amber had said, 'I'll understand.' A shining light in a dark world.

Tiffany had never seen the gates of the castle closed shut except at night. By day it was a mixture of the village hall, a place for the carpenter and the blacksmith to set up shop, a space for the children to play in when it rained and, for that matter, for temporarily storing the harvests of hay and wheat, at those times when the barns alone could not cope. There wasn't much room in even the biggest cottage; if you wanted a bit of peace and quiet, or somewhere to think, or somebody to talk to, you wandered over to the castle. It always worked.

At least by now the shock of the new Baron's return had worn off, but the place was still humming with activity when Tiffany entered, but it was rather subdued and people were not talking very much. Possibly the reason for this was the Duchess, Roland's mother-in-law-to-be, who was striding around in the great hall and occasionally prodding people with a stick. Tiffany didn't believe it the first time that she saw it, but there it was again – a shiny black stick with a silver knob on the end with which she prodded a maid carrying a basket of laundry. It was only at this point that Tiffany noticed, too, the future bride trailing behind her mother as if she was too embarrassed to go much closer to somebody who prodded people with sticks.

Tiffany was going to protest, and then felt curious as she glanced around. She stepped back a few paces and let herself disappear. It was a knack and a knack that she was good at. It wasn't invisibility, just that people didn't notice you. All unseen, she drifted close enough to hear what the pair of them were saying, or at least what the mother was saying and the daughter was listening to.

The Duchess was complaining. 'Been allowed to go to rack and ruin. Really, it needs a thorough overhaul! You cannot afford to be lax in a place like this!

Firmness is everything! Heaven knows what this family thought it was doing!'

Her speech was punctuated by the *whack* of the stick on the back of another maid who was hurrying, but clearly not hurrying fast enough, under the weight of a basket full of laundry.

'You must be rigorous in your duty to see that they are equally rigorous in theirs,' the Duchess went on, scanning the hall for another target. 'The laxity will stop. You see? You see? They do learn. You must never relax your guard in your pursuit of slovenliness, both in deed and manner. Do not suffer any undue familiarity! And that, of course, includes smiles. Oh, you may think, what could be so bad about a happy smile? But the innocent smile can so easily become a knowing smirk, and suggests perhaps the sharing of a joke. Are you listening to what I'm telling you?'

Tiffany was astonished. Single-handedly the Duchess had made her do something that she never thought she would do, which was to feel sorry for the bride-to-be, who at this point was standing in front of her mother like a naughty child.

Her hobby, and quite possibly one activity in life, was painting in watercolours, and although Tiffany was trying, against the worst of her instincts, to be generous to the girl, there was no denying that she *looked* like a watercolour – and not just a watercolour, but a watercolour painted by someone who had not much colour but large supplies of water, giving her the impression of not only being colourless but also rather damp. You could add, too, that there was so little of her that in a storm it might be quite possible that she would snap. Unseen as she was, Tiffany felt just the *tiniest* pang of guilt and stopped inventing other nasty things to think. Besides, compassion was setting in, blast it!

'Now, Letitia, recite again the little poem that I taught you,' said the Duchess.

The bride-to-be, not just blushing but melting in embarrassment and shame, looked around like a stranded mouse on a great wide floor, uncertain of which way to run.

'*If you,*' her mother prompted irritably, and gave her a prod with the stick.

'*If you . . .*' the girl managed. '*If you . . . if you grasp the nettle lightly, it will sting you for your pain, but if you grasp the nettle boldly, soft as silk it will remain. So it is with human nature, treat them kindly, they rebel, but if you firmly grasp the nettle, then your bidding they do well.*'

Tiffany realized, as the damp little voice faded away, that there was otherwise absolute silence in the hall and everybody was staring. She rather hoped that somebody might forget themselves sufficiently to start clapping, although that would probably mean the end of the world. Instead, the bride took one look at the open mouths and fled, sobbing, as fast as her very expensive but seriously impractical shoes would carry her; Tiffany heard them clicking madly all the way up the stairs, followed very shortly afterwards by the slamming of a door.

Tiffany walked away slowly, just a shadow in the air to anyone who wasn't paying attention. She shook her head. Why had he done it? Why in the world had Roland done it? Roland could have married anyone! Not Tiffany herself, of course, but why had he chosen that, well – not to be unpleasant – skinny girl?

And her father had been a duke, her mother was a duchess and she was a duckling – well, one might try to be charitable, but she did tend to walk like one. Well, she *did*. If you looked carefully you could see her feet stuck out.

And if you cared about these things, the dreadful mother and the soppy daughter *outranked* Roland! They could officially bully him!

The old Baron, now, had been a different sort of person. Oh yes, he liked it if the children gave a little bow or curtsied if he passed them in the lane, but he knew everybody's name, and generally their birthdays as well, and he was always polite. Tiffany remembered him stopping her one day and saying, 'Would you be so kind as to ask your father to come and see me, please?' It was such a gentle phrase for a man with such power.

Her mother and father used to argue about him, when they thought she was safely tucked up in bed. In between the symphony of the bedsprings she often heard them almost, but not exactly, having a row. Her father would say things like: 'It's all very well you saying he is generous and all that, but don't you tell me that his ancestors didn't get their money by grinding the faces of the poor!' And her mother would retort: 'I have never seen him grind anything! Anyway, that was the olden days. You've got to have someone to protect us. That stands to reason!' And her father would come back with something along the lines of: 'Protect us from who? *Another* man with a sword? I reckon we could do that by ourselves!'

And around this time the conversation would peter out, since her parents were still in love, in a comfortable type of way, and neither of them really wanted anything to change at all.

It seemed to her, looking down the length of the hall, that you didn't need to grind the faces of the poor if you taught them to do their own grinding.

The shock of the thought made her giddy, but it stayed in her mind. The guards were all local boys, or married to local girls, and what would happen if everybody in the village got together and said to the new Baron: 'Look, we will let you stay here, and you can even sleep in the big bedroom, and of course we'll give you all your meals and flick a duster around from time to time, but apart from that this land is ours now, do you understand?' Would it work?

Probably not. But she remembered asking her father to get the old stone barn cleaned up. That would be a start. She had plans for the old barn.

'You there! Yes! You there in the shadows! Are you lollygagging?'

This time she paid attention. All that thinking had

meant that she hadn't paid enough attention to her little don't-see-me trick. She stepped out of the shadows, which meant that the pointy black hat was not just a shadow. The Duchess glared at it.

It was time for Tiffany to break the ice, even though it was so thick as to require an axe. She said politely, 'I don't know how to lollygag, madam, but I will do my best.'

'*What? What! What did you call me?*'

The people in the hall were learning fast and they were scuttling as quickly as they could to get out of the place, because the Duchess's tone of voice was a storm warning, and nobody likes to be out in a storm.

The sudden rage overtook Tiffany. It wasn't as if she had done anything to deserve being shouted at like that. She said, 'I'm sorry, madam; I did not call you anything, to the best of my belief.'

This did not do anything to help; the Duchess's eyes narrowed. 'Oh, I know you. The witch – the witch girl who followed us to the city on who knows what dark errand? Oh, we know about witches where *I'm* from! Meddlers, sowers of doubt, breeders of discontent, lacking all morality, and charlatans into the bargain!'

The Duchess pulled herself right up and glowered at Tiffany as if she had just won a decisive victory. She tapped her cane on the ground.

Tiffany said nothing, but nothing was hard to say. She could sense the watching servants behind curtains and pillars, or peering around doors. The woman was smirking, and really needed that smirk removed, because Tiffany owed it to all witches to show the world that a witch could not be treated like this. On the other hand, if Tiffany spoke her mind it would certainly be taken out on the servants. This needed some delicate wording. It did not get it, because the old bat gave a nasty little snigger and said, 'Well, child? Aren't you going to try to turn me into some kind of unspeakable creature?'

Tiffany tried. She really tried. But there are times when things are just too much. She took a deep breath.

'I don't think I shall bother, madam, seeing as you are making such a good job of it yourself!'

The sudden silence was nevertheless peppered with little sounds like a guard behind a pillar sticking his hand over his mouth so that his shocked laughter would not be heard, and a splutter as – on the other side of a curtain – a maid almost achieved the same thing. But it was the tiny little click of a door high above that stayed in Tiffany's memory. Was that Letitia? Had she overheard? Well, it didn't matter, because the Duchess was gloating now, with Tiffany safely in the palm of her hand.

She shouldn't have risen to the stupid insults, whoever was listening. And now the woman was going to take terrible delight in making trouble for Tiffany, anyone near to her and quite probably everyone she'd ever known.

Tiffany felt chilly sweat running down her back. It had never been like this before – not even with the wintersmith; not even Annagramma being unpleasant on a bad day; not even the Fairy Queen, who was good at spite. The Duchess beat them all: she was a bully, the kind of bully who forces her victim into retaliation, which therefore becomes the justification for further and nastier bullying, with collateral damage to any innocent bystanders who would be invited by the bully to put the blame for their discomfiture onto the victim.

The Duchess looked around the shadowy hall. 'Is there a guard here?' She waited in delighted malice. 'I *know* there is a guard here *somewhere*!'

There was the sound of hesitant footsteps and Preston, the trainee guard, appeared from out of the shadows and walked a nervous walk towards Tiffany and the Duchess. Of course, it would have to be Preston, Tiffany thought; the other guards would be too experienced to risk a generous helping of the Duchess's wrath. And he was smiling nervously too, not a good thing to do when dealing with people like the Duchess. At least he had the sense to salute when he reached her, and by the standards of people who had never been told how to salute properly, and in any case had to do so very rarely, it was a good salute.

The Duchess winced. 'Why are you grinning, young man?'

Preston gave the question some serious thought, and said, 'The sun is shining, madam, and I am happy being a guard.'

'You will not grin at me, young man. Smiling leads

to familiarity, which I will not tolerate at any price. Where is the Baron?'

Preston shifted from one foot to the other. 'He is in the crypt, madam, paying his respects to his father.'

'*You will not call me madam!* "Madam" is a title for the wives of grocers! Nor can you call me "my lady", which is a title for the wives of knights and other riffraff! I am a duchess and am therefore to be addressed as "your grace". Do you understand?'

'Yes . . . m . . . your grace!' Preston threw in another salute in self-defence.

For a moment, at least, the Duchess seemed satisfied, but it was definitely among the shorter kinds of moments.

'Very well. And now you will take this creature' – she waved a hand towards Tiffany – 'and lock her in your dungeon. Do you understand me?'

Shocked, Preston looked to Tiffany for guidance. She gave him a wink, just to keep his spirits up. He turned back to the Duchess. 'Lock *her* in the dungeon?'

The Duchess glared at him. 'That is what I said!'

Preston frowned. 'Are you sure?' he said. 'It means taking the goats out.'

'Young man, it is not my concern what you do with the goats! I *order* you to incarcerate this witch immediately! Now, get on with it, or I will see to it that you lose your position.'

Tiffany was already impressed with Preston, but now he won a medal. 'Can't do that,' he said, ''cause of happy ass. The sergeant told me all about it. Happy ass. Happy ass corp ass. Means you can't just lock somebody away if they haven't broken the law. Happy ass corp ass. It's all written down. Happy ass corp ass,' he repeated helpfully.

This defiance seemed to push the Duchess beyond rage and into some sort of fascinated horror. This spotty-faced youth in ill-fitting armour was defying her over some stupid words. Such a thing had never happened to her before. It was like finding out that frogs talked. That would be very fascinating and everything, but sooner or later a talking frog has to be squashed.

'You will hand in your armour and leave this castle forthwith, do you understand? You are sacked. You have lost your position and I will make it my business to see that you never get a job as a guard ever again, young man.'

Preston shook his head. 'Can't happen like that, your lady grace. 'Cause of happy ass corp ass. The sergeant said to me, "Preston, you stick to happy ass corp ass. It is your friend. You can stand on happy ass corp ass."'

The Duchess glared at Tiffany, and since Tiffany's silence appeared to annoy her even more than anything she would have to say, she smiled and said nothing, in the hope that the Duchess might possibly explode. Instead, and as expected, she turned on Preston.

'How dare you talk back to me like that, you

scoundrel!' She raised the shiny stick with the knob on it. But suddenly, it seemed immovable.

'You will not hit him, madam,' said Tiffany in a calm voice. 'I will see your arm breaks before you strike him. We do not strike people in this castle.'

The Duchess snarled and tugged at the stick, but neither stick nor arm seemed to want to move.

'In a moment, the stick will come free,' said Tiffany. 'If you attempt to strike anyone with it again, I will break it in half. Please understand that this is not a warning – it is a forecast.'

The Duchess glared at her, but must have seen something in Tiffany's face that her own resolute stupidity could worry about. She let go of the stick and it fell to the floor. 'You have not heard the last of this, witch girl!'

'Just witch, madam. Just witch,' said Tiffany as the woman strutted at speed out of the hall.

'Are we going to get into trouble?' said Preston quietly.

Tiffany gave a little shrug. 'I will see to it that you don't,' she said. And she thought, And so will the sergeant. I'll make sure of it. She looked around the hall and saw the faces of the watching servants hurriedly turn away, as if they were afraid. There wasn't any real magic, she thought. I just stood my ground. You have to stand your ground, because it's *your* ground.

'I was wondering,' said Preston, 'if you were going to turn her into a cockroach and stamp on her. I've heard that witches can do that,' he added hopefully.

'Well, I won't say that it is impossible,' said Tiffany, 'but you won't see a witch doing it. Besides, there are practical problems.'

Preston nodded sagely. 'Well, yes,' he said. 'The different body mass for one thing, which would mean you would end up with either one enormous human-sized cockroach, which I think would probably collapse under its own weight, or dozens or even hundreds of people-shaped cockroaches. But the snag there, I think, might be that their brain might work very badly – though, of course, if you had the right spells, I suppose you could magic all the bits of the human that wouldn't fit into the cockroach into some kind of big bucket so they could use it to get them-selves bigger again when they were tired of being small. But the problem there would be what happened if some hungry dog came along when the lid was off. That would be quite bad. Sorry, have I said something wrong?'

'Er, no,' said Tiffany. 'Er, don't you think that you're a bit too smart to be a guard, Preston?'

Preston shrugged. 'Well, the lads all think that I am useless,' he said cheerfully. 'They think that there's got to be something wrong with someone who can pro-nounce the word "marvellous".'

'But, Preston . . . I know you are very clever and sufficiently erudite to know the meaning of the word "erudite". Why do you sometimes pretend to be stupid – you know, like "doctrine" and "happy ass corp ass"?'

Preston grinned. 'I was unfortunately born clever,

miss, and I've learned that sometimes it's not such a good idea to be all that clever. Saves trouble.'

Right now, it seemed to Tiffany that the clever thing would be not to be in the hall any longer. Surely the horrible woman couldn't do *too* much damage, could she? But Roland had been so strange, acting as if they had never been friends, sounding as though he believed every complaint against her . . . He had never been like that before. Oh, yes . . . he was mourning his father, but he just didn't seem . . . himself. And that dreadful old baggage had just bundled off to harry him while he was saying goodbye to his father in the coolness of the crypt, trying to find a way of saying the words that there had never been time for, trying to make up for too much silence, trying to bring back yesterday and nail it firmly to *now*.

Everyone did that. Tiffany had come back from quite a few deathbeds, and some were very nearly merry, where some decent old soul was peacefully putting down the weight of their years. Or they could be tragic, when Death had needed to bend down to harvest his due; or, well, ordinary – sad but expected, one light blinking off in a sky full of stars. And she had wondered, as she made tea, and comforted people, and listened to the tearful stories about the good old days from people who always had words left over that they thought should have been spoken. And she had decided that they weren't there to be said in the past, but remembered in the here and now.

'What do you think about the word "conundrum"?'

Tiffany stared at Preston, her mind still full of words people never said. 'What was that you asked?' she said, frowning.

'The word "conundrum"', Preston repeated helpfully. 'When you say the word, doesn't it look in your head like a copper-coloured snake, curled up asleep?'

Now, Tiffany thought, during a day like this, anyone who wasn't a witch would dismiss that as a bit of silliness, so that means I shouldn't.

Preston was the worst-dressed guard in the castle; the newest guard always was. To him were given chain-mail trousers that were mostly full of holes* and suggested, against everything we know about moths, that moths could eat through steel. To him was given the helmet that, no matter what size your head was, would slide down and make your ears look big; and this was not forgetting that he had also inherited a breastplate with so many holes in it that it might be more useful for straining soup.

But his gaze was always alert, to the point where it made people uneasy. Preston looked at things. *Really* looked at things, so intensely that afterwards they must have felt really looked at. She had no idea what went on in his head, but it was surely pretty crowded.

'Well, I must say I've never thought about that word "conundrum"', she said slowly, 'but it is certainly metallic and slithery.'

---

* In fact, chain-mail trousers are always full of holes, but they shouldn't be full of holes seven inches wide.

'I like words,' said Preston. '"Forgiveness": doesn't it sound like what it is? Doesn't it sound like a silk handkerchief gently falling down? And what about "susurration"? Doesn't it sound to you like whispered plots and dark mysteries? . . . Sorry, is something wrong?'

'Yes, I think *something* may be wrong,' said Tiffany, looking at Preston's worried face. 'Susurration' was her favourite word; she had never met anyone else who even knew it. 'Why are you a guard, Preston?'

'Don't like sheep very much, not very strong so I can't be a ploughman, too ham-fisted to be a tailor, too scared of drowning to run away to sea. My mother taught me to read and write, much against my dad's wishes, and since that meant I was no good for a *proper* job, I got packed off to be an apprentice priest in the Church of Om. I quite liked that; I learned a lot of interesting words, but they threw me out for asking too many questions, such as, "Is this really true or what?"' He shrugged. 'Actually, I quite like the guarding.' He reached down and pulled a book out of his breastplate, which in fact could have accommodated a small library, and went on, 'There's plenty of time for reading if you keep out of sight, and the metaphysics is quite interesting as well.'

Tiffany blinked. 'I think you just lost me there, Preston.'

'Really?' said the boy. 'Well, for example, when I'm on night duty and somebody comes to the gate, I have to say "Who goes there, friend or foe?" To which, of course, the correct answer is "Yes".'

It took Tiffany a moment to work this one out, and she began to have some insight into how Preston might have a problem holding down a job. He continued, 'The conundrum begins if the person at the gate says "Friend", since they may well be lying; but the lads who have to go out at night have very cleverly devised their own shibboleth with which to answer my question, and that is: "Get your nose out of that book, Preston, and let us in right now!"'

' "Shibboleth" being . . . ?' The boy was fascinating. It was not often you found somebody who could make nonsense sound wonderfully sensible.

'A kind of code word,' said Preston. 'Strictly speaking, it means a word that your enemy would be unable to say. For example, in the case of the Duchess, it might be a good idea to choose a word like "please".'

Tiffany tried not to laugh. 'That brain of yours is going to get you into trouble one day, Preston.'

'Well, so long as it's good for something.'

There was a scream from the distant kitchen, and one thing that makes humans different from animals is that they run *towards* a distress call, rather than away from it. Tiffany arrived only seconds behind Preston, and even they weren't the first. A couple of girls were comforting Mrs Coble the cook, who was sobbing on a chair while one of the girls was wrapping a kitchen towel around her arm. The floor was steaming and a black cauldron was lying on its side.

'I tell you, they were there!' the cook managed between sobs. 'All wriggling. I shall always remember it. And kicking and crying out "Mother!" I shall remember their little faces for as long as I live!' She began sobbing again, great big sobs that threatened to choke her. Tiffany beckoned to the nearest kitchen maid, who reacted as though she'd been struck and tried to cower back.

'Look,' said Tiffany, 'can someone please tell me what— *What* are you doing with that bucket?' This was to another maid, who was dragging a bucket up from the cellar and who, at the sound of a command on top of the turmoil, dropped it. Shards of ice flew across the floor. Tiffany took a deep breath. 'Ladies, you don't put ice on a scald, however sensible it seems. Cool some tea – but don't make it cold – and soak her arm in it for at least a quarter of an hour. Everybody understand? Good. Now, *what happened*?'

'It was full of frogs!' the cook screamed. 'They was puddings and I set them to boiling, but when I opened it up, they was little frogs, all shouting for their mother! I told everyone, I told them! A wedding and a funeral from the same house, that's bad luck, that is. It's witchcraft, that's what it is!' Then the woman gasped and clamped her free hand over her mouth.

Tiffany kept a straight face. She looked in the cauldron, and she looked around on the floor. There was no sign of any frogs anywhere, although there were two enormous puddings, still wrapped in their pudding cloths, at the bottom of the cauldron. When she picked them out, still very hot, and placed them on the table, she couldn't help noticing that the maids backed away from them.

'Perfectly good plum duff,' she said cheerily. 'Nothing to worry about here.'

'I have often noticed,' said Preston, 'that in some circumstances, boiling water can seethe in a very strange way, with water droplets appearing to jump up and down just above the surface, which I might suggest is one reason why Mrs Coble thought she was seeing frogs?' He leaned closer to Tiffany and whispered, 'And another reason may quite possibly be that bottle of finest cream sherry I can see on the shelf over there, which appears to be almost empty, coupled with the lone glass noticeable in the washing-up bowl over there.' Tiffany was impressed; she hadn't noticed the glass.

Everyone was watching her. Somebody ought to have been saying something, and since nobody was, it had better be her.

'I'm sure the death of our Baron has upset us all,' she began, and got no further, because the cook sat bolt upright in the chair and pointed a trembling finger at her.

'All except you, you creature!' she accused. 'I seed you, oh yes, I seed you! Everyone was sobbing and crying and wailing, but not you! Oh no! You were just strutting around, giving orders to your elders and betters! Just like your granny! Everybody knows! You was sweet on the young Baron, and when he chucked you over, you killed the old Baron, just to spite him! You was seen! Oh yes, and now the poor lad is beside himself with grief and his bride is in tears and won't come out of her room! Oh, how you must be laughing inside! People is saying that the marriage should be put off! I'd bet you'd like that, wouldn't you? That would be a feather in your black hat, and no mistake! I remember when you were small, and then off you went up to the mountains, where the folks are so strange and wild, as everybody knows, and what comes back? Yes, what comes back? What comes back, knowing everything, acting so hoity-toity, treating us like dirt, tearing a young man's life apart? And that ain't the worst of it! You just talk to Mrs Petty! Don't tell me about frogs! I know frogs when I sees them, and that's what I saw! Frogs! They must—'

Tiffany stepped out of her body. She was good at this now, oh yes. Sometimes she practised the trick on animals, who were generally very hard to fool: even if only a mind seemed to be there, they got nervous and eventually ran away. But humans? Humans were easy to fool. Provided your body stayed where you left it, blinking its eyes, and breathing, and keeping its balance, and all the other little things bodies are good at doing even when you are not there, other humans thought *you* were.

And now she let herself drift towards the drunken cook, while she muttered and shouted and repeated herself, spitting out hurtful idiocies and bile and hatred, and also little flecks of spittle that stayed on her chins.

And now Tiffany could smell the stench. It was faint

but it was there. She wondered: If I turn round, will I see two holes in a face? No, things weren't that bad, surely. Perhaps he was just thinking about her. Should she run? No. She might be running *to* rather than *from*. He could be anywhere! But at least she could try to stop this mischief.

Tiffany was careful not to walk *through* people; it was possible, but even though she was in theory as insubstantial as a thought, walking through a person was like walking through a swamp – sticky and unpleasant and dark.

She had got past the kitchen girls, who seemed hypnotised; time always seemed to pass more slowly when she was out of her body.

Yes, the bottle of sherry was almost empty, and *there was another empty one* just visible behind a sack of potatoes. Mrs Coble herself reeked of it. She had always been partial to a drop of sherry, and possibly another drop as well; it could be a work-related illness among cooks, along with three wobbly chins. But all that foul stuff? Where had that come from? Was it something she'd always wanted to say, or had *he* put it into her mouth?

I have done nothing wrong, she thought again. It might be useful to keep that firmly in mind. But I have been stupid too, and I shall have to remember that as well.

The woman, still hypnotising the girls with her ranting, looked very ugly in the slow-motion world: her face was a vicious red, and every time she opened her mouth her breath stank, and there was a piece of food stuck in her uncleaned teeth. Tiffany shifted sideways a little. Would it be possible to reach an invisible hand into her stupid body and see if she could stop the beating of the heart?

Nothing like that had ever occurred to her before, and it was a fact that you could not, of course, pick up anything when you were outside your body, but perhaps it would be possible to interrupt some little flow, some tiny spark? Even a big fat wretched creature like the cook could be brought down by the tiniest of upsets, and that stupid red face would shudder, and that stinking breath would gasp, and that foul mouth would shut—

First Thoughts, Second Thoughts, Third Thoughts, and the very rare Fourth Thoughts lined up in her head like planets to scream in chorus: *That's not us! Watch what you are thinking!*

Tiffany slammed back into her body, nearly losing her balance, and was caught by Preston, who was standing right behind her.

Quick! Remember that Mrs Coble had lost her husband only seven months ago, she told herself, and remember that she used to give you biscuits when you were small, and remember that she had a row with her daughter-in-law and doesn't get to see her grandchildren any more. Remember this, and see a poor old lady who has drunk too much and has listened to too much gossip – from that nasty Miss Spruce, for one. Remember this, because if you hit back at her, you will become what he wants you to be! Don't give him space in your head again!'

Behind her, Preston grunted, and said, 'I know it's not the right thing to say to a lady, miss, but you are sweating like a pig!'

Tiffany, trying to get her shattered thoughts together, muttered, 'My mother always said that horses sweat, men perspire, and ladies merely glow . . .'

'Is that so?' said Preston cheerfully. 'Well, miss, you are glowing like a pig!'

This caused a lot of giggling from the girls, already shaken up by the cook's ranting, but any laughter would be better than that and, it occurred to Tiffany, maybe Preston had worked that out.

But Mrs Coble had managed to get to her feet and waved a threatening finger at Tiffany – although she was swaying so much that for some of the time, depending on which way she was leaning, she was also threatening Preston, one of the girls and a rack of cheeses.

'You don't fool me, you evil-looking minx,' she said. 'Everyone knows you killed the old Baron! The nurse saw you! How dare you show your face in here? You'll take us all sooner or later, and I won't have that! I hope the ground opens up and swallows you!' the cook snarled. She tottered backwards. There was a heavy thud, a creak and, just for a moment until it was cut off, the beginning of a scream as the cook fell into the cellar.

## CHAPTER 10

# The Melting Girl

'Miss Aching, I must ask you to leave the Chalk,' said the Baron, his face wooden.

'I will not!'

The Baron's expression did not change. Roland could be like that, she remembered, and it was worse now, of course. The Duchess had insisted on being in his office for this interview, and had further insisted on having two of her own guards there, as well as two from the castle. That pretty much filled all the space in the study, and the two pairs of guards glared at each other in all-out professional rivalry.

'It is my land, Miss Aching.'

'I know I have some rights!' said Tiffany.

Roland nodded like a judge. 'That is a very important point, Miss Aching, but regrettably you have no rights at all. You are not a leaseholder, you are not a tenant and you own no land. In short, you have nothing on which rights are based.' He said all this without looking up from the foolscap paper in front of him.

Deftly, Tiffany reached across and snatched it from his fingers, and was back in her chair before the guards could react. 'How dare you talk like that without looking me in the eye!' But she knew what the words meant. Her father was a tenant of the farm. He had rights. She did not. 'Look,' she said, 'you can't just turn me out. I've done nothing wrong.'

Roland sighed. 'I really hoped that you would see reason, Miss Aching, but since you assert total innocence, I must spell out the following facts. Item: you admit that you took the child Amber Petty away from her parents and lodged her with the fairy folk who live in holes in the ground. Did you think this was the right place for a young girl? According to my men, there seemed to be a lot of snails in the vicinity.'

'Now just hold on, Roland—'

'You will address my future son-in-law as "my lord",' snapped the Duchess.

'And if I don't, will you hit me with your stick, your grace? Will you grasp the nettle firmly?'

'How dare you!' the Duchess said, her eyes blazing. 'Is this how you like your guests to be addressed, Roland?'

At least his bewilderment seemed genuine. 'I haven't the faintest idea what is being talked about here,' he said.

Tiffany pointed her finger at the Duchess, causing the Duchess's bodyguards to reach for their weapons, thus causing the castle guards to draw theirs too, so as not to be left out. By the time swords were safely disentangled and put where they belonged, the Duchess was already launching a counter-attack. 'You should not put up with this insubordination, young man! You are the Baron, and you have given this . . . this creature notice to leave your lands. She is not conducive to public order, and if she still wilfully insists on not leaving, do I need to remind you that her parents are your tenants?'

Tiffany was already seething because of 'creature', but to her surprise the young Baron shook his head and said, 'No, I cannot punish good tenants for having a wayward daughter.'

'Wayward'? That was worse than 'creature'! How dare he . . .! And her thoughts ran together. He wouldn't dare. He never had dared, not in all the time they'd known each other, all the time when she had been just Tiffany and he had been just Roland. It had been a strange relationship, mostly because it wasn't a relationship at all. They hadn't been drawn to one another: they had been pushed towards one another by the way the world worked. She was a witch, which meant that she was automatically different from the village kids, and he was the Baron's son, which automatically meant he was different from the village kids.

And where they had gone wrong was in believing, somewhere in their minds, that because two things were different, they must therefore be alike. Slowly finding out that this wasn't true hadn't been nice for either of them and there had been a certain number of things that both of them wished hadn't been said. And then it wasn't over, because it had never begun, not really, of course. And so it was best for both of them. Of course. Certainly. Yes.

And in all that time he'd never been like this, never so cold, never so stupid in such a meticulous kind of way that you couldn't blame it all on the wretched Duchess, although Tiffany would have loved to. No, there were other things happening. She had to be on her guard. And there, watching them watching her, she realized how a person could be both stupid and clever.

She picked up her chair, placed it neatly in front of the desk, sat down on it, folded her hands and said, 'I am very sorry, my lord.' She turned to the Duchess, bowed her head and said, 'And to you too, your grace. I temporarily forgot my place. It will not happen again. Thank you.'

The Duchess grunted. It would have been impossible for Tiffany to have thought any less of her but, well, a grunt? After a climb-down like that? Humbling an uppity young witch deserved a lot better than that — some remark so cutting that it blunted on the bone. Honestly, she might have made an effort.

Roland was staring at Tiffany, so nonplussed he was nearly minused. She confused him a little more by handing him the now-crumpled sheet of paper and saying, 'Do you want to deal with the other matters, my lord?'

He struggled for a moment, managed to flatten the paper on the desk to his satisfaction, smoothed it out and said, 'There is the matter of the death of my father and the theft of money from his strongbox.'

Tiffany fixed him with a helpful smile, which made him nervous. 'Anything else, my lord? I am anxious that everything should be dealt with.'

'Roland, she is up to something,' said the Duchess. 'Be on your guard.' She waved a hand towards the guards. 'And you guards should be on your guard as well, mind!'

The guards, having some difficulty with the idea of being even more on their guard when they were already – through nervousness – much further on their guard in any case than they had ever been before, strained to look a bit taller.

Roland cleared his throat. 'Ahem, then there is the matter of the late cook, who fell to her death almost coincidentally with, I believe, insulting you. Do you understand these charges?'

'No,' said Tiffany.

There was a moment of silence before Roland said, 'Er, why not?'

'Because they aren't charges, my lord. You are not declaring outright that you think I stole the money and killed your father and the cook. You are simply sort of waving the idea in front of me in the hope that I will burst into tears, I suppose. Witches don't cry, and I want something that probably no other witch has ever asked for before. I want a hearing. A proper hearing.

And that means evidence. And that means witnesses, and that means that the people who *say* have to say it in front of everybody. And that means a jury of my peers, which means people like me, and that means *habeas corpus*, thank you very much.' She stood up and turned towards the doorway, which was blocked by a struggling crowd of guards. Now she looked at Roland, and bobbed a little curtsy. 'Unless you feel *entirely* confident enough to have me arrested, my lord, I am leaving.'

They watched with open mouths as she walked up to the guards.

'Good evening, Sergeant, good evening, Preston, good evening, gentlemen. This won't take a minute. If you would just excuse me, I am leaving.' She saw Preston wink at her as she pushed past his sword, and then she heard the guards suddenly collapse in a heap.

She walked along the corridor to the hall. There was a huge fire in the even bigger fireplace, which was large enough to be a room all by itself. The fire was peat. It couldn't do much to heat most of the hall, which never got warm even in the heart of summer, but it was cosy to be close to, and if you have to breathe smoke, then you can't do better than peat smoke, which rose up to the chimney and drifted like a warm mist around the sides of bacon, which were hung up there to smoke.

It was all going to get complicated again, but for the moment Tiffany sat there simply for a rest and, while she was about it, to shout at herself for being so stupid. How much poison can he seep into their heads? How much does he *need* to?

That was the problem with witchcraft: it was as if everybody needed the witches, but hated the fact that they did, and somehow the hatred of the fact could become the hatred of the person. People then started thinking: Who are you to have these skills? Who are you to know these things? Who are you to think you're better than us? But Tiffany *didn't* think she was better than them. She was better than them at witchcraft, that was true, but she couldn't knit a sock, she didn't know how to shoe a horse, and while she was pretty good at making cheese, she had to have three tries to bake a loaf that you could actually bite into with your teeth. Everybody was good at something. The only wicked thing was not finding out in time.

There was fine dust on the floor of the fireplace, because there is nothing like peat for dust, and as Tiffany watched, tiny little footprints appeared in it.

'All right,' she said, 'what did you do to the guards?'

A shower of Feegles landed lightly on the seat beside her.

'Weel,' Rob Anybody said, 'personally I would have liked to take them to the cleaners, the mound-digging Cromwells that they are, but I could see where that might make it a wee bit difficult for ye, so we just tied their bootlaces together. Maybe they'll blame it on the wee mice.'

'Look, you're not to hurt anybody, all right? The guards have to do what they are told.'

'Nae, they didnae,' said Rob scornfully. 'That's nae errand for a warrior, doing what you're told. And what would they have done to ye, doing what they were told? That old carlin of a mother-in-law was glaring claymores at ye the whole time, bad cess to her! Hah! Let's see how she likes her bathwater tonight!'

The edge to his voice put Tiffany on the alert. 'You are not to hurt anybody, do you understand? Nobody at all, Rob.'

The Big Man grumbled. 'Och yes, miss, I've taken what you said on board!'

'And you promise on your honour as a Feegle not to throw it over the side as soon as my back is turned, do you?'

Rob Anybody started grumbling again, using crackling Feegle words that she had never heard before. They sounded like curses, and once or twice, when he spat them out, smoke and sparks came out with them. He was stamping his feet too, always a sign of a Feegle at the end of his tether. 'They came arrayed with sharp steel to dig up me home, dig up me clan and dig up me family,' he said, and his words were all the more menacing because they were so level and quiet. Then he spat a short sentence towards the fire, which burned green for a moment when the words hit the flames.

'I'll no' disobey the hag o' the hills, ye ken, but I put ye on firm notice that if I can see a shovel near my mound again, the owner will find it shoved up his kilt blunt end first, so that he hurts his hands trying to pull it out. And that will only be the start of his problems! And if there is any clearances here, I swear on my spog that it will be us that is doing the clearing!' He stamped up and down a bit, and then added: 'And what is this we are hearing about ye demanding the law? We is nae friends of the law, ye ken.'

'What about Wee Mad Arthur?' said Tiffany.

It was almost impossible to make a Feegle look sheepish, but Rob Anybody looked as if he was about to say 'Bah'. 'Oh, it's a terrible thing them gnomes did to him,' he said, looking sad. 'Do ye ken he washes his face every day? I mean, that sort of thing is OK when the mud gets too thick, but every day? I ask ye, how can a body stand it?'

One moment there were the Feegles, and then there was a faint *whoosh*, followed by a total lack of Feegles, and the next moment there was a more than adequate supply of guards. Fortunately they were the sergeant and Preston, stamping to attention.

The sergeant cleared his throat. 'Am I addressing Miss Tiffany Aching?' he said.

'It looks to me as if you are, Brian,' said Tiffany, 'but you be the judge.'

The sergeant looked around quickly and then leaned closer. 'Please, Tiff,' he whispered, 'it's all gone serious on us.' He straightened up quickly and then said, far louder than was necessary, 'Miss Tiffany Aching! I am commanded by my lord the Baron to inform you that it is his command that you must stay within the irons of the castle—'

'The what?' said Tiffany.

Wordlessly, his eyes on the ceiling, the sergeant handed her a piece of parchment.

'Oh, you mean the *environs*,' she said. 'That means the castle and the places around it too,' she told him helpfully. 'But I thought the Baron wanted me to leave?'

'Look, I'm just reading out what it says here, Tiff, and I am ordered to lock your broomstick in the dungeon.'

'That's an impressive errand that you have there, Officer. It's leaning against the wall, help yourself.'

The sergeant looked relieved. 'You're not going to make any . . . trouble?' he said.

Tiffany shook her head. 'Not at all, Sergeant. I have no quarrel with a man who is only doing his duty.'

The sergeant walked cautiously up to the broomstick. They all knew it, of course; they had seen it going overhead, and generally only *just* overhead, practically every day. But he hesitated, with his hand a few inches from the wood. 'Er, what happens when I touch it?' he said.

'Oh, then it's ready to fly,' said Tiffany.

The sergeant's hand very slowly drew back from the vicinity, or possibly the environs, of the broomstick. 'But it won't fly for me, right?' he said in a voice full of air-sickness and pleading.

'Oh, not very far or very high, probably,' said Tiffany, without looking round. The sergeant was well known to get vertigo simply by standing on a chair. She walked over to him and picked up the stick. 'Brian, what were your orders if I refused to obey your orders, if you see what I mean?'

'I was supposed to arrest you!'

'What? And lock me up in the dungeon?'

The sergeant winced. 'You know I wouldn't want to do that,' he said. '*Some* of us are grateful, and we all knew that poor old Mrs Coble was as drunk as a skunk, poor woman.'

'Then I won't put you to the trouble,' said Tiffany. 'So why don't I put this broomstick, which you seem so worried about, down in the dungeon and lock it in. Then I won't be going anywhere, yes?'

Relief flooded the sergeant's face, and as they walked down the stone steps to the dungeon he lowered his voice and said, 'It's not me, you understand, it's them upstairs. It seems like her grace is calling the shots now.'

Tiffany hadn't seen very many dungeons, but people said that the one in the castle was pretty good by dungeon standards and would probably earn at least five ball and chains if anybody ever decided to write a Good Dungeon Guide. It was spacious and well-drained, with a handy gutter right down the middle, which ended up in the inevitable round hole, which did not smell very bad on, as it were, the whole.

Neither did the goats, which unfolded themselves from their snug beds in piles of straw and watched her through slot eyes in case she did anything interesting, such as feeding them. They didn't stop eating, because being goats, they were already eating their dinner for the second time.

The dungeon had two entrances. One went straight outdoors: it was probably there to drag the prisoners in by, back in the old days, because that would save having to pull them across the great hall, getting the floor all mucky with blood and mud.

These days the dungeon was mostly used as a goat shed and, on racks higher up – high enough to be out of reach of all but the most determined goat – an apple store.

Tiffany lifted the broomstick up onto the lowest apple rack, while the sergeant petted one of the goats, taking care not to look up in case it made him feel dizzy. That meant he was entirely unprepared when Tiffany pushed him back out of the doorway, took the keys out of the lock, swung herself back into the dungeon and locked the door on the inside.

'I'm sorry, Brian, but, you see, it is you. Not just you, of course, and not even mostly you, and it was rather unfair of me to take advantage of you, but if I'm going to be treated like a criminal, I might as well act like one.'

Brian shook his head. 'We do have another key, you know.'

'Hard to use it if I blocked the keyhole,' said Tiffany, 'but look on the bright side. I'm under lock and key, which I think some people would rather like, so all you are worried about is the fine detail. You see, I think you might be looking at this the wrong way round. I'm safe in a dungeon. I haven't been locked away from you, the rest of you have been locked away from me.'

Brian looked as if he was about to cry and she thought, No, I can't do it. He's always been decent to me. He's trying to be decent now. Just because I'm cleverer than he is doesn't mean that he should lose his job. And besides, I already know the way out of here. That's the thing about people who have dungeons; they don't spend enough time in them themselves. She handed the keys back.

His face brightened with relief. 'Obviously we will bring you food and water,' he said. 'You can't live on apples all the time!'

Tiffany sat down on the straw. 'You know, it's quite cosy in here. It's funny how goat burps make everything sort of warm and comfortable. No, I won't eat the apples, but some of them do need turning or else they will rot, so I will take care of that while I'm in here too. Of course, when I'm locked in here I can't be out there. I can't make medicines. I can't clip toenails. I can't help. How is your old mum's leg these days? Still well, I hope? Would you mind leaving now, please, because I'd like to use the hole.'

She heard his boots on the stairs. It had been a bit cruel, but what else could she have done? She looked around and lifted up a pile of very old and very dirty straw that hadn't been touched for a long time. All sorts of things crawled, hopped or slithered away. Around her, now that the coast was clear, Feegle heads rose, bits of straw dropping off them.

'Fetch my lawyer, please,' Tiffany said brightly. 'I think he's going to like working here . . .'

\* \* \*

The Toad turned out to be quite enthusiastic, for a lawyer who knew that he was going to be paid in beetles.

'I think we will start with wrongful imprisonment. Judges don't like that sort of thing. If anyone's going to be put in prison, they like to be the ones who do it.'

'Er, actually I locked *myself* in,' said Tiffany. 'Does that count?'

'I wouldn't worry about that at the moment. You were under duress, your freedom of movement was being curtailed and you were put in fear.'

'I certainly was not! I was extremely *angry!*'

The Toad slapped a claw down on an escaping centipede. 'You were interrogated by two members of the aristocracy in the presence of four armed men, yes? Nobody warned you? Nobody read you your rights? And you say the Baron apparently believes on no evidence that you killed his father, and the cook, and stole some money?'

'I think Roland's trying hard not to believe it,' said Tiffany. 'Someone has told him a lie.'

'Then we must challenge it, indeed we must. He can't go around making allegations of murder when they can't be substantiated. He can get into serious trouble for that!'

'Oh,' said Tiffany, 'I don't want any harm to come to him!' It is hard to see when the Toad is smiling, so Tiffany had to take a guess. 'Did I say something funny?'

'Not funny at all, not really, but in its way rather sad and rather droll,' said the Toad. 'Droll, in this case, meaning somewhat bittersweet. This young man is making accusations against you which could, if true, lead to you being executed in many places in this world, and yet you do not wish him to be put to any inconvenience?'

'I know it's soppy, but the Duchess is pushing him all the time, and the girl he's going to marry is as wet as—' She stopped. There were footfalls on the stone stairs that led from the hall to the dungeon, and they certainly did not have the heavy ring of guards' hobnails.

It was Letitia, the bride-to-be, all in white and all in tears. She reached the bars of Tiffany's cell, hung onto them, and carried on crying: not big sobs, but just an endless snivelling, nose-dripping, fumbling-in-the-sleeve-for-the-lace-hanky-that-is-already-totally-soaking-wet kind of tears.

The girl didn't really look at Tiffany, just sobbed in her general direction. 'I'm so sorry! I really am very sorry! What can you think of me?'

And there, right there, was the drawback of being a witch. Here was a person whose mere existence had led Tiffany, one evening, to wonder about that whole business of sticking pins into a wax figure. She hadn't actually done it, because it was something that you shouldn't do, something that witches greatly frowned on, and because it was cruel and dangerous, and above all because she hadn't been able to find any pins.

And now the wretched creature was in some kind of

agony, so distraught that modesty and dignity were all being washed away in a rolling flood of gummy tears. How could they not wash away hatred as well? And, in truth, there had never been all that much hatred, more of a kind of *miffed* feeling. She'd known all along that she'd never be a lady, not without the long blonde hair. It was totally against the whole book of fairytales. She just hadn't liked being rushed into accepting it.

'I really never wanted things to happen like this!' gulped Letitia. 'I really am very, very sorry, I don't know what I could've been thinking about!' And so many tears, rolling down that silly, lacy dress and – oh no, there was a perfect snot balloon on a perfect nose.

Tiffany watched in fascinated horror as the weeping girl had a great bubbling blow and – oh no, she wasn't going to, was she? Yes, she was. Yes. She squeezed out the dripping handkerchief onto the floor, which was already wet from the incessant crying.

'Look, I'm sure things can't be as bad as all that,' said Tiffany, trying not to hear the ghastly blobby noises on the stone. 'If you would only stop crying for a moment, I'm sure everything can be sorted out, whatever it is.'

This caused more tears and some actual, genuine, old-fashioned sobs, the kind you never heard in real life – well, at least, up until now. Tiffany knew that when people cried, they said boo-hoo – or at least, that's how it was written down in books. *No one* said it in real life. But Letitia did, while projectile crying all over the steps. There was something *else* there too, and Tiffany caught the spill words as they were well and truly spilled, and read them as, somewhat soggy, they landed in her brain.

She thought, Oh, really? But before she could say anything, there was a clattering on the steps again. Roland, the Duchess, and one of her guards came hurrying down, followed by Brian, who had clearly been getting very annoyed about other people's guards clattering on his home cobbles, and so was making sure that whenever a clattering was taking place, he was fully involved.

Roland skidded on the damp patch, and threw his arms protectively around Letitia, who squelched and oozed slightly. The Duchess loomed over the pair of them, which left little looming space available for the guards, who had to put up with looking angrily at one another.

'What have you done to her?' Roland demanded. 'How did you lure her down here?'

The Toad cleared his throat and Tiffany gave him an undignified nudge with her boot. 'Don't you say a word, you amphibian,' she hissed. He might be her lawyer, but if the Duchess saw a *toad* acting as her legal counsel, then it could only make things worse.

As it happens, her not seeing the Toad did make things worse, because the Duchess screamed, 'Did you hear that? Is there no end to her insolence? She called me an *amphibian*.'

Tiffany was about to say, 'I didn't mean you, I meant the other amphibian,' but stopped herself in time. She sat down, one hand shovelling straw over the Toad and turned to Roland. 'Which question would you like me not to answer first?'

'My men know how to make you talk!' said the Duchess over Roland's shoulder.

'I already know how to talk, thank you,' said Tiffany. 'I thought that maybe she had come to gloat, but things seem to be more . . . afloat.'

'She can't get out, can she?' said Roland to the sergeant.

The sergeant saluted smartly and said, 'No, sir. I have the keys to both doors firmly in my pocket, sir.' He gave a smug look to the Duchess's guard when he said this, as if to say: *Some* people get asked important questions and come back with accurate and snappy answers around here, thank you so very much!

This was rather spoiled by the Duchess saying, 'He twice called you "sir" instead of "my lord", Roland. You must not let the lower orders act so familiarly to you. I have told you this before.'

Tiffany would cheerfully have kicked Roland for not coming back sharply on that one. Brian had taught him to ride a horse, she knew, and taught him how to hold a sword and how to hunt. Perhaps he should have taught him manners too.

'Excuse me,' she said sharply. 'Do you intend to keep me locked up for ever? I wouldn't mind some more socks and a couple of spare dresses, and, of course, some unmentionables if that is going to be the case.'

Possibly the mention of the word 'unmentionables' was what flustered the young Baron. But he rallied quite quickly and said, 'We, er . . . that is to say, I, er . . . feel we should perhaps keep you carefully but humanely where you can do no mischief until after the wedding. You do seem to be the centre of a lot of unfortunate events recently. I'm sorry about this.'

Tiffany didn't dare say anything, because it isn't polite to burst out laughing after such a solemn and stupid statement as that.

He went on, trying to smile, 'You will be made comfortable, and of course we will take the goats out, if you wish.'

'I'd like you to leave them in here, if it's all the same to you,' said Tiffany. 'I am beginning to enjoy the pleasure of their company. But may I ask a question?'

'Yes, of course.'

'This is not going to be about spinning wheels, is it?' Tiffany asked. Well, after all, there was only one way this stupid reasoning could be taking them.

'What?' said Roland.

The Duchess laughed triumphantly. 'Oh yes, it would be just like the saucy and all-too-confident young madam to taunt us with her intentions! How many spinning wheels do we have in this castle, Roland?'

The young man looked startled. He always did when his future mother-in-law addressed him. 'Er, I don't really know. I think the housekeeper has one, my mother's wheel is still in the high tower . . . there's always a few around. My father likes – *liked* – to see people busy with their hands. And . . . really, I don't know.'

'I shall tell the men to search the castle and destroy every single one of them!' said the Duchess. 'I shall call her bluff! Surely everyone knows about spiteful witches and spinning wheels? One little prick upon the finger and we'll all end up going to sleep for a hundred years!'

Letitia, who had been standing in a state of snuffle, managed to say, 'Mother, you know you've never let me touch a spinning wheel.'

'And you never will touch a spinning wheel, *ever*, Letitia, never in your life. Such things are there for the labouring classes. *You* are a *lady*. Spinning is for servants.'

Roland had gone red. 'My mother used to spin,' he said in a deliberate kind of way. 'I used to sit up in the high tower when she was using it sometimes. It was inlaid with mother-of-pearl. Nobody is to touch it.' It seemed to Tiffany, watching through the bars, that only someone with half a heart, very little kindness and no common sense at all would have said anything at this point. But the Duchess had no common sense, probably because it was, well, too common.

'I insist—' she began.

'No,' said Roland. The word wasn't loud, but it had a quietness that was somehow louder than a shout, and undertones and overtones that would have stopped a herd of elephants in their tracks. Or, in this case, one Duchess. But she gave her son-in-law a look which promised him a hard time when she could be bothered to think of one.

Out of sympathy, Tiffany said, 'Look, I only

mentioned about the spinning wheels to be sarcastic. That sort of thing just doesn't happen any more. I'm not sure that it ever did. I mean, people going to sleep for a hundred years while all the trees and plants grow up over the palace? How is that supposed to work? Why weren't the plants sleeping as well? Otherwise you would get brambles growing up people's nostrils, and I bet that would wake up *anybody*. And what happened when it snowed?' As she said this she fixed her attention on Letitia, who was almost screaming a very interesting spill word, which Tiffany had noted for later consideration.

'Well, I can see that a witch causes disruption wherever she walks,' said the Duchess, 'and so you will stay here, being treated with more decency than you deserve, until we say so.'

'And what will you tell my father, Roland?' said Tiffany sweetly.

He looked as if he'd been punched, and probably he would be if Mr Aching got wind of this. He'd need an awful lot of guards if Mr Aching found out that his youngest daughter had been locked up with goats.

'I'll tell you what,' said Tiffany. 'Why don't we say that I am staying in the castle to deal with important matters? I'm sure the sergeant here can be trusted to take a message to my dad without upsetting him?' She made this into a question and saw Roland nod, but the Duchess couldn't help herself.

'Your father is a tenant of the Baron and will do what he is told!'

Now Roland was trying not to squirm. When Mr Aching had worked for the old Baron, they had, as men of the world, reached a sensible arrangement, which was that Mr Aching would do whatever the Baron asked him to do. Provided the Baron asked Mr Aching to do what Mr Aching wanted to do and needed to be done.

That was what *loyalty* meant, her father had told her one day. It meant that good men of all sorts worked well when they understood about rights and duties and the dignity of everyday people. And people treasured that dignity all the more because that was, give or take some bed linen, pots and pans and a few tools and cutlery, more or less *all* they had. The arrangement didn't need to be talked about, because every sensible person knew how it worked: while you're a good master, I will be a good worker. I will be loyal to you, while you are loyal to me, and while the circle is unbroken, this is how things will continue to be.

And Roland was breaking the circle, or at least allowing the Duchess to do it for him. His family had ruled the Chalk for a few hundred years, and had pieces of paper to prove it. There was nothing to prove when the first Aching had set foot on the Chalk; no one had invented paper then.

People weren't happy about witches right now – they were upset and confused – but the last thing Roland could do with was Mr Aching seeking an answer. Even with some grey in his hair Mr Aching could ask some very hard questions. And I need to stay here now, Tiffany thought. I've found a thread, and what you do with threads is pull them. Aloud, she said, 'I don't mind staying here. I'm sure we don't want any little problems.'

Roland looked relieved about this but the Duchess turned to the sergeant and said, 'Are you sure she's locked in?'

Brian stood up straight; he'd been standing up straight already, and was probably now on tiptoe. 'Yes, m— your graceship, like I said, there's only one key to fit both the doors, and I have them in my pocket right here.' He slapped his right-hand pocket, which jingled. Apparently, the jingle was enough to satisfy the Duchess, who said, 'Then I think we might rest a little happier in our beds tonight, Sergeant. Come, Roland, and do take care of Letitia. I fear she needs her medicine again – goodness knows what the wretched girl said to her.'

Tiffany watched them go, all except Brian, who had the decency to look embarrassed. 'Could you come over here please, Sergeant?'

Brian sighed, and walked a little nearer to the bars. 'You're not going to make trouble for me, are you, Tiff?'

'Certainly not, Brian, and I hope and trust that you will not try to make trouble for me.'

The sergeant shut his eyes and groaned. 'You're planning something, aren't you? I knew it!'

'Let me put it like this,' said Tiffany, leaning forward. 'How likely is it, do you think, that I'm going to stay in the cell tonight?'

Brian went to pat his pocket. 'Well, don't forget I've got the—' It was terrible to see his face crumple up like a little puppy that's been given a sharp telling-off. 'You picked my pocket!' He looked at her pleadingly, like a little puppy who was now expecting much worse than a telling-off.

To the sergeant's shock and awe, Tiffany handed the keys back to him again, with a smile. 'You surely don't think a witch needs keys? And I promise you that I will be back in here by seven o'clock in the morning. I think you will agree, in the circumstances, that this is very good deal, especially since I will find some time to change the bandage on your mother's leg.'

The look on his face was enough. He grabbed the keys thankfully. 'I suppose it's no good me asking you how you intend to get out?' he said hopefully.

'I don't think you ought to ask that question in the circumstances, do you, Sergeant?'

He hesitated, and then smiled. 'Thank you for thinking about my mother's leg,' he said. 'It's looking a bit purple at the moment.'

Tiffany took a deep breath. 'The trouble is, Brian, you and I are the only ones thinking about your mother's bad leg. There's old folks out there who need someone to help them in and out of the bathtub. There's pills and potions that need making and taking to people in the hard-to-get-to places. There is Mr Bouncer, who can hardly walk at all unless I give him a good rubbing of embrocation.' She pulled out her diary, held together with bits of string and elastic bands, and waved it at him. 'This is full of things for me to do, because I am the witch. If I don't do them, who will? Young Mrs Trollope is due to have twins soon, I'm sure of it, I can hear the separate heartbeats. First-time births too. She is already scared stiff, and the nearest other midwife is ten miles away and, I have to say, a bit short-sighted and forgetful. You are an officer, Brian. Officers are supposed to be men of resource, so if the poor young mother comes looking for help, I am sure you will know what to do.'

She had the pleasure of seeing his face go very nearly white. Before he could stutter a reply she continued, 'But I can't help, you see, because the wicked witch must be locked up in case she gets her hands on a loaded spinning wheel! Locked up for a fairy story! And the trouble is, I think somebody might die. And if I let them die, then I am a bad witch. The trouble is, I am a bad witch anyway. I must be, because you have locked me up.'

She did actually feel sorry for him. He hadn't become a sergeant to deal with things like this; most of his tactical experience lay in catching escaped pigs. Should I blame him for what he's been ordered to do? she wondered. After all, you can't blame the hammer for what the carpenter does with it. But Brian has got a brain, and the hammer hasn't. Maybe he should try to use it.

Tiffany waited until the sound of his boots indicated that the sergeant had decided quite correctly that it might be a good idea to have a plausible distance between the cell and himself that evening, and also perhaps a little think about his future. Besides, the Feegles began to appear from every crevice, and they had a wonderful instinct for not getting spotted.

'You shouldn't have pick-pocketed his keys,' she said as Rob Anybody spat out a piece of straw.

'Aye? He wants to keep you locked up!'

'Well, yes, but he's a decent person.' She knew that sounded stupid, and Rob Anybody must have known that too.

'Oh aye, sure, a decent person who will lock you up at the bidding of that snotty old carlin?' he snarled. 'And what about that big wee strip o' dribbling in the white dress? I was reckoning we'd have to build guttering in front of her.'

'Was she one o' them water nymphs?' said Daft Wullie, but the majority view was that the girl was somehow made of ice and had been melting away. Lower down the steps, a mouse was swimming to safety.

Almost without her knowing it, Tiffany's left hand slid into her pocket and pulled out a piece of string, which was temporarily dropped onto Rob Anybody's head. The hand went back into her pocket and came back out with one interesting small key she had picked up by the side of the road three weeks ago, an empty packet that had once contained flower seeds, and a small stone with a hole in it. Tiffany always picked up small stones with holes in them, because they were lucky; she kept them in her pocket until the stone wore through the cloth and fell out, leaving only the hole. That was enough to make an emergency shamble, except that you usually needed something alive, of course. The Toad's dinner of beetles had entirely disappeared, mostly into the Toad, so she picked him up and tied him gently into the pattern, paying no attention to his threats of legal action.

'I don't know why you don't use one of the Feegles,' he said. 'They like this sort of thing!'

'Yes, but half the time the shamble ends up pointing me to the nearest pub. Now, just hang on, will you?'

The goats carried on chewing as she moved the shamble this way and that, searching for a clue. Letitia had been sorry, deeply damply sorry. And that last set of spill words was a set of words she wasn't brave enough to say but not quick enough to stop. They were: 'I didn't mean it!'

No one knew how a shamble worked. Everybody knew that it did. Perhaps all it did do was make you think. Maybe what it did do was give your eyes something to look at while you thought, and Tiffany thought: Someone else in this building is magical. The shamble twisted, the Toad complained and the silver thread of a conclusion floated across Tiffany's Second Sight. She turned her eyes towards the ceiling. The silver thread glittered, and she thought: Someone in this building is *using* magic. Someone who is very sorry that they did.

Was it possible that the permanently pale, permanently damp and irrevocably watercolouring Letitia was actually a *witch*? It seemed unthinkable. Well, there was no sense in wondering what was happening when you could simply go and find out for yourself.

It was nice to think that the barons of the Chalk had got along with so many people over the years that they'd forgotten how to lock anybody up. The dungeon had become a goat shed, and the difference between a dungeon and a goat shed is that you don't need a fire in a goat shed, because goats are pretty good at keeping themselves warm. You do need one in a dungeon, however, if you want to keep your prisoners nice and warm, and if you really don't like your prisoners then you'll need a fire to get them nasty and warm. Terminally hot. Granny Aching had told Tiffany once that when she was a girl there had been all kinds of horrible metal things in the dungeon, mostly for taking people apart a little bit at a time, but as it turned out there was never a prisoner bad enough to use them on. And, if it came to that, no one in the castle wanted to use any of the things, which often trapped your fingers if you weren't careful, so they were all sent down to the blacksmith for turning into more sensible things like shovels and knives, except for the Iron Maiden, which had been used as a turnip clamp until the top fell off.

And so, because nobody in the castle had ever been very enthusiastic about the dungeon, everybody had forgotten that it had a chimney. And that is why Tiffany looked up and saw, high above her, that little patch of blue which a prisoner calls the *sky*, but which she, as soon as it was dark enough, intended to call the *exit*.

It turned out to be a little more tricky to use than she had hoped; it was too narrow for her to go up sitting on the stick, so she had to hang onto the bristles and let the broomstick drag her up while she fended herself off the walls with her boots.

At least she knew her way around up there. All the kids did. There probably wasn't a boy growing up in the Chalk who hadn't scratched his name in the lead on the roof, quite probably alongside the names of his father, grandfathers, great-grandfathers and even great-great-grandfathers, until the names got lost in the scratches.

The whole point about a castle is that nobody should get in if you don't want them to, and so there were no windows until you got nearly to the top, where the best rooms were. Roland had long ago moved into his father's room – she knew that because she had helped him move his stuff in when the old Baron had finally accepted that he was too sick to manage the stairs any longer. The Duchess would be in the big guestroom, halfway between that room and the Maiden Tower – which really was its name – where Letitia would be sleeping. No one would draw attention to this, but the arrangement meant that the bride's mother would be sleeping in the room between the groom and the bride, possibly with her ears highly tuned at all times for any sound of hanky or even panky.

Tiffany crept quietly through the gloom and stepped neatly into an alcove when she heard footsteps coming up the stairs. They belonged to a maid, carrying a jug on a tray, which she very nearly spilled when the door to the Duchess's room was flung open and the Duchess herself was glaring at her, just to check nothing was going on. When the maid moved on again, Tiffany followed her, silently and, as she had the trick of it, invisibly too. The guard sitting by the door looked up hopefully when the tray arrived, and was told sharply to go downstairs and get his own supper; then the maid stepped into the room, the tray was placed beside the big bed, and the maid left, wondering for a moment whether her eyes had been playing tricks on her.

Letitia looked as though she was sleeping under freshly fallen snow, and it rather spoiled the effect when you realized that mostly it was screwed-up tissue paper. *Used* tissue paper, at that. It was very rare indeed on the Chalk, because it was quite expensive, and if you had any, it was not considered bad manners to dry it out in front of the fire for re-use later on. Tiffany's father said that when he was a little boy he had to blow his nose on mice, but this was probably said in order to make her squeal.

Right now, Letitia blew her nose with an unladylike honking noise and, to Tiffany's surprise, looked suspiciously around the room. She even said, 'Hello? Is there anybody there?' – a question which, considered sensibly, is never going to get you anywhere.

Tiffany pulled herself further into a shadow. She could sometimes fool Granny Weatherwax on a good day, and a soppy princess had no business sensing her presence.

'I can scream, you know,' said Letitia, looking around. 'There's a guard right outside my door!'

'Actually, he's gone down to get his dinner,' said Tiffany, 'which frankly I call very unprofessional. He should have waited to be relieved by another guard. Personally, I think your mother is more worried about how her guards look than about how they think. Even young Preston guards better than they do. Sometimes people never know he's there until he taps them on the shoulder. Did you know that people very seldom start screaming while someone is still talking to them? I don't know why. I suppose it's because we are brought up to be polite. And if you think you're going to do so now, I would like to point out that if I was planning to do anything nasty I would have done so already, don't you think?'

The pause was rather longer than Tiffany liked. Then Letitia said, 'You have every right to be angry. You *are* angry, aren't you?'

'Not at the moment. By the way, aren't you going to drink your milk before it gets cold?'

'Actually, I always tip it down the privy. I know that it's a wicked waste of good food and that there are a lot of poor children who would love a nightcap of warm milk, but they don't deserve mine because my mother makes the maids put a medicine in it to help me sleep.'

'Why?' said Tiffany incredulously.

'She thinks I need it. I don't, really. You have no idea what it's like. It's like being in prison.'

'Well, I think I know what that's like now,' said Tiffany. The girl in the bed started to cry again, and Tiffany hushed her into silence.

'I didn't mean it to get that bad,' said Letitia, blowing her nose like a hunting horn. 'I just wanted Roland not to like you so much. You can't imagine what it's like, being me! The most I'm allowed to do is paint pictures, and only watercolours at that. Not even charcoal sketches!'

'I wondered about that,' said Tiffany absent-mindedly. 'Roland once used to write to Lord Diver's daughter, Iodine, and *she* used to paint watercolours all the time too. I wondered if it was some kind of punishment.'

But Letitia wasn't listening. '*You* don't have to just sit and paint pictures. You can fly around all the time,' she was saying. 'Order people about, do interesting things. Hah, I wanted to be a witch when I was little. But just my luck, I had long blonde hair and a pale complexion and a very rich father. What good was that? Girls like that can't be witches!'

Tiffany smiled. They were getting to the truth, and it was important to stay helpful and friendly before the dam broke again and they were all flooded. 'Did you have a book of fairy stories when you were young?'

Letitia blew her nose again. 'Oh, yes.'

'Was it the one with a very frightening picture of the goblin on page seven by any chance? I used to shut my eyes when I came to that page.'

'I scribbled all over him with a black crayon,' said Letitia in a low voice, as if it was a relief to tell somebody.

'You didn't like me. And so you decided to do some magic against me ...' Tiffany said it very quietly, because there was something brittle about Letitia. In fact the girl did reach for some more tissue but appeared to have run out of sobs for a moment – as it turned out, only for a moment.

'I am *so* sorry! If only I had known, I would never have—'

'Perhaps I should tell you,' Tiffany went on, 'that Roland and I were ... well, friends. More or less the only friend the other one had. But in a way, it was the wrong kind of friendship. We didn't come together; things happened that pushed us together. And we didn't realize that. He was the Baron's son, and once you know that you're the Baron's son and all the kids have been told how to act towards the Baron's son, then you don't have many people you can talk to. And then there was me. I was the girl smart enough to be a witch and I have to say that this is not a job which allows you to have that much of a social life. If you like, two people who were left out thought they were the same kind of person. I know that now. Unfortunately Roland was the first to realize that. And that's the truth of it. I am the witch, and he is the Baron. And you will be the Baroness, and you should not worry if the witch and the Baron – for the benefit of everybody – are on good terms. And that is all there is to it, and in fact there isn't even an it, just the ghost of an it.'

She saw relief travel across Letitia's face like the rising sun.

'And that's the truth from me, miss, so I would like the truth from you. Look, can we get out of here? I'm afraid that some guards might rush in at any moment and try and put me in a place I can't get out of.'

Tiffany managed to get Letitia onto the broomstick with her. The girl fidgeted, but simply gasped as the stick sailed down gently from the castle battlements, drifted over the village and touched down in a field.

'Did you see those bats?' said Letitia.

'Oh, they often fly around the stick if you don't move very fast,' said Tiffany. 'You'd think they would avoid it, really. And now, miss, now we're both far from any help, tell me what you did that made people hate me.'

Panic filled Letitia's face.

'No, I'm not going to hurt you,' said Tiffany. 'If I was going to, I would have done it a long time ago. But I want to clean up my life. Tell me what you did.'

'I used the ostrich trick,' said Letitia promptly. 'You know, it's called unsympathetic magic: you make a model of the person and stick them upside down in a bucket of sand. I really am very, very sorry . . .'

'Yes, you already said so,' said Tiffany, 'but I've never heard of this trick. I can't see how it could work. It doesn't make sense.'

But it worked on me, she thought. This girl isn't a witch, and whatever she tried wasn't a real spell, but it worked on me.

'It doesn't have to make sense if it's magic,' said Letitia hopefully.

'It has to make some sense somewhere,' said Tiffany, staring up at the stars that were coming out.

'Well,' said Letitia, 'I got it out of *Spells for Lovers* by Anathema Bugloss, if that's any help.'

'That's the one with the picture of the author sitting on a broomstick, isn't it?' said Tiffany. 'Sitting on it the wrong way round, I might add. And it hasn't got a safety strap. And no witch I've ever met wears goggles. And as for having a cat on it with you, that doesn't bear thinking about. It's a made-up name too. I've seen the book in the Boffo catalogue. It's rubbish. It's for soppy girls who think all you need to do to make magic is buy a very expensive stick with a semiprecious stone glued on the end, no offence meant. You might as well pick a stick out of the hedge and call it a wand.'

Without saying anything, Letitia walked a little way down to the hedge that lay between the field and the road. There's always a useful stick under a hedge if you poke around enough. She waved it vaguely in the air, and it left a light blue line after it.

'Like this?' she said. For quite a while, there was no sound apart from the occasional hoot of an owl and, for the really good of hearing, the rustling of the bats.

'I think it's time we had a *proper* little chat, don't you?' said Tiffany.

# CHAPTER 11

# The Bonfire of the Witches

'I told you I always wanted to be a witch,' said Letitia. 'You don't know how hard that can be when your family lives in a great big mansion and is so old that the coat of arms has even got a few legs on it as well. All that gets in the way and, if you excuse me, I really wish that I had been born with your disadvantages. I only found out about the Boffo catalogue when I heard two of the maids giggling over it when I went into the kitchen one day. They ran away, still giggling, I might add, but they left it behind. I can't order as much stuff as I would want to, because my maid spies on me and tells Mother. But the cook is a decent sort, so I give her money and the catalogue numbers and they get delivered to her sister in Ham-on-Rye. I can't order anything very big, though, because

289

the maids are always dusting and cleaning everywhere. I would really like one of the cauldrons that bubble green, but from what you tell me it's just a joke.'

Letitia had taken a couple of other sticks from the hedge and stuck them in the ground in front of her. There was a blue glow on the tip of each one.

'Well, for everybody else it's a joke,' Tiffany said, 'but for you I expect it would produce fried chickens.'

'Do you really think so?' said Letitia eagerly.

'I'm not sure I can think at all if I am upside down with my head in a bucket of sand,' said Tiffany. 'You know that sounds a bit like wizard magic. This trick . . . it was in Mistress Bugloss's book, you say. Look, I'm sorry, but that really is boffo stuff. It's not real. It's just for people who think that witchcraft is all about flowers and love potions and dancing around without your drawers on – something I can't imagine any real witch doing . . .' Tiffany hesitated, because she was naturally honest, and went on, 'Well, maybe Nanny Ogg, when the mood takes her. It's witchcraft with all the crusts cut off, and real witchcraft is *all* crusts. But you took one of her silly spells for giggling housemaids and used it on me and it's worked! Is there a real witch in your family?'

Letitia shook her head and her long blonde hair sparkled even in the moonlight. 'I've never heard of one. My grandfather was an alchemist – not professionally, of course. He was the reason why the hall has no east wing any more. My mother . . . I can't imagine her doing magic, can you?'

'Her? Absolutely!'

'Well, I've never seen her do any and she does mean well. She says that all she wants is the best for me. She lost all her family in a fire, don't you know. Lost everything,' said Letitia.

Tiffany couldn't dislike the girl. It would be like disliking a rather baffled puppy, but she couldn't help saying, 'And did you mean well? You know, when you made a model of me and put it upside down in a bucket of sand?'

There must have been reservoirs in Letitia. She was never more than a teacup away from a tear.

'Look,' Tiffany said, 'I don't mind, honestly. Though frankly I wish I believed that it was just a spell! Just take it out again then, and we can forget all about it. Please don't start crying again, it makes everything so soggy.'

Letitia sniffed. 'Oh, it's just that, well, I didn't do it here. I left it at home. It's in the library.'

The last word in that sentence tinkled in Tiffany's head. 'A library? With books?' Witches were not supposed to be particularly bothered about books, but Tiffany had read every one she could. You never knew what you could get out of a book. 'It's a very warm night for the time of year,' she said, 'and your place is not too far, is it? You could be back in the tower and in bed in a couple of hours.'

For the first time since Tiffany had met her, Letitia smiled, genuinely smiled. 'Can I go on the front this time then?' she said.

\* \* \*

Tiffany flew low over the downs.

The moon was well on the way to full, and it was a real harvest moon, the copper colour of blood. That was the smoke from the stubble-burning, hanging in the air. How the blue smoke from burning wheat stalks made the moon go red, she didn't know, and she wasn't going to fly all that way to find out.

And Letitia seemed to be in some kind of personal heaven. She chattered the whole time, which was admittedly better than the sobbing. The girl was only eight days younger than herself. Tiffany knew that, because she had taken great care to find out. But that was just numbers. It didn't *feel* like that. In fact she felt old enough to be the girl's mother. It was strange, but Petulia and Annagramma and the rest of them back in the mountains had all told her the same thing: witches grew old inside. You had to do things that needed doing but which turned your stomach like a spinning wheel. You saw things sometimes that no one should have to see. And, usually alone and often in darkness, you needed to do the things that had to be done. Out in distant villages, when a new mother was giving birth and things had run into serious trouble, you hoped that there was an old local midwife who might at least give you some moral support; but still, when it came down to it and the life-or-death decision had to be made, then it was made by you, because you were the witch. And sometimes it wasn't a decision between a good thing and a bad thing, but a decision between two bad things: no right choices, just . . . choices.

And now she saw something speeding over the moonlit turf and easily keeping up with the stick. It kept pace for several minutes and then, with a spinning jump, headed back into the moonlight shadows.

*The hare runs into the fire,* Tiffany thought, and I have a feeling that I do too.

Keepsake Hall was at the far end of the Chalk, and it was *truly* the far end of the Chalk because there the chalk gave way to clay and gravel. There was parkland here, and tall trees – forests of them – and fountains in front of the house itself, which stretched the word 'hall' to breaking point, since it looked like half a dozen mansions stuck together. There were outbuildings, wings, a large ornamental lake, and a weathervane in the shape of a heron, which Tiffany nearly ran into. 'How many people live here?' she managed to say as she steadied the stick and landed on what she had expected to be a lawn but turned out to be dried grass almost five feet deep. Rabbits scattered, alarmed at the aerial intrusion.

'Just me and Mother now,' said Letitia, the dead grass crackling under her feet as she jumped down, 'and the servants, of course. We have quite a lot of them. Don't worry, they will all be in bed by now.'

'How many servants do you need for two people?' Tiffany asked.

'About two hundred and fifty.'

'I don't believe you.'

Letitia turned as she led the way to a distant door. 'Well, including families, there's about forty on the farm and another twenty in the dairy, and another twenty-four for working in the woodlands, and seventy-five for the gardens, which include the banana house, the pineapple pit, the melon house, the water-lily house and the trout fishery. The rest work in the house and the pension rooms.'

'What are they?'

Letitia stopped with her hand on the corroded brass doorknob. 'You think my mother is a very rude and bossy person, don't you?'

Tiffany couldn't see any alternative to telling the truth, even at the risk of midnight tears. She said, 'Yes, I do.'

'And you are right,' said Letitia, turning the door-knob. 'But she is loyal to people who are loyal to us. We always have been. No one is ever sacked for being too old or too ill or too confused. If they can't manage in their cottages, they live in one of the wings. In fact, most of the servants are looking after the old servants! We may be old-fashioned and a bit snobbish and behind the times, but no one who works for the Keepsakes will ever need to beg for their food at the end of their life.'

At last the cranky doorknob turned, opening into a long corridor that smelled of . . . that smelled of . . . that smelled of *old*. That was the only way to describe it, but if you had enough time to think, you would say it was a mix of dry fungi, damp wood, dust, mice, dead time and old books, which have an intriguing smell of their own. That was it, Tiffany decided. Days and hours had died quietly in here while nobody noticed.

Letitia fumbled on a shelf inside the door, and lit a

lamp. 'No one ever comes in here these days except me,' she said, 'because it's haunted.'

'Yes,' said Tiffany, trying to keep her voice matter-of-fact. 'By a headless lady with a pumpkin under her arm. She is walking towards us right now.'

Had she expected shock? Or tears? Tiffany certainly hadn't expected Letitia to say, 'That would be Mavis. I shall have to change her pumpkin as soon as the new ones are ripe. They start to get all, well, manky after a while.' She raised her voice. 'It's only me, Mavis, nothing to be frightened of!'

With a sound like a sigh, the headless woman turned and began to walk back up the corridor.

'The pumpkin was my idea,' Letitia continued chattily. 'She was just impossible to deal with before that. Looking for her head, you know? The pumpkin gives her some comfort, and frankly I don't think she knows the difference, poor soul. She wasn't executed, by the way. I think she wants everybody to know that. It was simply a freak accident involving a flight of stairs, a cat and a scythe.'

And this is the girl who spends all her time in tears, thought Tiffany. But this is *her* place. Aloud, she said, 'Any more ghosts to show me, just in case I want to wet myself again?'

'Well, not now,' said Letitia, setting off along the corridor. 'The screaming skeleton stopped screaming when I gave him an old teddy bear, although I'm not certain why that worked and, oh yes, the ghost of the first duke now sticks to haunting the lavatory next to the dining room, which we don't use very often. He has a habit of pulling the chain at inconvenient moments, but that's better than the rains of blood we used to have.'

'You are a witch.' The words came out of Tiffany's mouth all by themselves, unable to stay in the privacy of her mind.

The girl looked at her in astonishment. 'Don't be silly,' she said. 'We both know how it goes, don't we? Long blonde hair, milk-white skin, noble – well, a reasonably noble birth – and rich, at least technically. I'm officially a lady.'

'You know,' said Tiffany, 'maybe it's wrong to base one's future on a book of fairy stories. Normally, girls of the princess persuasion don't help out distressed headless ghosts by giving them a pumpkin to carry. As for stopping the screaming skeleton screaming by giving it a teddy bear, I have to say I am impressed. That is what Granny Weatherwax calls headology. Most of the craft is headology, when you get right down to it: headology and boffo.'

Letitia looked flustered and gratified at the same time, making her face blotch white and pink. It was, Tiffany had to agree, the kind of face that peered out of tower windows, waiting for a knight with nothing better to do with his time than save its owner from dragons, monsters and, if all else failed, boredom.

'You don't have to do anything *about* it,' Tiffany added. 'The pointy hat is optional. But if Miss Tick was here, she would definitely suggest a career. It is not good to be a witch alone.'

They had reached the end of the corridor. Letitia turned another creaky doorknob, which complained as the door opened, and so did the door. 'I've certainly found that out,' said Letitia. 'And Miss Tick is . . . ?'

'She travels around the country finding girls who have the talent for the craft,' said Tiffany. 'They say that you don't find witchcraft, it finds you, and generally it's Miss Tick who taps you on the shoulder. She's a witchfinder, but I don't suppose she goes into many big houses. They make witches nervous. Oh my!' And this was because Letitia had lit an oil lamp. The room was full of bookcases, and the books on them gleamed. These weren't cheap modern books; these were books bound in leather, and not just leather, but leather from clever cows who had given their lives for literature after a happy existence in the very best pastures. The books gleamed as Letitia moved around the large room lighting other lamps. She hauled them up towards the ceiling on their long chains, which swung gently as she pulled so that the shine from the books mixed with the gleam from the brasswork until the room seemed to be full of rich, ripe gold.

Letitia was clearly pleased by the way Tiffany stood and stared. 'My great-grandfather was a huge collector,' she said. 'Do you see all the polished brass? That's not for show, that's for the point-three-0-three bookworm, which can move so fast that it can bore a hole all the way through an entire shelf of books in a fraction of a second. Hah, but not when they run into solid brass at the speed of sound! The library used to be bigger, but my uncle Charlie ran away with all the books on . . . I think it was called erotica? I'm not sure, but I can't find it on any map. I may be the only one who comes in here now, anyway. Mother thinks that reading makes people restless. Pardon me, but why are you sniffing? I hope another mouse hasn't died in here.'

There is something very wrong about this place, thought Tiffany. Something . . . strained . . . straining. Maybe it's all the knowledge in the books, just bursting to get out. She had heard talk of the library at Unseen University – of the soulful books all pressed together in space and time so that at night, it was said, they spoke to one another and a kind of lightning flashed from book to book. Too many books in one place, who knew what they could do? Miss Tick had told her one day: 'Knowledge is power, power is energy, energy is matter, matter is mass, and mass changes time and space.' But Letitia looked so happy among the shelves and desks that Tiffany hadn't got the heart to object.

The girl beckoned her over. 'And this is where I do my little bits of magic,' she said, as if she was telling Tiffany this was where she played with her dollies.

Tiffany was sweating now; all the little hairs on her skin were trembling, a signal to herself that she should turn and run, but Letitia was chattering away, quite oblivious to the fact that Tiffany was trying not to throw up.

His stink was terrible. It rose in the cheery library like

a long-dead whale rising again to the surface, full of gas and corruption.

Tiffany looked around desperately for something to take her mind off that image. Mrs Proust and Derek had certainly benefited from Letitia Keepsake. She had bought the whole range, warts and all.

'But I only use warts at the moment. I think they have the right *feel*, without going overboard, don't you?' she was saying.

'I've never bothered with them,' said Tiffany weakly.

Letitia sniffed. 'Oh dear, I am so sorry about the smell; it's the mice, I think. They eat the glue out of the books, although I'd say that they must have found a particularly unpleasant book.'

The library was really beginning to upset Tiffany. It was like, well, waking up and finding a family of tigers had wandered in during the night and were fast asleep on the end of the bed: everything was peaceful at the moment, but at any minute now, somebody was going to lose an arm. There was the Boffo stuff, which was sort of witchcraft-for-show. It impressed people, and maybe helped a novice get into the mood, but surely Mrs Proust wasn't sending out stuff that actually *worked*, was she?

There was a clank of a bucket handle behind her as Letitia came round a bookcase, holding the bucket in both hands. Sand tipped out of it as she dropped it on the floor and she scrabbled in it for a moment. 'Ah, there you are,' she said, pulling out something that looked like a carrot which had been chewed by a mouse that wasn't really very hungry.

'Is that supposed to be me?' said Tiffany.

'I'm afraid I'm not very good at woodcarving,' said Letitia, 'but the book says it's what you're thinking that counts?' It was a nervous statement with a wiry little question clinging to the end of it, waiting to burst into tears.

'Sorry,' said Tiffany. 'The book has got that wrong. It's not as nice as that. It's what you *do* that counts. If you want to put a hex on someone, you need something that has belonged to them – hair, a tooth maybe? And you shouldn't mess about with it, because it's not nice and it's very easy to get wrong.' She looked closely at the very badly carved witch. 'And I see you've written the word "witch" on it in pencil. Er . . . you know I said it's easy to get it wrong? Well, there are times when "getting it wrong" just doesn't cover messing up somebody else's life.'

Her lower lip trembling, Letitia nodded.

The pressure on Tiffany's head was getting worse and the horrible stench was now so powerful that it felt like a physical thing. She tried to concentrate on the little pile of books on the library table. They were sad little volumes, of the sort that Nanny Ogg, who could be uncharacteristically scathing when she felt like it, called 'Tiddly Twinkle-Poo' for girls who played at being witches for fun.

But at least Letitia had been thorough; there were a couple of notebooks on the lectern which dominated the table. Tiffany turned to say something to the girl, but somehow her head did not *want* to stay turned. Her

Second Sight was dragging it back. And her hand rose slowly, almost automatically, and moved aside the little pile of silly books. What she had thought was the top of the lectern was in fact a much larger book, so thick and dark it seemed to merge with the wood itself. Dread trickled into her brain like black syrup, telling her to run and ... No, that was all. Just run, and go on running, and not stop. Ever.

She tried to keep her voice level. 'Do you know anything about *this* book?'

Letitia looked over her shoulder. 'It's very ancient. I don't even recognize the writing. Wonderful binding, though, and the funny thing is, it's always slightly warm.'

Here and now, thought Tiffany, it's facing me here and now. Eskarina said that there was a book of his. Could this possibly be a copy? But a book can't hurt, can it? Except that books contain ideas, and ideas can be dangerous.

At this point, the book on the lectern opened itself with a leathery creak and a little *flap* noise as the cover turned over. The pages rustled like a lot of pigeons taking flight, and then there it was, one page filling the midnight room with brilliant, eye-watering sunlight. And in that sunlight, running towards her, across the scorching desert, was a figure in black ...

Automatically, Tiffany slammed the book shut and held it shut in both hands, clutching it like a schoolgirl. He saw me, she thought. I know he did. The book jumped in her arms as something heavy hit it, and she could hear . . . words, words she was glad she couldn't understand. Another blow struck the book, and the cover bulged, nearly knocking her over. When the next thump came, she fell forward, landing with the cover under her and all her weight on the book.

Fire, she thought. He hates fire! But I don't think I could carry this very far and, well, you don't set fire to libraries, you just don't. And besides, this whole place is as dry as a bone.

'Is something trying to get out of the book?' said Letitia.

Tiffany looked up at her pink and white face. 'Yes,' she managed, and slammed the book down on the table as it jumped again in her arms.

'It's not going to be like that goblin in the fairytale book, is it? I was always so scared that it would squeeze itself out between the pages.'

The book sprang up into the air and slammed back down again on the table, knocking the wind out of Tiffany. She managed to grunt, 'I think this is a lot worse than the goblin!' Which was *our* goblin, she remembered inconveniently. They'd had the same book, after all. It wasn't a good book in many respects, but then you grow up and it's just a silly picture, but part of you never forgets.

It seemed to be something that happened to everybody. When she had mentioned to Petulia about being frightened by a picture in a book, the girl confessed that she had been hugely frightened by a happy-looking skeleton in a picture book when she was young. And it turned out all the other girls remembered something like that too. It was as if it was a fact of life. A book would start out by scaring you.

'I think I know what to do,' said Letitia. 'Can you keep it occupied for a while? I won't be a moment.' And with that she disappeared from view, and after a few seconds Tiffany, still straining to keep the book closed, heard a squeaking noise. She did not take much notice, because her arms, clinging tightly to the bouncing book, felt red-hot. Then, behind her, Letitia said quietly, 'Look, I'm going to guide you to the book press. When I say so, push the book in and get your hands out of the way really, really quickly. It is quite important that you do it quickly!'

Tiffany felt the girl help her turn, and together they edged along to something metallic waiting in the gloom, while all the time the book rocked with anger and thumped on her chest; it was like holding an elephant's heart while it was still beating.

She hardly heard Letitia's voice above the pounding as she shouted, 'Put the book down on the metal plate, push it a little way forward and get your fingers out of the way – right *now*!'

Something spun. In one pants-wetting moment Tiffany saw a hand thrust its way through the book's cover before a metal plate slammed down on it, clipping the ends of Tiffany's fingernails.

'Help me with this bar, will you? Let's tighten it down as far as we can.' That was from Letitia, who was leaning on . . . what? 'It's the old book press,' she said. 'My grandfather used to use it all the time when he was tidying up old books that got damaged. It helps when you have to glue a page back in, for example. We hardly use it except at Hogswatch. Very good for the precision cracking of walnuts, you see? Just wind the handle until you hear them start to crack. They look like tiny little human brains.'

Tiffany risked a look at the press, the top and bottom plates of which were now pressed tightly together, to see if any human brains were dripping down the outside. They weren't, but it didn't help very much at this point, as a small human skeleton walked out of the wall, through the library shelves as though they were smoke, and disappeared. It had been holding a teddy bear. It was one of those things that the brain files under 'something I would rather not have seen'.

'Was that some kind of ghost?' said Letitia. 'Not the skeleton – I told you about him, didn't I? Poor little thing. I mean, the other one. The one in the book . . .'

'He is, well, I suppose you could say that he is something like a disease, and also something like a nightmare that turns out to be standing in your bedroom when you wake up. And I think you may have called him. Summoned him, if you like.'

'I don't like either of those! All I did was a simple little spell out of a book that cost one dollar! All right, I know I must've been a silly girl, but I didn't mean anything like . . . that!' She pointed to the press, which was still creaking.

'Stupid woman,' said Tiffany.

Letitia blinked. '*What* did you say?'

'Stupid woman! Or silly woman, if you prefer. You're going to get married in a few days, remember? And you tried to do a spell on somebody out of jealousy. Did you see the *title* of that book? I did. It was right in front of me! It was *The Bonfire of the Witches!* It was dictated by an Omnian priest who was so mad that he wouldn't have been able to see sanity with a telescope. And you know what? Books live. The pages remember! Have you heard about the library at the Unseen University? They have books in there that have to be chained down, or kept in darkness or even under water! And you, miss, played at magic a matter of inches away from a book that boils with evil, vindictive magic. No wonder you got a result! I woke him up and ever since then he's been searching, *hunting* me. And you – with your little spell – have shown him where I was! You helped him! He's come back, and he's *found* me now! The witch-burner. And he is infectious, just as I told you, a kind of disease.'

She paused for breath, which came, and the torrent of tears, which didn't. Letitia just stood there as if she was thinking deeply. Then she said, 'I suppose that "sorry" isn't enough, right?'

'As a matter of fact, it would be rather a good start,' said Tiffany, but she thought: This young woman, who has never realized it's time to stop wearing girly dresses, gave a headless ghost a pumpkin to carry under its arm so that it would feel better and presented a screaming little skeleton with a teddy bear. Would I have thought to do that? It's absolutely something that a witch would do.

'Look,' she said, 'you have definitely got some magical talent, I really mean it. But you'll get into a terrible amount of trouble if you start mucking about when you don't know what you are doing. Although giving the teddy bear to the poor little skeleton was a stroke of genius. Build on that thought and get some training, and you might have quite a magical future. You will have to go and spend some time with an old witch, just like I did.'

'Well, that's wonderful, Tiffany,' Letitia said. 'But I have to go and spend some time getting married! Shall we get back now? And what do you suggest we do with the book? I don't like the idea of him being in there. Supposing he gets out!'

'He *is* out, already. But the book is . . . well, a kind of window that makes it easy for him to come through. To reach me. You get that sort of thing occasionally. It's a sort of way into another world, or perhaps somewhere else in this world.'

Tiffany had felt rather lofty when she explained this, and so was somewhat chastened when Letitia said, 'Oh yes, the bluebell wood with the cottage that sometimes has smoke coming out of the chimney and sometimes does not; and the girl feeding the ducks on the pond, where the pigeons on the house behind her are sometimes flying and sometimes perched. They are mentioned in H.J. Toadbinder's book *Floating Worlds*. Would you like it? I know where it is.' And before Tiffany could say a word, the girl hurried off among the bookshelves. She came back within a minute, much to

Tiffany's relief, and she was carrying a large, shiny leather volume which was suddenly dropped into Tiffany's hands.

'It's a present. You've been kinder to me than I was to you.'

'You can't give me that! It's part of the library! It'll leave a gap!'

'No, I insist,' said Letitia. 'I'm the only one who comes in here now, in any case. My mother keeps all the books of family history, genealogy and heraldry in her own room, and she's the only one who is interested in them. Apart from me, the only other person who ever comes in here these days is Mr Tyler, and I think I hear him now, making his last round of the night. Well,' she added, 'he's very old and very slow and it takes him about a week to go about his night watching, bearing in mind he sleeps through the day. Let's go. He'll have a heart attack if he actually finds anybody.'

There was indeed a creaking sound of a distant doorknob.

Letitia lowered her voice. 'Do you mind if we sneak out the other way? He really might have a nasty turn.'

A light was coming down the long corridor, although you needed to watch it for quite some time to see that it was moving. Letitia opened the door to the outer world and they hurried onto what would have been the lawn if anyone had mown it in the past ten years. Tiffany got the impression that lawn mowing here went at the same decrepit speed as Mr Tyler. There was dew on the grass, and a certain sense that daylight was a distinct possibility sometime in the future. As soon as they reached the broomstick, Letitia made yet another muttered apology and hurried back into the sleeping house via another door, coming out again five minutes later carrying a large bag. 'My mourning clothes,' she said as the broomstick rose into the soft air. 'It will be the old Baron's funeral tomorrow, the poor man. My mother always travels with her funeral clothes. She says you never know when someone is going to drop down dead.'

'That is a very interesting point of view, Letitia, but when you get back to the castle I would like you to tell Roland what you did, please. I don't care about anything else, but please tell him about the spell you did.' Tiffany waited. Letitia was sitting behind her and, right now, silent. Very silent. So much silence that you could hear it.

Tiffany spent the time looking at the landscape as it wound past. Here and there smoke rose from kitchen fires, even though the sun was still below the horizon. Generally speaking, women in the villages raced to be the first to show smoke; it proved you were a busy housewife. She sighed. The thing about the broomstick was that when you rode it you looked down on people. You couldn't help it, however much you tried. Human beings seemed to be nothing but a lot of scurrying dots. And when you started thinking like that, it was time you found the company of some other witches, to get your head straight. *You shall not be a witch alone*, the saying went. It wasn't so much advice as a demand.

Behind her, Letitia said, in a voice that sounded as though she had weighed out every word very carefully before deciding to speak, 'Why aren't you angrier with me?'

'What do you mean?'

'You know! After what I did! You are just being dreadfully . . . nice!'

Tiffany was glad the girl couldn't see her face and for that matter, she couldn't see hers.

'Witches don't often get angry. All that shouting business never really gets anybody anywhere.'

After another pause Letitia said, 'If that is true, then maybe I'm not cut out to be a witch. I feel very angry sometimes.'

'Oh, I *feel* very angry a lot of the time,' said Tiffany, 'but I just put it away somewhere until I can do something useful with it. That's the thing about witchcraft – and wizardry, come to that. We don't do much magic at the best of times, and when we do, we generally do it on ourselves. Now, look, the castle's right ahead. I'll drop you off on the roof, and frankly I'm looking forward to seeing how comfortable the straw is going to be.'

'Look, I really am very, very—'

'I know. You said. There's no hard feelings, but you have to clear up your own mess. That's another part of witchcraft, that is.' And she added to herself: And don't I know it!

# CHAPTER 12

# The Sin o' Sins

The straw turned out to be comfortable enough; little cottages usually do not have spare rooms, so a witch there on business, such as the birthing of a child, was lucky to get a bed in the cowshed. Very lucky, in fact. It often smelled better, and Tiffany wasn't alone in thinking that the breath of a cow, warm and smelling of grass, was a kind of medicine in itself.

The goats in the dungeon were nearly as good, though. They sat placidly chewing their supper over and over again, while never taking their solemn gaze off her, as if they expected her to start juggling or doing some kind of song-and-dance act.

Her last thought before falling asleep was that somebody must have given them the feed, and must therefore have noticed that the dungeon was minus one prisoner.

In that case, she was in more trouble, but it was hard to see how much more trouble she could be in. Possibly not that much, it seemed, because when she woke again, just an hour or so later, somebody had put a cover over her while she was asleep. What was happening?

She found out when Preston appeared with a tray of eggs and bacon, the eggs and bacon being slightly coffee-flavoured on account of slopping on their way down the long stone staircase. 'His lordship says it is with his compliments and apologies,' said Preston, grinning, 'and I'm to tell you that if you would like it, he could arrange for a hot bath to be waiting for you in the black-and-white chamber. And when you're ready, the Baron . . . the *new* Baron would like to see you in his study.'

The idea of a bath sounded wonderful, but Tiffany knew that there just wouldn't be any time, and besides, even a halfway useful bath meant that some poor girls had to drag a load of heavy buckets up four or five flights of stone stairs. She would have to make do with a quick swill out of a wash basin when the opportunity arose.* But she was certainly ready for the bacon and eggs. She made a mental note, as she wiped the plate, that if this was going to be a 'be nice to Tiffany day', she might try for another helping later on.

Witches liked to make the most of gratitude while it

---

* Witches always made certain that their hands were scrupulously clean; the rest of the witch had to wait for some time in the busy schedule – or possibly for a thunderstorm.

was still warm. People tended to become a little bit forgetful after a day or so. Preston watched with the expression of a boy who had eaten salt porridge for breakfast, and when she had finished said, carefully, 'And now will you go and see the Baron?'

He is concerned for me, Tiffany thought. 'First, I'd like to go and see the *old* Baron,' she said.

'He's still dead,' Preston volunteered, looking worried.

'Well, that's some comfort anyway,' said Tiffany. 'Imagine the embarrassment otherwise.' She smiled at Preston's puzzlement. 'And his funeral is tomorrow and that's why I should see him today, Preston, and right now. Please? Right now, he is more important than his son.'

Tiffany felt people's eyes on her as she strode towards the crypt with Preston almost running to keep up and clattering down the long steps after her. She felt a bit sorry for him, because he had always been kind and respectful, but no one was to think that she was being *led* anywhere by a guard. There had been enough of that. The looks that people gave her seemed rather more frightened than angry, and she didn't know if this was a good sign or not.

At the bottom of the steps she took a deep breath. There was just the usual smell of the crypt, chilly with a hint of potatoes. She smiled a little smile of self-congratulation. And there was the Baron, lying peacefully just as she had left him, with his hands crossed on his chest, looking for all the world as though he was sleeping.

'They thought I was doing witchcraft down here, didn't they, Preston?' she said.

'There was some gossip, yes, miss.'

'Well, I was. Your granny taught you about the care of the dead, right? So you know it's not right for the dead to be too long in the land of the living. The weather is warm, and the summer has been hot, and the stones that could be as chilly as the grave are not as chilly as all that. So, Preston, go and get me two pails of water, please.' She sat quietly by the side of the slab as he scurried away.

Earth and salt and two coins for the ferryman, those were the things that you gave to the dead, and you watched and listened like the mother of a newborn baby . . .

Preston came back, carrying two large pails with – she was pleased to see – only a limited amount of slopping. He put them down quickly and turned to go.

'No, stay here, Preston,' she commanded. 'I want you to see what I do, so that if anyone asks, you can tell them the truth.'

The guard nodded mutely. She was impressed. She placed one of the buckets beside the slab and knelt down by it, put one hand in the chilly bucket, pressed the other hand against the stone of the slab and whispered to herself, 'Balance is everything.'

Anger helped. It was amazing how useful it could be, if you saved it up until it could do some good, just as she had told Letitia. She heard the young guard gasp as the water in the bucket began to steam, and then to bubble.

He jumped to his feet. 'I understand, miss! I'll take the boiling bucket away and bring you another cold one, yes?'

Three buckets of boiling water had been tipped away by the time the air in the crypt once again had the chill of the midwinter. Tiffany walked up the steps with her teeth very nearly chattering. 'My granny would have loved to be able to do something like that,' Preston whispered. 'She always said the dead don't like the heat. You put cold into the stone, right?'

'Actually, I moved heat out of the slab and the air and put it in the bucket of water,' said Tiffany. 'It's not exactly magic. It's just a . . . a skill. You just have to be a witch to do it, that's all.'

Preston sighed. 'I cured my granny's chickens of fowl crop. I had to cut them open to clean up the mess, and then I sewed them up again. Not one of them died. And then when my mum's dog got run over by a wagon, I cleaned him up, pushed all the bits back and he ended up right as rain except for the leg I couldn't save, but I carved him a wooden one, with a leather harness and everything, and he still chases wagons!'

Tiffany tried not to look doubtful. 'Cutting into chickens to cure fowl crop hardly ever works,' she said. 'I know a pig witch who treats chickens when necessary, and she said it never worked for her.'

'Ah, but maybe she didn't have the knowin' of twister root,' said Preston cheerfully. 'If you mix the juice with a little pennyroyal, they heal really well. My granny had the knowing of the roots and she passed it on to me.'

'Well,' said Tiffany, 'if you can sew up a chicken's gizzard then you could mend a broken heart. Listen, Preston, why don't you get yourself apprenticed to be a doctor?'

They had reached the door to the Baron's study. Preston knocked on it and then opened it for Tiffany. 'It's them letters you get to put after your name,' he whispered. 'They are *very* expensive letters! It might not cost money to become a witch, miss, but when you need them letters, oh, don't you need that money!'

Roland was standing facing the door when Tiffany stepped in, and his mouth was full of spill words, tumbling over themselves not to be said. He *did* manage to say, 'Er, Miss Aching . . . I mean, Tiffany, my fiancée assures me that we are all the victim of a magical plot aimed at your good self. I do hope you will forgive any misunderstanding on our part, and I trust that we have not inconvenienced you too much, and may I add that I take some heart from the fact that you were clearly able to escape from our little dungeon. Er . . .'

Tiffany wanted to shout, 'Roland, do you remember that we first met when I was four years old and you were seven, running around in the dust with only our vests on? I liked you better when you didn't talk like some old lawyer with a broomstick stuck up his bum. You sound as if you are addressing a public meeting.' But instead, she said, 'Did Letitia tell you everything?'

Roland looked sheepish. 'I rather suspect that she did not, Tiffany, but she was very forthright. I may go so far as to say that she was emphatic.' Tiffany tried not to smile. He looked like a man who was beginning to understand some of the facts of married life. He cleared his throat. 'She tells me that we have been a victim of some kind of magical disease, which is currently trapped inside a book in Keepsake Hall?' It certainly sounded like a question, and she wasn't surprised he was puzzled.

'Yes, that's true.'

'And . . . apparently, everything is all right now she has taken your head out of a bucket of sand.' He looked truly lost at this point, and Tiffany didn't blame him.

'I think things may have got a bit garbled,' she said diplomatically.

'And she tells me she is going to be a witch.' He looked a little miserable at this point. Tiffany felt sorry for him, but not very much.

'Well, I think she's got the basic talent. It's up to her how much further she wants to take it.'

'I don't know what her mother will say.'

Tiffany burst out laughing. 'Well, you can tell the Duchess that Queen Magrat of Lancre is a witch. It's no secret. Obviously the queening has to come first, but she is one of the best there is when it comes to potions.'

'*Really?*' said Roland. 'The King and Queen of Lancre have graciously accepted an invitation to our wedding.' And Tiffany was sure she could see his mind working. In this strange chess game that was nobility, a real live queen beat just about everybody, which meant that the Duchess would have to curtsy until her knees clicked. She saw the spill words: *That would of course be very unfortunate.* Amazingly, Roland could be careful even with his spill words. However, he couldn't stop the little grin.

'Your father gave me fifteen Ankh-Morpork dollars in real gold. It was a gift. Do you believe me?'

He saw the look in her eye, and said, 'Yes!' immediately.

'Good,' said Tiffany. 'Then find out where the nurse went.'

Some small part of broomstick might still have been in Roland's bum when he said, 'Do you think my father understood the full worth of what he was giving you?'

'His mind was as clear as water up until the end, you know that. You can trust him, just as you can trust me, and you can trust me now when I say to you that *I will marry you.*'

Her hand clamped itself over her mouth just too late. Where had *that* come from? And he looked as shocked as she felt.

He spoke first, loudly and firmly to drive away the silence. 'I didn't quite hear what you just said, Tiffany . . . I expect all your hard work in recent days has over-whelmed your sensibilities in some way. I think we would all be a lot happier if we knew that you are having a good rest. I . . . love Letitia, you know. She is not very, well, complicated, but I would do anything for her. When she is happy, that makes me happy. And generally speaking, I am not very good at happy.' She saw a tear trickle down his face and, unable to stop herself, handed him a reasonably clean handkerchief. He took it and tried to blow his nose, laugh and cry all at the same time. 'And you, Tiffany, I am very fond of, really fond of . . . but it's as if you have a handkerchief for the whole world. You *are* smart. No, don't shake your head. You are smart. I remember once, when we were younger, you were fascinated by the word "onomatopoeia". Like making a name or a word from a sound, like cuckoo or hum or . . . ?'

'Jangle?' said Tiffany, before she could stop herself.

'That's right, and I remember that you said "humdrum" was the sound that boredom made, because it sounded like a very tired fly buzzing at the closed window of an old attic room on a boiling hot summer's day. And I thought, I couldn't understand that! It makes no sense to me, and I know you are clever and it makes sense to you. I think you need a special kind of head to think like that. And a special kind of clever. And I haven't got that kind of head.'

'What sound does kindness make?' said Tiffany.

'I know what kindness *is*, but I can't imagine it making a noise. There you go again! I just don't have the head that lives in a world where kindness has its own sound. I have a head that lives in a world where two and two makes four. It must be very interesting, and I envy you like hell. But I think I understand Letitia. Letitia is uncomplicated, if you see what I mean.'

A girl who once exorcized a noisy ghost from the

privy as if it was just another chore, Tiffany thought. Well, good luck with that one, sir. But she didn't say it out loud. Instead, she said, 'I think you have made a very wise match, Roland.' To her surprise, he looked relieved, and went behind his desk again as a soldier might hide behind the battlements.

'This afternoon, some of the more distant guests will be arriving here for the funeral tomorrow, and indeed some will be staying on for the wedding. Fortuitously' – that was another little piece of broom handle – 'Pastor Egg is passing through on the circuit, and has kindly agreed to say a few good words over my father, and he will remain with us as our guest to officiate at the wedding. He is a member of a modern Omnian sect. My future mother-in-law approves of the Omnians but, regrettably, not of this sect, so that is all a little strained.' He rolled his eyes. 'Moreover, I understand he is fresh from the city, and as you know, city preachers don't always do well here.*

'I would deem it a great favour, Tiffany, if you can

---

* There was no tradition of holy men on the Chalk, but since the hills were between the cities and the mountains, there was generally – in the good weather, at least – a steady procession of priests of one sort or another passing through who would, for a decent meal or a bed for the night, spread some holy words and generally give people's souls a decent scrubbing. Provided that the priests were clearly of the decent sort, people didn't worry unduly who their god was, so long as he – or occasionally she and sometimes it – kept the sun and moon spinning properly and didn't want anything ridiculous or new. It also helped if the preacher knew a little something about sheep.

help in any way to prevent any little difficulties and disturbances, especially those of an occult nature, in the trying days to come. Please? There are enough stories already going about.'

Tiffany was still blushing after her outburst. She nodded and managed to say, 'Look, about what I just said back then, I didn't—'

She stopped, because Roland had raised a hand. 'This is a bewildering time for all of us. There's a reason for all the superstitions. The time around weddings and funerals is fraught with stress for all concerned, except in the case of the funeral, for the chief, as it were, player,' he said. 'Let us just be calm and careful. I'm very pleased that Letitia likes you. I don't think she has many friends. And now, if you'll excuse me, I have more arrangements to supervise.'

Tiffany's own voice still bounced around in her head as she walked out of the room. Why had she said that about marrying? She'd always thought it was going to be true. Well, when she was a bit younger she had thought it was going to be true, but all that was past, wasn't it? Yes, it was! And to come out with something as wet and stupid as that was *so* embarrassing.

And where was she going now? Well, there were plenty of things to do, there always were. There was no end to the wanting. She was halfway across the hall when one of the maids approached her nervously and told her that Miss Letitia wanted to see her in her room.

The girl was sitting on her bed, twisting a

handkerchief – a clean one, Tiffany was pleased to see – and looking worried, which was to say more worried than her usual expression, which was that of a hamster that had had its treadmill stopped.

'So kind of you to come, Tiffany. Can I have a private word?' Tiffany looked around. There was no one else there. '*Privately*,' said Letitia, and gave the handkerchief another twist.

Hasn't got many friends of her own age, Tiffany thought. I bet she wasn't allowed to play with the village children. Doesn't get out much. Getting married in a couple of days. Oh dear. It wasn't a very difficult conclusion to reach. A tortoise with a bad leg could have jumped to it. And then there was Roland. Kidnapped by the Queen of the Elves, held in her nasty country for ages without growing older, bullied by his aunts, worried sick about his elderly father, finds it necessary to act as if he is twenty years older than he really is. Oh dear.

'How can I help you?' she said brightly.

Letitia cleared her throat. 'After the wedding we will have a honeymoon,' she said, her face shading to a delicate pink. 'What exactly is supposed to happen?' The last few words were mumbled quickly, Tiffany noticed.

'Do you have any . . . aunts?' she asked. Aunts were generally good at this sort of thing. Letitia shook her head. 'Have you tried talking about it with your mother?' Tiffany tried, and Letitia turned on her a face that was as red as a boiled lobster.

'Would you talk about *this* sort of thing with *my* mother?'

'I can see the problem. Well, broadly speaking, and I don't speak exactly as an expert here . . .' But she was.* A witch couldn't help being some kind of expert as to the ways people came and entered the world; by the time she was twelve the older witches had trusted her to go out to a birth by herself. Besides, she had helped lambs to be born, even when she was quite small. It came naturally, as Nanny Ogg said, although not as naturally as you might think. She remembered Mr and Mrs Hamper, quite a decent couple who had three children in a row before they worked out what was causing it. Ever since then she had tried to have a chat with the village girls of a certain age, just to be on the safe side.

Letitia listened like someone who was going to make notes afterwards, and possibly get tested on Friday. She didn't ask any questions until about halfway through, when she said, 'Are you *sure*?'

'Yes. I'm pretty certain,' said Tiffany.

'Well, er, it sounds reasonably straightforward. Of course, I suppose boys know all about this sort of thing . . . Why are you laughing?'

'It's a matter of opinion,' said Tiffany.

*Oh, now I see you. I see you, you filth, you plague, you noxious abomination!*

Tiffany looked at Letitia's mirror, which was big and

---

* If not through actual *personal* practice.

had around it lots of fat, golden cherubs who were clearly catching their death of cold. There was Letitia's reflection, and there was – faint but visible – the eyeless face of the Cunning Man. The outline of the Cunning Man began to thicken. Tiffany knew that nothing in her face had changed. She *knew* it. I won't answer him, she thought. I had almost forgotten all about him. Don't answer. Don't let him get a hold on you!

She managed to smile while Letitia hauled out from cases and chests what she called her trousseau which, in Tiffany's opinion, contained the world's entire supply of frilliness. She tried to focus on it, to let frilliness fill her mind and somehow chase away the words that came pouring from *him*. The ones she understood were bad enough; the ones that she didn't were worse. Despite everything, the creaking, choking voice got through again: *You think you have been lucky, witch. You hope you will be lucky again. You need to sleep. I never sleep. You have to be lucky time after time. I have to be lucky just once. Just once, and you will . . . burn.* That last word was soft, almost gentle, after the creaking, coughing, scraping words that came before. It sounded worse.

'You know,' said Letitia, looking thoughtfully at a garment that Tiffany knew she could never afford. 'While I am truly looking forward to being the mistress of this castle, I must say that the drainage system here smells dreadful. In fact, it smells like it has never been cleaned since the world began. Honestly, I could believe that prehistoric monsters have done their business in it.'

So she can smell him, Tiffany thought. She *is* a witch. A witch who needs training because without it she's going to be a menace to everybody, not least herself. Letitia was still prattling on – there was no other word for it. Tiffany, still trying to defeat the voice of the Cunning Man by sheer will, said aloud, 'Why?'

'Oh, because I think the bows look a lot more fetching than buttons,' said Letitia, who was holding up a nightdress of considerable splendour, another reminder to Tiffany that witches never really had any money.

*You burned before and so did I!* croaked the voice in her head, *but this time you will not take me! I will take you and your confederacy of evil!!!!!*

Tiffany thought she could actually see the exclamation marks. They shouted for him, even when he spoke softly. They jumped and slashed at his words. She could see his contorted face and the little flecks of foam that accompanied the finger-waving and shouting – gobs of liquid madness flying through the air behind the mirror.

How lucky for Letitia that she couldn't hear him yet, but her mind was currently full of frills, bells, rice and the prospect of being at the centre of a wedding. Not even the Cunning Man could burn his way through *that.*

She managed to say, 'It's not going to work for you.' And part of her kept repeating, inside her head: *No eyes. No eyes at all. Two tunnels in his head.*

'Yes, I think you're right. Possibly the mauve one

would look better,' said Letitia, 'although I have always been told that eau-de-nil is really my colour. By the way, could I make things up to you in some way by having you as my chief bridesmaid? Of course, I've already got a load of tiny distant cousins who I under-stand have been wearing their bridesmaids' dresses for the past two weeks.'

Tiffany was still staring at nothing, or rather, at two holes into nothing. At the moment, they were the most important things in her mind, and they were quite bad enough without adding tiny little cousins into the mixture. 'I don't think that witches are bridesmaid material, thank you all the same,' she said.

*Bridesmaids? A wedding?*

Tiffany's heart sank further. There was no help for it. She ran out of the room before the creature could learn anything more. How did it search? What was it looking for? Had they just given it a clue? She fled down to the dungeon, which was right now a place of refuge.

There was the book that Letitia had given to her. She opened it and began to read. She had learned to read fast up in the mountains, when the only books you could get were from the travelling library, and if you were late returning them they charged you an extra penny, an appreciable amount when your standard unit of currency is an old boot.

The book told stories of windows. Not ordinary windows, although some might be. And behind them . . . things – monsters, sometimes. A painting, a page in a book – even a puddle in the right place – could be a window. She remembered once more the nasty goblin in the old book of fairytales; sometimes it was laughing and at other times it was grinning. She had always been sure about that. It wasn't a big change, but it was still a change. And you always wondered: What was it like that last time? Did I remember it wrong?

The book rustled under Tiffany's hands like a hungry squirrel waking up in a hollow tree full of nuts. The author was a wizard, and a long-winded one at that, but the book was fascinating even so. There had been people who walked into a picture, and people who had walked out of one. Windows were a way of getting from one world into another, and anything could be a window and anything could be a world. She had heard that the sign of a good painting was that the eyes followed you around the room, but according to the book it was quite likely that they might follow you home and upstairs to bed, as well – an idea that she would rather not think about right now. Being a wizard, the author had tried to explain it all with graphs and charts, none of which helped in any way.

The Cunning Man had run towards her inside a book, and she had slammed it shut before he got out. She had seen his fingers just as the press had spun down. But he couldn't have been squashed inside the book, she thought, because he wasn't really in the book *at all*, except in some magical way, and he's been finding me in other ways too. How? Right now, those tiresome days of seeing to broken legs, bad stomachs and ingrown toenails suddenly seemed quite attractive.

She'd always told people that was what witchcraft was all about, and that was true, right up until the time something horrible could jump out of nowhere. That was when a poultice just wouldn't do the trick.

A piece of straw floated down and landed on the book. 'It's safe for you to come out,' said Tiffany. 'You are here, aren't you?'

And right by her ear a voice said, 'Oh aye, that we are.' They appeared from behind straw bales, spider webs, apple shelves, goats and one another.

'Aren't you Wee Mad Arthur?'

'Aye, miss, that is correct. I have to tell ye, to my embarrassment, that Rob Anybody is placing a big trust in me because I am a polisman and Rob appeared to think, ye ken, that if ye are dealing with bigjobs, a polisman will make them even more afeared. Besides, I can speak bigjob! Rob is spending more time up at the mound right now, ye ken. An' he doesnae trust yon Baron not tae come up there with shovels.'

'I will see that does not happen,' said Tiffany firmly. 'There has been a misunderstanding.'

Wee Mad Arthur did not look convinced. 'It is glad I am to hear you say that, miss, and so will the Big Man be, because I can tell ye that when the first shovel breaks into the mound there willnae be a living man left in yonder castle, and great will be the lamentation of the women, present company excepted.' There was a general murmuring from the other Feegles, on the broad theme of slaughter for whoever laid a hand on a Feegle mound, and how personally each and every one of them would regret what he would have to do.

'It's yon troosers,' said Slightly-Thinner-Than-Fat-Jock-Jock. 'Once a man gets a Feegle up his troosers, his time of trial and tribulation is only just beginning.'

'Oh aye, it will be a great time o' jumpin' and leapin' up and doon for such as them,' said Wee Jock o' the White Head.

Tiffany was shocked. 'When was the last time Feegles fought with bigjobs, then?'

After some discussion among the Feegles, this was declared to be the Battle o' the Middens when, according to Wee Jock o' the White Head, 'There was never such a screaming and rushing about and stamping on the ground, and pitiable sobbing, the like of which was never before heard, along with the coarse tittering of the ladies as the men scrambled to divest themselves of troosers that were suddenly no longer their friends, if ye ken what I'm saying.'

Tiffany, who had been listening to the tale with an open mouth, had the presence of mind to shut it, and then open it again to say, 'But have Feegles ever killed a human?'

This led to a certain amount of deliberate lack of eye contact among the Feegles, plus quite a lot of foot shuffling and head scratching, with the usual fallout of insects, hoarded food, interesting stones and other unspeakable items. In the end, Wee Mad Arthur said, 'Being as I am, miss, a Feegle who has only but recently learned that he is not a fairy cobbler, I ha' nae pride tae lose by telling ye that it is true that I have been speaking to my new brothers and learned that, when they lived up in the far mountains, they did have tae fight humans sometimes, when they came a-digging for the fairy gold, and a terror-err-able fighting did take place and, indeed, those bandits as were too stupid to run may have found themselves clever enough to die.' He coughed. 'However, in defence of my new brethren I must point out that they always made certain that the odds were fair and just, which is to say one Feegle to every ten men. Ye cannae say fairer than that. And it wasnae their fault that some men just wanted tae commit suicide.'

There was a glint in Wee Mad Arthur's eye that prompted Tiffany to ask, 'How *exactly* did they commit suicide?'

The policeman Feegle shrugged his small broad shoulders. 'They took a shovel to a Feegle mound, miss. I am a man who knows the law, miss. I never saw a mound until I met these fine gentlemen, but even so my blood boils, miss, it boils, so it does. My heart it does thump, my pulse it does race, and my gorge it arises like the breath of some dragon at the very thought of a bright steel shovel slicing through the clay of a Feegle mound, cutting and crushing. I would kill the man that does this, miss. I would kill him dead, and chase him through the next life to kill him another time, and I would do it again and again, because it would be the sin o' sins, to kill an entire people, and one death wouldnae be enough for recompense. However, as I am an aforesaid man of the law, I very much hope that the current misunderstanding can be resolved withoot the need for wholesale carnage and bloodletting and screaming and wailing and weeping and people having bits of themselves nailed to trees, such as has never been seen before, ye ken?' Wee Mad Arthur, holding his full-sized policeman's badge like a shield, stared at Tiffany with a mixture of shock and defiance.

And Tiffany was a witch. 'I must tell you something, Wee Mad Arthur,' she said, 'and you must understand what I say. You have come home, Wee Mad Arthur.'

The shield dropped out of his hand. 'Aye, miss, I ken that now. A policeman should not say the words I just said. He should talk about judges and juries and prisons and sentences, and he would say ye cannae take the law intae your own hands. So I will hand in my badge, indeed, and stay here among my own folk, although I have to say, with better standards o' hygiene.'

This got a round of applause from the assembled Feegles, although Tiffany wasn't sure that most of them fully understood the concept of hygiene or, for that matter, obeying the law.

'You have my word,' said Tiffany, 'that the mound will not be touched again. I will see to it, do you understand?'

'Och, weel,' said Wee Mad Arthur tearfully. 'That might be all very well, miss, but what will happen behind your back when ye are a-flying and a-whizzing aboot your verrae important business across the hills? What will happen then?'

All eyes turned to Tiffany, including those of the goats. She didn't do this kind of thing any more because she knew it was bad manners, but Tiffany picked up Wee Mad Arthur bodily and held him at eye level. 'I am the hag o' the hills,' she said. 'And I will vow to you and all other Feegles that the home of the Feegles will never be threatened with iron again. It will never be behind my back but will always be in front of my eyes. And while this is so, no living man will touch it if he wants to remain a living man. And if I fail the Feegles in this, may I be dragged through the seven hells on a broomstick made of nails.'

Strictly speaking, Tiffany admitted to herself, these were pretty much empty threats, but the Feegles did not think an oath was an oath if it didn't have lots of thunder and lightning and boasting and blood in it. Blood, somehow, made it official. I *will* see to it that the mound is never touched again, she thought. There is no way that Roland can refuse me now. And besides, I have a secret weapon: I have the trust and confidence of a young lady who is soon going to be his wife. No man can be safe in those circumstances.

In the glow of reassurance Wee Mad Arthur said happily, 'Well spoken, mistress, and may I take the opportunity on behalf of my new friends and relatives tae thank ye for explaining all aboot the business of the wedding nuptials the noo. It was verrae interesting to those of us who have little to do with such things. Some of us was wondering if we could ask questions?'

Being threatened by a spectral horror was terrible

enough right now, but somehow the thought of the Nac Mac Feegle asking questions about the facts of married life among humans was even worse. There was no point in explaining why she wasn't going to explain; Tiffany simply said 'No' in a tone of voice like steel and very carefully put him back down on the ground. She added, 'You shouldn't have been listening.'

'Why not?' said Daft Wullie.

'You just shouldn't! I'm not going to explain. You just shouldn't. And now, gentlemen, I'd like a bit of time to myself, if it's all the same to you.'

Some of them would follow her, of course, she thought. They always did. She went back up to the hall and sat down as close as possible to the huge fire. Even in late summer, the hall was cold. It was hung with tapestries as insulation from the chill of the stone walls. They were the usual sort of thing: men in armour waving swords and bows and axes at other men in armour. Given that battle is very fast and noisy, they presumably had to stop fighting every couple of minutes to give the ladies who were making the tapestry a little time to catch up. Tiffany knew the one nearest the fire by heart. All the kids did. You learned your history off the tapestries, if there was some old man around to explain what was going on. But generally, when she was a lot younger, it had been more fun to make up stories about the different knights, like the one who was desperately running to catch up with his horse, and the one who had been thrown by *his* horse, and, because he had a helmet with a point on it, was now upright head first in the ground, which, even as children, they had recognized was not a good position to be in on the battlefield. They were like old friends, frozen in a war whose name nobody on the Chalk could remember.

And ... suddenly there was another one, one that had never been there before, running *towards* Tiffany through the battle. She stared at him, her body demanding that she get some sleep right now, and whatever bits were still working in her brain insisting that she *did* something. In the middle of this her hand gripped a log on the edge of the fire and she raised it purposefully towards the tapestry.

The cloth had practically crumbled with age as it was. It would burn like dry grass.

The figure was walking cautiously now. She couldn't see any details yet and didn't want to. The knights on the tapestry had been woven in without any perspective; they were as flat as a child's nursery painting.

But the man in black, who had begun as a distant streak, was getting bigger as he approached and now ... She could see the face and the empty eyeholes, which even from here changed colour as he walked past the armour of knight after knight, and now he had started running again, getting bigger. And the smell was oozing towards her again ... How much was the tapestry worth? Did she have any right to destroy it? With that thing stepping out of it? Oh *yes*, oh *yes*!

Wouldn't it be nice to be a wizard and to conjure up those knights to fight one last battle!

Wouldn't it be nice to be a witch who wasn't here! She raised the crackling log and glared into the holes where the eyes should be. You had to be a witch to be prepared to stare down a stare that wasn't there, because somehow you felt that it was sucking your own eyeballs out of your head.

Those tunnels in the skull were hypnotic, and now he moved from side to side slowly, like a snake.

'Please don't.'

She wasn't expecting that; the voice was urgent but quite friendly – and it belonged to Eskarina Smith.

The wind was silver and cold.

Tiffany, lying on her back, looked up into a white sky; at the edge of her vision, dried grasses shook and rattled in the wind but, curiously, behind this little bit of countryside there was the big fireplace and the battling knights.

'It is really quite important that you don't move,' said the same voice behind her. 'The place where you are now has been, as we say, cobbled together for this conversation and did not exist until you arrived here, and will cease to exist the moment you leave. Strictly speaking, by the standards of most philosophical disciplines, it cannot be said to have any existence at all.'

'So it's a *magic* place, yes? Like the Unreal Estate?'

'Very sensible way of putting it,' said the voice of Eskarina. 'Those of us who know about it call it the travelling now. It's an easy way to talk to you in private; when it closes, you will be exactly where you were and no time will have passed. Do you understand?'

'No!'

Eskarina sat down on the grass next to her. 'Thank goodness for that. It would be rather disturbing if you did. You are, you know, an extremely unusual witch. As far as I can tell, you have a natural talent for making cheese, and as talents go, it is a pretty good talent to have. The world needs cheese-makers. A good cheese-maker is worth her weight in, well, cheese. So you were not born with a talent for witchcraft.'

Tiffany opened her mouth to reply before she had any idea what she was going to say, but that is not unusual among human beings. The first thing to push through the throng of questions was: 'Hang on, I was holding a burning brand. But now you have brought me here, wherever here is *exactly*. What happened?' She looked at the fire. The flames were frozen. 'People will notice me,' she said, and then, given the nature of the situation, she added, 'Won't they?'

'The answer is no; the reason is complicated. The travelling now is . . . tame time. It's time that is on your side. Believe me, there are stranger things in the universe. Right now, Tiffany, we are truly living on borrowed time.'

The flames were still frozen. Tiffany felt that they should be cold, but she could feel the warmth. And she had time to think too. 'And when I go back?'

'Nothing will have changed,' said Eskarina, 'except the contents of your head, which are, at the moment, very important.'

'And you've gone to all this trouble to tell me I have no talent for witchcraft?' Tiffany said flatly. 'That was very kind of you.'

Eskarina laughed. It was her young laugh, which seemed strange when you saw the wrinkles on her face. Tiffany had never seen an old person looking so young. 'I said you weren't *born* with a talent for witchcraft: it didn't come easily; you worked hard at it because you wanted it. You forced the world to give it to you, no matter the price, and the price is and will always be, high. Have you heard the saying "the reward you get for digging holes is a bigger shovel"?'

'Yes,' said Tiffany, 'I heard Granny Weatherwax say it once.'

'She invented it. People say you don't find witchcraft; witchcraft finds you. But you've found it, even if at the time you didn't know what it was you were finding, and you grabbed it by its scrawny neck and made it work for you.'

'This is all very . . . *interesting*,' said Tiffany, 'but I have got things I must be doing.'

'Not in the travelling now,' said Eskarina firmly. 'Look, the Cunning Man has found you again.'

'I think he hides in books and pictures,' Tiffany volunteered. 'And tapestries.' She shuddered.

'And mirrors,' said Eskarina, 'and puddles, and the glint of light on a piece of broken glass, or the gleam on a knife. How many ways can you think of? How frightened are you prepared to be?'

'I'm going to have to fight him,' Tiffany said. 'I think

I knew I would have to. He doesn't seem to me to be someone you can run away from. He's a bully, isn't he? He attacks where he thinks he will win, and so I have to find a way to be stronger than he is. I think I can work out a way – after all, he is a bit like the hiver. And that was really quite easy.'

Eskarina did not shout; she spoke very quietly and in a way that seemed to make more noise than a scream would have done. 'Will you persist in not recognizing how important this is, Tiffany Aching the cheese-maker? You have a chance to defeat the Cunning Man, and if you fail, witchcraft fails – and falls with you. He will possess your body, your knowledge, your talents and your soul. And for your own good – and for the good of all – your sister witches will settle their differences and take the pair of you into oblivion before you can do any more harm. Do you understand? This is *important*! You *have* to help yourself.'

'The other witches will *kill* me?' said Tiffany, aghast.

'Of course. You are a witch and you know what Granny Weatherwax always says: *We do right, we don't do nice*. It will be you or him, Tiffany Aching. The loser will die. In his case, I regret to say we might see him again in a few centuries; in your case, I don't propose to guess.'

'But hold on a moment,' said Tiffany. 'If they are prepared to fight him and me, why don't we all band together to fight him now?'

'Of course. Would you like them to? What is it you really want, Tiffany Aching, here and now? It's your choice. The other witches will not, I am sure, think any the worse of you.' Eskarina hesitated for a moment, and then said, 'Well, I expect they will be very *kind* about it.'

The witch who faced the trial and ran away? thought Tiffany. The witch they were kind to, because they knew she wasn't good enough? And if you think you're not good enough, then you are already no kind of witch. Aloud she said, 'I'd rather die trying to be a witch, than be the girl they were all kind to.'

'Miss Aching, you are showing an almost sinful self-assurance and overwhelming pride and certainty, and may I say that I wouldn't expect anything less of a witch.'

The world wobbled a bit and then changed. Eskarina vanished, even as her words were still sinking into Tiffany's mind. The tapestry was back in front of her again and she was still raising the burning log, but this time she raised it confidently. She felt as if she was full of air, lifting her up. The world had gone strange, but at least she knew that fire would burn dry tapestry like tinder the moment it touched it.

'I would burn this old sheet in an instant, mister, trust me. Back to where you came from, mister!'

To her astonishment the dark figure retreated. There was a momentary hiss and Tiffany felt as if a weight had dropped away, dragging the stench with it.

'That was all very interesting.' Tiffany spun round and looked into Preston's cheerful grin. 'Do you know,' he said, 'I was really worried when you went so stiff for a few moments. I thought you were dead. When I touched your arm – very respectfully, no hanky-panky – it felt like the air on a thundery day. So I thought, This is witch business, and decided to keep an eye on you, and then you threatened an innocent tapestry with fiery death!'

She stared at the boy's eyes as if they were a mirror. Fire, she thought. Fire killed him once, and he knows it. He won't go anywhere near fire. Fire is the secret. *The hare runs into the fire.* Hmm.

'Actually, I quite like fire,' said Preston. 'I don't think it's my enemy at all.'

'What?' said Tiffany.

'I'm afraid you were speaking just under your breath,' said Preston. 'I'm not going to ask what it was about. My granny said: *Don't meddle in the affairs of witches because they clout you around the ear.*'

Tiffany stared at him and made an instant decision. 'Can you keep a secret?'

Preston nodded. 'Certainly! I have never told anybody that the sergeant writes poetry, for example.'

'Preston, you have just told *me*!'

Preston grinned at her. 'Ah, but a witch isn't *anybody*. My granny told me that telling your secret to a witch is like whispering to a wall.'

'Well, yes,' Tiffany began and then paused. 'How do you *know* he writes poetry?'

'It was hard not to know,' said Preston. 'But, you see, he writes it on pages of the events ledger in the guard house, probably when he's on night duty. He carefully tears out the pages, and does it so neatly that you wouldn't guess, but he presses so hard with his pencil that it's quite easy to read the impression on the paper underneath.'

'Surely the other men notice?' said Tiffany.

Preston shook his head, which caused his oversized helmet to spin a little. 'Oh no, miss, you know them: they think reading is cissy stuff for girls. Anyway, if I get in early I tear out the paper underneath so that they don't laugh at him. I have to say, for a self-taught man he is a pretty good poet – good grasp of the metaphor. They are all written to somebody called Millie.'

'That would be his wife,' said Tiffany. 'You must have seen her in the village – more freckles than anyone I've ever seen. She is very sensitive about it.'

Preston nodded. 'That might explain why his latest poem is entitled "What Good Is The Sky Without Stars"?'

'You wouldn't know it from looking at the man, would you?'

Preston looked thoughtful for a moment. 'Excuse me, Tiffany,' he said, 'but you don't look well. In fact, no offence meant, you look absolutely dreadful. If you were somebody else and took a look at you, you would say that you were very ill indeed. You don't look as if you've had any sleep.'

'I had at least an hour's worth last night. And a nap the day before!' said Tiffany.

'Really?' said Preston, looking stern. 'And apart from

breakfast this morning, when did you last have a proper meal?'

For some reason Tiffany still felt full of light inside. 'I think I might have had a snack yesterday . . .'

'Oh really?' said Preston. 'Snacks and naps? That's not how somebody is supposed to live; it's how people die!'

He was right. She knew he was. But that only made things worse.

'Look, I'm being tracked by a horrible creature who can take over somebody else completely, and it's up to me to deal with it!'

Preston looked around with interest. 'Could it take *me* over?'

*Poison goes where poison's welcome*, thought Tiffany. Thank you for that useful phrase, Mrs Proust. 'No, I don't think so. I think you have to be the right kind of person – which is to say, the wrong kind of person. You know, somebody with a touch of evil.'

For the first time, Preston looked worried. 'I have done a few bad things in my time, I'm sorry to say.'

Despite her sudden tiredness, Tiffany smiled. 'What was the worst one?'

'I once stole a packet of coloured pencils off a market stall.' He looked at her defiantly, as if expecting her to scream or point the finger of scorn.

Instead, she shook her head and said, 'How old were you then?'

'Six.'

'Preston, I don't think this creature could ever find

341

its way into your head. Quite apart from anything else, it seems pretty crowded and complicated to me.'

'Miss Tiffany, you need a rest, a proper rest in a proper bed. What kind of witch can look after everybody if she's not sensible enough to look after herself? *Quis custodiet ipsos custodes.* That means: Who guards the guards, that does,' Preston went on. 'So who watches the witches? Who cares for the people who care for the people? Right now, it looks like it needs to be me.'

She gave in.

The fog of the city was as thick as curtains when Mrs Proust hurried towards the dark, brooding shape of the Tanty, but the billows obediently separated as she approached and closed again after her.

The warden was waiting at the main gate, a lantern in his hand. 'Sorry, missus, but we thought you ought to see this one before it gets all official. I know witches seem a bit unpopular right now, but we've always thought of you as family, if you know what I mean. Everyone remembers your dad. What a craftsman! He could hang a man in seven and a quarter seconds! Never been beat. We shall never see his likes again.' He went solemn. 'And may I say, missus, I hope I never see again the like of what you will be seeing now. It's got us rattled, and no mistake. It's right up your street, I reckon.'

Mrs Proust shook the water droplets off her cloak in the prison office and could smell the fear in the air. There was the general clanging and distant yelling that you always got when things were going bad in a prison:

a prison, by definition, being a lot of people all crammed together and every fear and hatred and worry and dread and rumour all sitting on top of one another, choking for space. She hung the cloak on a nail by the door and rubbed her hands together. 'The lad you sent said something about a breakout?'

'D wing,' said the warder. 'Macintosh. You remember? Been in here about a year.'

'Oh yes, I recall,' said the witch. 'They had to stop the trial because the jury kept throwing up. Very nasty indeed. But no one has ever escaped from D wing, right? The window bars are steel?'

'Bent,' said the warder flatly. 'You'd better come and see. It's giving us the heebie-jeebies, I don't mind telling you.'

'Macintosh wasn't a particularly big man, as I recall,' said the witch as they hurried along the dank corridors.

'That's right, Mrs Proust. Short and nasty, that was him. Due to hang next week too. Tore out bars that a strong man wouldn't have been able to shift with a crowbar and dropped thirty feet to the ground. That's not natural, that's not right. But it was the other thing he did – oh my word, it makes me sick thinking about it.'

A warder was waiting outside the cell recently vacated by the absent Macintosh, but for no reason that Mrs Proust could recognize, given that the man had definitely gone. He touched the brim of his hat respectfully when he saw her.

'Good morning, Mrs Proust,' he said. 'May I say it's an honour to meet the daughter of the finest hangman in history. Fifty-one years before the lever, and never let a client down. Mr Trooper now, decent bloke, but sometimes they bounce a bit and I don't consider that professional. And your dad wouldn't forego a well-deserved hanging out of the fear that fires of evil and demons of dread would haunt him afterwards. You mark my words; he'd go after them and hang them too! Seven and a quarter seconds, what a gentleman.'

But Mrs Proust was staring down at the floor.

'Terrible thing for a lady to have to see,' the warder went on.

Almost absentmindedly Mrs Proust said, 'Witches are not ladies *when* on business, Frank,' and then she sniffed the air and swore an oath that made Frank's eyes water.

'It makes you wonder what got into him, aye?'

Mrs Proust straightened up. 'I don't have to wonder, my lad,' she said grimly. 'I know.'

The fog piled up against the buildings in its effort to get out of the way of Mrs Proust as she hurried back to Tenth Egg Street, leaving behind her a Mrs Proust-shaped tunnel in the gloom.

Derek was drinking a peaceful mug of cocoa when his mother burst in to the strains, as it were, of a large fart. He looked up, his brow wrinkling. 'Did that sound like B-flat to you? It didn't sound like B-flat to me.' He reached into the drawer under the counter for his tuning fork, but his mother rushed past him.

'Where's my broomstick?'

Derek sighed. 'In the basement, remember? When

the dwarfs told you last month how much it would cost to repair, you told them they were a bunch of chiselling little lawn ornaments, remember? Anyway, you never use it.'

'I've got to go into the . . . country,' said Mrs Proust, looking around the crowded shelves in case there was another working broomstick there.

Her son stared. 'Are you sure, Mother? You've always said it's bad for your health.'

'Matter of life or death,' Mrs Proust mumbled. 'What about Long Tall Short Fat Sally?'

'Oh, Mother, you really shouldn't call her that,' said Derek reproachfully. 'She can't help being allergic to tides.'

'She's got a stick, though! Hah! If it's not one thing it's another. Make me some sandwiches, will you?'

'Is this about that girl who was in here last week?' said Derek suspiciously. 'I don't think she had much of a sense of humour.'

His mother ignored him and rummaged under the counter, coming back with a large leather cosh. The small traders of Tenth Egg Street worked on narrow margins, and had a very direct approach to shoplifting. 'I don't know, I really don't,' she moaned. 'Me? Doing good at my time of life? I must be going soft in the head. And I'm not even going to get paid! I don't know, I really don't. Next thing you know, I'll start giving people three wishes, and if I start doing that, Derek, I would like you to hit me very hard on the head.' She handed him the cosh. 'I'm leaving you in charge. Try to shift some of the rubber chocolate and the humorous fake fried eggs, will you? Tell people they are novelty bookmarks or something.'

And with that, Mrs Proust ran out into the night. The lanes and alleyways of the city were very dangerous at night, what with muggers, thieves and similar un-pleasantnesses. But they disappeared back into the gloom as she passed. Mrs Proust was bad news, and best left undisturbed if you wanted to keep all the bones in your fingers pointing the right way.

The body that was Macintosh ran through the night. It was full of pain. This didn't matter to the ghost; it wasn't his pain. Its sinews sang with agony, but it was not the ghost's agony. The fingers bled where they had torn steel bars out of the wall. But the ghost did not bleed. It never bled.

It couldn't remember when it had had a body that was really its own. Bodies had to be fed and had to drink. That was an annoying feature of the wretched things. Sooner or later they ran out of usefulness. Often, that didn't matter; there was always somebody – a little mind festering with hatred and envy and resentment that would welcome the ghost inside. But it had to be care-ful, and it had to be quick. Above all it had to be safe. Out here, on the empty roads, another suitable container would be hard to find. Regretfully, it allowed the body to stop and drink from the murky waters of a pond. It turned out to be full of frogs, but a body had to eat too, didn't it?

## CHAPTER 13

# The Shaking of the Sheets

Her proper bed in the castle's black-and-white chamber was so much better than the dungeon, even though Tiffany had missed the soothing burps of the goats.

She dreamed of fire, again. And she was being watched. She could *feel* it, and it wasn't the goats this time. She was being watched inside her head. But it wasn't bad watching; someone was caring for her. And in the dream the fire raged, and a dark figure pulled aside the flames as though they were curtains, and there was the hare sitting by the dark figure as if she was a pet. The hare caught Tiffany's eye and jumped into the fire. And Tiffany *knew*.

Somebody knocked at the door. Tiffany was suddenly awake. 'Who's there?'

A voice on the other side of the heavy door said, 'What sound does forgetfulness make?'

She hardly had to think. 'It's the sound of the wind in dead grasses on a hot summer's day.'

'Yes, I think that would about do it,' said Preston's voice from the other side of the door. 'To get right to the point, miss, there's a lot of people downstairs, miss. I think they need their witch.'

It was a good day for a funeral, Tiffany thought, looking out of the narrow castle window. It shouldn't rain on a funeral. It made people too gloomy. She tried not to be gloomy at funerals. People lived, and died, and were remembered. It happened in the same way that winter followed summer. It was not a wrong thing. There were tears, of course, but they were for those who were left; those who had gone on did not need them.

The staff had been up very early, and the long tables had been put out in the hall to make a breakfast for all-comers. That was a tradition. Rich or poor, lord or lady: the funeral breakfast was there for everyone, and out of respect for the old Baron; and also out of respect for a good meal, the hall was filling up. The Duchess was there, in a black dress that was more black than any black Tiffany had ever seen before. The dress gleamed. The black dress of the average witch was usually only *theoretically* black. In reality, it was often rather dusty, and quite possibly patched in the vicinity of the knees and somewhat ragged at the hems and, of course, very nearly worn through by frequent washings. It was what it was: working clothes. You couldn't imagine the Duchess delivering a baby in that dress . . . Tiffany blinked. She *could* imagine the Duchess doing just that; if it was an emergency, she *would*. She would bully and complain and order people around, but she would do it. She was that kind of person.

Tiffany blinked again. Her head felt crystal clear. The world seemed understandable but slightly fragile, as if it could be broken, like a mirror ball.

'Morning, miss!' That was Amber, and behind her, both her parents, Mr Petty looking scrubbed and sheepish and also quite bashful. He clearly didn't know what to say. Nor did Tiffany.

There was a stir at the main doors, and Roland hurried in that direction and came back with King Verence of Lancre and Magrat, his queen. Tiffany had met them before. You couldn't help meeting them in Lancre, which was a very small kingdom, and even smaller when you took into consideration that Granny Weatherwax lived there too.

And Granny Weatherwax was here, *right here and now*, with You* lying across her shoulders like a scarf, behind the King and Queen and just in front of a huge

---

* You had been a sad little white kitten when Tiffany had given her to the old witch. Now she was a queen, far more snobbish than the Duchess. She must have recognized Tiffany because she graciously condescended to blink at her and then look away as if bored. There were never any mice in Granny's cottage these days; You just stared at them until they realized how worthless they were and slunk away.

jolly voice that shouted, 'Watcha, Tiff! How's your belly off for spots!' which meant that a couple of feet below it, but hidden by reasons of size, was Nanny Ogg, rumoured by some to be cleverer than Granny Weatherwax, and clever enough at least not to let her find out.

Tiffany bowed to them as was the custom. She thought, They gather, do they? She smiled at Granny Weatherwax and said, 'Very pleased to see you here, Mistress Weatherwax, and a little surprised.'

Granny stared at her but Nanny Ogg said, 'It's a long bumpy ride down from Lancre, and so the two of us thought we'd give Magrat and her king a nice ride down.'

Possibly Tiffany was imagining it, but Nanny Ogg's explanation sounded like something she had been working on for a little while. It felt as if she were reciting a script.

But there was no more time to talk. The arrival of the king had triggered something in the air, and for the first time Tiffany saw Pastor Egg, in a black and white robe. She adjusted her pointy hat and walked over to him. He seemed quite glad of the company, which is to say that he gave her a grateful smile.

'Hah, a witch, I see.'

'Yes, the pointy hat is a bit of a giveaway, isn't it?' she said.

'But not a black dress, I notice . . . ?'

Tiffany heard the question mark as it went past. 'When I am old, I shall wear midnight,' she said.

'Entirely appropriate,' said the pastor, 'but now you wear green, white and blue, the downland colours, I can't help remarking!'

Tiffany was impressed. 'So, you're not interested in witchfinding, then?' She felt a bit silly for asking outright, but she was on edge.

Pastor Egg shook his head. 'I can assure you, madam, that the Church has not been seriously involved in that sort of thing for hundreds of years! Unfortunately some people have long memories. Indeed, it was only a matter of a few years ago that the famous Pastor Oats said in his renowned *Testament from the Mountains* that the women known as witches embody, in a caring and practical way, the very best ideals of Brutha the prophet. That's good enough for me. I hope it is good enough for you?'

Tiffany gave him her sweetest smile, which wasn't all that sweet, however hard you tried; she'd never really got the hang of sweet.

'It's important to be clear about these things, don't you think?'

She sniffed, and noticed no odour other than a hint of shaving cream. Even so, she was going to have to be on her guard.

It was a good funeral too; from Tiffany's point of view, a good funeral was one where the main player was very old. She had been to some – too many – where they were small and wrapped in a shroud. Coffins were barely known on the Chalk, and indeed nearly anywhere else. Decent timber was too expensive to be left to rot underground. A practical white woollen shroud did for most people; it was easy to make, not too expensive, and good for the wool industry. The Baron, however, went to his eternal rest inside a tomb of white marble which, him being a practical man, he had designed, bought and paid for twenty years ago. There was a white shroud inside it, because marble can be a bit chilly to lie on.

And that was the end of the old Baron, except that only Tiffany knew where he really was. He was walking with his father in the stubbles, where they burned the corn stalks and the weeds, a perfect late-summer's day, one never-changing perfect moment held in time . . .

She gasped. 'The drawing!' Even though she'd spoken under her breath, people around her turned to look. She thought, How selfish of me! And then thought, Surely it will still be there?

As soon as the lid of the stone tomb had been slid into place with a sound that Tiffany would always remember, she went and found Brian, who was blowing his nose; when he looked up at her he was pink around the eyes.

She took him gently by the arm, trying not to sound urgent. 'The room that the Baron was living in, is it locked?'

He looked shocked. 'I should say so! And the money is in the big safe in the office. Why d'you want to know?'

'There was something very valuable in there. A leather folder. Did that get put in the big safe too?'

The sergeant shook his head. 'Believe me, Tiff, after the' – he hesitated – 'bit of trouble, I did an inventory of everything in that room. Not a thing went out from there without me seeing it and putting it down in my notebook. With my pencil,' he added, for maximum accuracy. 'Nothing like a leather folder was taken out, I'm sure of it.'

'No. Because Miss Spruce had already taken it,' Tiffany said. 'That wretched nurse! I didn't mind about the money, because I never expected the money! Maybe she thought it had deeds in it or something!'

Tiffany hurried back to the hall and looked around. Roland was the Baron now, in every respect. And it was in respect that people were clustering around him, saying things like, 'He was a very good man,' and 'He'd had a good innings,' and 'At least he didn't suffer,' and all the other things people say after a funeral when they don't know what to say.

And now Tiffany headed purposefully towards the Baron, and stopped when a hand landed on her shoulder. She followed the arm up to the face of Nanny Ogg, who had managed to obtain the biggest flagon of ale that Tiffany had ever seen. To be precise, she noticed it was a half-full flagon of ale.

'Nice to see something like this done well,' said Nanny. 'Never knew the old boy, of course, but he sounds like a decent fellow. Nice to see you, Tiff. Managing all right?'

Tiffany looked into those innocent smiling eyes, and past them to the much sterner face of Granny Weatherwax, and the brim of her hat. Tiffany bowed.

Granny Weatherwax cleared her throat with a sound like gravel. 'We ain't here on business, my girl, we just wanted to help the king make a good entrance.'

'We are not here about the Cunning Man neither,' Nanny Ogg added cheerfully. It *sounded* like a simple and silly giveaway, and Tiffany heard a disapproving sniff from Granny. But, generally speaking, when Nanny Ogg came out with a silly, embarrassing comment by accident, it was because she had thought about it very carefully beforehand. Tiffany knew this, and Nanny certainly knew that Tiffany knew, and Tiffany knew that too. But it was often the kind of way that witches behaved, and it all worked perfectly if nobody picked up an axe.

'I *know* this is my problem. I will sort it out,' she said.

This was on the face of it a really stupid thing to say. The senior witches would be very useful to have at her side. But how would that look? This was a new steading, and she had to be proud.

You couldn't say, 'I have done difficult and dangerous things before,' because that was understood. What *did* matter was what you did today. It was a matter of pride. It was a matter of style.

And it was also a matter of age. In twenty years' time, perhaps, if she asked for help, people would think: Well, even an experienced witch can run up against something really unusual. And they would help as a matter of course. But now, if she asked for help, well . . . people would help. Witches always helped other witches. But everyone would think: Was she really any good? Can't she last the distance? Is she strong enough for the long haul? No one would say anything, but everyone would think it.

All this was the thought of a second, and when she blinked, the witches were watching her.

'Self-reliance is a witch's best friend,' said Granny Weatherwax, looking stern.

Nanny Ogg nodded in agreement, and added, 'You can always rely on self-reliance, I've always said so.' She laughed at Tiffany's expression. 'Do you think you are the only one to have to deal with the Cunning Man, love? Granny here had to deal with him when she was your age. She sent him back to where he came from in very short order, trust me on that.'

Knowing that it was useless, but attempting it anyway, Tiffany turned to Granny Weatherwax and said, 'Can you give me any tips, Mistress Weatherwax?'

Granny, who was already drifting purposefully towards the buffet lunch, stopped for a moment and turned and said, 'Trust yourself.' She walked a few steps further and stood as if lost in thought and added, 'And don't lose.'

Nanny Ogg slapped Tiffany on the back. 'Never met the bugger myself, but I hear he is pretty bad. Here, is the blushing bride having a hen night tonight?' The old lady winked and poured the remaining contents of the flagon down her throat.

Tiffany tried to think quickly. Nanny Ogg got on with *everyone*. Tiffany had only a vague idea of what a hen night was, but some of Mrs Proust's stock gave her a few clues, and if Nanny Ogg knew about them too, it was a certainty that alcohol was involved.

'I don't think it's appropriate to have a party like that on a night after a funeral, do you, Nanny? Though I think Letitia might enjoy a little talk,' she added.

'She's your chum, isn't she? I would have thought you'd have had a little talk with her yourself.'

'I did!' Tiffany protested. 'But I don't think she believed me. And you've had at least three husbands, Nanny!'

Nanny Ogg stared at her for a moment and then said, 'That's quite a lot of conversation, I suppose. All right. But what about the young man? When's his stag night going to be?'

'Ah, I've heard of those! It's where his friends get him drunk, take him a long way away, tie him to a tree and then ... I think a bucket of paint and a brush is involved sometimes, but usually they throw him in the pigsty. Why do you ask?'

'Oh, the stag night is always much more interesting than the hen night,' said Nanny, a look of mischief in her eye. 'Has the lucky groom got any chums?'

'Well, there are some nobby lads from other posh families, but the only people he really knows live here in the village. We all grew up together, you see? And none of them would dare throw the Baron in a pigsty!'

'What about your young man over there?' Nanny

gestured towards Preston, who was standing nearby. He always seemed to be standing nearby.

'Preston?' said Tiffany. 'I don't think he knows the Baron very well. And in any case—' She stopped and thought, *Young man?* She turned and looked at Nanny, who was standing with her hands behind her back and face turned towards the ceiling with the expression of an angel, although admittedly one who might have met a few demons in her time. And that was Nanny all over. When it came to affairs of the heart – or indeed, of any other parts – you couldn't fool Nanny Ogg.

But he's not my young man, she insisted to herself. He's just a friend. Who is a boy.

Preston stepped forward and removed his helmet in front of Nanny. 'I fear, madam, that it would be against the rules for me as a military man to lay a hand on my commanding officer,' he said. 'Were it not for that, I would do so with alacrity.'

Nanny nodded appreciatively at the polysyllabic response, and gave Tiffany a wink that made her blush to the soles of her boots. Nanny Ogg's grin was now so wide you could fit it onto a pumpkin. 'Oh dear, oh dear, oh dear,' she said. 'I can see this place needs a little fun. Thank goodness I'm here!'

Nanny Ogg had a heart of gold, but if you were easily shocked then it was best to stick your fingers in your ears when she said *anything*. Yet there had to be common sense, didn't there? 'Nanny, we're at a *funeral*!'

But her tone of voice would never make Nanny Ogg swerve. 'Was he a good man?'

Tiffany hesitated only for a moment. 'He grew into goodness.'

Nanny Ogg noticed everything. 'Oh yes, your Granny Aching taught him his manners, I believe. But he died a good man, then? Good. Will he be remembered with fondness?'

Tiffany tried to ignore the lump in her throat, and managed to say, 'Oh yes, by everybody.'

'And you saw to it that he died well? Kept the pain away?'

'Nanny, if I say it myself, he had a perfect death. The only better death would have been not to die.'

'Well done,' said Nanny. 'Did he have a favourite song, do you know?'

'Oh yes! It's "The Larks They Sang Melodious"', said Tiffany.

'Ah, I reckon that's the one we call "Pleasant and Delightful" back home. Just follow me, will you, and we'll soon get them in the right mood.'

And with that Nanny Ogg grabbed a passing waiter by the shoulder, took a full flagon from his tray, jumped up onto a table, as lively as a girl, and shouted for silence in a voice as brisk as a sergeant-major. 'Ladies and gentlemen! To celebrate the good life and easeful passing of our late friend and Baron, I have been asked to sing his favourite song. Do join in with me if you've got the breath!'

Tiffany listened, enthralled. Nanny Ogg was a one-woman masterclass, or rather mistressclass, in people.

She treated perfect strangers as if she had known them for years, and somehow they acted as if she really had. Dragged along, as it were, by an extremely good singing voice for one old woman with one tooth, perplexed people were raising their voices beyond a mumble by the second line, and by the end of the first verse were harmonizing like a choir, and she had them in her hand. Tiffany wept, and saw through the tears a little boy in his new tweed jacket that smelled of wee, walking with his father under different stars.

And then she saw the glisten of tears on the faces, including the faces of Pastor Egg and even the Duchess. The echoes were of loss and remembrance, and the hall itself breathed.

I should have learned this, she thought. I wanted to learn fire, and pain, but I should have learned people. I should have learned how not to sing like a turkey . . .

The song had finished, and people were looking around sheepishly at one another, but Nanny Ogg's boot was already making the table rock. '*Dance, dance, the shaking of the sheets. Dance, dance, when you hear the piper playing,*' she sang.

Tiffany thought, Is this the right song for a funeral? And then she thought, Of course it is! It's a wonderful tune and it tells us that one day all of us will die but – and this is the important thing – *we are not dead yet.*

And now Nanny Ogg had jumped off the table, grabbed a hold of Pastor Egg, and as she spun him round, she sang, '*Be assured no preacher can keep death away from any man,*' and he had the grace to smile and dance with her.

People applauded – not something Tiffany would ever have expected at a funeral. She wished, oh how she wished, to be like Nanny Ogg who *understood* things and knew how to hammer silence into laughter.

And then, as the applause died away, a male voice sang, '*Down in the valley, the valley so low, hang your head easy, hear the wind blow . . .*' And silence stood aside in the face of the unexpectedly silver voice of the sergeant.

Nanny Ogg drifted to where Tiffany was standing. 'Well, it looks like I've warmed them up. Hear them clearing their throats? I reckon the pastor will be singing by the end of the evening! And I could do with another drink. It's thirsty work, singing.' There was a wink, then she said to Tiffany, 'Human being first, witch second; hard to remember, easy to do.'

It was magic; magic had turned a hall full of people who mostly did not know very many of the other people there into human beings who knew they were among other human beings and, right now, that was all that needed to matter. At which point Preston tapped her on the shoulder. He had a curious kind of worried smile on his face.

'Sorry, miss, but I'm on duty, worst luck, and I think you ought to know we have three more visitors.'

'Can't you just show them in?' said Tiffany.

'I would like to do that, miss, only they are stuck on

the roof at the moment. The sound made by three witches is a lot of swearing, miss.'

If there had been swearing, the new arrivals had apparently run out of breath by the time Tiffany located the right window and crawled out onto the lead roof of the castle. There wasn't very much to hold onto and it was pretty misty, but she carefully made her way out there on her hands and knees and headed towards the grumbling.

'*Are* there any witches up here?' she said.

And out of the gloom came the voice of somebody not even *trying* to keep their temper. 'And what in the seven hells would you do if I said no, Miss Tiffany Aching?'

'*Mrs Proust?* What are *you* doing here?'

'Holding onto a gargoyle! Get us down right now, my dear, because these are not my stones and Mrs Happenstance needs the privy.'

Tiffany crawled a little further, well aware of the sheer drop an inch away from her hand. 'Preston has gone to fetch a rope. Do you have a broomstick?'

'A sheep crashed into it,' said Mrs Proust.

Tiffany could just make her out now. 'You crashed into a sheep in the air?'

'Maybe it was a cow, or something. What are those things that go *snuffle snuffle*?'

'You ran into a flying hedgehog?'

'No, as it happened. We were down low, looking for a bush for Mrs Happenstance.' There was a sigh in the gloom. 'It's because of her trouble, poor soul. We've stopped at a lot of bushes on the way here, believe me! And do you know what? Inside every single one of them is something that stings, bites, kicks, screams, howls, squelches, farts enormously, goes all spiky, tries to knock you over or does an enormous pile of poo! Haven't you people up here heard about porcelain?'

Tiffany was taken aback. 'Well, yes, but not in fields!'

'They would be all the better for it,' said Mrs Proust. 'I've ruined a decent pair of boots, I have.'

There was a clinking noise in the mist, and Tiffany was relieved to hear Preston say, 'I have forced open the old trapdoor, ladies, if you would be kind enough to crawl this way?'

The trapdoor opened into a bedroom, clearly one that had been slept in last night by a woman. Tiffany bit her lip. 'I think this is where the Duchess is staying. Please don't touch *anything*, she's bad enough as it is.'

'Duchess? Sounds posh,' said Mrs Proust. 'What kind of a duchess, may I ask?'

Tiffany said, 'The Duchess of Keepsake. You saw her when we had that bit of difficulty in the city. You know? At the King's Head? They've got a huge property about thirty miles away.'

'That's nice,' said Mrs Proust in a way that suggested that it probably wasn't going to be very nice but *would* be very interesting, and probably embarrassing to somebody who wasn't Mrs Proust. 'I remember her, and I remember thinking when I got back from all

that, Where have I seen you before, my lady? Do you
know anything about her, my dear?'

'Well, her daughter told me that a terrible fire took
away her property and her whole family before she
married the Duke.'

Mrs Proust brightened up, although it was the
brightness on the edge of a knife. 'Oh, really?' she said,
her voice all treacle. 'Just fancy that. I look forward
to meeting the lady *again* and offering my -
condolences . . .'

Tiffany decided that this was a puzzle she had no
time to unravel, but there were other things to think
about. 'Er . . . ?' she began, looking at the very tall lady
somehow trying to hide behind Mrs Proust, who
turned round and said, 'Oh dear me, where are my
manners? I know, I never had any to start with. Tiffany
Aching, this is Miss Cambric, better known as Long
Tall Short Fat Sally. Miss Cambric is being trained by
old Mrs Happenstance, who was the one you briefly
saw hurrying down the stairs with one aim in mind.
Sally suffers terribly from tides, poor thing. I had to
bring them both because Sally had the only working
broomstick I could find and she wouldn't leave Mrs
Happenstance behind. It was the devil, keeping the
broomstick trim. Don't worry, she'll be back to about
five foot six in a few hours. Of course, she's a martyr
to ceilings. And Sally, you'd better get after Mrs
Happenstance right now.'

She waved a hand and the younger witch scurried
off, looking nervous. When Mrs Proust gave orders,

they tended to be obeyed. She turned back to Tiffany. 'The thing that is after you has got a body now, young lady. He has stolen the body of a murderer locked up in the Tanty. You know what? Before the bloke got out of the building he killed his canary. They *never* kill their canary. It's what you don't do. You might beat another prisoner over the head with an iron bar in a riot, but you *never* kill a canary. That would be *evil*.'

It was a strange way to introduce the subject, but Mrs Proust didn't do small talk or, for that matter, reassurance.

'I thought something like this would happen,' said Tiffany. 'I *knew* it would. What does he look like?'

'We lost him a couple of times,' said Mrs Proust. 'Calls of nature, and so on. He might have broken into a house for better clothes, I couldn't say. He won't care about the body. He'll run it until he finds another one or it falls to pieces. We'll keep an eye out for him. And this is your steading?'

Tiffany sighed, 'Yes. And now he is chasing me like a wolf after a lamb.'

'Then if you care about people, you must get rid of him quick,' said Mrs Proust. 'If a wolf gets hungry enough it will eat *anything*. And now, where are *your* manners, Miss Aching? We're cold and wet, and by the sound of it there is food and drink downstairs, am I right?'

'Oh, I'm sorry, and you've come all this way to warn me,' said Tiffany.

Mrs Proust waved a hand as if it wasn't important.

'I'm sure Long Tall Short Fat Sally and Mrs Happenstance would like some refreshment after our long ride, but I'm just tired,' she said. And then, to Tiffany's horror, she flung herself backwards and landed on the Duchess's bed with only her boots sticking off the end, dripping water. 'This Duchess,' she said, 'has she been giving you any more grief at all?'

'Well, yes, I'm afraid so,' said Tiffany. 'She doesn't seem to have any respect for anybody lower than a king, and even then I suspect that's only a maybe. She bullies her daughter too,' she added, and as an after-thought pointed out, 'One of your customers, in fact.' And then she told Mrs Proust everything about Letitia and the Duchess because Mrs Proust was the kind of woman you told everything to, and as the story unfolded, Mrs Proust's grin grew wider, and Tiffany needed no witch skill to suspect that the Duchess was going to be in some trouble.

'I thought so. I never forget a face. Have you ever heard of the music hall, my dear? Oh, no. You wouldn't have, not out here. It's all about comedians and singers and talking-dog acts – and, of course, dancing girls. I think you are getting the picture here, are you not? Not such a bad job for a girl who could shake a handsome leg, especially since after the show all the posh gentlemen would be waiting outside the stage door to take them out for a lovely dinner and so on.' The witch took off her pointy hat and dropped it on the floor beside the bed. 'Can't abide broomsticks,' she said. 'They give me calluses in places where nobody should have calluses.'

Tiffany was at a loss. She couldn't demand that Mrs Proust get off the bed; it wasn't *her* bed. It wasn't *her* castle. She smiled. In fact it really wasn't her problem. How nice to find a problem that wasn't yours.

'Mrs Proust,' she said, 'could I persuade you to come downstairs? There are some other witches down here who I would really like you to meet.' Preferably when I'm not in the room, she thought to herself, but I doubt if that would be possible.

'Hedge witches?' Mrs Proust sniffed. 'Although there's nothing actually wrong with hedge magic,' she went on. 'I met one once who could run her hands over a privet hedge and three months later it had grown into the shape of two peacocks and an offensively cute little dog holding a privet bone in its mouth, and all this, mark you, without a pair of shears being anywhere near it.'

'Why did she want to do that?' said Tiffany, astounded.

'I doubt very much that she actually *wanted* to do it, but someone asked her to do it, and paid good money too and, strictly speaking, topiary is not actually illegal, although I rather suspect that one or two folk are going to be the first up against the hedge when the revolution comes. Hedge witches – that's what we call country witches in the city.'

'Oh, really,' said Tiffany innocently. 'Well, I don't know what we call city witches in the country, but I am sure that Mistress Weatherwax will tell you.' She knew she should have felt guilty about this, but it had been a long day, after a long week, and a witch has got to have some fun in her life.

The way downstairs took them past Letitia's room. Tiffany heard voices, and a laugh. It was Nanny Ogg's laugh. You couldn't mistake that laugh; it was the kind of laugh that slapped you on the back. Then Letitia's voice said, 'Does that really work?' And Nanny said something under her breath that Tiffany couldn't quite hear, but whatever it was, it made Letitia almost choke with giggling. Tiffany smiled. The blushing bride was being instructed by somebody who had probably never blushed in her life, and it seemed quite a happy arrangement. At least she was not bursting into tears every five minutes.

Tiffany led Mrs Proust down into the hall. It was amazing to see that all people needed to make them happy was food and drink and other people. Even with Nanny Ogg no longer chivvying them along, they were filling the place with, well, people being people. And, standing where she could see very nearly everybody, Granny Weatherwax. She was talking to Pastor Egg.

Tiffany drifted up to her carefully, judging from the priest's face that he wouldn't mind at all if she intruded. Granny Weatherwax could be very forthright on the subject of religion. She saw him relax as she said, 'Mistress Weatherwax, may I introduce to you Mrs Proust? From Ankh-Morpork, where she runs a remarkable emporium.' Swallowing, Tiffany turned to

Mrs Proust and said, 'May I present to you Granny Weatherwax.'

She stepped back as the two elderly witches looked at one another and then held her breath. The hall fell silent and neither of them blinked. And then – surely not – Granny Weatherwax winked and Mrs Proust smiled.

'Very pleased to make your acquaintance,' said Granny.

'How very nice to see you,' said Mrs Proust.

They exchanged a further glance and turned to Tiffany Aching, who suddenly understood that old, clever witches had been older and cleverer for much longer than her.

Granny Weatherwax almost laughed when Mrs Proust said, 'We don't need to know one another's names to recognize one another, but can I suggest, young lady, that you start breathing again.'

Granny Weatherwax lightly and primly took Mrs Proust's arm and turned to where Nanny Ogg was coming down the stairs, followed by Letitia, who was blushing in places where people don't often blush, and said, 'Do come with me, my dear. You must meet my friend, Mrs Ogg, who buys quite a lot of your merchandise.'

Tiffany walked away. For a brief moment in time, there was nothing for her to do. She looked down the length of the hall, where people were still gathering in little groups, and saw the Duchess by herself. Why did she do it? Why did she walk over to the woman?

Maybe, she thought, if you know you are going to be facing a horrible monster, it is as well to get in a little practice. But to her absolute amazement, the Duchess was crying.

'Can I help in any way?' said Tiffany.

She was the immediate subject of a glare, but the tears were still falling. 'She's all I've got,' said the Duchess, looking over at Letitia, who was still trailing Nanny Ogg. 'I'm sure Roland will be a very considerate husband. I hope she will think that I have given her a good grounding to get her safely through the world.'

'I think you've definitely taught her many things,' said Tiffany.

But the Duchess was now staring at the witches, and without looking at Tiffany she said, 'I know we've had our differences, young lady, but I wonder if you can tell me who that lady is up there, one of your sister witches, talking to the remarkably tall one.'

Tiffany glanced around for a moment. 'Oh, that's Mrs Proust. She's from Ankh-Morpork, you know. Is she an old friend of yours? She was asking about you, only a little while ago.'

The Duchess smiled, but it was a strange little smile. If smiles had a colour, it would have been green. 'Oh,' she said. 'That was, er' – she paused, swaying a little – 'very kind of her.' She coughed. 'I am so glad that you and my daughter appear to be close chums and I would like to tender you my apologies for any hastiness on my part in recent days. I would also very much like to tender you and the hard-working staff here my apologies for what may have appeared to be high-handed behaviour, and I trust you will accept that these stemmed from a mother's determination to do the very best for her child.' She spoke very carefully, the words coming out like children's coloured building blocks, and between the blocks – like mortar – were the unspoken words: *Please, please, don't tell people I was a dancer in a music hall. Please!*

'Well, of course, we're all on edge,' said Tiffany. 'Least said, soonest mended, as they say.'

'Regrettably,' said the Duchess, 'I don't think I said least.' Tiffany noticed that there was a large wine glass in her hand, and it was almost empty. The Duchess watched Tiffany for a while and then continued, 'A wedding almost straight after a funeral, is that right?'

'Some people think that it's bad luck to move a wedding once it's planned,' said Tiffany.

'Do you believe in luck?' said the Duchess.

'I believe in not having to believe in luck,' said Tiffany. 'But, your grace, I can tell you in truth that at such times the universe gets a little closer to us. They are strange times, times of beginnings and endings. Dangerous and powerful. And we feel it even if we don't know what it is. These times are not necessarily good, and not necessarily bad. In fact, what they are depends on what *we* are.'

The Duchess looked down at the empty glass in her hand. 'For some reason, I think I should be taking a nap.' She turned to head towards the stairs, nearly missing the first step.

There was a burst of laughter from the other end of the hall. Tiffany followed the Duchess, but stopped to tap Letitia on the shoulder.

'If I was you, I'd go and talk to your mum before she goes upstairs. I think she'd like to talk to you now.' She bent down and whispered in her ear, 'But don't tell her too much about what Nanny Ogg said.'

Letitia looked about to object, saw Tiffany's expression, thought better of it and intercepted her mother.

And now, suddenly, Granny Weatherwax was at Tiffany's side. After a while, as if addressing the air, Granny said, 'You have a good steading here. Nice people. And I'll tell you one thing. *He* is near.'

Tiffany noticed that the other witches – even Long Tall Short Fat Sally – were now lining up just behind Granny Weatherwax. She was the focus of their stares, and when a lot of witches are staring at you, you can feel it like the sun. 'Is there something you want to say?' said Tiffany. 'There is, isn't there?'

It wasn't often, and in fact now Tiffany came to think of it, it wasn't *ever* that she had seen Granny Weatherwax look worried.

'You are certain that you can best the Cunning Man, are you not? I see you don't wear midnight yet.'

'When I am *old*, I shall wear midnight,' said Tiffany. 'It's a matter of choice. And Granny, I know why you are here. It is to kill me if I fail, isn't it?'

'Blast it,' Granny Weatherwax said. 'You are a witch, a good witch. But some of us think that it might be best if we *insisted* on helping you.'

'No,' said Tiffany. 'My steading. My mess. My problem.'

'No matter what?' said Granny.

'Definitely!'

'Well, I commend you for your adherence to your position and wish you . . . no, not luck, but certainty!' There was a susurration among the witches and Granny snapped sharply, 'She has made her decision and that, ladies, is *it*.'

'No contest,' said Nanny Ogg with a grin. 'I very nearly pity him. Kick him in the— Kick him anywhere you can, Tiff!'

'It's your ground,' said Mrs Proust. 'How can a witch do anything but succeed on her own home ground?'

Granny Weatherwax nodded. 'If you have let pride get the better of you, then you have already lost, but if you grab pride by the scruff of the neck and ride it like a stallion, then you may have already won. And now I think it's time for you to prepare, Miss Tiffany Aching. Do you have a plan for the morning?'

Tiffany looked into the piercing blue eyes. 'Yes. Not to lose.'

'That's a good plan.'

Mrs Proust shook Tiffany with a hand that was prickly with warts and said, 'By happy accident, my girl, I think I should go and slay a monster myself . . .'

# CHAPTER 14

# Burning the King

Tiffany knew she wouldn't go to sleep that night, and didn't try. People sat together in little groups, talking, and there was still food and drink on the tables. Possibly because of the drink, the people didn't actually notice how fast the food and drink were disappearing, but Tiffany was certain she could hear faint noises in the beams high above. Of course, witches were proverbially good at stuffing food into their pockets for later, but probably the Feegles outdid them by sheer numbers.

Tiffany moved aimlessly from group to group, and when the Duchess finally left to go upstairs, she didn't follow her. She was quite emphatic to herself that she wasn't following. She just happened to be going in the same direction. And, when she darted across the stone

373

floor to reach the door of the Duchess's room, just after it closed behind the woman, she wasn't doing this in order to eavesdrop. Certainly not.

She was just in time to hear the beginning of an angry scream, and then Mrs Proust's voice: 'Why, Deirdre Parsley! Long time, no sequins! Can you still high-kick a man's top hat off his head?' And then there was silence. And Tiffany left hurriedly, because the door was very thick and someone would be bound to notice if she stood there any longer with her ear pressed to it.

So she went back down in time to talk to Long Tall Short Fat Sally and Mrs Happenstance, who she now realized was blind, which was unfortunate but not – for a witch – too much of a tragedy. They always had a few extra senses to spare.

And then she went down into the crypt.

There were flowers all around the old Baron's tomb, but not on it because the marble lid was so beautifully made that it would be a shame even to cover it with roses. On the stone, stonemasons had carved the Baron himself, in armour and holding his sword; it was so perfectly done that it looked as if he might, at any moment, get up and walk away. At the four corners of the slab, candles burned.

Tiffany walked to and fro past other dead barons in stone. Here and there was a wife, carved with her hands peacefully folded; it was . . . strange. There were no gravestones on the Chalk. Stone was too precious. There were burying grounds, and in the castle somewhere was an ancient book of faded maps that showed where people had been put. The only common person to have a memorial, who was in most respects an extremely uncommon person, was Granny Aching; the cast-iron wheels and pot-bellied stove that were all that remained of her shepherding hut would certainly survive for another hundred years. It had been good metal, and the endlessly nibbling sheep kept the ground around it as smooth as a tabletop, and besides, the grease from the sheep's fleeces as they rubbed up against the wheels were as good as oil for keeping the metal as fine as the day it was cast.

In the old days, before a knight became a knight, he would spend a night in his hall with his weapons, praying to whichever gods were listening to give him strength and good wisdom.

She was sure she heard those words spoken, at least in her head if not in her ears. She turned and looked at the sleeping knights, and wondered if Mrs Proust was right, and stone had a memory.

And what are *my* weapons? she thought. And the answer came to her instantly: pride. Oh, you hear them say it's a sin; you hear them say it goes before a fall. And that can't be true. The blacksmith prides himself on a good weld; the carter is proud that his horses are well turned out, gleaming like fresh chestnuts in the sunshine; the shepherd prides himself on keeping the wolf from the flock; the cook prides herself on her cakes. We pride ourselves on making a good history of our lives, a good story to be told.

And I also have fear – the fear that I will let others down – and because I fear, I will overcome that fear. I will not disgrace those who have trained me.

And I have trust, even though I am not sure what it is I am trusting.

'Pride, fear and trust,' she said aloud. And in front of her the four candles streamed fire, as if driven by the wind, and for a moment she was certain, in the rush of light, that the figure of an old witch was melting into the dark stone. 'Oh, yes,' said Tiffany. 'And I have fire.'

And then, not knowing exactly why, she said, 'When I am old, I shall wear midnight. But not today.'

Tiffany held up her lantern and the shadows moved, but one, which looked very much like an old woman in black, faded completely. And I know why the hare leaps into the fire, and tomorrow . . . No, today, I am leaping into it too. She smiled.

When Tiffany got back in the hall, the witches were all watching her from the stairs. Tiffany had wondered how Granny and Mrs Proust would get on, given that both of them were as proud as a cat full of sixpences. But they seemed to be getting on well enough in a talking-about-the-weather, the-manners-of-young-people-these-days and the-scandalous-price-of- cheese sort of way. But Nanny Ogg looked unusually worried. Seeing Nanny Ogg looking worried was *worrying*. It was past midnight – technically speaking, the witching hour. In real life every hour was a witching hour, but nevertheless the way the two hands on the clock stood straight up was slightly eerie.

'I hear that the lads came back from their stag-night fun,' said Nanny, 'but it seems to me they've forgotten where they left the groom. I don't think he is going to go anywhere, though. They are pretty certain they took his trousers down and tied him to something.' She coughed. 'That's generally the usual procedure. Technically the best man is supposed to remember where, but they found him and he can't remember his own name.'

The clock in the hall struck midnight; it was never on time. Each strike may as well have hit Tiffany's backbone.

And there, marching towards her, was Preston. And it seemed to Tiffany that for quite some time, wherever she had looked, there was Preston, looking smart and clean and – somehow – hopeful.

'Look, Preston,' she said. 'I haven't got time to explain things, and I'm not certain you would believe them – no, you probably *would* believe them if I told you them. I have to go out there to kill that monster before it kills me.'

'Then I will protect you,' said Preston. 'Anyway, my commander-in-chief might be out there somewhere in the pigsty with a sow sniffing his unmentionables! And I represent the temporal power here!'

'*You?*' Tiffany snapped.

Preston stuck out his chest, although it didn't go very far. 'As a matter of fact, yes: the lads made me officer of the Watch so that they could all have a drink, and right now the sergeant is in the kitchen, throwing up in the sink. He thought he could outdrink Mrs Ogg!' He saluted. 'I'm going out there with you, miss. And you can't stop me. No offence meant, of course. However by virtue of the power invested in me by the sergeant, in between him throwing up into the sink, I would like to commandeer you and your broomstick to assist me in my search, if that is all right with you?'

It was a dreadful question to ask a witch. On the other hand, it was being asked by Preston. 'All right then,' she said, 'but do try not to scratch it. And there is one thing that I have to do first. Do excuse me.' She walked a little way over to the open door of the hall and leaned against the cold stonework. 'I know there are Feegles listening to me,' she said.

'Oh aye,' said a voice about one inch from her ear.

'Well, I don't want you to help me tonight. This is a hag thing, you understand?'

'Oh aye, we seen the big posse of hags. It's a big hag night the noo.'

'I must—' Tiffany began. And then an idea struck her. 'I have to fight the man with no eyes. And they are here to see how good a fighter I am. And so I mustn't cheat by using Feegles. That's an important hag rule. Of course, I respect the fact that cheating is an honourable Feegle tradition, but hags don't cheat,' she went on, aware that this was a huge lie. 'If you help me, they will know, and all the hags will put me to scorn.'

And Tiffany thought, And if I lose, it will be Feegles

versus hags, and that's a battle that the world will remember. No pressure, eh?

Aloud, she said, 'You understand, right? This once, just this once, you will do as I tell you and *not help me.*'

'Aye, we understand ye. But ye ken that Jeannie says we must look out for ye at all times, because ye are our hag o' the hills,' said Rob.

'I'm sorry to say that the kelda is not here,' said Tiffany, 'but I am and I have to tell you that if you help me this once I will no longer be your hag o' the hills. I'm under a geas, ye ken. It's a hag geas, and that's a big geas indeed.' She heard a group groan, and added, 'I mean it. The chief hag is Granny Weatherwax and you know *her.*' There was another groan. 'There you are then,' said Tiffany. 'This time, please, let me do things my way. Is that understood?'

There was a pause, and then the voice of Rob Anybody said, 'Och aye.'

'Very well,' said Tiffany, and took a deep breath and went to find her broomstick.

Taking Preston with her didn't seem such a good idea as they rose above the roofs of the castle.

'Why didn't you tell me that you were scared of flying?' she said.

'That's hardly fair,' said Preston. 'This is the first time I've ever flown.'

When they were at a decent height, Tiffany looked at the weather. There were clouds above the mountains, and the occasional flash of summer lightning. She could hear the rumble of thunder in the distance. You were never far from a thunderstorm in the mountains. The mist had lifted, and the moon was up; it was a perfect night. And there was a breeze. She had hoped for this. And Preston had his arms around her waist; she wasn't sure whether she had hoped for that or not.

They were well down onto the plains at the foot of the Chalk now, and even by moonlight Tiffany could see dark rectangles where earlier fields had been cleared. The men were always meticulous about not letting the fires get out of hand; nobody wanted wild-fire – there was no telling what that would burn. The field they reached was the very last one. They always called it the King. Usually when the King was burned, half the village was waiting to catch any rabbits that fled the flames. That should have happened today, but everybody had been . . . otherwise occupied.

The chicken houses and the pigsty were in a field just above it at the top of a bank, and it was said that the King grew such bountiful crops because the men found it much easier to cart the mulch onto the King rather than take it all to the lower fields.

They landed by the pigsties, to the usual ferocious screaming of piglets, who believed that no matter what is actually happening, the world is trying to saw them in half.

She sniffed. The air smelled of pig; she was sure, absolutely sure, that she would nevertheless smell the ghost if and when he was here. Mucky though they were, the pigs nevertheless had a natural smell; the smell of the ghost, on the other hand, would make a pig smell like violets by comparison. She shuddered. The wind was getting up.

'Are you sure you can kill it?' whispered Preston.

'I think I can make it kill itself. And Preston, I absolutely forbid you to help me.'

'I'm sorry,' said Preston. 'Temporal power, you understand. You can't give me orders, Miss Aching, if that's all right by you.'

'You mean your sense of duty and your obedience to your commander means that you must help me?' she said.

'Well, yes, miss,' said Preston, 'and a few other considerations.'

'Then I really need you, Preston, I really do. I *think* I could do this myself, but it will make it so much easier if you help me. What I want you to do is—'

She was almost certain that the ghost would not be able to overhear, but she lowered her voice anyway, and Preston absorbed her words without blinking and simply said, 'That sounds pretty straightforward, miss. You can rely on the temporal power.'

'*Yuck! How did I end up here?*'

Something grey and sticky and smelling very much of pig and beer tried to pull itself over the pigsty wall. Tiffany knew it was Roland, but only because it was highly improbable that *two* bridegrooms had been thrown into the pigsty tonight. And he rose like something nasty from the swamp, dripping . . . well, just dripping; there was hardly any necessity to go into details. Bits of him splashed off.

He hiccupped. 'There appears to be an enormous pig in my bedroom, and it would seem that I have mislaid my trousers,' he said, his voice baffled by alcohol. The young Baron peered around, understanding not so much dawning as bursting. 'I don't think this is my bedroom, is it?' he said, and slowly slipped back into the sty.

*She smelled the ghost.* Over and above the mix of smells coming from the pigsty it stood out like a fox among chickens. And now the ghost spoke, in a voice of horror and decay. *I can feel you here, witch, and others too. I do not care about them, but this new body, while not very robust, has . . . a permanent agenda of its own. I am strong. I am coming. You cannot save everybody. I doubt if your fiendish flying stick can carry four people. Who will you leave behind? Why not leave them all? Why not leave the tiresome rival, the boy who spurned you, and the persistent young man? Oh, I know how you think, witch!*

But I don't think that way, Tiffany thought to herself. Oh, I might have liked to see Roland in the pigsty, but people aren't just people, they are people surrounded by circumstances.

But you aren't. You're not even people any more.

Beside her, with a horrible sucking noise, Preston pulled Roland out of the pigsty, against the protest of the sow. How lucky for both of them that they couldn't hear the voice.

She paused. *Four people? The tiresome rival?*

But there was only herself, Roland and Preston, wasn't there?

She looked towards the far end of the field, in the moon shadow of the castle. A white figure was running towards them at speed.

It had to be Letitia. *Nobody* around here wore so much billowing white all the time. Tiffany's mind spun with the algebra of tactics.

'Preston, off you go. Take the broomstick.'

Preston nodded and then saluted, with a grin. 'At your service, miss.'

Letitia arrived in a flurry and expensive white slippers. She stopped dead when she saw Roland, who was sober enough to try to cover, with his hands, what Tiffany knew she would always now think of as his passionate parts. This simply made a squelching noise, since he was thickly encrusted in pig muck.

'One of his chums told me they threw him in the pigsty for a laugh!' Letitia said indignantly. 'And they call themselves his friends!'

'I think *they* think that's what friends are for,' said Tiffany absentmindedly. To herself she thought, Is this going to work? Have I overlooked something? Have I understood what I should do? Who do I think I'm talking to? I suppose I'm looking for a sign, just a sign.

There was a rustling noise. She looked down. A hare looked up at her and then, without panicking, lost herself in the stubbles.

'I'll take that as a yes, then,' said Tiffany, and felt panicked herself. After all, *was* that an omen, or was it just a hare who was old enough not to run instantly when she saw people? And it wasn't good manners, she was sure, to ask for a second sign to tell you if the first sign wasn't just a coincidence, was it?

At this point, this *very* point, Roland started to sing, possibly because of drink, but also perhaps because Letitia was industriously wiping him down while keeping her eyes closed so that, as an unmarried woman, she wouldn't see anything unseemly or surprising. And the song that Roland sang went: '*Tis pleasant and delightful on the bright summer's morn, to see the fields and the meadows all covered in corn, and the small birds were singing on every green spray, and the larks they sang melodious, at the dawning of the day . . .*' He paused. 'My father used to sing that quite a lot when we walked in these fields . . .' he said. He was at that stage when drunken men started to cry, and the tears left little trails of pink behind as the muck was washed from his cheeks.

But Tiffany thought, Thank you. An omen was an omen. You picked the ones that worked. And this was the big field, the field where they burned the last of the stubbles. And *the hare runs into the fire*. Oh, yes, the omens. They were always so important.

'Listen to me, both of you. I am not going to be argued with by you, because you, Roland, are rascally drunk and you, Letitia, are a witch' – Letitia beamed at that point – 'who is junior to me, and therefore both of you *will do what I tell you*. And that way, all of us may get back to the castle alive.'

They both stopped and listened, Roland swaying gently.

'When I shout,' Tiffany continued, 'I want you to each grab one of my hands and *run*! Turn if I turn, stop if I stop, although I doubt very much that I shall want to stop. Above all, don't be afraid, and *trust me*. I'm almost sure I know what I'm doing.' Tiffany realized that this wasn't the best assurance, but they didn't seem to notice. She added, 'And when I say leap, leap as if a devil is behind you, because it *will* be.'

The stink was suddenly unbearable. The sheer hatred in it seemed to beat on Tiffany's brain. By the pricking of my thumbs, something wicked this way comes, she thought as she stared into the night-time gloom. By the stinking of my nose, something evil this way goes, she added, to stop herself gibbering as she scanned the distant hedge for movement.

And there was a figure.

There, heavy-set, walking towards them down the length of the field. It moved slowly, but was gathering speed. There was an awkwardness about it. '*When he takes over a body, the owner of the body becomes a part of him too. No escape, no release.*' That's what Eskarina had told her. Nothing good, nothing capable of redemption, could have thoughts that stank like that. She gripped the hands of the arguing couple and dragged them into a run. The . . . creature was between them and the castle. And was going more slowly than she'd expected. She risked another look and saw the glint of metal in its hands. *Knives.*

'Come on!'

'These aren't very good shoes for running in,' Letitia pointed out.

'My head aches,' Roland supplied as Tiffany towed them towards the bottom of the field, ignoring all complaints as dry corn stalks snatched at them, caught hair, scratched legs and stung feet. They were barely going at a jog. The creature was following them doggedly. As soon as they turned to run up towards the castle and safety, it would gain on them . . .

But the creature was having difficulties as well, and Tiffany wondered how far you could push a body if you didn't feel its pain, couldn't feel the agony of the lungs, the pounding of the heart, the cracking of the bones, the dreadful ache that pushed you to the last gasp and beyond. Mrs Proust had whispered to her, eventually, the things that the man Macintosh had done, as if saying the words aloud would pollute the air. Against that, how did you rank the crushing of the little songbird? And yet somehow that lodged in the mind as a crime beyond mercy.

There will be no mercy for a song now silenced. No redemption for killing hope in the darkness. I know you.

You are what whispered in Petty's ear before he beat up his daughter.

You are the first blast of the rough music.

You look over the shoulder at the man as he picks up the first stone, and although I think you are part of us all and we will never be rid of you, we can certainly make your life hell.

No mercy. No redemption.

Glancing back, she saw its face looming bigger now and redoubled her efforts to drag the tired and reluctant couple over the rough ground. She managed a breath to say, 'Look at him! Look at it! Do you want him to catch us?' She heard a brief scream from Letitia and a groan of sudden sobriety from her husband-to-be. The eyes of the luckless Macintosh were bloodshot and wide open, the lips stuck in a frenzied grin. It tried to take advantage of the sudden narrowed gap but the other two had found fresh strength in their fear and they were almost pulling *Tiffany* along.

And now there was a clear run up the field. It all depended on Preston. Amazingly, Tiffany felt confident. He is trustworthy, she thought, but there was a horrible gurgle behind them. The ghost was driving its host harder, and she could imagine the swish of a long knife. Timing had to be everything. Preston *was* trustworthy. He had understood, hadn't he? Of course he had. She could trust Preston.

Later on, what she remembered most was the silence, broken only by the crackling of the stalks and the heavy breathing of Letitia and Roland and the horrible wheezing of their pursuer. In her head the silence was broken by the voice of the Cunning Man.

*You are setting a trap. Filth! Do you think I can be so easily caught again? Little girls who play with fire will get burned, and you will burn, I promise you, oh you will burn. Where then will be the pride of witches! Vessels of iniquity! Handmaidens of uncleanliness! Defilers of all that is holy!*

Tiffany kept her eyes fixed on the end of the field as tears streamed out. She couldn't help it. It was impossible to keep the vileness out; it drizzled in like poison, seeping into her ears and flowing under her skin.

Another swish in the air behind them made all three runners find redoubled strength, but she knew it couldn't go on. Was that Preston she saw in the gloom ahead? Then who was the dark figure beside him, looking like an old witch in a pointy hat? Even as she stared at it, it faded away.

But suddenly fire burst up and Tiffany could hear the crackling as it spread like a sunrise across the field towards them, sparks filling the sky with extra stars. And the wind blew hard and she heard the stinking voice again: *You will burn. You* will *burn!*

And the wind gusted and the flames blew up, and now a wall of fire was racing through the stubbles as fast as the wind itself. Tiffany looked down and the hare was back, running along beside them without any apparent effort; she looked at Tiffany, flicked up her legs and ran, ran directly towards the fire now, seriously ran.

'Run!' Tiffany commanded. 'The fire will not burn you if you do what I say! Run fast! *Run fast! Roland, run to save Letitia. Letitia, run to save Roland.*'

The fire was almost on them. I need the strength, she thought. I need the power. And she remembered

Nanny Ogg saying: 'The world changes. The world flows. There's power there, my girl.'

Weddings and funerals are a time of power . . . yes, weddings.

Tiffany grasped their two hands even tighter. And here it came. A crackling, roaring wall of flame . . .

'Leap!'

And as they leaped, she screamed: '*Leap, knave. Jump, whore.*' She felt them lift as the fire reached them.

Time hesitated. A rabbit sped past beneath them, fleeing in terror from the flames. He *will* flee, she thought. He will *run* from the fire, but the fire will run to him. And the fire runs much faster than a dying body.

Tiffany floated in a ball of yellow flame. The hare drifted past her, a creature happy in her element. We are not as fast as you, she thought. We will get singed. She looked right and left at the bride and groom, who were staring ahead as if hypnotised, and pulled them towards her. She understood. I *am* going to marry you, Roland. I said I would.

She would make something *beautiful* out of this fire.

'Back to the hells you came from, you Cunning Man,' she yelled above the flames. '*Leap, knave! Jump, whore!*' she screamed again. '*Be married now for ever more!*' And this is a wedding, she said to herself. A fresh start. And for a few seconds in the world, this is a place of power. Oh yes, a place of power.

They landed, rolling, behind the wall of fire. Tiffany was ready, stamping out embers and kicking the small flames that remained. Preston was suddenly there too, picking up Letitia and carrying her out of the ash. Tiffany put an arm round Roland, who had had a soft landing (possibly on his head, part of Tiffany thought), and followed him.

'Looks like very minor burns and some frizzled hair,' said Preston, 'and as for your old boyfriend, I think his mud is now baked on. How did you manage it?'

Tiffany took a deep breath. 'The hare jumps through the flames so fast that she barely feels them,' she said, 'and when she lands, she lands on hot ash mostly. A grass fire burns out quickly under a strong wind.'

There was a scream from behind them, and she imagined a lumbering figure trying to outrun the wind-driven flames bearing down on it, and failing. She felt the pain of a creature that had twisted through the world for hundreds of years.

'The three of you, stay right here. Do not follow me! Preston, look after them!'

Tiffany walked across the cooling ash. I have to see, she thought. I have to witness. I have to know what it is that I have done!

The dead man's clothes were smouldering. There was no pulse. He did terrible things to people, she thought: things that made even the prison warders sick. But what was done to him first? Was he just a much worse version of Mr Petty? Could he ever have been good? How do you change the past? Where does evil begin?

She felt the words slide into her mind like a worm:

*Murderer, filth, killer!* And she felt she should apologize to her ears for what they had to hear. But the voice of the ghost was weak and thin and querulous, sliding backwards into history.

You can't reach me, she thought. You are used up. You are too weak now. How hard was it, forcing a man to run himself to death? You can't get in. I can feel you trying. She reached down into the ash and picked up a lump of flint, still warm from the fire; the soil was full of it, the sharpest of stones. Born in the chalk, and so in a way was Tiffany. Its smoothness was the touch of a friend.

'You never learn, do you?' she said. 'You don't understand that other people think too. Of course you wouldn't run into the fire; but in your arrogance you never realized that the fire would run to you.'

Your power is only rumour and lies, she thought. You bore your way into people when they are uncertain and weak and worried and frightened, and they think their enemy is other people when their enemy is, and always will be, *you* – the master of lies. Outside, you are fearsome; inside, you are nothing but weakness.

Inside, *I* am flint.

She felt the heat of the whole field, steadied herself and gripped the stone. How *dare* you come here, you worm! How *dare* you trespass on what is mine! She felt the flint get hotter in her hand and then melt and flow between her fingers and drip onto the soil as she concentrated. She had never tried this before and she took a deep breath of air that somehow the flames had cleansed.

And if you come back, Cunning Man, there will be another witch like me. There will *always* be another witch like me, because there are always going to be things like you, because we make space for them. But right now, on this bleeding piece of earth, *I* am the witch and *you* are nothing. *By the blinking of my eyes, something wicked this way dies.*

A hiss in her mind faded away and left her alone among her thoughts.

'No mercy,' she said aloud, 'no redemption. You forced a man to kill his harmless songbird, and somehow I think that was the greatest crime of them all.'

By the time she had walked back up the field, she had managed to become, once again, the Tiffany Aching who knew how to make cheese and deal with everyday chores and didn't squeeze molten rock between her fingers.

The happy but slightly singed couple were beginning to take some notice of things. Letitia sat up. 'I feel cooked,' she said. 'What's that smell?'

'Sorry, it's you,' said Tiffany, 'and I'm afraid that wonderful lace nightshirt might just about be usable to clean windows from now on. I'm afraid we didn't leap as fast as the hare.'

Letitia looked around. 'Is Roland . . . is he all right?'

'Right as rain,' said Preston cheerily. 'The wet pig muck really helped.'

Letitia paused for a moment. 'And that . . . thing?'

'Gone,' said Tiffany.

'Are you *sure* Roland is all right?' Letitia insisted.

Preston grinned. 'Absolutely tickety boo, miss. Nothing important has been burned away, although it might be a little painful when we take the crusts off. He's somewhat baked on, if you get my meaning.'

Letitia nodded and then turned, slowly, to Tiffany. 'What was that you said when we were jumping?'

Tiffany took a deep breath. 'I married you.'

'You, that is to say *you*, married, which is to say, wedded . . . *us*?' said Letitia.

'Yes,' said Tiffany. 'That is to say, certainly. Jumping over the fire together is a very ancient form of marriage. Doesn't need any priests either, which is a great saving on the catering.'

The possible bride weighed this one up. 'Are you sure?'

'Well, that's what Mrs Ogg told me,' said Tiffany, 'and I've always wanted to try it.'

This seemed to meet with Letitia's approval, because she said, 'Mrs Ogg is a very knowledgeable lady, I must admit. She knows a surprising number of things.'

Tiffany, keeping her face as straight as possible, said, 'A *surprising* number of surprising things.'

'Oh, yes . . . Er.' Letitia cleared her throat rather hesitantly and followed up 'er' with an 'um'.

'Is something wrong?' said Tiffany.

'That word you used about me while we were jumping. I think it was a *bad* word.'

Tiffany had been expecting this. 'Well, apparently it's traditional.' Her voice almost as hesitant as Letitia's, she added, 'And I don't think Roland is a knave, either. And, of course, words and their usage do change over the years.'

'I don't think that one does!' said Letitia.

'Well, it depends on circumstance and context,' said Tiffany. 'But frankly, Letitia, a witch will use any tool at hand in an emergency, as you might learn one day. Besides, the way we think about some words does change. For example, do you know the meaning of the word "buxom"?' She thought to herself, Why am I making this small talk? I know: because it's an anchor, and reassures me that I am a human being among other humans, and it helps wash the terror out of my soul . . .

'Yes,' said the bride-to-be. 'I'm afraid I'm not, very, um, large in that department.'

'That would have been a bit unfortunate a couple of hundred years ago because the wedding service in those days required a bride to be buxom towards her husband.'

'I'd have had to push a cushion down my bodice!'

'Not really; it used to mean kind, understanding and obedient,' said Tiffany.

'Oh, I can do those,' said Letitia. 'At least, the first two,' she added with a grin. She cleared her throat. 'What is it, apart from getting married, of course – and I am very amused about that – that we have just done?'

'Well,' said Tiffany. 'You have helped me trap one of the worst monsters that has ever fouled the world.'

The new bride brightened up. 'Did we? Well, that's

good,' she said. 'I'm very glad *we* did that. I don't know how we can repay you for all *your* help though.'

'Well, clean used linen and old boots are always welcome,' said Tiffany seriously. 'But you don't have to thank me for being a witch. I'd much prefer that you thanked my friend Preston. He put himself in real danger for the pair of you. At least we were together. He was out here all by himself.'

'That is, in point of actual fact,' said Preston, 'not entirely *accurate*. Apart from anything else, all my matches were damp, but fortuitously Mr Daft Wullie and his chums were very kind enough to lend me some. And I've been told to tell ye that that was OK, because they was helping me, not ye! And although there are ladies present, I have to say that they did assist in getting things going quickly by flapping the flames with their kilts. A sight, I may say, that once seen is *never* forgotten.'

'I would very much have liked to have seen it,' said Letitia politely.

'Anyway,' said Tiffany, trying to get the mental picture out of her mind, 'it might be best to concentrate on the fact that you will be somewhat more acceptably married by Pastor Egg tomorrow. And you know something very important about tomorrow? It's *today*!'

Roland, who was holding his head and groaning, blinked and said, 'What is?'

## CHAPTER 15

# A Shadow and a Whisper

It was, on the whole, a pretty good wedding in Tiffany's opinion, a pretty good wedding. Pastor Egg, aware of the unusual number of witches in the audience, kept the religion to a minimum. The blushing bride walked up the hall, and Tiffany saw her blush a little more when she caught sight of Nanny Ogg, who gave her a cheerful thumbs-up as she passed. And then there was the throwing of the rice, followed of course by the careful sweeping up of the rice, because it was wicked to waste good food.

Then there was general cheering and congratulations and, to the surprise of some, a happy, beaming Duchess, who chatted merrily, even to the maids, and appeared to have a kind and reassuring word for everybody. And only Tiffany knew why the woman shot occasional nervous glances towards Mrs Proust.

Tiffany left then, to sneak away and help Preston in the King field, where he was digging a hole deep enough so that the plough would never find the charred remains that were collected and thrown down it. They washed their hands with vicious lye soap, because you could never be too careful. It was not, strictly speaking, a very romantic occasion.

'Do you think he will ever come back?' said Preston as they leaned on their shovels.

Tiffany nodded. 'The Cunning Man will, at least. Poison is always welcome somewhere.'

'What will you do now he's gone?'

'Oh, you know, all the exciting stuff; somewhere there is always a leg that needs bandaging or a nose that needs blowing. It's busy, busy all day long.'

'It doesn't sound very exciting.'

'Well, I suppose so,' said Tiffany, 'but compared to yesterday that kind of day suddenly seems to be *a very good day*.' They headed towards the hall, where the wedding breakfast was now being served as lunch. 'You are a young man of considerable resourcefulness,' Tiffany said to Preston, 'and I thank you very much for your help.'

Preston nodded happily. 'Thank you very much for that, miss, thank you very much indeed, but with just one little – how can I put it – correction. You are, after all, sixteen, more or less, and I am seventeen, so I think you will conclude that calling me young man . . . I will own up to a cheerful and youthful disposition, but I am older than you, my girl.'

There was a pause. Then Tiffany said carefully, 'How do you know how old I am?'

'I asked around,' said Preston, his eager smile never leaving his face.

'Why?'

Tiffany didn't get an answer because the sergeant came out of the main door with confetti cascading off his helmet. 'Oh, *there* you are, miss. The Baron's been asking after you, and so has the Baroness.' He paused to smile and said, 'Nice to have one of them again.' His gaze fell on Preston and the sergeant frowned. 'Lollygagging again, as usual, Lance Private Preston?'

Preston saluted smartly, 'You are correct in your surmise, Sergeant; you have voiced an absolute truth.' This got Preston the puzzled glare he always got from the sergeant, and there was also a disapproving grunt, which meant: One day I'll work out what it is you are saying, my lad, and then you'll be in trouble.

Weddings can be rather similar to funerals in that, apart from the main players, when it's all over, people are never quite sure what they should be doing next, which is why they see if there is any wine left. But Letitia was looking radiant, which is compulsory for brides, and the slightly frizzled bits of her hair had been neatly concealed by her brilliant, sparkly tiara. Roland had also scrubbed up quite well, and you had to be quite close to him to smell pig.

'About last night . . .' he began nervously. 'Er, it did happen, didn't it? I mean, I remember the pigsty, and we

398

were all running, but . . .' His voice faded away.

Tiffany looked at Letitia, who mouthed the words, 'I remember *everything*!'

Yes, she really *is* a witch, Tiffany thought. That's going to be interesting.

Roland coughed. Tiffany smiled. 'Dear Miss Aching,' he said, and for once Tiffany forgave him his 'public meeting' voice, 'I am well aware that I have been party to a miscarriage of natural justice vis-à-vis your good self.' He stopped to clear his throat again and Tiffany thought, I really hope that Letitia can wash some of the starch out of him. 'With this in mind, I spoke to young Preston here, who talked to the kitchen girls in his cheery way and found out where the nurse had gone. She had spent some of the money, but most of it is here and it is, I am happy to say, yours.'

At this point somebody nudged Tiffany.

It was Preston, who hissed, 'We've found this too.'

She looked down, and he pressed a worn leather folder into her hand. She nodded in grateful thanks and looked at Roland. 'Your father wanted you to have this,' she said. 'It may be worth more to you than all that money. I would wait until you are alone before you look at it.'

He turned it over in his hands. 'What is it?'

'Just a memory,' said Tiffany. 'Just a memory.'

The sergeant stepped forward then and tipped a heavy leather bag onto the table, among the glasses and flowers. There was a gasp from the guests.

I'm being watched like hawks by my sister witches, thought Tiffany, and I am also being watched by practically everyone I know, and who know me. I've got to do this right. And I've got to do this so that everybody remembers it.

'I think you should keep it, sir,' she said. Roland looked relieved, but Tiffany went on, 'However, I have a few simple requests on behalf of other people.'

Letitia nudged her husband in the ribs and he spread out his hands. 'This is my wedding day! How can I refuse any request?'

'The girl Amber Petty needs a dowry which, incidentally, would allow her young man to buy his indenture to a master craftsman, and you might not be aware that he sewed the gown that is currently adorning your beautiful young wife. Have you ever seen anything finer?'

This got an immediate round of applause, along with whistles from Roland's chums, who whimsically called out things like, 'Which one? The girl or the dress!' When that was over, Tiffany said, 'And furthermore, sir, and with your indulgence, I would like your pledge that any boy or girl from the Chalk with such a similar request will find you obliging. I think you will agree that I am asking for a lot less than I am returning to you?'

'Tiffany, I believe you are correct,' said Roland, 'but I suspect you have more up your sleeve?'

'How well you know me, sir,' said Tiffany and Roland, just for a moment, went pink.

'I want a school, sir. I want a school here on the Chalk. I've been thinking about this for a long time – in fact for longer than I had worked out the name for what I wanted. There's an old barn on Home Farm that isn't being used right now and I think we could make it quite acceptable in a week or so.'

'Well, the travelling teachers do come through every few months,' said the Baron.

'Yes, sir, I know, sir, and they're useless, sir. They teach facts, not understanding. It's like teaching people about forests by showing them a saw. I want a proper school, sir, to teach reading and writing, and most of all thinking, sir, so people can find what they're good at, because someone doing what they really like is always an asset to any country, and too often people never find out until it's too late.' She deliberately looked away from the sergeant, but her words had caused a susurration around the room, Tiffany was glad to hear. She drowned it out with, 'There have been times, lately, when I dearly wished that I could change the past. Well, I can't, but I can change the present, so that when it becomes the past it will turn out to be a past worth having. And I'd like the boys to learn about girls and I'd like the girls to learn about boys. Learning is about finding out who you are, what you are, where you are and what you are standing on and what you are good at and what's over the horizon and, well, everything. It's about finding the place where you fit. I found the place where I fit, and I would like everybody else to find theirs. And may I please propose that Preston is the school's first teacher? He pretty much knows everything there is to know as it is.'

Preston bowed low with his helmet off, which got a laugh.

Tiffany went on, 'And his reward for a year's teaching

401

work for you will be, yes, enough money for him to buy the letters to go after his name so that he can become a doctor. Witches can't do *everything* and we could do with a doctor in these parts.'

All this got a big cheer, which is what generally happens when people have worked out that they are likely to get something that they won't have to pay for. When that had died down, Roland looked the sergeant in the eye and said, 'Do you think you can manage without Preston's military prowess, Sergeant?'

This precipitated another laugh. That's good, Tiffany thought; laughter helps things slide into the thinking.

Sergeant Brian tried to look solemn, but he was concealing a smile. 'It would be a bit of a blow, sir, but I think we might just about manage, sir. Yes, I think I can say that the departure of Lance Private Preston will enhance the overall efficiency of the squad, sir.'

This caused more general applause from people who hadn't worked it out and laughter from those that did.

The Baron clapped his hands together. 'Well then, Miss Aching, it would appear that you have got everything you asked for, yes?'

'Actually, sir, I haven't finished asking yet. There is one more thing and it won't cost you anything, so don't worry about that.' Tiffany took a deep breath, and tried to make herself look taller. 'I require that you give to the peoples known as the Nac Mac Feegle all the downland above Home Farm, that it should be theirs for ever in law as well as in justice. A proper deed can be drawn up, and don't worry about the cost – I know a toad that will do it for a handful of beetles – and it will say that for their part the Feegles will allow all shepherds and sheep untrammelled access to the downs but there will be – and this is important – no sharp metal beyond a knife. All this will cost you nothing, my lord Baron, but what you and your descendants, and I hope you are intending to have descendants—' Tiffany had to stop there because of the gale of laughter, in which Nanny Ogg took a large part, and then she continued, 'My lord Baron, I think you will assure yourself of a friendship that will never die. Gain all, lose nothing.'

To his credit, Roland hardly hesitated, and said, 'I would be honoured to present the Nac Mac Feegle with the deeds to their land and I regret, no, I apologize for any misunderstandings between us. As you say, they deserve their land by right and by justice.'

Tiffany was impressed by the short speech. The language was slightly stuffy, but his heart was in the right place, and slightly stuffy language suited the Feegles very well. To her joy there was yet another susurration in the beams high over the castle's hall. And the Baron, looking a lot more like a real baron now, went on, 'I only wish that I could tell them this personally right now.'

And from the darkness above came one mighty cry of:

# 'CRIVENS!'

The wind was silver and cold. Tiffany opened her eyes, with the cheer of the Feegles still ringing in her ears. It was replaced by the rattle of dried grass in the wind. She tried to sit up but got nowhere, and a voice behind her said, 'Please don't wriggle, this is very difficult.'

Tiffany tried to turn her head. 'Eskarina?'

'Yes. There is somebody here who wants to talk to you. You may get up now; I have balanced the nodes. Don't ask questions, because you would not understand the answers. You are in the travelling now, again. Now and again, you might say. I will leave you to your friend . . . and I am afraid you cannot have much time, for a given value of time. But I must protect my son . . .'

Tiffany said, 'You mean you've got—' She stopped, because a figure was forming in front of Tiffany and became a witch, a classic witch with the black dress, black boots – rather nice ones, Tiffany noted – and, of course, the pointy hat. She had a necklace too. On the chain was a golden hare.

The woman herself was old, but it was hard to say how old. She stood proudly, like Granny Weatherwax, but like Nanny Ogg she seemed to suggest that old age, or something, wasn't really being taken seriously.

But Tiffany concentrated on the necklace. People wore jewellery to show you something. It always had a meaning, if you concentrated.

'All right, all right,' she said, 'I have just one question: I'm not here to bury you, am I?'

'My word, you are quick,' said the woman. 'You have immediately devised a remarkably interesting narrative and instantly guessed who I am.' She laughed. The voice was younger than her face. 'No, Tiffany. Interestingly macabre though your suggestion is, the answer is no. I remember Granny Weatherwax telling me that when you get right down to it, the world is all about stories, and Tiffany Aching is extremely good at endings.'

'I am?'

'Oh yes. Classic endings to a romantic story are a wedding or a legacy, and you have been the engineer for one of each. Well done.'

'You *are* me, right?' said Tiffany. 'That's what the "you have to help yourself" business was about, yes?'

The older Tiffany grinned, and Tiffany could not help noticing that it was a very nice grin. 'As a matter of fact, I only interfered in a few small ways. Like, for example, making certain the wind really did blow very hard for you . . . although, as I recall, a certain colony of little men added their own special excitement to the venture. I'm never quite certain if my memory is good or bad. That's time travel for you.'

'You can travel in time?'

'With some help from our friend Eskarina. And only as a shadow and a whisper. It's a bit like the don't-see-me thing that I . . . that *we*— You have to persuade time not to take any notice.'

'But why did you want to talk to me?' said Tiffany.

'Well, the infuriating answer is that I remembered that I did,' said old Tiffany. 'Sorry, that's time travel again. But I think I wanted to tell you that it all works out, more or less. It all falls into place. You've taken the first step.'

'There's a second step?' said Tiffany.

'No; there's another first step. Every step is a first step if it's a step in the right direction.'

'But hold on,' said Tiffany. 'Won't I be you one day? And then will I talk to me now, as it were?'

'Yes, but the you that you talk to won't exactly be you. I'm very sorry about this, but I am having to talk about time travel in a language that can't really account for it. But in short, Tiffany, according to the elasticated string theory, throughout the rest of time, somewhere an old Tiffany will be talking to a young Tiffany, and the fascinating thing is that every time they do they will be a little bit different. When you meet your younger self, you will tell her what you think she needs to know.'

'But I have got a question,' said Tiffany. 'And it's one I want to know the answer to.'

'Well, do be quick,' said old Tiffany. 'The elasticated

string thingy, or whatever it is that Eskarina uses, does not allow us very much time.'

'Well,' said Tiffany, 'can you at least tell me. Do I ever get—?'

Old Tiffany faded, smiling into nothingness, but Tiffany heard one word. It sounded like, '*Listen.*'

And then she was in the hall again, as if she'd never left it at all, and people were cheering and there seemed to be Feegles everywhere. And Preston was by her side. It was as if ice had suddenly melted. But when she got her balance back, and stopped asking herself what had just happened, had *really* happened, Tiffany looked for the other witches, and saw that they were talking amongst themselves, like judges adding up a score.

The huddle broke up, and they came towards her purposefully, led by Granny Weatherwax. When they reached her they bowed and raised their hats, which is a mark of respect in the craft.

Granny Weatherwax looked at her sternly. 'I see you have burned your hand, Tiffany.'

Tiffany looked down. 'I didn't notice,' she said. 'Can I ask you now, Granny? Would you all have killed me?' She saw the expressions of the other witches change.

Granny Weatherwax looked around and paused for a moment. 'Let us say, young woman, we would have done our best not to. But all in all, Tiffany, it seems to us that you've done a woman's job today. The place where we looks for witches is at the centre of things. Well, we looks around here and we see that you is so central that this steading *spins* on you. You are your own mistress, nevertheless, and if you don't start training somebody, that will be a waste. We leave this steading in the best of hands.'

The witches clapped, and some of the other guests joined in, even though they did not understand what those few sentences had meant. What they *did* recognize, however, was that these were mostly elderly, experienced, important and scary witches. And they were paying their respect to Tiffany Aching, one of *them*, their witch. And she was a very important witch, and so the Chalk had to be a very important place. Of course, they had known that all along but it was nice to have it acknowledged. They stood a little straighter and felt proud.

Mrs Proust removed her hat again, and said, 'Please don't be afraid to come back to the city again, Miss Aching. I think I can promise you a thirty per cent discount on all Boffo products, except for perishables or consumables, an offer not to be sneezed at.'

The group of witches raised their hats in unison again and walked back into the crowd.

'You know all that just now was organizing people's lives for them,' said Preston behind her, but as she spun round he backed away laughing and added, 'But in a good way. You are the *witch*, Tiffany. *You are the witch!*'

And people drank a toast and there was more food, and more dancing and laughter and friendship and tiredness, and at midnight Tiffany Aching lay alone on her broomstick high above the chalk hills and looked up at the universe, and then down on the bit of it that belonged to her. She *was* the witch, floating high over everything but, it must be said, with the leather strap carefully buckled.

The stick rose and fell gently as warm breezes took it and as tiredness and darkness took her, she stretched out her arms to the dark and, just for a moment, as the world turned, Tiffany Aching wore midnight.

She didn't come down until the sun was crusting the horizon with light. And she woke up to birdsong. All across the Chalk the larks were rising as they did every morning in a symphony of liquid sound. They did indeed sing melodious. They streamed up past the stick, paying it no attention at all, and Tiffany listened, entranced, until the last bird had got lost in the brilliant sky.

She landed, made breakfast for an old lady who was bed-bound, fed her cat, and went to see how Trivial Boxer's* broken leg was doing. She was stopped halfway there by the neighbour of old Miss Swivel, who had apparently become suddenly unable to walk overnight, but Tiffany was fortunately able to point out that she had regrettably put both feet through one knicker leg.

Then she went down into the castle to see what else needed doing.

After all, she *was* the witch.

---

* Mr and Mrs Boxer had been slightly more educated than was good for them, and thought that 'trivial' was a good name for their third child.

EPILOGUE

# Midnight by Day

It was the scouring fair again, the same noisy hurdy-gurdy, the bobbing for frogs, the fortune-telling, the laughter, the pickpockets (though never of a witch's pocket), but this year, by common consent, no cheese rolling. Tiffany walked through it all, nodding at people she knew, which was everybody, and generally enjoying the sunshine. Had it been a year? So much had happened, it all swam together, like the sounds of the fair.

'Good afternoon, miss.'

And there was Amber, with her boy – with her husband . . .

'Nearly didn't recognize you, miss,' said Amber cheerfully, 'what with you not having your pointy hat on, if you see what I mean.'

410

'I thought I'd just be Tiffany Aching today,' said Tiffany. 'It is a holiday after all.'

'But you are still the witch?'

'Oh yes, I'm still the witch, but I'm not necessarily the hat.'

Amber's husband laughed. 'I know what you mean, miss! Sometimes I swear that people think I'm a pair of hands!' Tiffany looked him up and down. They had met properly when she had married him to Amber, of course, and she had been impressed; he was what they called a steady lad and as sharp as his needles. He would go far, and take Amber with him. And after Amber finished her training under the kelda, who knows where *she* would take *him*?

Amber hung on his arm as if it was an oak. 'My William done a little present for you, miss,' she said. 'Go on, William, show her!'

The young man proffered the package he had been carrying, and cleared his throat. 'I don't know if you keep up with the fashions, miss, but they are doing wonderful fabrics now down in the big city, so when Amber suggested this to me I thought of them. But it also has to be washable, for a start, with perhaps a split skirt for the broomstick and leg-of-mutton sleeves, which are all the go this season, and with buttons tight at the wrists to keep them out of the way, and pockets on the inside and styled to be hardly noticeable. I hope it fits, miss. I'm good at measuring without a tape. It's a knack.'

Amber bounced up and down at his side. 'Put it on, miss! Go on, miss! Put it on!'

'What? In front of all these people?' said Tiffany, embarrassed and intrigued at the same time.

Amber was not to be denied. 'There's the mother-and-baby tent, miss! No men in there, miss, no fear! They'd be afraid that they would have to burp some-body, miss!'

Tiffany gave in. The package had a *rich* feel to it; it felt soft, like a glove. Mothers and babies watched her as she slid into the dress and she heard the envious sighs that interspersed burps.

Amber, on fire with enthusiasm, pushed her way in through the flap, and gasped.

'Oh, miss, oh, miss, it does suit you so! Oh, miss! If only you could see yourself, miss! Do come and show William, miss, he'll be as proud as a king! Oh, miss!'

You couldn't disappoint Amber. You just couldn't. It would be like, well, kicking a puppy.

Tiffany felt different without the hat. Lighter, per-haps. And William gasped and said, 'I wish my master was here, Miss Aching, because you are a masterpiece. I just wish you could see yourself . . . miss?'

And just for a moment, because people shouldn't get too suspicious, Tiffany stood outside herself and watched herself twirl the beautiful dress as black as a cat full of sixpences, and she thought: I shall wear mid-night, and I will be good at it . . .

She hurried back to her body and shyly thanked the young tailor. 'It's wonderful, William, and I will happily fly over to show your master. The cuffs are wonderful!'

Amber was jumping up and down again. 'We'd better

hurry if we're going to see the tug-of-war, miss – it's Feegles versus humans! It's going to be fun!'

And in fact, they could hear the roar of the Feegles warming up, though they had made a slight alteration to their traditional chant: 'Nae king, nae quin, nae laird! One baron – and underrr mutually ag-rreeeed arrr-angement, ye ken!'

'You go on ahead,' said Tiffany. 'I'm waiting for some-body.'

Amber paused for a moment. 'Don't wait too long, miss, don't wait too long!'

Tiffany walked slowly in the wonderful dress, won-dering if she would dare wear it every day and . . . hands came past her ears and covered her eyes.

A voice behind her said, 'A nosegay for the pretty lady? You never know, it might help you find your beau.'

She spun round. 'Preston!'

They talked as they strolled away from the noise, and Tiffany listened to news about the bright young lad that Preston had trained to take over as the school's new teacher; and about exams and doctors and the Lady Sybil Free Hospital who had – and this was the really important part – just taken on one new apprentice, this being Preston, possibly because since he could talk the hind leg off a donkey, he might have a talent for surgery.

'I don't reckon I'll get many holidays,' he said. 'You don't get many when you're an apprentice and I shall have to sleep under the autoclave every night and look after all the saws and scalpels, but I know all the bones by heart!'

'Well, it's not too far by broomstick, after all,' said Tiffany.

Preston's expression changed as he reached into his pocket and pulled out something wrapped in fine tissue, which he handed to her without saying a word.

Tiffany unwrapped it, knowing – absolutely knowing – that it would be the golden hare. There was no possibility in the world that it wouldn't have been. She tried to find the words, but Preston always had an adequate supply.

He said, 'Miss Tiffany, the witch . . . would you be so good as to tell me: what is the sound of love?'

Tiffany looked at his face. The noise from the tug-of-war was silenced. The birds stopped singing. In the grass, the grasshoppers stopped rubbing their legs together and looked up. The earth moved slightly as even the chalk giant (perhaps) strained to hear, and the silence flowed over the world until all there was was Preston, who was always there.

And Tiffany said, 'Listen.'

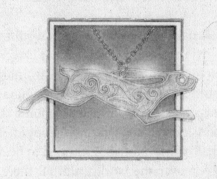

# A Feegle Glossary
adjusted for those of a delicate disposition

*(A Work In Progress By Miss Perspicacia Tick, witch)*

*Bigjobs:* human beings

*Big Man:* chief of the clan (usually the husband of the kelda)

*Blethers:* rubbish, nonsense

*Boggin:* to be desperate, as in 'I'm boggin for a cup of tea'

*Bunty:* a weak person

*Carlin:* old woman

*Cludgie:* the privy

*Crivens!:* a general exclamation that can mean anything from 'My goodness!' to 'I've just lost my temper and there is going to be trouble'

*Dree your/my/his/her weird:* facing the fate that is in store for you/me/him/her

*Een:* eyes

*Eldritch:* weird, strange; sometimes means oblong too, for some reason

*Fash:* worry, upset

*Geas:* a very important obligation, backed up by tradition and magic. Not a bird

*Gonnagle:* the bard of the clan, skilled in musical instruments, poems, stories and songs

*Hag:* a witch, of any age

*Hag o' hags:* a very important witch

*Hagging/Haggling:* anything a witch does

*Hiddlins:* secrets

*Kelda:* the female head of the clan, and eventually the mother of most of it. Feegle babies are very small, and a kelda will have hundreds in her lifetime

*Lang syne:* long ago

*Last World:* the Feegles believe that they are dead. This world is so nice, they argue, that they must have been really good in a past life and then died and ended up here. Appearing to die here means merely going back to the Last World, which they believe is rather dull

*Mudlin:* useless person

*Pished:* I am assured that this means 'tired'

*Schemie:* an unpleasant person

*Scuggan:* a really unpleasant person

*Scunner:* a generally unpleasant person

*Ships:* woolly things that eat grass and go baa. Easily confused with the other kind

*Spavie:* see *Mudlin*

*Special Sheep Liniment:* probably moonshine whisky, I am very sorry to say. No one knows what it'd do to sheep, but it is said that a drop of it is good for shepherds on a cold winter's night and for Feegles at any time at all. Do not try to make this at home

*Spog:* a small leather bag at the front of a Feegle's kilt, which covers whatever he presumably thinks needs to be hidden, and generally holds things like something he is halfway through eating, something he'd found that now therefore belongs to him, and quite often – because even a Feegle can catch a cold – it might hold whatever he was using as a handkerchief, which might not necessarily be dead

*Steamie:* only found in the big Feegle mounds in the mountains, where there's enough water to allow regular bathing; it's a kind of sauna. Feegles on the Chalk tend to rely on the fact that you can only get so much dirt on you before it starts to fall off of its own accord

*Waily:* a general cry of despair

# Author's Note

My job is to make things up, and the best way to make things up is to make them out of real things . . .

When I was a small boy, just after the last Ice Age, we lived in a cottage that Tiffany Aching would recognize: we had cold water, no electricity, and took a bath once a week, because the tin bath had to be brought in from its nail, which was outside on the back of the kitchen wall; and it took a long time to fill it, when all my mother had to heat water with was one kettle. Then I, as the youngest, had the first bath, followed by Mum and then Dad, and finally the dog if Dad thought it was getting a bit niffy.

There were old men in the village who had been born in the Jurassic period and looked, to me, all the same, with flat caps and serious trousers held up with very thick leather belts. One of them was called Mr Allen, who wouldn't drink water from a tap because, he said, 'It's got neither taste nor smell.' He drank water from the roof of his house, which fed a rain barrel.

Presumably he drank more than rainwater, because he had a nose that looked like two strawberries that had crashed into one another.*

Mr Allen used to sit out in the sun in front of his cottage on an old kitchen chair, watching the world go by, and we kids used to watch his nose, in case it exploded. One day I was chatting to him, and out of the blue he said to me, 'You seen stubbles burning, boy?'

I certainly had: not near our home, but when we drove down to the coast on holiday, though sometimes the smoke from the burning stubbles was so thick that it looked like a fog. The stubbles were what was left in the ground after most of the corn stems had been cut. The burning was said to be good for getting rid of pests and diseases, but the process meant lots of small birds and animals were burned. The practice has long since been banned, for that very reason.

One day, when the harvest wagon went down our lane, Mr Allen said to me, 'You ever seen a hare, boy?'

I said, 'Yes, of course.' (If you haven't seen a hare, then imagine a rabbit crossed with a greyhound, one that can leap magnificently.) Mr Allen said, 'The hare ain't afraid of fire. She stares it down, and jumps over it, and lands safe on the other side.'

I must have been about six or seven years old, but I

* My dad told me it's called 'Drinker's Nose', but he was probably wrong, as the condition, I'm told, is a type of adult acne (called Rhinophyma, but I suspect that this is too much information).

remembered it, because Mr Allen died not long afterwards. Then when I was much older, I found in a
second-hand bookshop a book called *The Leaping
Hare* written by George Ewart Evans and David
Thomson, and I learned things that I would not have
dared to make up.

Mr Evans, who died in 1988, spoke – during his
long life – to the men who worked on the land: not
from the cab of a tractor, but with horses, and they
saw the wildlife around them. I suspect that maybe
they had put a little bit of a shine on the things they
told him, but everything is all the better for a little bit
of shine, and I have not hesitated to polish up the
legend of the hare for you. If it is not the truth, then it
is what the truth ought to be.

I dedicate this book to Mr Evans, a wonderful man
who helped many of us of us to learn about the depths
of history over which we float. It is important that we
know where we come from, because if you do not
know where you come from, then you don't know
where you are, and if you don't know where you are,
then you don't know where you're going. And if you
don't know where you're going, you're probably going
wrong.

*Terry Pratchett*
*Wiltshire*
*27 May 2010*